Keepers of the Shield

BY

Sandy Kelly

Dedication

This labour of love is dedicated to my sons: Travis, Spencer, Jason, and Adam.

Acknowledgment

I would like to acknowledge my second cousin, Ginny, for giving me the courage to pursue the dream of authorship. Writing has always been a passion, but it was her kind words that pushed me forward. Thank you, Ginny — much love.

Here's to the memory of Trooper, a lost and then found German Shepherd, who was a loyal friend and a protector of cats and little girls.

About The Author

The author began online gaming in the early days, when her four teenage sons would come home from school and disappear for hours. Curious about what they were doing while sequestered in their bedrooms, she started watching them play their online games—and then she began playing with them. She was fascinated by the graphics and the storylines.

Many years later, she has shifted her focus to writing, though she still loves the thrill of gaming—despite the dangers of entrapment. These days, it's easier to step away and write about the experience, rather than be trapped in a dungeon raid or pulled into an all-nighter.

Book 1

Chapter 1

I can't believe this is happening

Not much surprised Elder Nexlucimus anymore, but this astonished him.

"Are you sure, Breeze?" Nexlucimus asked the essence, trying hard to understand how this could have happened. *"First this mortal boy is found to possess red magic, and now you tell me that he is a Finding as well. Curious, very curious indeed."*

"Yes, Milord, I thought you would feel that way. Do you or the gods have any further instructions for me?"

"Yes, Breeze," the Elder paused, as he listened to something only he could hear. *"The gods have been waiting for us to learn of these talents. Now we need to increase the urgency of your dreams to the lad."*

"Why have the gods been waiting? Why not just tell us? I'm sorry... I don't mean to question the gods. I fear that I may have offended, but it would have saved time, considering the seriousness of the quest."

"The only answer they give us," Nexlucimus said to her, *"is that they have their reasons, and we will learn all things when the time is upon us. Now, my young Shadow Dream, away with you. Jesse must be prepared—especially with these new developments."*

Breeze circled once around Nexlucimus' head before she vanished to tend to her assignment—Jesse Finch, a mortal youth. She sighed.

"How could this be possible? And why do I feel so… attracted to him? It doesn't make sense. Not now… after so many millennia."

In the meantime, fifteen-year-old Jesse Finch struggled with his own problems.

"Jesse, stop! Where are you going?" Sally Robinson called to her son as he stormed out of the house.

"Don't know, don't care. I just need to get away from… him," Jesse said, pointing an accusatory finger at his stepfather.

"Jesse, please, can't we talk about this?" Sally cried out to her son as he jumped on his bike and bolted from the yard.

"Please…" she pleaded, watching him disappear, ignoring the tears that rolled down her face.

"Come in, Sally," Bill, Jesse's stepfather, said as he gently guided his wife back into the house. "He has his phone. You can call him later, after he's had time to cool off. It was a shock and a surprise for all of us."

Jesse rode long and hard, as a traitorous tremor of doubt and fear tried breaking through to his thoughts. His brain felt heavy and tortured, but he refused to acknowledge it.

Pounding the road with reckless abandon, he began wondering, *Where can I go?*

It was getting dark, and despite the workout, he was starting to chill. He hadn't grabbed a coat in his rush to leave the house, and the fall weather was starting to cool dramatically.

Jesse considered his options. Except for Cami Chambers, his only real friend, and Tommy Tam, whom he had just met, there were no options. Except for… Gran.

Jesse groaned. "I guess Gran is my only real choice."

Pearl, Jesse's grandmother—his mum's mum—lived five miles away from Jesse's house, in the opposite direction of where he'd already been pedaling for a good ten minutes. Reluctantly, he turned around.

"Gran's going to ask questions. What can I tell her? The truth? That the Army is transferring Bill to Germany? How could my life get any more messed up!" Jesse shouted at the wind. "As if Mum marrying again just two years after Dad's death wasn't bad enough. It's like my feelings don't matter. And another Army guy too! How thick can one person be!"

Jesse's anger began building again, and he pedaled faster.

"Slow down, dude," he tried to reason with himself. *"Think about something else."*

A rebellious grin played at Jesse's lips. *"Maybe Gran will let me escape into the game when I get there."*

Bill didn't like online games, and Jesse loved doing things that Bill didn't like. Giving his mum grief because it irritated Bill was fun. It was her fault really, for marrying such a stupid, controlling jerk. Plus, Gran loved online games.

When Jesse got to Gran's place, he was tired. Despite being sweaty and breathing hard, he was shivering.

Stopping just outside the gate to the yard, Jesse surveyed the surroundings. On the porch was Rambo, Gran's rooster.

"Stupid, pit bull wannabe," Jesse mumbled. *"Where's Brutus? Ah... asleep, on his pillow, as usual. Worthless watchdog. What can you expect from something the size of a guinea pig?"*

Rambo had seen Jesse and was marching in his direction.

"Uh-oh... discovered."

"Hey, Rambo, old buddy, what's up?" Jesse smiled.

The rooster just stood there, glaring at Jesse. Then he hiccupped. A smoke ring escaped his beak.

"I'm just going to pretend that I didn't see that," Jesse said, watching the big bird, who was watching him as he, Jesse, decided what to do.

"I'm coming in now, is that OK? I need to talk to Gran."

The rooster hiccupped again—sparks this time. Brutus, who had joined Rambo, growled.

"OK, there's more than one way to storm the castle," Jesse said, pulling out his cell phone and texting: **GRAN I'M AT THE FRONT GATE PLEASE RESCUE ME FROM YOUR ARMY.**

Shortly after sending the text, his short, rather plump grandmother came out.

"Jesse, dear, this is unexpected," she grinned. "Come on in. It's OK, Rambo, let him pass. Brutus, go back to the porch."

Jesse watched the two animals as they retreated to their stations—Rambo patrolling the yard and Brutus snuggling back into his porch pillow, watching Jesse with one eye, growling softly.

"This is a wonderful surprise," Pearl said as they walked to the front door. "What brings you to this part of town? I would've thought that you'd be home, enjoying supper. Is everything OK? Are you hungry?'

"I just pulled a pizza out of the oven. It's even your favorite—Italian meatball delight with extra cheese and a side salad. There's a carton of cold milk in the refrigerator to go with it. You'd think I knew you were coming," she winked.

"Thanks, Gran."

"What are grandmothers for but to feed grandsons? And be a listening ear, if you want one. I made a fresh batch of cookies today too. Hope you're hungry."

She opened the door, and they walked into the delicious smells. Jesse's mouth watered.

Sitting down, they ate in silence. Then Jesse noticed something unusual.

"How come Rambo and Brutus aren't eating? I thought they ate with you."

"Normally they do. I like the company. But since you're here, I put their food outside on the porch. I had a special pizza made just for them," Gran whispered conspiratorially. "Lots of meat and a gluten-free crust. Wheat gives Brutus gas and... whew!" she chuckled, waving a hand in front of her face.

Jesse studied his strange little grandmother for a moment, then smiled and returned to his pizza. At home, she was often the topic of discussion with her purple camouflage and spiked red hair. Her short, round stature made her look like an eggplant with a sunburn. The thought made him smile again.

"Now, are you going to tell me what's going on, or do I need to call your mother?" Pearl asked as they finished the pizza. Standing, she refilled his milk glass and placed a plate of cookies between them. Pearl studied her grandson while returning to her seat across from him. She was always good at getting right to the point.

"I can't stand living in that house one more day, Gran. Ever since Mum married Bill, it's been a living nightmare for me. Curfews, chores, bedtimes, time limits on internet access, no cell phone after 9 p.m." He took a couple of deep breaths, trying to calm himself. "No friends at the house on school nights. That's not a problem, but it's the principle. I'm sick of being treated like a kid. I'll be sixteen in two weeks. And that's another thing—Bill says I can't drive until I'm eighteen unless I get straight A's. I can't believe this is happening. I'm in prison."

He waved his arms in the air for emphasis, then buried his face in his hands, gathering his thoughts.

"Then today, after school, they told me Bill received a new assignment. He's being transferred to Germany. The orders are in a rush. They'll leave in two weeks! GERMANY—in two weeks! I HATE him, and Mum just does whatever he says. I hate it there." Jesse slumped in his chair, crossing his arms over his chest, scowling. "You know what bothers me the most? I can't talk to Mum about any of this because it's all about Bill."

Pearl sat there for a moment, watching him. "Jesse, dear, how would you feel about moving in here with me, to help take care of the house while you finish school?"

Jesse immediately brightened, sitting up. "Are you serious? Can I move in tonight? I don't ever want to see either one of them again. I mean, I love Mum—or the Mum before Bill—but I can't stand Bill."

"It wouldn't be a free ride, Jesse. You'd have chores, curfews, and other rules too. Think you could handle it?"

"Yeah, I guess. What kind of rules?"

"Well, we'd have to figure that out, but there would be some. Another thing—I need to be on the game more than before. I'd like you to join me. It's important. Things are happening that I can't explain right now. I talked to your mum this morning when she called to tell me about Bill's transfer."

"You talked to Mum? And she was okay with it?" Jesse asked, surprised.

"Well, she's okay with everything—except the game, of course. I didn't mention that. You know what they think about online games. Close your mouth, dear; it's distractive."

"Sorry. Can I stay here tonight?"

"Since it's Friday, yes. But you need to call your mother and explain what you're doing. I'm sure she's worried, the way you dashed out of the house in a huff."

"How did you know about that? Did Mum call you?"

"No, actually. You just said that you were unhappy. The fact that you showed up at my gate, out of breath and sweaty, said a lot. Now help me clean up, and after you call your mum, we'll get on the game. You need to level up more and become better with your character. It's important."

"Why? I mean, I love the game, but why is it so important?" Jesse questioned.

"It's preparation for something big. A new boss. But we'll talk about that when Mr. Chambers can help explain."

Mr. Chambers was Jesse's best friend, Cami's dad, and Jesse's math teacher at the high school.

Gran could sure be mysterious, Jesse thought, as he dunked a cookie in milk and shoved it into his mouth, whole. He was feeling much better excited even.

After the meal had been cleaned up, Jesse decided it would be better to talk to his mum in person, since Bill had night duty and wouldn't be there. Gran offered to drive him to the house, since it was five miles away and dark.

"I'll go visit the Slaters while you talk. They're not too far away. You call me when you're ready to leave. Grab some of your clothes and personal items while you're at it."

"Yes ma'am, will do," he replied as they walked out the door toward Gran's car. Rambo was still patrolling, and Brutus was on his cushion, watching them as they drove away.

Jesse was nervous as he approached his mum's front door. He'd never been so mad at her before. Bill just generated so much friction and anger—just thinking about him made Jesse's blood boil. Jesse felt like he should knock before entering, but he didn't. That would be too weird. The door creaked as he pushed it open. He heard footsteps approaching as he stepped in.

"Hello?" Sally called out, flipping on the entryway light.

"Hi, Mum," Jesse said, blinking at the sudden brightness. "You really should lock the doors when you're here alone at night. Bill's always telling you that." Jesse's stepdad's name felt nasty in his mouth.

His mum ran the last ten steps and hugged him fiercely.

"Oh Jesse, I've been so worried! Where have you been? I…" She started to cry. Jesse never knew what to do when she cried, and she cried a lot. Lately, she cried when she was happy, or sad, or excited, or nervous. You name it—she cried for it.

"Mum, come on, everything's okay. Mum, get a grip." He pushed her away; his shirt front was wet now. Why did she have to do that?

"Everything isn't okay, Jesse," she said, brushing away the tears. "You yelled at me. You wouldn't let me explain things, and then you raced out of here. Why did you do that? What's wrong with you? With us? We could always talk before…"

"Before Bill," Jesse cut her off. "He's the answer to all the above problems, Mum. All of them."

"Jesse, that's not fair. Come into the kitchen; I'll make some hot cocoa, and we'll talk."

She turned around, heading to the kitchen. Jesse had no choice but to follow. He was impressed with how much his mum and Gran were alike—always placing food out like a peace offering. Well, it wasn't going to work this time. He needed to stay focused on the problem, and he wasn't going to let hot cocoa and cookies distract him.

They sat at the table, holding their mugs of hot cocoa, a plate of cookies between them. Jesse thought of all the hurt he had felt in the last year and a half since the wedding. He started to boil again.

"Why did you have to marry Bill? We were happy, weren't we? And why another Army guy?" He glared at her. She looked down sadly and took a deep breath, letting it out slowly.

"This is going to sound like a cheap budget movie, Jesse," she paused, watching him, trying to judge his reaction before she continued. "I was lonely."

"Lonely? Why were you lonely? I was here most of the time. We did things together. We talked," he responded hotly. "Until Bill." Jesse realized that he too was sounding like the same movie, but he didn't care.

"Jesse, you aren't my little boy anymore. Please don't interrupt," she said quickly, as he opened his mouth. "You will always be my son, but you're growing up—well, getting bigger at least. My point is this," she pushed on before he could interrupt again, "in two more years, you'll be off to college. Then what for me?"

Jesse sat there, not sure what to say.

"I met Bill at the Army hospital where I work as a nurse. You know the story. He was the medic working alongside the duty doctor and me. He was kind, smart, and funny. I fell in love—again. Honestly, Jesse, he reminded me of your father."

This upset Jesse. "He's nothing like Dad. He's bossy, controlling, demanding—and since he got here, I've been living in prison. A rule for everything, and everything in a rule. It's maddening, and I hate it. I hate him, and I can't live here anymore. That's why I went to Gran's, and I want to stay there forever, if necessary. I'm not coming back if Bill's here, and I don't care what you say."

Jesse stood, heading for the door. He turned briefly, expecting his mum to stop him. She didn't. She sat there looking at her hands, tears running down her face.

That was it. Apparently, she had moved on. Bill was more important to her. It didn't feel like his home anymore.

He left, slamming the front door. He felt abandoned.

Jesse walked down to the corner store, fuming, and called Gran. "I'm ready to go. I'm at the corner store. And Gran—I forgot to get my clothes."

***

Jesse hadn't noticed the shimmering mist that followed him. Breeze, they called her—a being of pure thought. Introducing Jesse to her world and its people was Breeze's assignment, and she smiled. Not at Jesse's pain, but at how nicely this development played into the quest. Master Nexlucimus would be pleased.

She left to report.

She would return later to give Jesse more dreams. It was crucial—especially now.

Chapter 2

What gladiator did you steal those from?

Jesse's mum and stepdad left the following month. Pearl went to see them off at the airport, but Jesse didn't. As far as he was concerned, that chapter of his life was over. He still had pleasant memories of the times when his father was alive, and before Bill. That was enough.

Jesse found it strange, but during the last couple of weeks since arriving at Gran's, he'd had a recurring dream involving his dad in a strange place—almost like the game. He figured it was because he missed his dad so much, especially now, and also because he and Gran were on their computers all the time. In fact, the only times they weren't online together were while he was at school, eating, doing homework, or finishing chores. Jesse didn't mind the dreams, but they did leave him feeling tired and confused.

An incredible sidelight to all the playing was that Cami, his closest friend, and Tommy Tam, a new acquaintance at school, also played the same online game. Mr Chambers—Cami's dad and Jesse's maths teacher—had been playing the game along with two of Gran's neighbours, Jim and Sara Slater, for many years. It was amazing how many people Jesse met who played one role-playing adventure or another. Lately, around the school, there had been a lot of talk about the game that he and Gran played.

A new Boss had recently appeared, unexpectedly, during the past few months. He was an odd Boss—not even part of a new expansion. Instead of staying in one spot, he wandered around with his minions, randomly starting fights, creating instances and dungeons (places where battles took place). There was also a new option, where players could join the Boss's minions. That seemed to appeal to specific types at school, and there was definite excitement among what Jesse called 'the bully bunch.' He didn't like that choice in the game because it meant more PVP—or player versus player—interaction, and he hated that. First-person shooter formats never appealed to Jesse either, though tons of people enjoyed them.

One weird thing being talked about at school and on social media was the fact that several people who played the game had suddenly disappeared. The authorities were getting involved. Jesse didn't mind it too much, because one of the people missing was a humongous, annoying bully named Rusty Daniels.

Rusty had tormented Jesse since Year Six. Two of his thug friends were still around, giving people grief, but Jesse just avoided them when he saw them, and that pretty much took care of the problem. They seemed to prefer targeting the younger kids anyway. He secretly hoped that they would join Rusty among the missing.

That day after school, Jesse hurried home—Gran had said she had some tactical training she wanted him to do. She wouldn't elaborate any further, only that it contained valuable lessons needed for the game.

When Jesse got home, Gran was sitting on the porch swing waiting for him. Rambo was patrolling the yard, and Brutus was asleep on his pillow, as usual. Gran invited Jesse into the house for a snack.

"I got a call from your mother this morning," Gran said casually, watching Jesse. "She's enjoying Europe. She was wondering how you were doing. How are you doing, Jesse? What can I tell her? Would you like to talk to her sometime? We can call over Instant Messenger or Skype."

Jesse put down the sandwich he was eating, took a big drink of milk, wiped his mouth with a napkin, then took a deep breath, letting it out slowly, trying to calm himself.

"Gran, I know what you're trying to do, but it won't work. I'm not interested in what's going on in 'their world.' No, I don't want to talk to her. No, I don't want to Skype. I love being here with you. No drama, no long list of rules and regulations, no ridiculous anything else. I'm at peace here, and I don't want to complicate things with tears and regrets—and that's all I'd get from Mum. Don't get me wrong, I love her, and I wish her the best, but I can't stand Bill, and if he's there, I don't want to be.

"Now, what were you going to show me?"

Pearl sat there for a moment, studying her grandson. Then she sighed, pushed herself away from the table, and started putting away the makings of Jesse's snack.

"Well, OK then. We'll get started with the tactical training. Follow me."

"What do you mean by tactical training, Gran?"

"Oh, you'll see, dear. I hope you had enough to eat, because you're going to need all your energy."

Puzzled, he followed her into the computer room, thinking that the tactical training meant something on the computer. He was surprised at what he saw. There, in the middle of the computer room floor, was an antique trunk—massive in size. Jesse had never seen it before. He watched as she hefted the lid and began digging around in its depths. Grunting and mumbling, Gran threatened to topple headfirst into its vastness. She set aside tattered robes, strange bottles with powders and liquids, old books, and assorted other oddities—including a tarnished longsword and a battered shield.

"Where'd that trunk come from, Gran?" Jesse asked, suspicious.

Not answering, Gran pushed herself out, expressing a snort of satisfaction. To Jesse's surprise, she held a large, rusty, spiked metal and leather harness, with an attached length of heavy chain.

They appeared ancient and probably weighed at least twenty-five pounds.

"Wow, what gladiator did you steal those from, Gran?" Jesse asked, curious.

Pearl chuckled as she hefted the weighty apparatus and staggered out of the room.

"You're going to have some fun, specialised training for the game. Follow me," Gran said, grunting her way out of the room.

"What do you mean, specialised training?" Jesse probed as he followed her, eyeing the equipment warily. "How could those possibly be fun?"

"You'll see. For online role-playing games," Gran puffed, stumbling towards the front door, "you need mind control and focus—for every aspect. From your spell rotation, and understanding the mechanics of team play, to surviving when there's dangerous stuff on the ground."

"Do you need help with that, Gran?"

"No, dear, I'm just peachy. Would you mind opening the front door for me?"

Jesse scrambled for the door. He doubted she was okay, given how she was staggering, her face red and sweaty. He was afraid she might collapse or something.

She continued walking and talking between breaths. "Since multi-tasking is vital to mind control and focus, we'll start there. I want you to take Brutus for a walk."

"What? Gran, I thought you said this house was my game classroom," Jesse said, puzzled, pointing to the house behind them. "How's taking Brutus for a walk—with that rusty old whatever-it-is—going to be training? You do realise he weighs, at most, four pounds, don't you? How is that thing going to work?"

Finally reaching her destination in the middle of the large front yard, Gran dropped the hefty contraption. Wiping her sweat-stained face on her apron, she motioned for Jesse to join her.

"I'm sorry, dear. Did I neglect to mention that the yard and grounds were part of your training area too? Well, just like in the game and its expansions, life is full of little surprises, isn't it?"

The understatement of the year, Jesse thought. Especially living here. Strange things happened all the time. In addition to a rooster that hiccupped smoke rings, now a mysterious trunk had appeared.

"Hurry, dear—this activity is Brutus' favourite."

"Gran, how is this going to work? That gizmo probably outweighs Brutus by twenty pounds." Brutus bounced up to Pearl, wagging his fluffy tail, turning tight little circles and yipping.

"Likeable little guy. Too bad he's so friendly with the pitbull wannabe rooster," Jesse mumbled.

"Jesse, come here and put this harness on Brutus, please."

"How's that possible?" Jesse grumbled.

"You'll see, dear. One thing you must never forget: a good team member always does what the team leader says, without question. Understood?"

"Yes, ma'am, but how—?"

"Jesse, you're questioning me, and that makes Rambo nervous. He gets restless around insubordination."

Standing motionless, not five feet away, Rambo intently glared at Jesse. The rooster hiccupped, and a smoke ring—followed by a spark—issued from his beak. Jesse trotted to Gran, who pointed to the metal item now resting at her feet. She instructed him to pick up the substantial contraption, and to Jesse's surprise, Brutus ran to him, leaping around even more excitedly. Sitting down, Brutus wagged his tail with anticipation.

Gran grinned at Jesse, turned quickly, and jogged back to the porch. She had evidently recovered from hauling out the heavy equipment.

Jesse looked down at the tiny dog, now standing and looking up at him expectantly, still wagging his fluffy little tail. He glanced over at the front porch where Gran had retreated. He shrugged and hoisted the rusty apparatus, slipping it over Brutus' head.

Strange things began to happen.

First came an awful smell—like burnt popcorn mixed with dirty socks—then greenish smoke snaked out from under the little dog's feet, lifting him slightly. Brutus turned from purest white to darkest brown and started to grow. The now-huge dog filled the harness, which itself enlarged even more. Jesse could only stand there in shock and stare. He was on the verge of either fainting or running when another creepy thing happened.

Apparently in response to his urge to flee, the length of heavy chain twisted around his left wrist, firmly attaching itself. It was impossible to push it off. Jesse tried.

"Whoa... Gran! W—what's going on?" Jesse sputtered, very alarmed now.

"It's perfectly okay, dear."

"NO, no it's not! What's happening?"

"Oh, I forgot to tell you," Gran said sweetly, evading Jesse's question. "There's a bucket of doggy treats and a tennis racket by the shed out back. They'll help you get Brutus back home. And Jesse—don't step in anything he leaves on the ground. It won't be pleasant. Trust me. Just think of this as the game... on steroids."

"Gran!" Jesse yelled, digging at the attached chain and feeling panic grip him.

"Have an enjoyable walk, dear. I'll have a hot bath ready for you when you get back." She then stepped into the house, closing the door. He saw her peeking out through the curtains.

Rambo resumed his strutting around the yard, and Jesse was left facing one of the biggest, nastiest-smelling dogs he'd ever seen anywhere.

"Now what do I do?" he shrieked, to no one.

Brutus whimpered and gave Jesse a slurpy lick with an enormous purple tongue before running off through the trees towards the shed, knocking Jesse off his feet and dragging him unceremoniously through the yard into the woods.

"Ouch! Ow! Slow down! Eww! Geez, dog—do you have to… aww, gross! Brutus, you are so dead!"

Brutus stopped at the garden shed near a bucket of dog snacks and whined, wagging his enormous tail. The thump rattled the side of the small building. Jesse rolled to a stop not too far behind Brutus—smack in the middle of a puddle of nasty-smelling green slime.

It made Jesse think of diarrhoea and smelled a whole lot worse.

Jesse was drenched from head to toe in the stuff, which also included leaves, twigs, and pieces of gravel. He was bruised, beaten up, and hurt everywhere. He struggled to his feet, panting. The arm wrapped with the chain felt a foot longer than the other, and his hand was numb.

"Well, that was fun. I'm going to go puke now," Jesse said, glaring at the massive mutt while wiping the disgusting matter off his face with his now-ragged T-shirt.

Watching the dog, Jesse noticed that every time Brutus lifted his foot and placed it back down, he deposited a puddle of the foul goo. Jesse figured he'd hit every single pool as he was dragged to the shed. The awful smell was attracting some large, circling flies. They started to bite, leaving welts.

Brutus danced around howling, making more puddles and drawing more flies.

Jesse seized the tennis racket hanging on the shed wall and started whacking the insects. Swatting flies and clutching the treat bucket, Jesse led Brutus away from the shed.

Getting the hang of sidestepping Brutus' slime deposits, Jesse directed Brutus with the biscuits while beating off flies with the racket. Then Brutus spied a rabbit—and took off. Once again, Jesse was pulled through more muck, deep into the woods. A thick carpet of wet leaves cushioned the ground, making it easier for Brutus to drag Jesse over small boulders and around bushes.

"Ouch! Ow! Geez, Brutus—gross! Slow down! Oh man, let me get on my feet—STOP, BRUTUS!"

Surprisingly, the beast stopped. Jesse lay there a few moments, wondering what was happening and how this could possibly be real—except that he hurt everywhere and stank. Brutus started whining. Jesse slowly got to his feet and considered the colossal mutt and the situation. An idea hit him as he brushed off his bruised and battered body.

Removing his ripped and disgusting T-shirt, Jesse secured what remained of it around the dog's eyes. Brutus whimpered, but Jesse hoped that would stop the rabbit-chasing.

Astonished that he still had the treat bucket—and that he wasn't dead after the wild trip into the woods—Jesse decided to try an experiment. He pitched a couple of biscuits ahead of them and watched. Brutus sniffed the air and followed his nose. How the mutt could smell anything with all that disgusting green stuff everywhere was a mystery.

Understanding how to control Brutus helped considerably, and the tennis racket took care of the flies nicely. Since Jesse was already covered in slimy goop, avoiding puddles seemed pointless. They just needed to get back home.

Suddenly, there was an enormous clap of thunder, and heavy, cold rain began to fall—mixed with hail the size of marbles.

"Great," Jesse groaned.

The rain at least discouraged the large flies. The irritating part was that marble-sized hail really hurt when it struck his bruised and bare skin. Both he and the huge mutt were soaked, and the smell of wet dog now overpowered even the stink of the green muck—which was saying something.

"Brutus, do you know the way home?" Jesse asked, gagging.

Brutus responded eagerly, wagging his tail, sniffing the air, and leading out excitedly. Trusting that the dog knew the way, Jesse controlled their pace with the treats. After a few moments, the path back to the house came into view. Jesse felt like he had things under control.

Abruptly, everything changed—for the worse, as it often did in the game world.

Most of the reeking puddles turned into flaming pools of harsh-smelling liquid. A few of the smaller ones remained as stinking green slime. The flying insects transformed into large spiders that spun webs around everything—and Brutus was no longer friendly.

"Whoa…!" Jesse yelped, trying to back away from a snarling Brutus. But the leash still connected them.

Jesse noticed the treats were nearly gone. This was no time to panic.

"Think, Jesse, think," he told himself, as Brutus snapped at him, spiders converged, and smoke rose from the flaming ground. Inspiration struck.

Throwing the snarling Brutus a few biscuits, Jesse quickly removed his torn, stinky T-shirt from the monster's head. Wrapping it around the tennis racket and touching it to the flaming liquid, he fashioned a torch. Brutus backed away.

"Outstanding!" Jesse cried out, smiling.

Despite the heavy rain, Jesse was still covered in goo that seemed oddly resistant to water. Swinging the torch at the spiderwebs, he created mini bonfires—and fried the gnarly spiders at the same time.

"Excellent!" he yelled.

Unfriendly Brutus seemed to understand that following Jesse meant more treats. Walking in front of the unpleasant mutt helped Jesse avoid the flaming pools the dog was leaving behind. After a long, painful, and disgusting journey, the house finally came into view.

Brutus, growling, wanted to run—but Jesse didn't fancy being dragged again. He'd probably lose some skin. Since Jesse controlled the treats, he won. They walked the rest of the way, Brutus whining whenever he wasn't snarling.

Gran sat on the front porch swing, protected from the rain, stroking Rambo like a lapdog. In the yard, an old-fashioned clawfoot bathtub full of steaming, lavender-scented water awaited.

"I wonder where that came from?" Jesse mused, shaking his head.

Gran stood, beaming at him. "Well done, dear—and in record time too! You finished in"—she consulted her watch—"only forty-seven minutes. Excellent indeed. Take that gadget off Brutus and have yourself a nice soak. You deserve it. You'll find everything you need in the big box by the tub. After you finish, wrap yourself in the towel from the box and come inside. Get dressed, and we'll have some hot cocoa and cookies while we discuss your lesson. Oh, by the way, leave your clothes on the grass. We'll burn them later."

She stood and walked into the house. Rambo returned to patrolling.

Jesse unbuckled the harness and—just like that—both the snarling dog and the equipment shrank back to their regular sizes. Brutus was purest white again—and friendly. He didn't even stink.

"Not fair," Jesse chortled, as the little dog bounced around his feet, carefully avoiding the slime that dripped from Jesse's clothes.

Surprising Jesse, Rambo strutted over to Brutus. The big bird squawked and clucked. Brutus ran straight to his bed, scratched, circled twice, and lay down. He looked happy to be home. Jesse watched as Rambo resumed his patrol.

"Brutus is following his team leader," Jesse realised in astonishment. *"Just like in the game."*

After bathing and dressing, Jesse joined Gran in the kitchen, where she handed him a large mug of hot chocolate with floating mini marshmallows. They sat at the table, a plate of her famous homemade cookies between them.

"What do you think the purpose of that lesson was, dear?" Gran inquired, adding more mini marshmallows to her mug.

"I don't know—maybe how to control a monster mutt and other nasties? Or it might help me learn how to stay out of stuff on the ground," he guessed, smirking as he dunked a cookie into his mug.

"Excellent, yes," she smiled. "Controlling the circumstances and not allowing them to control you—that's primary. You did superbly, by the way."

"Thanks, Gran. It was challenging—not knowing what to expect. Kind of like the game when you first start."

Jesse and Pearl spent the next hour talking about what he had learned, and how it applied to their online gaming.

Breeze smiled as she watched the scene. Things were proceeding nicely. Once again, she left to report—but she would return later that night. There were more dreams to give before Jesse would be ready.

Chapter 3

Could my life get any weirder?

A few days later, Jesse, who had been in a deep sleep, crashed to the floor tangled in his bedding. His mind wasn't registering what his body was desperately trying to escape. As he lay on the carpet, staring up at the ceiling and trying to figure out what the heck had just happened to him, Rambo jumped on his chest and delivered his most excellent rendition of cock-a-doodle-doo perfection.

Once again, Jesse's body reacted violently to the experience. He nearly wet himself.

"Rambo, you BIG, FAT, STUPID chicken," Jesse yelled, trying to grab the huge bird. "Get out of here, or I swear I'll wring your neck with my bare hands and throw you into Gran's soup pot—feathers and all. I don't care what she says."

The big rooster clucked twice, strutting to the open bedroom door, swishing his long, reddish-green iridescent tail feathers. He glanced back at Jesse, who was trying to untangle himself from his bedding. Satisfied that Jesse would remain conscious, Rambo exited.

Peeved, Jesse threw a handy shoe at the retreating bird, missing by a long shot. Every part of Jesse's body was complaining about the abrupt and rude awakening. He rolled back over, covering his head.

"Same senseless dream, over and over, with Dad trying to tell me something—and now Rambo crows me awake. Could my life get any weirder?"

"Jesse, dear, it's time to get up. Your food is getting cold," Gran called to him from the hallway.

Jesse groaned. "I'm getting up," he yelled, pushing himself off the floor. "Hey, Gran, tell your attack rooster he needs to go on a diet. He's way too fat for a chicken! And why was he in my bedroom, crowing?"

He heard Gran chuckling as she walked back to the kitchen.

"I sent Rambo in there because you're a sound sleeper. I wasn't sure if you slept in the buff, and I didn't want to, um… embarrass anyone," she snickered.

"I don't sleep in the buff," Jesse retorted. "But I might start sleeping with that old shotgun I saw hanging in the shed."

"Rambo did what his team leader asked," Pearl said. "Now move it, or I'll send Brutus in to finish the job."

"OK, OK…" Jesse said, thinking of the huge, snarling dog Brutus had become. "I'm coming, sheesh."

Picking up his bedding, now scattered all over the floor, Jesse discovered his missing alarm clock under the bed and noticed the time.

"Hey Gran, it's only six-thirty in the morning. What's the problem? It's Saturday, for Pete's sake."

"I know, dear. However, Mr Chambers and Cami will arrive around noon, and I have some things I need you to take care of before then."

"Oh yeah," Jesse remembered, yawning big again as he pulled on his clothes, staggering against his dresser.

With his mind on the perplexing dream, Jesse stumbled down the hall to the bathroom. Turning too soon, he banged into the doorframe, stubbing his big toe. Fully awake now, he yelped in pain.

"Good heavens, what are you doing?" Pearl yelled.

"Nothing, I just walked into the wall," Jesse said, examining his toe.

"Are you feeling OK?"

"Yeah. Just tired. I'll be out in a minute."

"OK, dear," Gran said.

As Jesse entered the kitchen, the smell of bacon and French toast greeted him. Rambo and Brutus were already at the table, gobbling down plates of food. Jesse thought it was odd that they ate at the table, but it was Gran's house. He glared at the big rooster as he sat in the chair as far away from the two animals as possible. Rambo and Brutus ignored him.

After everyone had their food, Pearl joined them at the table with a plate for herself.

"Are you ready for some more tactical training today, Jesse?"

"That's uncertain," Jesse said. "I want some answers before I commit to anything else. What's going on here, Gran? And don't give me any lame responses. I want the truth."

Pearl studied him and then sighed, pushing her plate away.

"OK, I think that's fair. But before I answer, let me ask you a quick question first. What do you imagine is going on here? Give it your wildest guess."

"Honestly, I don't know," Jesse responded. "I'm trying hard to make sense of everything—and nothing, absolutely nothing, makes any logical sense. Plenty of it makes no sense at all."

Jesse noticed that both Rambo and Brutus were staring at him now, their food forgotten.

"Wildest guess," Gran said again.

"OK, you want my wildest guess? Magic. I can't believe I just said that out loud, but it's the only thing that makes any sense—and that makes no sense at all."

"And why can't you believe that it's magic?" Pearl asked.

"I don't know. I guess because magic is right up there with Santa Claus, the Easter Bunny, and the Tooth Fairy—and all the other make-believe stuff people conjure for kids. I mean, magic wands and stuff like that can't be real."

"Jesse, what is it that you enjoy about the game so much? Why do you play? Is it just about levelling, or is it something else?"

"You know, Gran, I've tried to figure that out myself, and the best answer I can come up with is—I don't know. In some ways, it gives me a place to hide, but I love the idea of a world of fantasy. Where magic is possible, and people are united in black-and-white causes. So much in this world is grey. I wish aliens were real, and families stayed together forever."

His head drooped sadly at the thought of forever families, and he sighed heavily.

"Maybe that's my answer."

"Jesse, dear, this world that we live in is, in many ways, dying. People don't trust each other. There was a time when that wasn't true. Everyone had faith, were honourable, and believed in some form of magic. When imagination dies—except in the mind and heart of a child, or in books, games, and stories—life can become stagnant and stale, like an old piece of bread or pond water."

"Can that be changed, Gran? Can we save this world, make it honourable again, and bring back imagination and magic?"

"Yes, we can. All it takes is people that believe, and that's where the answer to your question rests. I'm going to tell you something—something so outrageous that you're going to think I imagined it or made it up."

Jesse shifted in his seat. Rambo and Brutus stayed at the table, watching; neither moved.

"A little over a year ago, while Mr Chambers and I played the game together—me here, and him at his house—we both felt someone watching us. Not in a creepy way. More like a guardian angel peeking over our shoulder. Since then, we've had contact with people from another world. A world of fantasy. Where magic is real, and the people are immortal. But they have a, um… situation, and they need people from our world to help them solve it. The problem is dire. It requires people who are familiar with the Internet, role-playing games, and who believe in magic. Real magic. That's why they monitored us. That's why there's a big push in the game right now."

Jesse didn't know what to say. He was in shock.

"They're aliens? Why do they need assistance? Are they the ones that make all the weird stuff around here happen?"

"We'll wait for Mr Chambers, dear. He can explain it better."

"So you're just going to leave me hanging like that?" Jesse asked, sceptically.

"I'm afraid so. You'll see why once Mr Chambers gets here. In the meantime, we'll continue with the lessons. I think you're going to enjoy this next one."

Jesse's brain was struggling. It felt overloaded and sluggish as it tried to wrap itself around what Gran had said. He drew in a big breath and let it out slowly. He was disappointed that she wouldn't give him more details, but without any other options, he had to trust her.

"What's the next lesson?" Jesse asked, resignedly. "I hope it doesn't include disgusting slime or biting flies."

"No," she tittered. "I'm going to show you another way to solve problems. I call it 'outside the box'. Let me show you—but first, I think Rambo and Brutus should go outside for a while."

Both animals jumped down and walked to the front door. She let them out.

"OK Jesse, let's go into the family room," she said as she walked that way.

From the middle of the room, she beckoned him to her. Jesse followed her cautiously, tensely watching for the unexpected. She faced him, hands on her ample hips and a big smile on her face. Jesse noticed that she seemed relaxed, and yet there was a hint of mischief in her eyes. For some reason, this made him feel uneasy.

Gesturing him closer, Pearl widened her stance and calmly said, "Take a punch at me, Jesse."

He honestly felt unnerved at the request. "Gran, I'm not going to hit you."

"Trust me," she smiled. "Give it a crack. Like you're the champ boxer and I'm your student."

"OK," Jesse responded, unsure. "But if you get a black eye, don't tell Mum I've been beating you up."

"It's a deal. Now give it your best shot."

Jesse approached Gran and lifted his arm to comply, but his knees buckled.

"Once more," she shouted at him. Again, he tried—and again, he went down.

"Jesse… really try this time."

"I am trying, Gran," he snapped, frustrated. "It's weird. I don't know what's happening to me."

"Swing," she bellowed.

His third attempt also failed.

"OK, I think that's enough to make my point," she said, giving him a hand up.

"What do you think just happened there, dear?"

"You kicked my butt without lifting a finger, that's what happened."

"No, you kicked your butt, without lifting a finger."

"Huh?" Jesse said, stumped.

"Sweetheart, I merely suggested—through telepathic thought—that you'd rather fall down than hit me. You didn't want to hit me in the first place, which helped. Your mind took the suggestion, and your body reacted, knocking you down."

"Good thing the carpet's thick," Jesse mused, flatly.

"Indeed," she chuckled. "Mind control is an ancient way of getting what you want. It takes many forms, such as 'brainwashing' and subconscious suggestion. Cults practise it with their followers. All governments employ variations of it. The media tries, but I consider their way the sloppiest. When they want to influence a person, group or country, they put the chosen side into a favourable light and blacklist the other—or they just flat out embellish the facts. It's deceptive and crude, but effective, especially when people don't reason things out for themselves. It's called 'yellow journalism'. When you get a chance, look it up."

"I don't understand, Gran. I can't remember thinking I should fall. How did you do that?"

"I pictured it. Every time you tried to hit me. It was that simple. I've been doing it for years," Gran chuckled at a memory. "As a teenager, your mother always volunteered to do things she didn't want to do—like cleaning the cat box or weeding the garden. It's all about practice, practice, and more practice. I'm going to teach you how to do it. Let's go outside."

She started toward the door but then thought of something else.

"One more thing—I know you wouldn't do this—but you can't get a person or animal to do anything contrary to their nature. In other words, I couldn't make you kill someone or rob a bank unless it was already in your mind to do so. We can compare it to hypnotism. A person usually won't do anything while hypnotised that they wouldn't do while awake."

"Wow, Gran, when do we start?" Jesse asked excitedly, starting for the door.

"Right now. I'll have you work on this until lunch, or until the Chambers arrive."

"Outstanding. What's first?"

"You're going to pet Rambo."

"What…!" Jesse choked, stopping dead in his tracks. "How is that going to help me with my playtime, or to learn magic? Gran, I don't think this is a good idea. Besides—"

"Jesse," Pearl said, cutting him off. "Rambo is an important part of this equation, and the sooner you understand that and stop your grumbling, the better it will go for you. You did want to learn mind control, didn't you? Now, follow me, dear."

Gran walked outside and sat on the grass in the front yard. She patted the ground for Jesse to sit next to her. He sulked his way over and plopped down. He was not looking forward to this, no matter what she thought he would learn.

"I want you to picture Rambo climbing into your lap, and you petting him. That's all. No words, or hand movement—just thoughts. You must keep your mind clear of everything but the task. Do you understand?"

"Yes, ma'am," he mumbled.

"Do you need a drink or the bathroom? You'll probably be here a long time."

"Yeah, sure. I'll be right back." Jesse stood, petulantly, and walked back to the house, kicking clumps of grass as he went.

When he returned, Gran showed him a meditation pose to sit in, with his eyes closed. Then she retreated inside. The position felt comfortable for a while, but then his legs started to tingle and go numb. He kept at it, determined to succeed despite his reservations. Every few minutes he peeked through his eyelashes, checking on Rambo. Nothing changed. No big surprise there.

Time passed, and he couldn't feel his legs anymore. He changed his thoughts to his legs. He imagined the blood flowing back into the numb areas and feeling returning. To his surprise, it worked—and there were no pins and needles!

He decided to refocus on Rambo, visualising differently from what Gran had said. Jesse pictured Rambo tired and stiff from all his walking, wanting a nice, comfortable lap to sit in. He saw himself stroking the big bird and imagined the relaxing effect it could have on them both.

After a few moments of concentration in this fashion, Jesse felt a soft peck on his pant leg. Shocked, he watched as Rambo climbed into his lap, settling down. Slowly, Jesse moved his right hand over the big rooster, gently caressing the silky feathers. Rambo made a soft clucking sound Jesse could only describe as a rooster's purr. Relaxing, Jesse felt completely safe and comfortable in Rambo's presence. To his surprise, he found himself enjoying the experience.

Gran came out of the house to the front porch. Glancing up, Jesse smirked at her. Her profound astonishment was etched deep on her face. Silently, she returned inside the house.

Not sure how long he sat with Rambo, listening to the soft sound, Jesse continued stroking the resting bird. After a while, Rambo climbed out of Jesse's lap and nodded once—in what could have been a bow—before returning to his patrol. Jesse smiled after the big rooster, sad that this time with Rambo was over. He was amazed at how entirely his opinion of the bird had changed. Why? Was that part of the activity too?

Stretching out on his back, Jesse studied the returning clouds, thinking about the experience. What had he done? Stroking a chicken was not unusual. Getting one to sit in your lap by imagining it—that was very strange. Jesse chuckled. Strange described many things around here over the last few months.

Noticing the shortening shadows, he hurried in to eat something before the Chambers' arrival. Jesse was very anxious about their visit—not just to see his closest friend, Cami, but to get many of his questions answered.

He and Cami had been friends since the sixth grade, right before she'd been in a terrible car accident that killed her mother and twin sister, Chloe. The accident had crushed Cami's spine, leaving her paralysed from the waist down. Cami had been a great football player, and she and Jesse had paired up all the time before that tragic day.

The following year was the year Jesse's dad died in Iraq. They helped each other a great deal throughout that time, and their friendship deepened. Now they had the game. Jesse found peace with Gran and their guild family—but best of all, in the game, Cami could run again.

Chapter 4

Oh man! Creep alarm going off!

Walking into the kitchen, Jesse observed Gran sitting at the table, her head bowed. Her hands rested on a strange crystal globe that emitted soft lights and a whirring sound. It was about the size of a bowling ball and slightly egg-shaped.

Not wanting to disturb her, Jesse quietly washed and dried his hands at the kitchen sink. Moving to the table, he sat down and started eating the sandwiches and grapes she had placed there for him. At least, his rumbling stomach hoped they were his. He watched her as he ate.

Gran finally raised her head, looking at him, ashen-faced. Jesse stopped eating.

"What's wrong, Gran? Are you sick?"

"No, dear, just shocked. Jesse, we need to have a serious talk, but I want you to finish eating. Do you need another sandwich or an apple?"

"Gran, what's that thing, a crystal egg?" he smirked.

"It's a telewave, a way to talk to the fantasy world. It's like television, but more like Skyping—only very long distance. It's probably a million years old or more. No one knows. Mr Chambers has one too."

"Wow, that's incredible. A million years?"

"Or more. Finish eating, dear; then we'll talk."

He studied her as she gathered the telewave. Understanding flooded his mind.

"It's about the rooster, right?"

"Eat, dear. We'll talk in a little while."

She walked into her room with the telewave in her arms, closing the door.

"That's so weird," he thought. Then, shrugging, he resumed eating his sandwiches.

As he finished and cleaned up, he heard a soft knocking at the front door. Remembering the Chambers', he ran to let them in.

What greeted him as the door swung open surprised him exceedingly. There stood a snow-white griffin and a reddish-green iridescent dragon. Shaken, Jesse clambered back into the room.

"Master Jesse," the dragon addressed him in a soothing voice from the doorway. "Be not alarmed. We mean you no harm, but we must talk to you."

Unable to stand any longer, Jesse collapsed into a nearby chair.

"Who... who are you?" Jesse stammered.

"You know us by our other forms," the dragon stated nonchalantly. "I am Rambo, and this," he nodded towards the griffin, "is Brutus. May we come in?" They bowed slightly.

Jesse couldn't imagine how to refuse. He nodded, and the two fantasy creatures entered, shrinking to accommodate the room.

"The Elders have decided that your training must continue in our world, Xanthara. You are too gifted for the mortal world, and your life may be at risk. We will transport you to that realm as soon as possible," the dragon said, nodding again slightly.

"What do you mean, transport me to your world? And who are the Elders?" Jesse asked nervously. He watched Rambo and inwardly groaned at the thought of holding this creature on his lap—or worse, threatening him with Gran's soup pot and calling him names.

Gran entered the room. Rambo and Brutus both bowed and stepped aside.

"You are precocious, dear, and the Elders are the leaders of that world, Xanthara," she said, sitting down. "Now, before Mr Chambers gets here, I will try to answer some of your questions. No one has ever communicated with a dragon through thought alone—unless an elf, or if they had extensive training."

"I didn't know he was a dragon. I only tried to do what you wanted me to do. An elf?" Jesse's emotions jumped all over—scared, excited, anxious, curious.

"Yes, dear, an elf. And that's why it's so incredible. If Rambo were merely a rooster, the task would have been difficult at best. But you penetrated the mind of a dragon." She cleared her throat and shifted her weight.

"Let me put it this way. The focus of a chicken is on survival. Once you get past their need to eat, sleep, mate, and protect their young, there isn't much left for them to consider. A dragon, on the other hand, is intelligent—not to mention a creature of magic. Entering Rambo's mind the way you did can be compared to sending a single BB through a ten-inch-thick piece of titanium steel. Then, after you gained access, you convinced him that the request was worthwhile."

Jesse glanced at Rambo, who was staring at him with a toothy, dragon sort of grin. It was unnerving.

"I'm sorry, dear; I never expected you to succeed. I considered it an exercise to strengthen your mental muscle—to teach you how to improve your focus," Gran stated sheepishly.

"Then all that talk about 'mind control' was a farce?" Jesse asked, dubiously.

"Oh no, dear, it's real. After this, I have no doubt about your abilities. However, I'm not sure it's a good idea, because of the possibility of abusing the talent."

"Abusing the talent?" Jesse questioned, curious.

"Yes. Imagine tormenting those boys that teased you in school—just because you could."

Jesse grinned despite himself. Gran didn't miss his reaction.

"Bingo," she said, pointing at him. "That's what I'm talking about."

Jesse blushed at his guilt. "What happens now, Gran?"

"When I first contacted Xanthara—or the fantasy world—I was told that you would journey to the capital city of Rodashu immediately, as Rambo said. Master Nexlucimus, the leading Elder and High Priest, has since decided you will remain here for the time being. You will continue your training with me—unless something else happens. "

"He wants you to come for orientation immediately, however. That way, you will know what we're facing with this quest. I told him we expected Mr Chambers and Cami today. That pleased him. He mentioned someone else would be coming as well. I don't know who."

A knock at the front door diverted their attention. Rambo and Brutus returned to their conventional forms.

Gran let them out as Mr Chambers and Cami walked in. Tommy Tam, Jesse's new friend from school, was also with them. As Rambo walked past Tommy, he bowed. Tommy returned the action. Jesse watched the exchange curiously but said nothing.

"Hey Tommy, I didn't know you'd be here. Gran, this is the guy from school I mentioned to you. I guess this means you know about these fantasy guys too?"

"Yeah, you might say that," Tommy smiled.

"Are there others from school?" Jesse asked.

"Yes, dear," Gran answered. "Plus others from around the world—wherever the games are played. You will shortly learn about the problem."

Gran invited them into the family room.

"Please, have a seat."

They all sat, except Tommy, who stepped into the middle of the floor.

"Mrs Smith and Jesse, before we begin, I want to show you something."

Jesse glanced at Gran, who looked as confused as he felt.

"First off, my name isn't Tommy Tam, and I'm not from your world."

Jesse looked over at Cami and Mr Chambers, but they were intently watching Tommy. "Let me show you what I mean," Tommy said, waving his hands outward. His image flickered and then changed. He was now a full head shorter, with dark tan skin and shoulder-length silver hair. He had delicate, slightly pointed features and wore leather from head to toe.

"Oh my," Gran whispered, bringing her hands to her heart. "A wood elf."

"Holy crap!" Jesse gulped, jumping up, alarmed. Tommy grinned at him.

Cami and her father didn't react. Jesse wondered why, as he sat down, embarrassed.

"*My* real name is Tomitobas Silverrod, and I am one part of the Rodashu Council. I share that honour with my uncle Nexlucimus, my father Heralon, and twelve others. We are the ruling body of our world."

Shocked, speechless, Jesse just gaped. Then something clicked into place in the back of his mind. A shadow emerged out of his brain fog, carrying his dreams with it.

"Wait a minute! I remember now. Marble buildings, people like you, and creepy little furballs. Several nights in a row, my dad tried to explain it to me, but nothing made sense."

All of them, except Tommy, appeared stunned by Jesse's revelation.

"I've never heard of anyone shown this in a dream," Mr Chambers stated.

Tommy smiled. "Jesse has superior talents that the Council of Elders need for this quest. We wanted him prepared for our world when he saw it. A Shadow Dream introduced him to Xanthara and our people through dreams. She also identified him as a Finding."

Gran gave another surprised gasp, moving her hands to her mouth. Jesse watched her, perplexed.

"I don't understand," Jesse said.

"Don't be concerned, Jesse," Tommy stated. "This will all be explained soon. We need to proceed with the orientation. Cami, would you please show Jesse the talisman?"

Jesse's head snapped around, and he stared at her as she moved toward him, her motorised wheelchair gliding smoothly over the thick carpet. Holding out her left hand, Cami showed Jesse a ring in the shape of a white dragon with a glowing red eye.

"This is a talisman, Jesse. I'm sorry, I couldn't say anything to you before this," she said, sheepishly, her cheeks radiant with embarrassment. "I've watched Dad play the games for years, and just recently, I learned of the Elders. They asked us to watch for others with magical talent, but they wanted us to guard the fact. The talisman senses magic, or the ability to learn magic. Its eye glows red when I'm close to you. I've known about your talent for some time. The Xantharaians were stunned when I told them you were red. My ability is white magic, my dad is yellow, and your grandmother is brown."

"That's insane. You've known about this for a while, and you couldn't tell me? Why? And why do we have different colours?" Jesse questioned, feeling hurt that his friend had kept such a huge secret.

"Jesse, you'll understand shortly why Cami or your grandmother, for that matter, couldn't tell you anything more before now. The colours indicate different strengths and abilities," Tommy explained. "Red and gold are the strongest, and until you, only immortals had those colours. The other colours are white, blue, yellow, brown, and black in that order."

"Why would I be red?"

"We aren't sure; there are several things unusual about you."

"So bizarre!" Jesse thought to himself.

"Now, with your permission, Jesse, Elder Nexlucimus would like to meet with you to explain our quest. By the way, there's a surprise waiting for you on the other side," Tommy said, grinning widely.

"This whole thing is a surprise," Jesse thought.

"Cami, would you be so kind?" Tommy asked.

"Jesse, please stand in front of me and take my hands," Cami said, holding her hands out.

Nervously, Jesse stood and moved closer to Cami, taking her hands. She closed her eyes and lowered her head, then started to hum. The air in the room changed. It felt heavier, like before a storm—snapping and crackling, charged with electricity.

Then the impossible happened. Cami stood, still holding Jesse's hands. He was so shaken he nearly broke contact, but he was attached to her like a piece of steel trapped by a powerful magnet. Her head lolled back, and her eyes opened. What he saw then startled him even more. Cami's eyes radiated a soft white glow, like dim flashlights.

Jesse began to tremble. *"Oh man! Creep alarm going off!"*

Slowly, she reached out with her left hand, placing the talisman on his head. A shiver ran down his spine. She spoke in a soft, confident voice. "We, the Keepers of the Shield, present to you, esteemed Elders, Jesse Finch."

An intense white light encased them, radiating to everyone in the room, making faces shine and the air sparkle. Jesse felt warmth permeating his entire body, soothingly. He relaxed. Willingness to submit to whatever happened overcame him. He was impressed that he should bow to greatness. Before he could act on this thought, however, the room disappeared into melting, swirling colours, streaking people, furniture, and wall hangings into molten trails of painted light. The coloured veins were the only movement, but something extraordinary was happening.

After a few moments, Jesse sensed he was falling. Cami was no longer there holding his hands. Throwing his arms out to stabilise himself, he gently settled to the ground, standing.

"Jesse Finch?" A gentle, disembodied female voice asked him.

"Yes," Jesse peeped, his voice cracking.

"Behold, and welcome to the world of Xanthara."

Chapter 5

Whoa!

Jesse's vision cleared, and he stood in a strange yet familiar place, unsure if he was actually there or still dreaming. All around him were gold- and silver-streaked white stone buildings, two or three stories tall. Beautifully carved wooden doors decorated with golden inlays of intricate patterns enhanced the entries. Narrow streets, paved with crystal cobblestones, sparkled in the warm air. Furry balls of various sizes and colours raced past him. Startled, Jesse jumped aside, only then realising that he stood inside a clear bubble.

Cautiously, he reached out to touch his encasement. It felt and wobbled like gelatin, only more plastic. Since breathing was no problem, Jesse guessed it was a filter. Many sounds captured his attention—animal noises and talking. Carefully taking a few steps, he discovered that walking was easy. He glided. The bubble stayed just beyond his feet, but he could feel the cobblestones through his sneakers.

Walking a short distance, Jesse entered a marketplace, lined with street vendors and people shopping and visiting with each other. The individuals Jesse saw were the kind you might read about in a book of fairy tales. Maybe you'd see them in an animated movie. Perhaps you would interact with them online, in a game full of computer-generated characters—of all sizes, shapes, and colours.

Jesse experienced a déjà vu feeling. He was having a difficult time getting his mind to accept what he saw, yet it all seemed so familiar. Then, with a jolt, he understood why. It was the world of his dreams. Only this time, he was feeling it tangibly. *"How could that be?"* he wondered.

Jesse noticed people watching him. Some seemed astonished, others amused; some were waving shyly. He waved back. They pointed him out to their children—at least, he thought they were children. They were smaller and looked like the bigger ones. A little blue boy approached him.

"You're one of the new Keepers, aren't you?"

"Yes," Jesse said. He'd known the answer, without understanding the question.

"When I get bigger, I will join the Keepers too. My name is Jamison."

"I'm pleased to meet you, Jamison. I'm Jesse," Jesse smiled, as the retreating young man waved goodbye.

Abruptly, Jesse remembered Tommy's words: "There will be a surprise waiting on the other side."

"Jesse?" The deep, painfully familiar voice—almost a whisper—spoke from behind. Jesse whirled around, and his legs gave way. He toppled to the ground inside his bubble.

"Dad?" Jesse stammered, shocked. "Is that you? Or is this another dream?"

"Yes, son, it's me, and no, this is not a dream."

"How can this be?" Jesse choked on his words. "How is this possible? You're dead."

"Only my body is dead. My essence will always be alive."

"Your essence?" Jesse asked, confused.

"The part that lives when the body dies. Some call it the spirit."

"You look just like I remember, only younger."

"Our spirits are a perfect version of our mortal bodies, with deformities and age removed."

"Dad… is this heaven? Can I touch you?"

"No, this isn't heaven. It's the world of Xanthara, and this is the capital city of Rodashu. You can't touch me, Jesse, because I have no physical body, but I will soon. The only reason you can see me now is because of the magic here."

"How come you didn't go to Heaven, Dad? I thought you said when we die, we go to Heaven."

"I had a choice, Jesse."

"What do you mean, you had a choice?" Jesse sounded uncertain.

"Jesse, heaven isn't a place where people go to play harps and lie around," his father said. "It's a busy place, where people are coming and going. They are returning from the mortal world to become immortal. Some are spirits, getting ready to be born into mortality. Essences like me can help those being prepared to go to Earth. Or we can help the people still in the mortal world get back, like guardian angels. That's putting it simply. I decided I wanted to help people, especially you and your mother."

"Mum's married again," Jesse said dryly.

"I know, son. I helped it happen."

"You what?!" Jesse was shocked.

"Your stepdad is a great man, Jesse. He'll be good for your mother. He would have been good for you too if you'd let him." Jesse opened his mouth to reply but was cut off by his father.

"We need to leave, Jesse. We can chat about this later."

"Where are we going?"

"To meet with the head Elder, Master Nexlucimus. He needs to explain the quest to you."

"Oh yeah, I forgot," Jesse said awkwardly. David, his father, chuckled.

Jesse tried to stand, but when he leaned against the wall of the bubble, it moved. He tripped, his long legs tangled in the spongy material. David watched and then suggested, "Why don't you get out of that thing? You'll be able to travel faster."

"I can get out of it?" Jesse asked, concerned. "Can I breathe out there?"

"I can breathe out here," his father said.

"Yeah, but you're dead," Jesse smirked.

David laughed. "Good point. Yes, you can come out. This air is better than any you'd breathe back home. You're in that thing so you don't contaminate the environment. A word of warning though: when you come out, you'll be attacked."

Jesse blanched and surveyed the area around them cautiously. "What will attack me?" he asked nervously.

"Skeedlers," his father grinned. "You don't see them until it's too late."

"What will they do to me? Will it hurt?" Jesse asked fearfully, remembering the distressing furballs from his dream that seemed to eat people.

"Nope, but you'll never be as clean again. They won't hurt you; it tickles."

"I hate tickling," Jesse winced.

"Well then, mighty warrior, it's time to meet your masters." David looked around and called to a vendor.

"Excuse me, ma'am, would you be so kind as to burst my son's bubble, please?"

The plump little lady, with lavender skin and bright pink braids, nodded. "It would be an honour to assist a young Keeper start on his journey, good sir." She shyly approached and then gingerly poked a small hole in Jesse's bubble with a knife, ripping it open. She stepped back quickly, retreating to her booth.

At first, nothing happened. Then, there was a low rumble, like distant thunder. Suddenly, the area exploded with a rush of furry balls. Hundreds of them. Every possible colour, and a few colours Jesse had never seen before. They piled in on him, filling the bubble and stretching it, almost to bursting. Jesse yelled, and they filled his mouth, gagging him.

From the outside, it looked like a clear plastic bag, gyrating with furry balls. Jesse was completely covered. The Skeedlers could smell invading dirt, germs, or even the thought, from miles away. Jesse and his earthly garments were the filthy trespassers, contaminating the environment. They had work to do, and he was that work. They scrubbed and scoured every speck of him, crawling inside his shirt, pants, and shoes. When they finished, he glistened. Places not shown in public even glowed, and his breath was minty fresh. Then abruptly, they were gone, along with the bubble.

Jesse was humiliated but squeaky clean. There was no chance that anyone could catch a germ from him now. In fact, he doubted there were any microbes on the entire planet, with the Skeedlers on duty. He glanced at his father, who was doubled over with laughter, trying desperately to catch his breath.

"You know, Dad," Jesse said, trying to sound dignified under the circumstances. "I don't remember you having such a wicked sense of humour."

Jesse shook a leg, tugging at the seat of his pants, dislodging a wedgie, as he strode off. His father, regaining his composure, trotted after him and redirected him to the proper path.

"Sorry, Jesse. I should've given you more warning," his father stated, still trying to control his snickers.

"At least you could've told me what you meant by 'attack' before they hit me," Jesse said, smirking. "It's hard to believe I'm here with you," Jesse continued. "This whole experience is incredibly weird. It's unreal to hear you laugh and speak my name again."

"I know, it's wonderful to see you again too. I've missed talking to you," David smiled.

As they walked, David pointed out places of interest, and Jesse's amazement grew with every step. His mum would love it here. Quaint homes with big yards and walkways lined with flowering plants. Boxes filled with herbs and blossoms decorated many windows. It was so different from home. Well-tended vegetable gardens and fruit trees laden with ripe fruit reminded Jesse how hungry he was. His stomach growled.

"Mum would love this place," Jesse told his dad. "She was always trying to grow stuff."

"I know," David responded. "She looked forward to moving to Europe. I wish I had been the one to take her there." David sounded pensive. Jesse studied him for a moment.

Skeedlers darting all over the place distracted Jesse. He eyed them suspiciously, but they never came close again. Jesse breathed a sigh of relief and shivered at the thought.

They walked past a zoo and a park with many large families. Food vendors were all around them, offering their merchandise. People watched Jesse and his father, curious. Some waved and greeted them. All were smiling.

From the shadows, Jesse noticed a beautiful, green-tinted girl with golden hair. She smiled and waved shyly before flying off with gossamer wings, reminding him of a dragonfly. Jesse was stunned and smitten at the same time, suddenly forgetting how to walk. His father, walking slightly ahead of him, turned back.

"You okay, son?"

"Oh, yeah, Dad," Jesse replied dreamily. "I'm just fine. This is a very cool place."

"Good. Hurry up, we don't want to keep the High Priest waiting."

"Oh, sure," Jesse said, looking back over his shoulder to where the girl had been, as he trotted to where his dad waited. Eventually, they came to a massive building. David called it the Great Library. It reminded Jesse of a castle, except it was made of gold- and silver-veined white stone and crystal walls. Gilt leafing surrounded the windows and doors, accenting the patterns and intricate designs carved into the wood. Gemstone studs created delicate shapes that flowed like a sparkling river on the walls of the building, complementing the beauty of the workmanship. Jesse felt more than a little intimidated as he walked up to this magnificent edifice. His stomach churned; he wasn't sure if it was nerves or hunger.

"Dad, who is this High Priest, Head Elder guy? Is he like a king or something? Will I have to bow or do other weird stuff?"

"Don't worry; he's very nice. You'll know what to do when the time comes," David said, trying to reassure him.

"How much do you want to bet I'll embarrass myself?" Jesse groaned.

David just smiled at his son as they moved toward the remarkable building. Climbing the crystal entry stairs, they each retreated into their own thoughts. The outer doors opened automatically as they approached and stepped through.

The Great Library was massive inside. When Jesse thought it enormous from the outside, he had significantly underestimated its size. He wondered how anyone could walk from one end of it to the other in an hour. As he thought this, a little man floated by on a circular disk with handlebars.

"Wow, what's he riding?" Jesse asked his father.

"That's a teledisk, Jesse. People use them in these expansive capital buildings. They will transport you while here or teleport you between buildings. Just tell it where you want to go."

"Outstanding! Can we try one?"

"Not this trip, maybe another time."

"Bummer," Jesse moaned.

As they walked through the central courtyard with its huge, vaulted ceiling, they couldn't miss a magnificent crystal fountain. In the centre stood the statue of a beautiful white dragon, frozen in the purest white stone. She carried a gleaming silver sword in her talons.

To think of the dragon as female just felt right to Jesse. She was in the act of taking flight, her large, delicate wings extended. Jesse wondered how anyone could carve something so gentle, so beautiful. She radiated a soft light to the surrounding area.

Watery fountainheads of misty spray sprang to life at her feet, changing shapes and colours, creating the look of flowing clouds of every hue. They were surrounded by soft music that made Jesse think the dragon was humming. He was awestruck. This was the same dragon as Cami's talisman, only Cami's dragon wasn't trying to fly, and it didn't have a sword.

"David and Jesse Finch?" a soft, commanding voice called to them. They turned.

David immediately fell to one knee. Seeing this, Jesse did the same.

"Master Nexlucimus," David said, in humble reverence.

"Please, stand, my friends. It's pleasant to see you again, David."

"You too, sir," David nodded toward the Elder.

"Young Jesse, you are most welcome to Xanthara, and our fair city, Rodashu."

"Thank you, sir," Jesse tried to sound braver than he felt.

The Elder looked younger than what Jesse had pictured in his mind. He had imagined a wise old wizard, with flowing silver hair and a beard. This man seemed the same age as his dad, a little shorter and slightly plump. He had dark brown shoulder-length hair, a neatly trimmed beard, and a moustache. His dark brown eyes had a mischievous twinkle, and he wore dark blue robes, sprinkled with silver swirls, no hat, and shiny cloth slippers of the same colour.

"I am pleased to meet you, my young friend. I have heard much about you. You have admirers in our world," Nexlucimus said, with a cheerful grin.

Jesse, astonished, looked at his father, who only shrugged, also mystified.

"Now, will you please walk with me to my council chambers?" Elder Nexlucimus said, as he turned and motioned toward some stairs. After climbing several sets of stairs, they walked down a grand corridor, lined with many paintings, all framed in gold. The building seemed to be a museum of art, as well as a library, and it went on forever. There were statues of people, animals, and flowers along the way. Each piece of art was placed on a crystal pedestal. They looked so lifelike. Jesse was tempted to touch one but resisted. Everywhere he looked, there was something delicate. It was astonishing. Never had Jesse seen a building so elaborately decorated.

"Geez, something would probably break in here if I sneezed, or worse, farted," he thought, and had to concentrate hard so he wouldn't start laughing. Something would probably shatter if he did.

Walking down several long hallways, Jesse observed many rooms with rows of shelves laden with books. It was very silent. Only the echo of his footsteps on the marble floor and the swish of the Elder's robes were heard.

They finally stopped at high doors, covered in carvings of creatures that appeared to be storybook fairies trying to hide behind the exotic fruit carved on the door, or he thought it was fruit. It was gold, with silver leaves.

"Ah, here we are," Master Nexlucimus said, as he waved his hand, and the solid doors swung open smoothly and silently, as if by a soft zephyr. Jesse marvelled, and his mouth dropped open.

"Close your mouth, son," David whispered in Jesse's ear, smiling.

"Sorry," Jesse breathed back, snapping his mouth shut.

"Please come in," the High Priest invited.

Jesse and his dad followed the Elder into the large chamber, marvelling at the room's immense beauty. Jesse felt small indeed. Pillars lined both sides of the cavernous room, holding up a gilded ceiling that was vaulted at least forty feet. Polished stones covered the floor, and all along one wall were tall stained-glass windows depicting fanciful scenes that let in sunbeams, gleaming with shiny sparkles. Jesse found his thoughts wandering. "Obviously, the sparkles can't be dust or those Skeedlers would be all over this place. I wonder who that shy green girl by the food vendors was. She looked close to my age. She sure was pretty."

As they continued into the enormous room, Jesse wondered how many people could fit in the space. If the floor was grass, he was sure you could play a football game in the centre. A glass, oval-shaped table filled a sizable section of the central area. Several smaller, golden-edged crystal tables and long crystal benches lined the outer walls. "Wow, this place is impossible!" Jesse mused. "How could anyone make, and then move, a table that big?"

Overstuffed chairs covered in soft tan fur begged for someone to sit on them. They snuggled against the table, moving slightly. Jesse stepped closer for a better view. One of the chairs slid silently away from the table, inviting him to sit in the comfort it offered.

"Whoa!" Jesse jumped back, startled. The seat replaced itself, almost sadly. Jesse noticed the Elder and his dad watching him, with smiles on their faces.

"You can sit there if you wish, Jesse," Master Nexlucimus said. "But there are other, more comfortable chairs over here." Jesse noticed that the fur-covered chair stamped a leg, as if it were pouting. Jesse smiled.

The Elder and his dad were standing by a smaller, yet still grand, golden-edged, crystal table located near one of the large windows. Several plump chairs, covered in fabric of continually changing colours, glimmered in the beams of sunlight that caressed their surface.

"Please be seated," the Elder invited. He waved his hand in the direction of the seats. They moved slightly, plumping themselves further, to be even more comfortable for the visitors. Jesse selected a chair and sank into the luxurious softness. His dad and the Elder did the same.

"I love this room," Nexlucimus said, with a sigh. "It contains some very fond memories."

Enjoying the warm coziness he sat in, Jesse felt his tiredness keenly. Overwhelmed with the relaxing atmosphere and all the revelations of that day, there was no holding back his yawns. He gave in, trying to be discreet as he yawned into the bend of his elbow. "*Man, I'm tired,*" Jesse thought.

"I see, young one, we have extended your limits of tolerance," the Elder said kindly. "We, not tied to mortal bodies, sometimes forget that sleep is vital for human survival. Forgive me for overlooking your physical needs."

"No worries, sir," Jesse yawned again. "I'll be okay. I want to understand what's…"

Before Jesse could finish his sentence, he felt a prick on his forearm. Surprised, he saw a minuscule blue dart, and without a word, he collapsed.

Chapter 6

The Quest

Nexlucimus and David let Jesse sleep until he woke on his own, a couple of hours later.

Stretching and rubbing the sleep from his eyes, Jesse yawned. "Man, what happened? I didn't think I was that tired. Maybe it was all the fresh air or something," he said, stifling another yawn.

"I'm afraid it was my fault, Jesse," the Elder admitted, his cheeks flushing slightly. "You were slipped a potion of sleeping."

"Wow, when did you do that, sir?" Jesse asked, impressed.

"I didn't do it myself," Nexlucimus grinned, almost sheepishly. "It was one of the fairies at my door. Apparently, when I said that sleep was vital for mortal survival, one of them sent an invisible dart of searching, dipped in a potion of sleeping, toward the only possible target in the room… you."

"Those fairies are real? I thought they were carvings," Jesse said, amazed.

Nexlucimus chuckled. "The fairies are very much alive, and always on guard. They like to hide amongst the carvings."

"I guess I'd better be careful with what I say around here. What did you say put me to sleep, sir?" Jesse asked.

"An invisible dart of searching. It is a small dart which, when dipped in a potion—such as the sleeping one—and then thrown or launched from a bow or atlatl, becomes invisible. The dart searches for the intended target, like the heat-seeking missiles of your world," the Elder said patiently.

"Oh wow, that must have been that small blue dart that hit right before I dropped off," Jesse said, wide-eyed with curiosity and thoroughly enthralled.

"Indeed," the Elder chuckled. "Now that you have rested, I must explain the quest and send you back to your world. First, however, I don't know about you, Jesse, but I'm starving. Would you like some refreshment?"

"Oh, absolutely, sir. I'm starving too. What about you, Dad?"

David sighed. "Sadly, Jesse, food would do me no good since I have no physical body."

Nexlucimus touched a bright spot on the table that Jesse hadn't noticed before. A skinny little man about four feet tall, with dark circles under his beady green eyes, popped into the room, bowing and making Jesse jump.

"Wow! More surprises!" Jesse thought, grinning, warming up to this new environment.

Nexlucimus addressed the small man. "Clocks, I believe our guest needs some refreshment. Would you be so kind as to bring us a pepperoni pizza, with extra cheese please?"

"They have pizza here? Awesome!"

"What would you like to drink, Jesse?" the Elder queried.

"I don't know, sir—no clue," Jesse shrugged, not sure what to request.

"What do you like to drink in your world?"

"I like milk with my pizza, sir."

"You heard him, Clocks. A cold pitcher of milk, please."

"As you wish, Milord," Clocks said, sneering slightly in Nexlucimus' direction before vanishing with a soft pop.

"Sir, how did he just pop in and out like that?" Jesse asked, puzzled.

"You must remember, Jesse, that this is a world of magic. Things not possible in the mortal world—because of unbelief—are considered ordinary here. Now, I must ask for silence as we review the quest."

Jesse, self-conscious now, tried shrinking into the folds of his comfortable chair. Sensing Jesse's temporary embarrassment, the armchair wrapped around him, concealing all but his face. Jesse smiled to himself and relaxed into its embrace, like a chick under a hen's wing.

The Elder, noticing the actions of the chair, reconsidered his words.

"I beg your pardon, Jesse. I forget who I am addressing. Please ask questions as you feel impressed to do so. I understand that there is little that you comprehend, and much to tell," Nexlucimus sighed sorrowfully.

Wiggling free of the chair's reassuring hug, unable to stop himself, Jesse braved further comment. "Thank you, sir. I do have many questions."

David rolled his eyes at his son, but smiled despite himself.

"What? He said it was okay," Jesse said, looking at his dad.

"It is fine, David. Ask your questions, Jesse."

"What did you mean when you said that magic wasn't possible in my world because of unbelief?" Jesse asked.

"Most people in your world don't believe in real magic anymore. If you don't believe in something, chances are it will not happen. In the early history of your world, people not only believed in, but also practised magic. Ancient shamans and other healers were the key groups of practising mortals, but there were others, with greater powers. The Druids of Britain and the Nordic people practised magic. The Asian peoples and many of the islanders and Aboriginal people believed in magic. The Africans, and of course, the native people of the Americas had many magical ceremonies. But modern people think of all that as superstitious, evil, or just plain myth. In fact, the very thought frightens many of them."

"Pardon me, Master Nexlucimus." It was the beady-eyed little man with a delicious-smelling pizza and a cold jug of milk. He had appeared so quietly that both Jesse and his father jumped.

"Geez! That guy is sneaky!"

"Ah, the refreshment," the Elder smacked his lips.

Clocks handed Nexlucimus the pizza, setting the jug of milk on the crystal table. Peering through heavy eyebrows, he stole a side glance at Jesse, then popped back out of the room.

Nexlucimus set the pizza down, serving himself a piece from the golden platter. Plates, glasses, and utensils appeared on the table with the advent of the food. Pouring a large glass of milk, the Elder settled back into his chair, enjoying the delicious fare.

"Please help yourself, Jesse."

"Who is that guy? He gives me the creeps," Jesse asked, serving himself and then taking a huge bite of pizza, guzzling half a glass of the cold milk. Napkins appeared on the table as Jesse dribbled milk from his too-full mouth.

Nexlucimus chuckled, wiping his mouth and smoothing his neat beard.

"He's my scribe, and I've been working him very hard this past season, as I searched and prepared the records of learning. He's a good man, just overworked."

Jesse noticed his dad sitting quietly. "So, you really can't eat any food, Dad?"

"Nope, not a bite. It would serve no purpose."

"Wow, that sucks to be you right now."

"It sure does. I do miss pizza."

Jesse snickered at his father as he grabbed another piece of pizza. He made a big production of smacking his lips and groaning in pleasure as he ate. David rolled his eyes and smiled at his son.

"I guess that gets me back for not giving you more warning about the Skeedlers."

"Maybe," Jesse replied, taking another huge bite.

"Enjoy it now, boy, because someday soon, I'm going to have a body. And when I do, I'll wrestle you down and tickle you until you puke."

"Ha, you wish, old man. You'll have to catch me first."

The Elder watched the playful exchange as he ate, smiling warmly at them.

"Now," Master Nexlucimus said, as they finished eating and the table cleared itself, "let me tell you about our urgent quest."

Settling deeper into his cushioned chair, the Elder waved his hand, and a large flat-screen monitor appeared, suspended in the air — but it didn't come on.

"Please pay close attention. What you will witness is vital information."

"Yes, sir," Jesse said, feeling nervous and excited at the same time.

Elder Nexlucimus snapped his fingers, and the monitor flashed to life. The voice coming from the screen, narrating the presentation, was that of the Elder himself. He began by explaining that what they were about to watch was the creation of their world, and some of its subsequent history. He stated that this was an accurate account, taken from his own memories, as he had witnessed it. It played out before them like a documentary.

Jesse watched the screen, astounded, quickly realising that what he was seeing was impossible—except, here they were, with Nexlucimus, experiencing the magic.

"Man," Jesse whispered to his father, "the scientists have sure got it wrong."

"Indeed," David whispered back, equally awestruck.

Jesse observed the creation of Earth and Xanthara. He learned that each time the gods of the mortal worlds created a new world, the gods of the immortal worlds created a world of fantasy to go with it. They always went together. It had always been so.

He observed that fantasy was necessary to teach mortals how to dream and imagine. Without dreams, they wouldn't advance. They needed imagination to progress and develop. Mortals, when deprived of those gifts, would stagnate, never grow, or change—like primitive tribes left alone to live in their old traditions and habits.

Jesse thought of Gran's words ("like stale bread and pond water") and wondered if she too had seen this presentation.

He learned of a rebellion in the heaven of Earth, and of their gods deciding that all their spirit children needed to prove their loyalty, with human weaknesses. A veil of forgetfulness would shroud their minds, making sure that what they did was genuine, and not the result of memory.

He saw that there had been no rebellion in the heaven of the immortals. They were all deemed worthy of immortality from the start of their lives. They were given the responsibility of teaching and inspiring mortals. It was a charge they took seriously, with great pleasure and honour. They proved their loyalty through this service and their worthiness to progress before their gods.

Jesse observed worlds and galaxies without number co-existing, scattered across a tapestry of dark sky—glittering, silver specks of fine sand.

As the presentation progressed, Jesse became aware of another, smaller world, created between his world and the world of Xanthara. It was a place where specific forms of creativity lived the life breathed into them by mortals through their stories and games. It was a world where these ideas—gifted to them through the whisperings of the immortals—grew and developed.

The mortals believed that the places and characters contained in their stories and games existed solely for their amusement. They thought them something to be used and then tossed away or stored. They never understood that what they created existed. They didn't appreciate the fact that, unless ended by the artist or author, it continued to live even when they weren't enjoying it. To them, the world of fantasy only existed in the imagination of their minds.

Jesse sat spellbound by what he was seeing and learning. It made perfect sense, and yet, it was all so strange. The histories of Nexlucimus continued.

Jesse noticed a young man, not much older than himself, but clearly immortal. He was casting spells and wore the robes of a mage. He had a bright face and sweet smile. There were many scenes of this boy with his parents and siblings. It showed that they were a happy family who intensely loved each other. Jesse heard the boy's family call him by the name of Tazeron.

As Tazeron advanced in his skills, he travelled with others of his world into the world of mortals. They disguised themselves, performing tasks to aid their charges. In many cases, they assisted with the construction of buildings and cities. Jesse saw grand palaces, ancient walls and even the pyramids, created under this alien guidance.

These extraterrestrials suggested—through dreams and visions—ways for mortals to improve and expand their lives and existence. Many ideas, including irrigation, shipbuilding, electricity, and medical procedures, were studied and implemented. Ancient healers, contemporary doctors, engineers, and scientists—along with everyday citizens—were all inspired and gifted with visions.

It disappointed Tazeron that these Earthlings weren't always willing to accept the advice given to them, no matter how it was suggested.

Jesse watched as the young man stood by himself, growing dissatisfied with his service, viewing it as degrading and pointless. He considered these people to be snivelling, destructive beings—ruining their beautiful world and their chances of returning to their gods.

Tazeron obsessed over the choices made on the beautiful planet. He wanted more than anything to take control. He reasoned that if he were in charge, things would be better for everyone.

He gathered followers, and what Tazeron and his followers desired made the gods of both worlds unhappy. It would nullify all that the gods were trying to do. The mortals needed to make decisions of their own free will. They had to prove their worthiness through the way they lived their lives, in order to return to their gods at the end of their mortal experience.

Force was not acceptable.

After a time, Tazeron and his sympathisers were brought before the High Council of Xanthara in Rodashu and told to stop. They refused, no matter what the Council said to persuade them otherwise. The gods decreed that Tazeron and his followers could no longer live among the immortals or freely travel among the mortals. They directed that Tazeron and the other dissenters be stripped of their bodies and banished into outer darkness, where they would no longer be a threat.

Before this could happen, however, Tazeron and his followers escaped into the world of stories and games and continued with their schemes to destroy the independent will of those on Earth during this exile. Jesse watched as the gods placed a magical shield or barrier within the world of games to contain Tazeron and his followers from achieving their goals. Jesse saw Tazeron and his minions' intense grief at their containment—but no remorse for their actions or desires.

The screen went blank and then disappeared. For several minutes, they sat in silence, each lost in their thoughts.

"Master Nexlucimus," Jesse spoke quietly. "I remember my grandmother telling me a story like this one. She said that another being tried to do something similar."

"Indeed, Jesse. There is, however, a distinction between the two stories. When the mortal gods banished that being, he ended up on your Earth with all his followers—and no bodies. Even though they seem to be pursuing the same goal, this situation is unique."

"How is it different? And didn't your gods see this coming?" Jesse asked, confused.

"The difference is that Tazeron and his followers still have their bodies, giving them a power that the other beings do not possess. Tazeron and his supporters have many options, whereas the others do not."

"As you saw, they scheme to enter the mortal domain and take charge. If they had not escaped into the game world, our gods could have controlled them. But as soon as they entered the game world, the mortal gods saw it as another way to test."

"They were now in human territory, since that sphere was, in a sense, created by people. There was an agreement between the gods of both worlds: they would leave this problem to be solved by our two realms, as they—the gods of both dominions—watched."

Nexlucimus paused, gathering his thoughts.

"To answer the rest of your question—yes, they did know that this was a possibility. What I'm going to tell you now will perhaps surprise you."

Chapter 7

Keepers Revealed

Jesse leaned forward so he wouldn't miss a single word as the Elder continued.

"Even though we of Xanthara, and all the other worlds of fantasy, were born immortal, we also needed a test. This trial will prove our loyalty, beyond merely performing our duties.

While we are not perfect, we did not suffer a fall from immortality through a pre-life rebellion. We, like you mortals, are learning how to serve our gods. We do that by performing the tasks given to us from the beginning, which is assisting the persons of your world in their development. Mortals, on the other hand, serve their gods by following the gods' teachings and helping each other.

Just as the anti-gods of your world are tools in the hands of the mortal gods, Tazeron and his followers are tools in the hands of the immortal gods. They both whisper evil and seductive thoughts to unsuspecting minds, to test them for the gods. These wicked ones have lost the vision of who they were in the eternal plan of things. As such, they have lost their inheritance with the gods.

Although this is painful to us, it is necessary. As this unfolds, the gods are watching very closely—all of them, both sets. They, the gods, have allowed this puzzle to happen, and they are leaving it up to us to solve. Before this is over, my young friend, this trial will test us all."

"Do they know how all of this is going to end, sir?" Jesse asked earnestly.

Nexlucimus smiled kindly at Jesse. "Yes, my young friend, they do. They are gods. However, unlike that bodiless being and his followers—where the ending is known to all—this time, the immortal and mortal gods aren't revealing the outcome. Even I am as blind as anyone. It is, after all, an assessment of our loyalty."

Jesse marvelled at this revelation, and then he had another thought.

"Do you know Tazeron, sir?"

"Yes, Jesse, I do," Nexlucimus sighed sadly. "He is the child of my sister—my nephew. And he was a mighty mage of the highest order. What he tried to do pains all of us more than I could ever express. I sorrow that we could not change him, and we tried most earnestly.

We cannot allow Tazeron to enter your world, Jesse. It would mean the destruction of everything good, by taking away all free will." The Elder sighed, an unhappy, haggard expression on his face.

"Sir, is that possible?"

"Sadly, Jesse, there are ways—but it requires help from people of your world."

"What!" Jesse exclaimed, shocked. "Why would anyone want to do that?"

"Tazeron and his followers can be very charming and manipulative. People do not understand who—or what—they are. Like the anti-gods of your world that influence people. It is possible because many individuals in the human world are looking to belong. They are easily swayed through propaganda, flattery, and greed. I believe your grandmother called it 'brainwashing.' There are many types. The internet games are a perfect stage for Tazeron's lies and blandishments."

"You know about these games and how they work?" Jesse asked the Elder.

Master Nexlucimus smiled at Jesse and his father. "Yes, my young friend, we know. We plant ideas, and sometimes where they go amazes even us. The people of your world are the most intelligent, valiant, righteous, and noble of all the mortal worlds ever created. Sadly, they can also be some of the meanest and most wicked. Nowhere else has there been a world of games designed like this one. That is why this challenge was given here, now. We are the only ones who can solve it—by working together."

"How can we keep them out of our world?" Jesse asked, disturbed.

"Jesse, most of these questions will be answered later, back in our world, with training," David interjected.

"It is all right, David, I do not mind. But we must send you back home soon, Jesse."

Master Nexlucimus stood and paced, becoming very solemn as he faced Jesse.

"My young friend, I cannot stress what I am about to tell you enough. This is critical, and you must take this very seriously." He paused, then continued. "There has been a magical shield placed around Tazeron in the world of games, as was shown in the history. It acts as a barrier between that world of games and the mortal world. But there is one path we cannot block. That path is called emotions."

Jesse knitted his eyebrows, twisting his face, looking puzzled. "Emotions?"

"Yes, Jesse. When people play their games, they project all their extreme sentiments, moods, and passions into those games. Tazeron can sense them. Even you have felt the anger, happiness, frustration, joy, pleasure, and accomplishment as you played with others, I am sure. Using those intense feelings as a tracking signal, Tazeron can pull a person physically into the world of the games. That opens a portal—or pathway—between the two worlds.

But there is one more feature that Tazeron must tap to enter the mortal world. That factor is something we have yet to discover. As far as we know, he hasn't figured it out either. For now, however, while we contemplate all the puzzle pieces, guarding the Shield is of vital importance. That is the mission of the Keepers. That is your quest—along with saving as many of the unfortunate victims physically drawn into the games as possible."

"Sir," Jesse asked, "how are we going to do this? How will we know what to do?"

Nexlucimus took a deep breath and let it out slowly.

"We will bring you and the other Keepers here. We will teach you the magic that the talisman says you can learn. You will become Game Masters. You will learn how to survive in the real, live world of games. And you will learn how to rescue.

Soon, my young friend, you must confront Tazeron and his followers. They are always searching for the way out of that realm. We cannot do it for you, but you will not be alone. We will be with the Keepers every step of the way—watching, teaching, guiding, and encouraging."

"Why can't immortals take care of this themselves?" Jesse asked.

"We have no special abilities there. The Keepers will have all the magic of the games at their disposal. Right now, Tazeron and his followers are prisoners in that strange realm. We have no idea for sure what will happen if they manage to get through the Shield. Sadly, we feel that someday they will figure it out. The Keepers must be there when that happens—to stop them."

Jesse was stunned, once again overwhelmed by what he had learned. He tried desperately not to panic under the weight of it all. He glanced over at his dad, who, he noticed, was intently studying the Elder's face.

"How do you figure into this, Dad?" Jesse asked.

David thought for a moment. "I'll be a technical advisor, son. Because of my military experience, and my desire to help. There will be many others besides me. I am here now because I requested to be with you."

There was a soft knock at the door. Nexlucimus, David, and Jesse turned to face it.

"Enter," said Nexlucimus.

A small woman opened the door. She was about four feet tall, with pale lavender skin and waist-length silver hair that was tied back with golden ribbons. She looked like an elf, with her delicate features—but couldn't be, because she was lavender-skinned with sheer pink wings, which carried her closer to where they were waiting. Dressed in brown leather from her headband to her boots, Jesse guessed her to be either a Hunter or a Druid.

Jesse and David stood. Jesse thought she was the most beautiful woman he had ever seen—except for the gorgeous green girl in the marketplace, of course.

"What is she, Dad?" Jesse whispered, hoping no one else heard him.

"She's a wood nymph. They're fairies," David whispered back to his son.

"I wonder if that's what the pale green girl was... and if all fairies have those darts?" he mused, as he scooted closer to Nexlucimus.

"I am sorry to interrupt you, Nexi, but we have much to discuss during the refreshing," said the woman gently.

"Ah, Zeela, my dear, come in and meet my guests." Nexlucimus was instantly cheerful. He smiled warmly at her, his face shining. "David and Jesse, may I present to you my dear wife, Zeela."

"My pleasure, Milady," David said, bowing. Jesse also bowed.

"The pleasure is mine. I have heard much of you."

"You have heard of us... Milady?" Jesse asked nervously, blushing slightly.

"Yes, Jesse. All of us on Xanthara know of the Keepers, especially here in Rodashu."

Seeing his confusion, she continued, "Keepers like you will help us do something we cannot do ourselves. Many of our people are willing to help, but the Keepers will have the power this time. Not us," she smiled sadly.

Nexlucimus turned to Jesse. "It's time for you to go back, Jesse. I believe you understand what our purpose is. The rest is up to you—and the Keepers. I encourage you to learn quickly. There isn't much time. Tazeron is growing stronger, and his minions are increasing as his influence spreads. You and the others may indeed be our only hope."

Jesse stood silent, overwhelmed—and yet, at the same time, he was feeling a spirit of adventure and responsibility. A wave of purpose and desire was building in him. It was scary and exciting all at once.

David turned to his son. "Jesse, I'll be with you, but you won't see me again until you return here. I'm proud of you. I always have been. I love you, son."

"I love you too, Dad. I'll learn fast, so I can come back to you—and together we can kick some evil butt."

Jesse waved goodbye as the room began to swirl and melt into a collage of colours. He felt dizzy as the room disappeared.

Chapter 8

Mind Control and Shadow Dreams

Jesse was falling, but this time he landed gently on his feet in the family room. Since time moved differently on Xanthara, it was much later, and only Tommy remained.

"Welcome back, Jesse."

"Hey Tommy, where is everyone?"

"Well, since it's almost two in the morning, I sent everyone else home, or to bed."

"Wow, it wasn't night there," Jesse said, surprised.

"Yes, there is a difference between the two worlds. Clearly, my uncle had much to tell you."

"Awesome experience. Especially the fairies, and their searching thingy's," Jesse said, laughing.

"Seriously," Tommy smirked. "Tell me everything that happened. If you have any other questions, perhaps I can answer them."

Jesse told him about his trip to Rodashu, the bubble, and meeting up with his dad. He talked about his experience with Skeedlers, fairies, and the dart dipped in sleep potion. He reflected on the history lesson with Nexlucimus. Jesse mentioned the Elder's charge to learn the games, and to get ready to defend the Shield.

"Impressive trip," Tommy stated. "Don't you just love the Skeedlers? Even I get greeted by those energetic little fellows' every time I go back. It's hard to warn about Skeedlers. I knew you would enjoy seeing your dad."

"It was incredible seeing my dad," Jesse said with a huge grin, and then he became serious. "I was wondering Tommy, what's your part in all of this? Now that I think about it, I didn't meet you until right before I started living with Gran and playing the game with her and Mr. Chambers. Another thing, why was Cami able to stand? It's been five years since the accident."

Tommy sighed and invited Jesse to sit so they could talk.

"As I told you Jesse, I am part of the Council of Elders of Xanthara. There are fifteen of us; my uncle Nexlucimus is the head Elder. We are the ruling body of our world. Our headquarters are in the capital city of Rodashu. It was us that tried to stop my brother, Tazeron, and his followers. Once we identified you as a Finding, the council decided that someone should oversee your training. We would give you additional protection, as needed. Such as those bullies at your school. They haven't troubled you much lately, have they?" Tommy smiled and winked at Jesse. "My uncle and I have been advising your grandmother, even though she's quite talented on her own."

"Tazeron is your brother...?" Jesse asked, shocked.

"Yes...my elder brother, whom I looked up to, and followed around as a youth," Tommy's countenance darkened, and he paused. "He was a wonderful person. He was kind and loving, always willing to help me progress in my skills. That is, until he started down this path he is traveling now. It's hard to see him this way. It's difficult being against him, knowing how it must end so that our two worlds will survive. Our parents have suffered greatly because of him, and that angers me.

Tazeron is very selfish to seek this power. He ruins not only his immortal life but the lives of all that follow him to their destruction. It is my hope that we can yet save some of them," Tommy grew quiet, struggling with emotions.

"I don't know what I would do, if I were in your shoes, Tommy," Jesse said, concerned. "What do you mean by 'a Finding'? And how are Findings identified?" Jesse asked, changing the subject to perhaps something less painful for his friend.

"A Finding is someone with extraordinary magical talent, and often they manifest traits of an elf, such as stronger intuition, and an affinity for animals and magic. The term was coined by the elves many millennia ago, after an interplanetary situation, where whole villages of their people disappeared. Efforts were put forth to find the lost ones, but they had vanished. For reasons known only to them, the gods were silent concerning the issue. No one remembers the details; too much history has happened since then. Time has erased much of the hidden ancestry, but genetics have prevailed. Shadow Dreams often uncover lost abilities. Those talents are apparent in you, my friend, and we aren't sure why."

"Close your mouth dear, it's distracting," Gran said, chuckling as she stepped into the room.

Both Jesse and Tommy stood, turning to face her.

"I'm sorry Mrs. Smith; did we wake you?" Tommy asked.

"No dear, I needed a drink and heard you talking. You were late getting back Jesse. I'm sure you'll have lots to tell me later. I was interested in what you had to say. Tommy, do you mind if I join this conversation? And please call me Pearl."

"Thank you, Pearl, it would be my pleasure to have you join us. I was explaining what a Finding was, and that brings me to Shadow Dreams. Jesse, I believe it's time for you to meet the one assigned to you, but first I will invite Rambo in if you don't mind Pearl."

Gran didn't care, in fact, she opened the door for Rambo to enter. He approached in his smaller dragon form.

"Rambo, would you please call Breeze to us."

"Indeed, Master Silverrod," Rambo said.

"Please, not so formal here Rambo. Call me Tommy." Tommy said, flushing some, his dark skin taking on a rusty glow.

"As you wish...Tommy," Rambo shivered like he'd eaten something nasty. He bowed his head and started humming. A silver mist formed around his head and then moved to his shoulder.

"Jesse, this is Breeze," Tommy said. "She is the essence of a fairy kind. She is the one that discovered you as a Finding and reported back to us. From time to time, it is necessary for the gods, or head Elder of a world, to educate or direct someone in a different world. Shadow Dreams are assigned to give these unique messages. Your communications were the result of a unanimous vote of the Council, under the direction of the head Elder, my uncle, Nexlucimus. These messages are always in the form of dreams. Findings are very rare. Mostly they are immortals, but occasionally a mortal."

"That's crazy. Essence...? Does that mean that she's dead like my dad?"

"No. Breeze is a soul of pure thought and energy waiting to be born into her immortal body. Individual essences, before they are born, can be called into service by the gods. It depends on their ability to learn while in that form, and their innate tendencies toward stronger intuition and affinity with others. Only these excellent spirits, with outstanding abilities, are chosen for these important assignments."

"Can I talk to her?"

"Yes, you can, if she wishes."

"Breeze, I'm pleased to meet you and..." Jesse was stunned, as Breeze quickly settled on his shoulder, caressing his head with her essence. She spoke to his mind.

"Jesse, it has been my fondest wish that we could meet. I have become much attached to you, as I have given you your dreams. I wish we had more time to visit; perhaps we will have another day."

Breeze slipped off his shoulder and left the room, leaving Jesse feeling lonely and missing her, for some odd reason.

"Wow, that was so cool. Will I see Breeze again soon?"

"I believe you will Jesse," Tommy smiled.

"Tommy, why did the Council think I needed the extra protection? Was it because I mind talked to Rambo, or because of the red magic, or because they consider me a Finding?"

"All of those are very rare in a mortal. Anyone of them would have sent warning bells to the Council, but to have all three in one person is highly unusual. You are very special, my friend. We of the Council can't wait to see what you can do once you start your training on Xanthara, and then go into the game world, for real."

Gran leaned over and whispered in Jesse's ear, "Close your mouth dear, it's not dignified."

Jesse snapped his loosely hinged mouth shut, embarrassed. Tommy didn't seem to notice and continued.

"Now about Cami and why she can stand. It happens every time she summons the Elders. We believe that it is a blessing, given to her by the power that she uses through the talisman. That energy opens the damaged nerve paths in her spine and allows her to stand. It only happens at that time."

"Is there any chance that it could become permanent?" Jesse wondered.

"Nothing is impossible Jesse, sometimes it takes time, however, and belief. Now, my friends, I must tend to other duties. Pearl, I have a need for Brutus. Rambo will remain here in your service for a while yet."

"No offense dude, but it's weird listening to you talk like you have been. I'm so used to you just being a kid." Jesse smirked.

Tommy chuckled, "It took me a long time to learn how to communicate like a mortal youth. I might revert once we get into the game. That would be totally wicked."

Jesse chuckled as they stood to escort Tommy out to Brutus, who was now an impressive full-sized snow-white griffin with his eagle head, forelegs and wings and his lion back legs and tail. They watched Tommy climb aboard, and launch into the early morning air, disappearing.

After the Griffin had left with his rider, Gran and Jesse sat on the porch swing, cozy under a quilt, chatting. Surprising everyone, Breeze made an impromptu visit to Rambo who was standing nearby. She quickly left again.

"Breeze tells me; we have visitors out by the shed Pearl. I will investigate with your permission."

"Indeed, my friend, we'll come if needed."

They watched as he reverted to his rooster form and walked out into the dark yard. After a few moments, there was a rooster crow and a brilliant flash of light by the shed.

"What the devil!" Gran exclaimed, grabbing a flashlight from a nearby hook and dashing off the porch. "Stay here Jesse," she said, as she ran toward the commotion.

"No way," Jesse muttered, following her into the dark.

As he ran in the direction of the shed, Jesse had visions of green slime and big spiders. He shuddered hoping they didn't see anything like that.

What they found surprised them and only added to the mystery of the night. Lying on the ground by the shed, were two boys, slightly scorched and unconscious.

"Jesse dear, do you know these two?" Gran asked.

"Yep, I sure do. These are a couple of the losers that used to make my life hell at school. They haven't bothered me much lately. They prefer to pick on the younger students. Scummy creeps. There was another, but he is part of the missing ones at school," Jesse explained.

"Now Tommy's words about not being bothered by the bully's make sense," he smiled at the thought.

They walked to the side of the shed hidden from the house and driveway. There were big black words scrawled where the two had attempted to graffiti the shed wall before Rambo distracted them.

"Are you sure you don't want me to mind control these maggots, Gran?" Jesse spat.

"No dear, I think we'll let the law take care of them for us. One of our guild members, Jim Slater, is a local officer, and he won't question the antics of an over-exuberant rooster," she chuckled.

"My question to you is what were they trying to say with this graffiti?" She shone the light on the shed wall where the hooligans had written, 'time to flee little bird, before…" and that was as far as they got.

"I'm not sure what they were trying to say, but the little bird part is just something they thought was funny, because of my last name. They're just jerks, always looking for a way to torment people."

"Unfortunately, there are always going to be jerks and bullies, sad creatures. Shall we go in, and call our friendly, game playing officer, while faithful Rambo keeps guard?" Gran asked.

"Gran, can I please try some mind control? I'd love to give them an itch they couldn't scratch."

"No dear," she tittered. "Not this time, maybe if there's a next time. I'll tell Rambo to let you have them before he blazes all their hair off. Besides, it doesn't work on the unconscious."

"Ah, that sucks."

Gran snickered as they started toward the house, not realizing that someone else was watching as well. Rambo noticed, however, and bowed to Breeze as she drifted nearby. She swirled around his head once and was gone. He chuckled softly to himself as he stood guard. Jesse turned back to see Rambo bow to the shimmering mist before she disappeared. Again, he had that lonely, missing her feeling.

When they got to the house, Gran called the cell phone of Jim Slater. He was just getting off duty and would come right over. Gran and Jesse sat on the swing as they waited. He arrived ten minutes later.

"Jim Slater, this is my grandson, Jesse Finch. Jesse this is the best neighbor you could ever have. He's always willing to come to the aid of a helpless, little old widow lady in need," Gran introduced him, in a fake, shaky old lady voice.

Jesse laughed, "Nice to meet you, Jim."

"It's nice to meet you in person too Jesse. By the way," he grinned at Gran. "This little old widow lady is a beast. No need for protection here. She does keep the Mrs. and me fat with all her cookies, however," he patted his middle as he winked at Pearl.

Now Pearl, if you would show me these dastardly fiends, who had the audacity to trespass on the property of a helpless, little old widow lady AND, assault a defenseless rooster," he guffawed. "They're lucky Rambo didn't extra crispy their nuggets."

They showed him the graffiti, and where the two were. They were starting to rouse.

"My, my, McKay Palmer and Troy Peterson," he said, chuckling softly. "I understand Rusty Daniels, who was the ringleader, is one of the missing. The Department is searching, but no clues so far. With what we are learning about the game and Tazeron, I doubt they will have any luck. I can't very well tell them what I know. We will just have to hope we get this development settled soon".

Jesse wasn't surprised to learn that Jim knew about Tazeron, he was sure that many gamers were learning about the quest. He was curious about Jim's knowledge of these two losers, however.

"You know these Jerks then, Jim?" Jesse asked.

"You bet. McKay and Troy both have records with the law. I don't think anyone ever lassoed them as neatly as Rambo, however. Well done my man." He bowed in Rambo's direction. Rambo returned the gesture. Jim called the station, and they waited for an officer to come and collect the two pranksters.

After the squad car had pulled away, Gran suggested that they all go in for hot chocolate.

"Not a bad idea," Jim said. "The nights have been getting cold early this year. Maybe we could talk Rambo into roasting some marshmallows for us, smores sound good too."

Rambo squawked once, catching them all by surprise. Flipping his tail against Jim's leg as he turned, Rambo strutted back to the house.

"And then, maybe not," Jim snorted.

Sitting at the kitchen table with hot chocolate and cookies, they visited mostly about the game, swapping stories. After about an hour, Jim said he needed to get home to his wife Sara, who would be waking up soon to go to work. Gran packed up some cookies for Sara, before they walked Jim out to his car, and watched him pull away.

"I like him, Gran. And his wife plays the game too?" Jesse asked as they walked back into the house.

"Yes, she does, probably more than she should," Gran said, as she sat down on the couch in the front room inviting Jesse to sit next to her.

Jesse looked at her puzzled, "What do you mean by that Gran?"

"They lost a baby about two years ago, and Sara has had a difficult time, poor dear. They haven't been able to have another. You'll find that people use the games for a variety of reasons, but most of them are running away from something. Non-gamers that don't understand their reasons would say that they were running away from life, while some of the gamers would say that life has abandoned them."

"Gran, how did you get started in the games?"

"Are you sure you wouldn't like to wait until you get caught up on your sleep?" Gran asked.

"Nope, I'm awake now. It's been an exciting night. Besides, I had a nap," He smiled, remembering fairies, hiding behind the large carved fruit.

"You'll have to fill me in later today," Gran said, noticing Jesse's smile. "You may be awake, but I still need more sleep."

Chapter 9

Another Dream

Gran considered Jesse's question about why she started playing the games. She studied her hands for a moment before she spoke.

"About fifteen years ago, I was looking for something to do, to fill in my time. I was a new widow and bored. I didn't want to scrapbook or make quilts, and I was too young for senior citizens. Surprisingly, I was talking to the mailman one day, and he was the one who introduced me to online gaming. I fell in love with the incredible graphics and the challenge and excitement of levelling up with battles and quests. You just never know when you're going to meet people who play. I've met many wonderful people from around the world, but I've also met some real jerks."

Gran became pensive for a moment before letting out a big sigh. She continued.

"I was one of the people on the game running away from life. I was trying to replace loneliness with adventure, and it worked for me. One day, while volunteering at the school library, I met Mr. Chambers. I don't remember how it happened, but we started talking about the benefits and problems of gaming. We discovered that we played the same game on the same server, and my gaming took on a whole new dimension. He introduced me to his guild and a whole new group of friends. Now I'm one of the leaders—who would've believed it?" She smiled at the thought.

"Well, dear, I'm going to go back to bed and try to get some more sleep. I suggest that you do the same thing. We'll get to the game later and get some more experience for you after I wake up."

"Gran, where does Rambo sleep at night?"

"He has a box on the porch next to Brutus' pillow. You've probably seen it. Why do you ask?"

"Well, I was wondering if he would like to move into my room, now that Brutus is gone."

"I don't know. Why don't you ask? It's OK with me if Rambo doesn't mind."

Jesse stood and walked into his room, sitting on the edge of the bed. Gran followed him, watching. Jesse thought of Rambo, cold and lonely, with Brutus gone. He pictured the big bird warm and snug at the foot of the bed on Brutus' sleeping pillow. Gran watched curiously. Soon, she heard a soft tap at the door. Smiling, Pearl went to let in Rambo. Thinking Rambo would like Brutus' sleeping pillow, she grabbed that too.

"Thanks, Gran," Jesse yawned big. He stroked the rooster's silky feathers as the sleepy bird settled into the pillow, emitting the soft purring sounds Jesse enjoyed. "I hope you don't mind that I suggested you grab the sleeping pillow while you were out there."

"You did that?" she asked, surprised.

"Yep, sorry, it just seemed to make sense."

Gran just smiled, shaking her head as she stepped out of his room, closing the door.

"Good night, dear."

"Night, Gran." He changed his clothes, climbed into bed, and was instantly asleep.

The night brought a new dream to Jesse, as Breeze visited him once again. He dreamed of himself in midnight blue magician's robes, standing in a vast valley before a large gathering of others dressed for battle. He was talking to them about the war; at his side was a fabulous red and iridescent green dragon.

Across the throng, an ageless young man landed on a snow-white griffin. His expression was urgent. In the distance, Jesse saw a glowing oval of light; it shimmered and pulsated. He knew that they must travel to that oval; it held the clue to solving a mystery. The one they searched for wasn't the one they sought.

The wind started blowing, swirling dust and mist and magic into every crevice. The sky turned green, streaked with purple and gold. In the expanse above him, he could see others caught in the wind of the shifting sky. They were drifting and swaying like marionettes, flopping without their strings to give them direction. He knew these others, caught in the air, dangling. They were calling for help. He had to decide: release the one who would open the path for all, or continue to travel an endless trail of lies.

The ageless young man had the answer and was frantically waving at him. Jesse wondered how to cross the distance. The red dragon nudged him. Jesse climbed aboard, and they took to the sky—but not into the wind. The ones caught in the wind never got any closer.

Arriving at the rendezvous, Jesse recognised his friend. With unspeakable joy, he grasped the hands of the one he knew and knelt, overcome with relief and happiness.

The young man's voice sounded in Jesse's ear. "We must abandon the ones we know and love, no matter the pain. We must let the one go to save us all."

Jesse woke up with Rambo sitting on his chest, staring at him, clucking softly. At least he hadn't squawked or crowded, and he wasn't as weighty as that first time. The sun was shining brightly outside.

"What's up, boy?"

Rambo jumped down and walked over to the door.

"Oh, I bet you need to visit the little rooster's room. OK, just a second."

Jesse slipped into his jeans and grabbed a shirt, opening the bedroom door and then the front door as he and Rambo went outside. Gran wasn't up yet; their day had gotten flipped around because of last night. Pulling on his long-sleeved shirt against the cold morning air, Jesse sat on the porch swing under the quilt and considered yet another dream.

"This time, I'm telling Gran as soon as she wakes up," Jesse thought.

Later, as Jesse described his dream, Gran listened intently. She immediately went to her room and retrieved the telewave.

"We need to tell Master Nexlucimus about your dream; perhaps he can make sense of it."

Gran carried out the opaque, egg-shaped globe, which was roughly the size of a bowling ball, and placed it on a small stand. After it was positioned and settled, she covered it with a green cloth. She tapped it with a pattern like the old Morse code Jesse remembered from Scouts. There was a soft pop, and she pulled off the cloth as the Great Library of Learning came into view. It was like watching a small oval TV.

Gran held a small golden device in her hand, reminding Jesse of a remote control. Depending on where she pointed the controller, they could travel around in the globe's surroundings. They explored the interior of the library and down a couple of corridors until they found the object of their search.

Master Nexlucimus was visiting with a few other people, engaged in a lively discussion. Pearl wasn't sure if she wanted to interrupt, but the Elder sensed them. He directed Pearl and Jesse to his private chambers to wait for him, reassuring them that it wouldn't take long.

While they waited, they snooped around a bit. Pearl and Jesse checked open side rooms with tables and chairs and shelves laden with books and decorative items. Closets ajar contained robes and soft leather boots. Wishing they could open drawers, they drifted to a large window where they saw an enormous piazza with peacocks strutting, vendors, and families having picnics on the grass. There was a pond with different waterfowl swimming. Nearby, many children played a type of tag with several Skeedlers. They told themselves that it was okay to poke around, because they were on a fact-finding mission, and you never knew what you might discover.

A few moments later, Elder Nexlucimus opened the door, and they both jumped like a couple of guilty children.

"I'm glad he can't see us, Gran," Jesse whispered.

"Ah... but I can hear quite well, young sir." Nexlucimus smiled.

Jesse groaned. Gran patted his arm, smiling.

"Nexlucimus, Jesse has something to tell you, a dream he had last night. It's different from his others. I thought you might be interested."

The Elder raised an eyebrow at this news and settled himself in a chair.

"Proceed, Jesse. Tell me of this dream."

Jesse explained his strange dream as the Elder sat listening intently.

"Thank you for sharing this with me, Jesse. I believe another piece of the puzzle has just dropped into place. I need to consult with my Council, and then I promise to reveal all that we know. Pearl, I want you to set the alarm on the telewave to notify you when I return. In the meantime, Jesse, continue your studies of the game with urgency. Until then, my friends, I must leave you. There is much going on, and many concerned citizens."

The telewave went dark, and Pearl sat back in her seat.

"This is growing more mysterious every day," Pearl said, more to herself than to Jesse.

"Well, dear, shall we have some breakfast and then resume our gameplay?"

"Yeah, sure, Gran. What do you think this all means? Any ideas?" Jesse asked as he stood to help her with preparations.

"I don't have a clue. I wish I did."

After they ate and cleaned up, Pearl changed out of her robe and bunny slippers, and they met in the computer room to continue Jesse's game training.

Logging onto their computers, Pearl was surprised to see Mr. Chambers, Jim, and Sara Slater. She introduced Jesse to Mr. Chambers' female barbarian cleric, 'Puff,' Jim Slater's ogre warrior, Twotoes, and Sara Slater's azure elf druid, 'Sassy.' Gran got on her dwarf hunter, Olive, and Jesse played his high elf red mage, 'Nophule.' With a full party, they could synchronise their levels. They were all able to play at Jesse's lower level, even with their higher-level characters. Usually, they were limited to players within two levels of themselves, but not if they agreed to match the lowest level.

They logged into live chat on their headphones so they could talk and not have to type their conversations. Live chat was quite handy, especially when someone yelled, "Run! I just pulled the entire room of zombies and beetles, and they're coming your way."

That only happened once, and they all laughed about it, making Jesse feel a little better about his playing ability.

"Ah, what are newbie peeps for, if not to bring frustration and laughter to the game arena?" Twotoes said, increasing the hilarity.

The group was incredible to adventure with, and Jesse enjoyed himself immensely. They played for several hours, and Jesse gained many levels. Mr. Chambers and Jim tried to explain the math behind the stats of each of the classes. They explained how important it was for healers and other magic casters to have intelligence, spirit, and spell power. Then they explained how warriors and hunter types needed a certain ratio of agility, dexterity, strength, and stamina to perform their abilities and talents to the maximum. It was interesting, but Jesse had a hard time grasping all the complexities of the classes, different from his own. They gave him several websites that he could visit to learn more.

Gran talked about the different foods, drinks, and armour, and the stats they each added to the equation. She also mentioned that alcohol was available but, if not used carefully, it could lower your intelligence for a real-time hour.

"Wow, you can get booze for these toons?" Jesse marvelled.

"Well, every character is over twenty, even if the person on the other side of the screen is six or ninety, and that never changes. There are no age restrictions at the game pubs," Gran explained.

"Excellent," Jesse grinned.

Pearl's eyebrows shot to her hairline and her eyes rolled at her grandson.

"But your job isn't to see how drunk you can get, it's to fight the evil guys, remember," she said. "We need you sober, and walking straight, with all your intelligence intact. Believe me, you can get so drunk that your computer screen tunnels out and gets all blurry. I fell off a fishing dock once and was nearly eaten by a shark because... well, never mind. It was a guild party, lots of fun. One of the guild members made a big batch of 'Old Sweaty's Firewater' to level his brewmaster skills, and the guild, bless their hearts, helped him get rid of it," she laughed.

"I remember that party," Mr. Chambers chuckled. "I couldn't walk straight for a long time, and my typing was gibberish. And let me tell you, logging off won't help. You're still drunk when you log back on. Dueling was interesting, lots of fun with all the mishaps," he smiled at the memories.

"Oh man, I miss all the great parties. What's a real-time hour, by the way?" Jesse questioned.

"Real-time is Earth time. Game time goes faster than real time by about twenty minutes per hour. An hour on the game is only forty minutes in real time," Jim explained.

Sara was quiet for the most part, adding comments only when asked a specific question. Jesse figured it was because she was shy, or because the others were so adamant and loud. They played until the afternoon, clearing out several dungeons and higher-level areas. Since most of them had errands, they decided to regroup after dinner. Gran went to do some chores.

Jesse decided to explore the game world on his own. When he joined a pickup group that needed a mage, he decided to give it a try. Since his understanding of the game had increased after the morning, he felt comfortable venturing out on his own. Playing with pickup groups of unknown people gave him a different perspective, and his confidence flourished. He had a remarkable time. The details of the graphics and the intricacy needed to create the world such as the game contained were spectacular.

When Gran called him for something to eat, he felt like a changed player. It was all falling into place, amazingly. He couldn't wait to talk to her about it.

"It was incredible, Gran," Jesse said, taking a huge bite of his ham and cheese sandwich. "The first group didn't like me too much and kicked me out, but the second and third groups gave me tons of pointers that helped a lot. I can't wait to get back on."

"That's great, dear. I'm happy you had such a good time. Just remember that everything you are learning about the game now will be real someday. If you find something that works for you, learn it well. Some of those people have had years of experience playing as a mage. While the rest of us have played the game for a long time, learning from another of the same class will help you tremendously."

"I know," he said, subdued. "Gran, do you ever feel panic about the 'real someday' part?"

Gran sighed before answering. "I feel concern, with a twinge of terror, but I try to remember that we won't be alone. Now finish eating your lunch. I have some chores for you outside. Then you can get back in the game if you wish."

"Sure, Gran, as long as I don't have to clean up green slime or battle giant flies and spiders."

"No," she chuckled. "Just rake some leaves and finish painting the garden fence. I might have you paint over the graffiti those boys left on the shed wall. It shouldn't take you long."

Chapter 10

Dragon Blessed

After Jesse finished his chores, he went inside and noticed Gran watching the telewave with a worried look on her face.

"What do you think is happening, Gran?"

"I have no idea. It's unusual for Nexlucimus to take this long. I hope everything is OK."

"Yeah, me too. Hey, Gran, unless you need me for something else, I'm going to ride my bike down to the lake. It's been a long time since I've done anything like that."

"I think that would be a marvellous idea, dear. Try to be back before dark. Trouble brews faster after the sun goes down."

"Yes, ma'am," Jesse chuckled, thinking that Gran sounded just like his mum, or perhaps it was his mum who sounded like Gran. Jesse found his thoughts drifting to his mum and Bill more often, and to his surprise, he realised that he missed them. He felt sadness for the family he had lost because of his… what? His selfishness? His stubbornness? His childish concern for himself and disregard for his mum and her happiness? He had a crazy desire to visit them, to apologise. He missed the simplicity of that life, where all he had to think about was school and his one or two friends. He wasn't sure he liked this new grown-up world of responsibility and decisions. He was uncomfortable with the idea that people thought of him as the hero type. He wasn't. His dad was, and maybe even

Bill. He would never know, because he never gave Bill a chance. His dad also said that Bill would be helpful for him, if he would let him. What could Bill have shown him? This new role he was being tossed into scared him. He was terrified of the computer world becoming real. He even wondered what Rusty Daniels was doing right now, as part of the 'lost ones'. He secretly wished that he could disappear, and that someone else would have to take his place as the Red Mage with special powers. People depended on him, and that paralysed him on so many levels.

Putting on his hoodie, Jesse headed out to the shed for his bike. It was a beautiful autumn afternoon. The trees were just starting to change colours, and flocks of geese flew overhead, honking their way south for warmer waters. Jesse wondered what it would be like to fly south for the winter – to see land far below you, to be a goose, leaving all cares behind.

He pedalled slowly, drinking in the crispness of the air, with its feel of impending early snow. He imagined small animals in the woods, preparing for the cold months ahead. He could almost sense them and their urgency.

Letting his senses and mind wander freely over the sights that stimulated him, Jesse felt the stress of the last few days ease up a little. Peace washed over him, covering some of the fear and doubt.

Throwing his arms into the air, he hooted loudly, feeling carefree as he pedalled faster, breathing deeply. Only slowly did he become aware of a soft flapping behind him. He looked over his shoulder and stopped in his tracks. He waited for the small red dragon to catch up. He grinned widely, extending a hand of greeting.

"Rambo, my friend, what are you doing? Aren't you supposed to be guarding the home front?"

The dragon landed, careful not to get too close. "Your grandmother is an accomplished mistress of magic, Jesse. She can stand alone. I was curious. Do you mind if I accompany you on this journey to the lake?"

"I would enjoy your company. Let me stash my bike over there in the brush, and we can walk together."

He buried his bike in a thicket, being careful to cover it entirely, and jogged back.

"Rambo, aren't you afraid of someone seeing you in this form?"

"Mortals only notice what I want them to. Only persons with magic would see me thus; all others would observe a big red dog."

"They would see a large red dog flying?"

"No," Rambo smiled. "I fly close to the ground, and it looks like I'm running."

"Awesome," Jesse chuckled softly. "Rambo, I was curious about something. What is your exact size? I've seen you smaller, like now, and as a rooster, and larger when you were with Brutus at the house."

"Since you asked, I will show you."

Rambo shimmered and then morphed into a remarkable red dragon, with scales that glimmered in the clean autumn air like mirrors, reflecting the light. He was at least eighteen feet tall at the shoulders. His four strong legs gave him balance and grace, as he moved his massive body. Two mighty wings reached out, spanning at least twenty-five feet. He was the size of an airplane, but far more agile, able to fly higher and for longer distances. His thick neck and shoulders supported his massive head, with its small crown of spikes. Dinosaurs briefly came into Jesse's mind, but Rambo seemed more sleek than that, more graceful. Rambo's soft brown eyes gave the appearance of wisdom and experience, and despite his size, gentleness. He was a splendid example of ancient myth and majesty.

Several small birds fluttered to his head, some landing on his shoulders. Rambo greeted them with soft whispers and loving kindness.

Jesse was thoroughly awed at the sight of this new friend and smiled at his gentle display.

"Even the birds are impressed with your splendour."

"What a spectacular creature. I can't believe I'm standing here with this beautiful dragon. I wonder if it was Rambo that I saw in my dream."

"Yes, it was I in your dream," Rambo spoke to Jesse's mind.

"You spoke to my mind?" Jesse asked aloud, stunned.

"Indeed, we are connected that way now. I will explain more shortly. Breeze also shared the dream with me," Rambo said. "We will have many adventures together in the unfolding of time. I was wondering, would you permit me to give you something that will help you in the future?" Rambo bowed and then reduced in size.

Jesse was surprised and curious. "Of course, Rambo, what did you have in mind?"

"A gift from the gods."

Jesse stood there speechless at first, unsure of what that meant. He felt calmness prevail. "Yes, my friend. You have my permission."

Rambo softly hummed a tune as he reached forward with his nimble, clawed wing. Touching Jesse's head, Rambo sent shivers through every molecule of Jesse's being, and Jesse closed his eyes in response. When he opened his eyes again, the world looked different.

"What have you done to me, Rambo?" Jesse gasped softly, turning slowly, taking in the grandeur of what he saw. Colours were a hundred times crisper, and butterflies and other winged creatures he hadn't seen before surrounded them. Fairies sat on Rambo's shoulder, where Jesse had seen only birds before. A centaur stepped out of the woods with another creature Jesse couldn't identify, but he was impressed with thoughts of Sasquatch.

"I have removed the last vestige of doubt from your mind, Jesse. You now see the world through eyes that believe. The veil of darkness is gone. Breeze informed me that the gods felt this was necessary, and they gave me permission to do this. Only a chosen few are dragon-blessed."

Jesse felt humbled; he couldn't find words to express himself.

"We are brothers now, friends through this life, and the one that awaits you, if you wish," Rambo said, smiling.

"I can't adequately express my honour at having you by my side, Rambo. Thank you."

"The honour is mine."

"You talked to my mind just a minute ago, when I thought of my dream. Can you understand my thoughts as well?" Jesse asked.

"We can communicate thus, yes. You broke down the barriers when you first reached my mind through your meditation. It happens rarely, and never the way it did. I will only touch your thoughts when there is a need, or my name is mentioned. You have the soul of an elf, Jesse, which means that you will feel a closeness with all essences—mortal and immortal, beast and non-beast. It is an ability given to you before birth, a gift previously reserved only for elves. It's as if the White Druid kissed you herself. But that is impossible. She has been missing for many generations."

"Who was she, Rambo?"

"An elf so pure and noble, she was a delightful soul—kind and gentle. It was hard to imagine her strength and untiring stamina in battle. A wonder to behold. She had complete control of magic, a great leader. As a member of royalty, she was chosen to guide her people, and then she disappeared. No one knows for sure where she went. Some speculate that she was taken to live with the gods, reserved to come at a time of their choosing."

"It sounds like you knew her personally, Rambo," Jesse was astounded. "My world has opened so much over the last few months. I find myself stumbling over all the new thoughts and feelings that I'm having."

"I did know her, Jesse. Perhaps someday I will tell you the story. Yes, we have expanded you, and now, we better hurry, or it will be late, and your grandmother will worry. Might I give you a ride?" Rambo morphed into his larger size.

"Are you serious?! That would be totally amazing! Outstanding, in fact. How do I get up there?"

Rambo chuckled, a musical sound.

"No need for you to worry, I will help you."

With a lift from Rambo, Jesse found himself comfortably seated in a natural cradle behind Rambo's wing joints. A golden bridle appeared, giving him a handhold and creating a restraint of sorts. The place where he sat was soft and silky, as if rooster feathers padded it. Jesse smiled at the thought. Rambo gave a gentle little jump, and they were airborne, flying just below the high clouds. Drifting silently, they sailed over the beautiful palette of fall colours. Oranges, reds, yellows, purples, and violets were all peppered with the greens of pines and firs—colours he had never noticed from the ground.

Jesse observed another flock of geese and asked Rambo if they could fly with them for a while. Rambo banked slightly, falling into line with the group. The geese didn't seem to notice. Things couldn't get any better than this. Jesse's heart swelled with delight. Before long, the lake came into view. Rambo spoke to Jesse's mind.

"Jesse, as your brother, I would trust you with my life. Would you honour me likewise? Know that I would never do you harm."

"Of course, I would. Why do you ask?"

"I want to show you something about faith, my friend. It's important that we have confidence in each other, especially during times of battle."

"But we aren't in battle."

"This is the best time—when you are safe."

"My life is in your keeping, Rambo. I believe you."

To Jesse's surprise, he was encased in a bubble while on Rambo's back. It was like the one on Xanthara when Jesse first landed and met up with his dad, only smaller. They were flying over the lake, and then, without warning, Rambo went into a steep dive towards the water.

"Rambo, what are you doing?!" Jesse yelled, alarmed.

"Trust me, my friend."

They entered the water at high speed. Jesse was surprised that there was still water left in the lake. Sitting on Rambo's back as they moved smoothly through the water felt like flying. The protective bubble kept him dry and comfortable, and his sight was crystal clear. It was an underwater wonderland. He was astonished—he could even smell the environment. It was fresh, like spring rain, with a hint of grass or water plants. He heard soft whistles, pops, swishes, creaking, and pings, which surprised him. The underwater community was very vocal.

The lake was enormous. There were sunken trees, ghost-like in their appearance, leaves and bark long gone. Their skeletal branches appeared to reach for the sky. Many schools of fish swam in the crystal water—some green with red stripes, others spotted with purple and yellow. Schools of smaller rainbow-coloured fish darted in and out of plants and debris. Jesse guessed that the colours of the fish were more intense because of the dragon blessing. Rambo took great delight in chasing the fish, and they seemed to enjoy the activity as well.

Jesse saw sunken boats and even an old house, although not much was left of the wooden structures. In one of the deeper, darker chasms, there were several strange creatures, snakelike with large, flippered feet. They appeared to be sleeping. It felt to Jesse like he and Rambo were on a different planet, and in some ways, they were.

Chapter 11

Trust and Responsibility

Jesse thoroughly enjoyed himself as he and Rambo flew through the lake, and he was disappointed when Rambo headed for the surface. As they emerged, he was surprised to see grey clouds gathering and how late it seemed. Flying over the forest of trees, Jesse watched the beautiful kaleidoscope of colours beneath him, with the sun's rays peeking through grey clouds and bouncing off the fluttering autumn leaves. He felt as light as a feather and happier than he'd been in a long time.

"Rambo, thank you for that. It was amazing; words cannot describe it. I will never doubt you again. I hope to earn your trust completely someday."

"It was my pleasure, Jesse. I'm sure we will have many opportunities to trust each other soon."

When they reached the house, Gran was standing on the front porch, watching as Rambo and Jesse landed. She had her hands on her hips and a pout on her face.

"You've been holding out on me, you overinflated lizard. How come you never offered me a ride around town?" Gran huffed.

Rambo roared his musical laugh and bowed toward Gran.

"Welcome aboard, Milady."

"Oh, now he's kissing up. Miserable excuse for a rooster," Gran mumbled under her breath. She gladly accepted a lift, settling her ample backside into the cradle behind Rambo's wings. Then she yelled, "Giddy up, you flying turkey. Let's see what you can do."

Rambo launched into the air. Jesse could hear Rambo's guffaws and Gran's screeches for a full ten minutes before they landed on the front grass. Her neatly spiked hair was twisted, making her look like a ruffled red cactus. Her face was flushed with excitement, and a fire Jesse had never noticed before was in her eyes. Gran had a grin plastered on her face that threatened to split her head in two.

"Nothing like dragon flight to empty a full bladder. It must've been the altitude change. Jesse, you might want to hose Rambo off, while I change. Sorry about that, Rambo dear, but it was your fault. I am an old lady, after all. Pardon me for a minute or two, while I go to recover the pride that I lost over Slater's place."

Jesse and Rambo were laughing hard as Gran shook out a leg and gingerly walked into the house. Jesse went to get the hose, as Rambo morphed to a smaller, more manageable size.

Once Rambo was hosed off and Gran was showered and changed, she fixed them some dinner. They chatted about their day while eating, including Jesse and Rambo's flight through the lake. The dragon elected to return outside after supper so he could keep watch.

"I remember when they decided to create that lake," Gran reminisced. "Your grandpa and I knew the people who lived in the house. They were a quiet couple and kept some unusual pets. I'm sure those snakelike creatures you saw were some of their critters."

"You know, Gran, I don't remember Gramps. What was he like?" Jesse asked curiously.

"He was a quiet man who didn't make friends readily. The couple of friends that he did have were just like him. He kept to himself most of the time. I think that's why I enjoyed the games so much. I finally had a social life and some adventure. For a long time, I was a very lonely person, even before he died. I wish I could say it was different, but that's the truth."

Gran and Jesse decided not to play the computer game since the Elder hadn't called, and they didn't know when he would do so. After their relaxing supper and chat, Jesse pulled out the Scrabble board and set it up while Gran popped corn and made fudge for a snack. They were just entering their second game when there was a musical sound coming from the telewave. Gran trotted in to get the globe. She placed it on the table as Jesse moved their Scrabble board out of the way.

"Greetings, my friends. I know I took longer than expected, but much is happening here in preparation for the arrival of the Keepers. Many of the citizens here have concerns," Nexlucimus sighed sadly.

"How is your game training going, Jesse?"

"Um... it's going okay, I think. Is that right, Gran?"

"He's doing very well. It takes time, and we all know that he doesn't have much, which increases the pressure. He worries too much."

"As soon as preparations are complete, we will bring everyone to Xanthara," Nexlucimus said. "Being here will improve your magic, and polish up everything else that we can help with, to prepare for the future. Now, Jesse, I will tell you about your dream, what we think it means and what we plan to do about it. I know that Tommy introduced you to your Shadow Dream, Breeze. She is an essential part in all of this. She, as you know, gave you the visions related to the magic, Xanthara, the upcoming war, and the dream you had last night, all of it.

Most of the dreams were given by my command to prepare you for what was coming. The vision last night, however, comes directly from the gods," he said, amazement engraved deeply on his face.

"What?!" Jesse said, stunned.

"We have never heard of such a thing happening before. In the past, the gods have only talked to the leading Elder. He, in turn, passes along the information to those who need it. This time, however, they have sent Breeze to you directly. She brought you a vital piece of the puzzle, a clue that only you can discover the meaning of, with those of your choosing. It gives you a position of power.

We are uncovering many parts of this upcoming war with Tazeron, and much is pointing to you, my young friend. There are parts we cannot regulate, and that is terrifying to those of us who are usually in control. We shake our collective heads and wonder who you are and what is happening to our world."

Jesse was finding it difficult to breathe. He looked at Gran. She was ghost-white and trembling, with her hands to her mouth and tears tracing down her face.

"Gran," Jesse squeaked, "What am I going to do?"

"You, sir..." Nexlucimus said, with authority, "are coming to Xanthara immediately. This dream and its mysteries prove that we cannot wait. I am no longer speaking to a mere mortal youth, but to a war captain, a man of decision and a leader, a Chief comparable to your great Native American ancestors of the Red Hawk Clan.

You, Jesse, are the pivotal player in this game of life and death, quite possibly the saviour of millions of immortal souls. We have faith in you, and it's imperative that we begin your training immediately."

Jesse was shocked to hear these words, but their truth touched his very essence. Nexlucimus trusted him. The gods were sending him messages. Rambo had blessed him. Jesse hoped he could do this. Whatever it took, he would gladly give—even his life.

Jesse stood. They had faith in him. He would believe in himself. He felt a spark of confidence—blessed by magic, strengthened by the word, and gifted with the soul of an elf. As if taught by the dragons of ancient times, he would learn how to rally the troops. They would press forward and be undivided in their battle against the growing evil, just like the game. Only for real. He shuddered. He hoped the doubts and fear he felt wouldn't show through and cripple him. He prayed he could overcome them and do this. He needed to do this.

He bowed to Nexlucimus.

"At your service, Milord," Jesse whispered, trying hard not to show his trembling.

"So it is, and so it begins," Nexlucimus bowed back.

***

Jesse found it difficult to say goodbye to Gran. How do you say goodbye to someone who has saved your life? Or to someone who has helped you age at many levels, and then baked the best 'fish head stew' in the world? You don't. You log off the computer and hug them goodbye for real. That's what he did. Pearl had just a couple of things to show him in the game before he left.

"I'm sure going to miss you, Gran, and all the fun stuff around here. I mean, who could forget green diarrhoea slime from dog feet, large flies, spiders, or bullying tormentors and their graffiti? Also, let's not forget the total insanity, with a massive, stinking dog and a fire-breathing rooster. Oh, wait, the rooster's going with me. I can't wait until you can join Dad and me, with the guild on

Xanthara. Maybe I can have my seventeenth birthday party there with the guild. I'm going to miss you, Gran. I hope it isn't too long until you come."

"I'm already missing you too, dear. We'll keep in contact one way or another. Remember to focus and learn your lessons well. I guess I better check you out of school," she chuckled. Jesse hadn't even thought about that. The school was a very distant thought. Now his time would be consumed with learning of a different type.

Jesse hugged Pearl one last time, and then he and Rambo launched into the night sky for a dragon's journey into fantasy.

Rambo encased Jesse in a bubble, like the one he used when they dove into the lake. Jesse would stay warm. He could stretch out and get some sleep. That was a bonus. His golden seatbelt moved with him, holding him secure, but not binding. The trip was going to take much longer than it did with Cami's talisman.

"You OK out there, Rambo? Does the atmosphere bother dragons? I mean, is there air for you to breathe?"

Jesse could feel the vibrations of Rambo's laughter through his bubble.

"I'm doing well, Jesse. The magic protects me. Now relax and get some sleep. We are flying faster than sound or light, by mortal calculations, but it will still take us many hours."

"Just two more questions, Rambo, then I promise I'll be quiet. First, why do you become a rooster? Is that a normal ability for a

dragon? And why, if you're going to change forms, not a lion or something more impressive? Second, how did you get your name? I mean, Rambo isn't a typical dragon name, is it?"

Rambo sighed. *"My form has many functions, Jesse. First, roosters are a common sight in your part of the world. There aren't many lions roaming around your grandmother's neighbourhood. I could be a lion if I wanted, but I rather like roosters. Besides, food is never a problem for roosters; they can eat almost anything smaller than themselves.*

When I was first given the assignment of being your grandmother's companion in preparation for the coming quest, it was decided that I be granted the shape-shifter ability. Very few are blessed with that skill. Down through mortal history, dragons haven't been well received by most people. There have been a few exceptions, of course. The Chinese and other Asians, for example. I am a dragon; that is my natural form, either large or small. The rooster appearance, as well as the red dog illusion, is for the benefit of the mortals who might see me by chance.

Regarding my real name, it is something that the mortal tongue would have great difficulty pronouncing. Very few people know that name, and even fewer have ever used it. When I arrived at your grandmother's service, I let her decide what she would call me. I understand that she is a fan of old movies. She allowed me to observe the old film that this name came from, and I think it fits.

Would you like to see me flex my muscles?" Jesse could feel him laughing.

"Thanks, maybe tomorrow. I think I'll go to sleep now."

"As you wish, young master. Sleep well. One more thing, Jesse, when we arrive, the Elders have a short assignment for me. Don't be concerned if I'm not with you at first. I won't be gone long."

"I understand, my friend. I'm sure there are many important things for you to do."

Jesse yawned as he stretched out on his back to study the incredible display of innumerable stars. He wished he had a telescope, but it was remarkable just the way it was. Now and then, a falling star appeared, displaying a tail of fire. He tried to identify some of the constellations, but with so many stars, it was difficult.

As Jesse rested there, nagging little uncertainties started creeping into his thoughts. He wondered about Tommy and Cami and all the other guild members. He worried about the battle with Tazeron. He tried not to think about fighting a dungeon or whatever in the real-life game situation. The very idea was weird and complicated to get his mind around. How was he ever going to learn everything?

He wondered what preparations needed to be made to gather everyone to Xanthara. How were they going to get everyone there? Surely dragons weren't an option. He speculated about how many people there would be. The thought of what he might have to do conjured a churning stomach. But the Elder said they had faith in him. Now he had to have confidence in them to teach him all that he needed to know. He died in the game all the time. Would that still happen? His mind felt tortured.

"Jesse," Rambo's soft, soothing voice filled his head, sending all other thoughts scurrying.

"Sleep, my friend. You will need your energy for the new day. You will learn all things with time, and you have the skills and talent you need within you. Remember, I can see deep into the fabric of who you are, almost to your very essence, and there beats the heart of a champion.

There will be hard times ahead, maybe life-threatening, but we, you and I, will survive. Think about this also: you won't be doing this on your own. Your father will be there, your friends will be there, and I will be there. And of course, the gods are always cheering for the honourable side. Now sleep, be at peace."

Rambo's words spoke comfort to his troubled mind, and Jesse drifted off into a dreamless sleep.

When he woke up, they had landed on Xanthara, and he was lying within his bubble, on a very comfortable bed. Rambo was not there. In fact, no one was there that he could see. He could feel someone, however, and he wondered if it was *Breeze*.

"I can sense someone here, who are you? Please come out so we can meet."

A soft vapour glowed in an upper part of the ceiling. It approached and pulsated near his face.

"Is that you, Breeze? Can we talk?"

There was a soft knock on the door, just before it opened. *Breeze* jetted back to her lookout spot.

"Good morning, young sir," said a tall man, bringing in a tray of food that looked and smelled delicious. "I had no idea what you might like to eat, so I took the liberty of choosing for you. I hope it is agreeable."

He turned to leave but then added, "You will need to remove the bubble before you can eat. I suggest you do it soon before the food gets cold." With that, he stepped out.

Jesse knew what happened next. He wasn't excited at the thought, but he didn't relish starving to death either. He wondered if there was some way to keep the Skeedlers away from this room, but then he wouldn't be able to leave.

"Whimp! What are you afraid of?" Jesse chided himself. *"You'll have to face them sooner or later. How are you going to save the world if you're afraid of a few hundred furballs? Geez, I guess this is the new normal for me. Ok, Rambo, you are my inspiration."* With those words, Jesse ripped the bubble and stepped out.

"Come and get me... you mutant, clean freaks! Breakfast is served!"

At first, he didn't hear anything, and he started to think maybe they'd miss him. Then came the familiar rumble, growing louder and louder until it burst through the door.

"Holy cow! There are more of them this time! I must really stink!"

Just like before, they were all over him. He kept his mouth shut, remembering how they almost jumped down his throat, gagging him last time. They scrubbed and scoured every inch—inside and out of his clothes. They even removed a stain he had on his shirt front. "Mum would be impressed. In my whole life, I don't think she ever saw me this clean. I wonder if it would be faster if I were naked. Don't laugh, Jesse, or they'll be down your throat."

Finally, there were fewer of them, and many were leaving. Except for one fuzzy little guy, who was resolutely hanging from the end of Jesse's nose, tapping Jesse's lips. Groaning, Jesse reluctantly opened his mouth, and the happy little scrubber went to work, cleaning Jesse's teeth better than any hygienist ever came close to doing. Then, the little fella too was gone.

Jesse knew that he could travel anywhere now and be presentable. He sat down to eat the delicious-smelling food but remembered Breeze.

"Breeze, are you still there?" he asked, testing. There was no response. He checked his impressions and found that he could barely detect her, farther away. His stomach gave a huge rumble. *"I'll search for her later."*

The food was fantastic and very filling. He wondered what it was—cooked cereal, toast with jam, and an odd piece of purple fruit that tasted like bananas and raspberries combined. The tray had a flower arrangement that he didn't think he was supposed to eat, but he decided to try a sample. Surprisingly, the flower tasted delicious, so he ate the whole thing, stem and all.

He heard a snicker coming from somewhere. *"I guess people don't eat the flowers here."* Jesse wondered who was laughing, and thinking of fairies, he was instantly on guard. "Hello... who are you? Will you come out so I can see you?"

To his surprise, two small children—a boy about nine and a girl about four (he could only guess)—stepped through the door and addressed him in musical voices.

"Good morning, Master Jesse," the boy said. "I am Ramekin, and this is my youngest sister, Fairlese." They bowed and curtsied. "Our mother, Willa, is the head steward of this building. She sent us to show you to the place of learning. Please come with us."

"It is a pleasure to make your acquaintance, Ramekin and Fairlese. I would be honoured to follow you to the place of learning."

Before following the two children, Jesse grabbed the last flower, shoving it into his front pocket. It looked like a rumpled boutonnière.

"It wouldn't hurt to have a snack for later," he thought.

Chapter 12

You have got to be kidding

Jesse followed the two children through many halls. The building looked and felt new. The walls were light blue, and there were many tapestries and other wall hangings depicting scenes from Earth's peasant life. There were small towns and farms, with people working in fields. Another view showed a horse with an old-fashioned plough and a quaint barn with chickens and cows.

Jesse thought how strange it was to see the landscapes, with ordinary people and animals. Even if they seemed strange, they were cool to look at. Another hall had pictures of African people thrashing grain of some kind. There were zebras and lions. Jesse saw folk art from Asia, with people dancing. The islands were represented, with palm trees and turtles swimming in the ocean, surrounded by other sea creatures.

"Ramekin, what building is this, and where are these pictures from?" Jesse asked, his curiosity overcoming him.

"This is the lodging house for the Keepers, sir, and these pictures are from your world. The Elders wanted the Keepers to feel more comfortable."

"Are there other Keepers in the building?"

"No, sir, you are the first."

Jesse was surprised at that answer, and as they continued to walk, he tried to imagine how many people this large building would house. He wondered when the other Keepers would be arriving.

"Ramekin, do you know when the other Keepers will arrive?"

"No, sir, I do not know that answer. Your trainer might, however."

After a while, they went down some stairs and entered a large arena with a packed dirt floor covered in straw. Practice dummies surrounded the perimeter.

There were different weapons grouped on stands: fearsome-looking axes, spears, and crossbows. On a wall in another area, bows, swords, shields, and knives of all types were mounted. Further down the same wall were several items that looked like small cannonballs with spikes, each attached to clubs with chains.

Jesse thought that these seemed primitive for advanced people. Then he had an awakening thought. These were the weapons of the games. He winced, wondering how they were going to teach him the magic he used. Even though he had practiced on a dummy while setting up his spell rotations and changing his statistics, he used a keyboard and mouse or a video controller to project the spells. He didn't see any of those hanging on the walls. He certainly hoped that he didn't have to use these other weapons.

Then Ramekin spoke, distracting him from his thoughts. "This is the place of learning, sir. Your trainer will be here shortly. We will leave you now. We wish you well."

The two children bowed and curtsied before running off. He waved goodbye to them and then returned to studying the impressive armament displayed around the room.

As he ventured into a side room, there were various types of protective clothing displayed on racks, shelves, and stands. He saw shiny plate armour, just like suits of armour, and chainmail that seemed a bit flimsy in comparison. There were leathers of all varieties, some smooth and supple, others thick and scaly or covered in soft or coarse fur. He saw cloth of every description, in a wide range of colours and textures. Each type of covering had appropriate helms, bracers, gloves, leggings, tabards, chest and back pieces, earrings, rings, trinkets, and relics. It was like the wardrobe of a movie set or a shopping mall in the game.

After a short period, Jesse heard footsteps approaching. He stepped into the main room and turned his attention in that direction. Two women and a man were walking toward him, and as they got closer, he recognised Nexlucimus' wife, Zeela, as one of the women.

"Good morning, Jesse," Zeela addressed him. "I hope you slept well."

"Yes, Milady," he wasn't sure if he should bow, kneel, or what he should do. He settled for a quick bow and felt his cheeks flush slightly.

Sensing his discomfort, Zeela said, "Jesse, politeness is always welcomed, but formality is not necessary on the field of battle. Please consider me a friend and partner, as we work to strengthen your considerable talents and advance you into the game world."

"Yes, ma'am, and thank you. I never know what I should do."

Zeela smiled warmly at him and then introduced the other two.

Pointing to the woman first, "This is my dear friend, Wolfa. She is a master magician and will oversee your training as a mage. And this is Andrazen, he is also a friend," Zeela said, indicating the man. "He is a master healer, accomplished in alchemy. He will show you which plants are helpful, and what potions increase and protect your health, and, of course, your stats."

They both nodded, and then Wolfa spoke. "It is my pleasure to finally meet you, Jesse. I am sure you will learn quickly, and I hope that my unique teaching style will not embarrass you. I find that when teaching someone such as you, it is better to start at their level of understanding. I will enlist the help of my son Meriloc, who is also a young mage, and I will train the two of you together."

Jesse felt his excitement growing, along with his shaky nerves. It would be helpful to have someone else to train with; he looked forward to that.

"I look forward to learning alongside your son."

"It is agreed then. I must leave you now, but Meriloc and I will join you later, after the refreshing. We will begin your training then." She bowed slightly, and with the swish of green satin robes, she turned and left the room.

Andrazen stepped forward and spoke next. "I consider it a pleasure to meet you, Jesse, and to teach you about the plants you will find both here and in the game. I understand that Zeela wants to give you a tour of the city before we begin. She will point out key locations that will be important to you and the other Keepers. We will commence our lessons later today, after your session with Mistress Wolfa. Until then, enjoy our fair city." Bowing slightly, Andrazen also left. Jesse turned to face Zeela, the wife of the High Priest, and found her smiling at him.

"Jesse, I can tell that you are finding everything a bit overwhelming."

"Ah, yeah… I mean, yes, ma'am, totally overwhelming," he tried to smile.

"That's why I thought it would be a good idea to show you around before the lessons began. That way, you can better process being here. First, however, we must dress you correctly for one of your classes. Please come with me."

She led Jesse to the armory. After a short time of measuring and fitting, she picked out his apparel and left Jesse to dress. He was familiar with most of the items she chose for him from his time in the game. It was just so odd to see and feel them. A soft robe of dark blue satin (he guessed the material), leggings (more like long socks), slippers, bracers, gloves, and back and chest pieces of the same dark blue fabric, only much thicker.

There were earrings, but he wasn't sure about getting his ears pierced, so he left those on the table. There were rings and a flat blue stone attached to a leather cord, with red lines crisscrossing its surface. There were trinkets and other small stone relics, all of which he knew were storage spaces for spell knowledge and energy. He would stash them in hidden pockets he found in the folds of his robes until someone imbued them.

It didn't take too long for him to dress in his new clothes, but he was very uncomfortable walking around. His mum would have a fit seeing him dressed like this, and his dad was going to have a heart attack from laughing. He stepped out into the room with Zeela. She checked him over to make sure everything fit correctly and was in the right place.

"You look very respectable, Jesse. Oh, you forgot the earrings. I'll get them." She stepped back into the room to retrieve the earrings. Returning, she placed them on his ears, causing a slight sting.

Feeling his ears and the stone earrings, he was horrified at how big and dangly they were.

"Congratulations, Jesse, you look like a magician. How does it feel?" she asked, with a pleased smile.

"I feel ridiculous, to be honest. Do I seriously need to wear a dress and these dangly earrings? I mean, I understand why I need all this stuff, but wearing it in the game and then for real is very strange."

Zeela chuckled. "They will feel more comfortable as you get used to them. Perhaps we can find something a bit more to your liking. You will, however, choose the robes later, because of the added stat bonuses. For now, as you learn, I believe breeches and a shirt will do."

They stepped back into the armory. Zeela picked out a pair of pants that looked like his mum's nylon stockings, without feet and thicker. Then she picked out a shirt with puffy sleeves. He wasn't sure these would be any better, but he decided to give them a try. Zeela left, and again he changed his clothes. Wiggling into the tights, he wondered how his mum, or other girls for that matter, ever got into nylons. Then he put on the shirt with puffy sleeves.

He checked himself out in a shiny shield, turning from side to side. *"You have got to be kidding me!"*

While the pants didn't swish, they were so tight that there was no room for boxers (or imagination), and the short shirt didn't come anywhere near covering him enough.

After some painful deliberation, he took off the tights and puffy shirt, putting back on the robes, which still felt like a dress. He walked out, trying to keep his pride from jumping overboard and running away, screaming.

Zeela smiled at him. "I know it's uncomfortable now, Jesse, but with time, you'll be glad that you got used to the robes at the beginning of your training. I can change the earrings." She touched them briefly, and they were no longer as big and didn't dangle.

"We will need to have the earrings, neckpiece, trinkets, and relics imbued. I'll have Nexi do that later; he's a master enchanter. Now let me introduce you to our fair city, as Andy called it."

Walking out of the building, Jesse tripped twice on his robes before realising that he needed to lift them slightly so he wouldn't step on them as he climbed the stairs. They were comfortable, but he missed his jeans and T-shirt. *"Dang, I forgot the flower."*

The morning was bright and sunny, bustling with people who greeted them with cheerful smiles and waves. Zeela pointed out the market and its many vendors. She said he and the other Keepers could get anything they needed at no cost.

In their discussion, Jesse learned that no one had to pay for anything. It was part of their society. They all contributed what they could and used what they needed. He stopped by a vendor and took a giant sandwich with tasty meat and some fruit on a stick to munch on.

As they walked, Zeela talked about the history of Xanthara. She mentioned that they were in the process of preparing for a splitting.

"As explained in Nexi's history, a new world of humans requires a world of fantasy to accompany it. Our gods choose one of the most populated of our worlds. A group of more experienced people is split off or separated to populate the new immortal world. They then help the new mortal world as its inhabitants grow and develop."

"That is so cool," Jesse said, amazed. "That way, you never get overpopulated."

"That's correct. With this splitting, Nexi, I, and many others were chosen to go. However, with all that's happening, Nexi and I elected to stay here. As head Elder, he has been preparing all the records that must go with the splitting. All the important books from the Great Library are copied, some by hand. It's a difficult undertaking that must be done with exactness."

"Wow, I wondered why the scribe was so cranky. I'm glad you both decided to stay. Was that a hard decision?"

"Not really," Zeela answered. "It is an honour to help you and the other Keepers. We will have another opportunity for a splitting in a few millennia."

Jesse gaped at her. "No offence, but it's so strange being around people who live forever."

Zeela smiled at him. "I'm sure it is, but given time, you will see that we are not so unusual."

Jesse glanced at Zeela with her lavender skin and pink wings and wondered if he would ever not consider her unusual. She was indeed strikingly beautiful and exotic, but never unusual.

Their tour continued with Zeela showing Jesse a portal into the games. After passing the saluting guard, they stepped in. It made Jesse think of a funhouse tunnel at a carnival, with swirling, sparkly air and flashing lights. When the door opened with a pop less than a second later, he was in a desert canyon. In the distance, Jesse could see the lush green of a forest. Snakes, spiders, and other wildlife scurried out of their way; birds flew overhead. Jesse was surprised at how much like the game it was. But, of course, it would be, since this was the game.

After a while, they approached the end of the narrow canyon, where it opened to the forest. Just out of sight, Jesse could hear noises, whisperings, and animal sounds. Zeela pulled out a small bow that he hadn't noticed her carrying and fitted it with a tiny silver dart.

"Is that one of those darts of searching?" he whispered.

"Indeed, it is. This area is a dangerous place, even though it is close to the portal entrance. If we get noticed, my barb of confusion will cause the attacker to run away, pulling any friends along."

"That is so cool. Can I see it work?" Jesse asked.

She chuckled. "Perhaps later in training. Right now, I think we need to head back before we start trouble."

She turned and started jogging back. Jesse followed.

"Zeela, how come you aren't using your wings? I remember you flying with wings when we first met in Master Nexlucimus' council room."

"Sometimes I like to walk or run, Jesse, but if I am tired, flying is easier. We need to hurry; it is almost the refreshing, and I told Nexi that we would join him for a meal."

Anticipating his next question, she added, "I will explain the refreshing when we get there; we must hasten now."

Zeela decided to fly after a while, and Jesse had to run to keep up with her. Eventually, they arrived at the Great Library of Learning.

Panting with the effort to keep up, Jesse was glad when they saw the magnificent building. Just as they went through the massive front doors, and the courtyard with the white dragon fountain came into view, there was an enormous clap of thunder. Jesse was tempted to look out the doors, but Zeela, sensing his thoughts, grabbed his arm, shook her head, and turned to go up the stairs. Jesse followed her, wondering about this refreshing, as another huge clap of thunder shook the floor he jogged on.

Finally, they arrived at the council chambers, and Zeela knocked and entered as the Elder called out to them. Jesse took a closer look at the fairies, who were trying to hide behind the gold and silver-leaf fruit. One of them waved to him, and several others giggled. He waved back as he stepped through the door.

Standing in the room, Jesse was surprised to see not only the Elder but his father.

"Dad...!" Jesse shouted, forgetting where he was, and then listened to his voice ping off the walls for at least ten seconds.

"Sorry, I guess I shouldn't shout in here, " he said sheepishly.

They all chuckled at him, and then Nexlucimus invited them to sit and eat. It was a remarkable feast—roasted meats, bread, many different fruits and vegetables, and several kinds of desserts. The table was large, and that was a good thing. Most of the serving platters and bowls moved around the table, making reaching for the food more accessible. Jesse discovered that all he had to do was point, and a plate or bowl would come to him so he could serve himself. He felt sorry for his dad.

"Does it bother you that you can't eat, Dad?"

"Not really, it's like I'm full all the time."

Jesse tried to imagine what that would be like, as his stomach growled loudly.

"By the way, Master Jesse, you look stunning in your mage robes. Very professional," the Elder complimented, as he filled his plate.

To Jesse's amazement, they all agreed, even his father, whom he thought would die laughing.

"Thank you," Jesse said, embarrassed. "I'm getting used to them. It felt weird at first, but I seem to fit in better dressed like this."

As they ate, Jesse asked his ever-present questions.

"Are there more portals than just the one into the game world?"

David answered that question.

"Yes, the portals are scattered throughout Xanthara to allow access by the different races that patrol the game world. They have been trained to assist the Keepers in keeping the Shield in good repair and functioning. While they can't use the magic of the games like the Keepers can, they can still use their other skills. We mostly use the tank and melee types for that work. That is one of my responsibilities as an advisor. We post guards on this side of the portal so only authorised personnel can enter. As you get more comfortable with your magic, we'll take you deeper into the games so that you can practise in that setting, just like you did while you were at Gran's."

"Outstanding, I can't wait. Will Rambo be coming with us into the game world?" Jesse asked.

"Yes, he will. He has an advantage because his magic is different from ours, and as such, he is not affected by the magical barrier, as other immortals are," Zeela answered.

"Excellent, I was hoping he could come. Will he be a rooster or a dragon?"

"That is up to him, but I rather suspect he will retain his dragon form most of the time," Nexlucimus smiled.

Another clap of thunder rang out, not as loud or long this time. Jesse also noticed that the rain wasn't hitting the windows as heavily. They could see out a little better.

"What's the deal with this refreshing, as you call it?" Jesse asked.

"The refreshing happens every day at the same time," the Elder answered. "Imagine a one-thousand-mile broad line, going from pole to pole. That is the refreshing. It travels around our world at roughly one thousand miles per hour at the equator, and slightly slower toward the poles. By mortal calculations, since our world is about the same size as the human world, it takes about twenty-four hours to circle the globe at the equator. It's always the same. It never changes. It refreshes the air and fills the lakes, rivers, and streams, giving us water for all our needs. It's like a thunderstorm in your world, Jesse, but it never gets out of control, and it happens with regularity.

"It's best not to be caught in it, although you could go out if it were an emergency," Zeela added. "Most people use this time to be inside with their family or take a nap or engage in other quiet, private activities. I like to do my baking or potion-making during this period; my recipes turn out better."

"Indeed, they do," Nexlucimus beamed. "Zeela is an excellent cook, as my middle will witness."

Zeela flushed a deeper shade of lavender, which only increased her beauty, Jesse thought. He enjoyed being around these people, and he looked forward to learning his magic in this world. Jesse was anxious for the refreshing to end so he could meet Meriloc and get started. He wondered if Meriloc would be close to his age.

Chapter 13

Whoa! Did I do all that?

After the meal was completed and cleared, Zeela and Nexlucimus walked over to a small sofa by the window and sat, chatting quietly. Jesse and his dad wandered out of the room and down a hall to leave them alone. As they walked, they caught up on things since they last saw each other.

Jesse asked about the preparations, and David told him as much as he could. He didn't know much about what the Xantharaians were doing with the Keepers, except that they were rounding everyone up. David explained to his son that his area of responsibility was patrolling the game world, with selected guards for shield security and getting ready for the Keepers to arrive.

Skirmishes were becoming more common, and there seemed to be more mortals with Tazeron, which was not a good sign. Tazeron appeared to be doing more recruiting or something, but David wasn't sure.

"Dad, I just remembered something. There was a new option for players to join with Tazeron's minions. This selection caught on with certain types, mostly the bully people at school."

This information surprised David. "That would explain the increase. I will mention this to the guards at the shield to watch for more coming through."

David revealed that there would be over a hundred Keepers arriving in the next couple of days, and he would be busy. Jesse was surprised by this news.

Jesse told his dad about the training he had with Gran, and they enjoyed a good chuckle. When Jesse mentioned Rambo's blessing, David was shocked.

"Have you told anyone about this, Jesse?" he asked.

"No, sir. I haven't had a chance yet. Do you think I should?"

"Yes, I do. In fact, I believe we need to go back and tell Nexlucimus right away."

They hurried down the hall to the council chambers. Zeela and Nexlucimus were just coming to find them.

"Master Nexlucimus, Jesse has something to tell you that might be significant."

"Go on, Jesse," Nexlucimus said, as he took a chair and invited the others to do the same.

"Yesterday, while I was out for a walk with Rambo, he gave me a blessing. He said that the gods had suggested it and authorised it."

There was stunned silence.

"My goodness, this just gets more and more curious. Jesse, this means magic will not be a problem for you in any realm, and that you now have an amazing friend for life. I think that this drops the ball in our court, as you mortals would say."

"He also said that I had the soul of an elf and that it was as if the White Druid had kissed me at birth."

Now the silence was intense; no one made a sound for a full minute, and they barely breathed.

"What else did he tell you?" Nexlucimus asked when he found his voice.

"He told me who she was and that the dragon statue in the courtyard downstairs was to honour her. He said that no one knew where she was or what had happened to her, and that he had personally known her. It almost seemed like he was in love with her. Did you know her, sir?"

"There is much more to this story, Jesse, but I think Rambo is the one who should tell you. It will be his choice, and I would ask you not to push him on this matter. That is imperative. Do you understand?"

"Yes, sir. I understand." Jesse was surprised and very curious—just one more mystery.

"Come, Jesse; it's time to meet up with Wolfa and her son," Zeela urged.

Interested, Nexlucimus asked which of Wolfa's sons she was using for the training. Zeela told him that it was Meriloc, and the Elder nodded his approval.

"An excellent choice. That family has many talented magicians, and Meriloc will be one of the best, I believe. You will learn much working with him, Jesse. Enjoy your lessons."

"Yes, sir. It was good to see you again."

David decided to accompany Jesse to the place of learning and observe his training. Zeela agreed but cautioned David not to interfere. He had no problem with that, and once they arrived, David found a seat on an upper level, overlooking the arena.

Wolfa and her son weren't at the training site when they arrived, but Zeela assured Jesse that they would be there soon. In the meantime, Zeela suggested they sit on a nearby bench while they waited.

Soon, they heard footsteps, and Wolfa entered with a boy that appeared to be five years old. Jesse couldn't believe it. Would he be training with a five-year-old? Jesse felt deflated and embarrassed, as if he'd been sent back to kindergarten. But as he thought about it, maybe that was where he needed to be. He stood to meet them. As Wolfa and Meriloc approached, Jesse noticed that Meriloc wore the same robes. He was glad that he had decided against the tights.

"Jesse, may I introduce my son, Meriloc."

The boy bowed. "I'm pleased to meet you, sir. It will be an honour to be learning alongside one of the Keepers."

"I look forward to working with you, Meriloc. Your uncle Nexlucimus speaks highly of you."

The boy looked pleased and smiled widely at Jesse.

Zeela excused herself and joined David. Wolfa invited both of her students to sit on a bench while she gave them instructions.

"Since Meriloc has known the magic from birth, Jesse, there are advantages for him that you will now learn. One of these is learning how to control the fire within you, which often displays as impulsiveness. Self-discipline, focus, and magic control are the lessons you must learn first. For right now, I want you to watch."

Jesse watched as first Wolfa and then Meriloc torched several practice dummies, while the other tried to distract. At one point, Wolfa grabbed Meriloc and tickled him. Jesse was surprised to see that the boy still hit his target before collapsing into gales of laughter. Jesse felt the seeds of doubt swelling inside him.

"This kid is incredible! I have so much to learn. Rambo, I wish we could talk."

"Jesse, my friend, know that you are not alone and that you have the heart of a champion and the strength of a dragon beside you. Be brave, my friend, fear not, doubt not, and you will succeed."

"Rambo! Where are you?"

"Close enough to hear your thoughts. I will return soon. In the meantime, focus and learn well from Wolfa. She, of all people, knows the power we face. Farewell until later."

"Jesse? Are you well?" Wolfa was beside him, looking concerned.

"I'm sorry, Mistress Wolfa. I was distracted."

"Indeed, you were, and that, my young mage, must never happen. It could cost you your life. Now get up, it's your turn. Let's see what magic you have in you."

"What do I do first?" Jesse asked, self-conscious.

"You must search within. I know the meditation exercises that your grandmother taught you and how you could communicate with Rambo. Don't look so surprised," she smiled, noticing his reaction to her disclosure. "We teachers must know our students. I want you to do the same thing here. Find the magic as it swirls inside you, and then channel it, releasing it through your hands. Be careful; the first time could be intense."

Wolfa and Meriloc moved far away from him.

Remembering his lessons from Gran, he looked deep inside. To his surprise, he saw many ribbons of red light swirling, just as Mistress Wolfa had said. He pictured these ribbons gathering to his arms and hands as heat pulsated just under his skin. He began to feel hot. In fact, he started to sweat.

When he felt like he was becoming a volcano, Jesse selected a practice dummy and released the fire. He was blown backward fifteen feet, rolling over and over in the straw before skidding to a stop. His robes were twisted in knots around his legs. His leggings bunched around his ankles, and he had no idea where his slippers ended up. He struggled to sit up, spitting dirt and pieces of straw out of his mouth. The dummy and a good chunk of the wall behind it were gone. His robes sustained scorched holes, his eyebrows, eyelashes, and hair were singed, and his hands smoked.

"Whoa, did I do all that?" Jesse asked Wolfa, shaking his head as peals of husky, choking laughter erupted from above. His slippers floated down from the balcony, where David and Zeela sat.

"Indeed, you did, Jesse, and I must say, you certainly have much magic inside you." Jesse could tell she was struggling to stay composed and not laugh. Meriloc had his back turned toward them, but his shoulders were shaking.

"Now comes the challenge—you must learn to control it. If you were to release that much magic in the game world, you would be dead before your target. Everything within aggro or aggression radius would suddenly sense you and attack. No amount of taunting by your tanks, or healing from your healers, would save you. In fact, most people would just step back and let you die. It would take less mana or energy to resurrect you than to try and save you with healing. Moderation kills a mob faster than uncontrolled blasting ever did. When the target is almost two-thirds dead, then you can blast away. Always remember that. Now that we know what you can do…" Wolfa glanced at the smoking hole in the wall. "I will have an improved approach to your training."

Over the next few hours, Jesse focused on the swirling magic inside of him. He sent it out in smaller batches, sometimes just singeing the target, other times scorching it, or burning it down. Wolfa had him and Meriloc playing a game of magical dot-to-dot. They had to connect the dots with their magic on a large dot-covered square by taking alternating turns. The object was to block your opponent while trying to get to the end of the pattern. Meriloc won every time, which only encouraged Jesse to work harder.

They played tic-tac-toe, and Jesse had the advantage there. All in all, it was a fun afternoon. Jesse felt like he had learned a lot. Wolfa suggested that he come to the learning place and practice mind control, paying attention to detail. She showed him patterns to burn into an area on the wall, to increase his focus development. She told him that, as his magical intelligence increased, his attention span and spell control would also improve. She suggested that he have Nexlucimus imbue some of his gear. He needed to add intelligence, focus, and some dexterity.

"Jesse, I believe that is enough for this day. It was a pleasure. Shall we meet again tomorrow, after the morning meal?"

"I would like that very much."

Before they left, Jesse taught Meriloc how to grasp hands and then bump knuckles, which he explained was a manly thing to do in the mortal world. Meriloc grinned like he'd learned a great secret. Jesse smiled to himself as he watched the boy and his mother departing hand in hand.

Zeela and his dad rejoined him. Zeela suggested that he change into fresh robes. As soon as he entered the clothing area, he was greeted by an army of Skeedlers. Apparently, they weren't allowed on the training field. This time, he stripped naked, putting his dirty clothes in a bin marked for cloth only. Another bunch of Skeedlers attacked the dirty laundry. His 'bath' went much faster this time. Freshly scoured and smelling spring-fresh in new robes, Jesse joined his father and Zeela for a quick trip to the vendors and some refreshments.

Zeela took some fruit, and Jesse grabbed one of the delicious sandwiches, some fruit on a stick, and an enormous, probably sixty-four-ounce, pineapple slushy drink. They walked to a nearby park to enjoy their snack and discuss the training he'd just experienced.

"I must say, son, I was impressed with your display," David chuckled.

"Honestly, Dad, your laughing was rude," Jesse said, through a full mouth.

David snorted again. "I think once you stop blowing holes in the wall, losing your clothes, and burning all your hair off, you'll do just fine."

"I didn't burn it all off. I saved some for tomorrow," Jesse chuckled, taking another huge bite of his sandwich.

"After we finish eating, Jesse, we will find Andy for your herbalism lesson. Your father and I will accompany you on this lesson as well, since Andy would like to take you into the game," Zeela said.

"Excellent, I'm excited. Hey, how long does it take to enchant stuff?"

"Not long. I'll take the pieces you need to be imbued to Nexi when we finish. I'll have them back to you by tomorrow."

"That would be awesome, thank you."

"Finish eating, Jesse. I told Andrazen that we would meet him by the third portal, where his gardens are. We probably should hasten, so he doesn't have to wait long for us." Zeela stood, gathering her bag and notes.

"We can go right now," Jesse said. "I'm done."

They walked toward the third portal, which was close to the one that Jesse and Zeela had entered that morning. David explained that, because they would be travelling deeper into the game, they would assume their game character or toon forms. Jesse was excited to hear that perhaps he would be able to practise his magic in a real situation.

As they approached the gardens, Zeela noticed Andrazen squatting near a small purple tree, full of little fruit.

"Greetings, Andy!" Zeela shouted as she waved. Andrazen stood and waved them over to where he was.

"Welcome, Zeela, David, and young Jesse. I want to show you some unusual creatures." He pointed to some furry, orange insects. They carried a piece of dried fruit down a hole in the ground.

"Wow, those are some strange-looking ants," Jesse said, surprised.

"These are spike ants, Jesse. They keep our plants healthy. They do this by carrying away dropped fruit to be decomposed underground. They maintain the root systems of all the plants on Xanthara. You must be careful around them, however. When agitated, they can shoot spikes that have a toxin, which causes considerable discomfort, as well as swelling of the flesh. Think of them as little porcupines."

Jesse backed up, causing Andrazen to jump towards him and grab his arm.

"They are everywhere, Jesse. You just missed stepping on some behind you. It's a good lesson in paying attention to your surroundings. Always beware of where you are, and what you might step in."

Jesse was reminded of the green slime and grimaced. "I will be more careful, sir."

"While we are here, I will tell you about this tree and its fruit. The Dumplumba tree and its fruit are in almost all our tonics, except those of offence. It removes all internal impurities and pollutants we might contact from travelling to other worlds. Every traveller needs to carry Dumplumba. A person can live on this fruit for many days, and since it is sweeter and more condensed in its dried form, it is highly suited for pockets or bags. The spike ants enjoy it too. It is the mainstay of their diet. So, if you pick it up off the ground, check closely for young spikes, as they are just as potent as the adults."

They walked to another part of the garden as Andrazen pointed out herbs used in potions of defence, offence, and healing. When they came to a small silver tree, Andrazen bowed to the tree, waited a minute, and then spoke some words. To Jesse's surprise, the tree shook violently, dropping about ten small silver fruits. Andrazen reverently picked these up, placing them gently into a fur-lined pouch. He motioned for the party to follow him to a stone table, where he took one of the fruits and laid it on a small square of leather. Carefully, he removed a silver knife from another pouch and cut the fruit into four equal sections, handing one to each of them.

"Eat the fruit of the Naqisha tree with reverence, Jesse. It is the mother of all healing herbs. We are honoured to have three of these trees scattered throughout our gardens. They are very rare, and as such, only certain people are authorised to collect from them. No one can gather the fruit without the tree's permission. If you try, it is considered a severe crime.

The elves gave these three trees to us as a gift from the White Druid, many millennia ago. They are the ones that taught us to use them, and only a few have learned how to do so. Zeela is a master alchemist, and she is one of the few, along with me. She will assist you in learning how to make your potions. Please eat your fruit, so you do not dishonour the tree."

As Jesse bit into the soft, bitter fruit, he felt a tingle spread from his mouth through his whole body. He was surprised when he touched his face; all his pimples had vanished.

"This is awesome, Master Andrazen," Jesse said, smiling.

"Please, call me Andy."

They continued to the portal, and as they arrived, Andy, David, and Zeela chatted with a guard named Tares before they entered.

Travelling through the portal was uneventful. Once again, several lizards, snakes, and spiders scurried off the path. Jesse saw shadows of more significant creatures in the brush, but nothing of concern.

As they exited the narrow canyon, which looked like a tunnel to Jesse, they entered a bright green forest of dense trees. Zeela and his father equipped their weapons. Jesse noticed that his father had changed in appearance to a much larger man, muscled and wearing shiny chainmail armour.

"Wow, Dad, you look cool."

"Thanks, Jesse, you're impressive yourself."

Jesse hadn't noticed anything different, but when he felt his face, it was smooth and softer, and his ears had grown longer and pointed. He wished he had a mirror and made a mental note to bring one the next time. He did feel slightly taller. Andy led them down a path toward a green patch of ground, covered in small golden flowers.

"These are called golden dreams; we steep them into a powerful sleeping potion."

Jesse noticed Zeela picking some and placing them carefully in a special pouch with compartments. As they ventured deeper into the forest, it opened to a beautiful valley, covered with waving grain of some kind, and ponds of water. Birds, like big ducks and swans, were swimming and diving beneath the surface. Jesse was sure that many fish also called it home, since every time a diving bird reappeared, it had a squirming fish in its bill.

"We steer clear of open areas like this, Jesse," David told him. "We are too exposed, and many beasts lay in wait for passing meals. I don't plan on being anyone's meal today. When you are on the game at home, you can travel to these places if you are high enough level, but not so here."

"Interesting," Jesse commented. "Dad, in the game back home I died all the time. After running around as a ghost for a while, we got our bodies back, or we received a resurrection. How does that work here?"

"It's pretty much the same here; after all, this is the game world. Some things haven't changed, while other things have. Travelling with experienced players will help your learning curve. As for the death issue, the difference is that you will feel it this time. A slow death by poison, for instance, isn't pleasant. It's best to be careful and remember that even though you are wearing a game body, you are still mortal to a degree."

"Wow, that's something I never thought about before."

Suddenly, there was a loud screech, and several birds took flight from a distant thicket. David pulled Jesse down into a crouch, while Zeela instantly positioned herself in a similar stance, holding a dart-equipped bow.

Chapter 14

Blood Fairies and Trouble

"Don't make any noise, and stay down," Zeela whispered, glancing nervously around her. She pulled a small bottle from her pouch and took a sip. Her image shimmered as she launched herself, flying off. She became invisible.

"Wow, that was so cool," Jesse whispered to his father.

"Normally, as a druid, she would shapeshift, but she has no magic in the game world. Potions are the only thing she can use."

Jesse noticed Andy equipping a small tube with a tiny silver dart.

"Is that one of those darts of searching?" Jesse asked.

"No, only fairies can use those. This is an ordinary blow dart, dipped into a potion of confusion, just in case Zeela returns with some nasties. As a healer, I can carry few weapons, but these darts are very useful and easy to bring," he smiled grimly.

Waiting was not an easy thing for Jesse. Just out of curiosity, and because he was bored, he decided to explore the area with his mind. Exploring was something he had thought about doing but hadn't yet. He found it surprisingly easy. As he projected his mind farther and farther from their location, he saw a surrounding grove of trees, and a large gathering of characters, including ogres, trolls, humans, dust whelps, and bog witches. As he watched, Jesse was shocked to also see blood fairies and tried to pull away. The blood-red nymphs, however, had noticed his spying and started talking animatedly, pointing in his direction. Several were fitting tiny silver darts.

"Crap!" Jesse thought as he tried to pull his mind back quickly.

"Dad, I have to get out of here now!" Jesse said urgently. "I just saw blood fairies, and they saw me. Quick, show me the way out!"

David was startled. "How could you see them?"

"Mind travels. I have no time to explain; please hurry. Lead me out of here, now!"

David stood and began running, with Jesse in hot pursuit. Andy followed. With the tunnel entrance in sight, Jesse felt a burning sting in his left ankle and collapsed to the ground, writhing in pain. Jesse had never felt pain like this before; it was consuming him. It was worse than when his broken leg had to be set, without anaesthesia. Or the time he spilled boiling water down his front when he was nine. His mum had put him in a bathtub of lukewarm water while they waited for the ambulance. On a scale of one to ten, he would say later that this pain was a twenty. It felt like being set on fire or standing in lava, and it was spreading slowly up his leg, consuming his mind. He screamed and screamed, clawing at David, who picked Jesse up and carried him to the portal. David could bring him no farther before becoming an essence.

Before he passed out, Jesse saw Andy at his side, removing caps from several bottles and dumping them onto a cloth. Jesse remembered no more.

****

Jesse dreamed of a faraway place covered in fiery embers. Blood-red nymphs danced around him, laughing and singing. He burned, and nothing chased away the heat. He was changing into a charcoal briquette, searing everything he touched, including himself. No one knew what to do. No one could help him. The only thing everyone wanted to do was laugh at him for being so stupid.

Then a reassuring and refreshing voice penetrated the heat.

"Jesse, it is me, Breeze. Please come back. Fight the magic. See the fire and control it. That is the only way. Andy and Zeela can do no more; it is up to you. I am begging with my whole essence, take the snow and ice I am sending and contain the fire."

Jesse saw a tunnel of icy blue light, peaceful and soothing. A freezing wind blew across a field of frost, and he was covered in soft, caressing flakes of snow that encased the fire inside him. With the blaze contained, he forced his mind open and rejected the pain. The ice allowed him to seize control once again. He began travelling the tunnel of light, reaching out to anything that didn't burn.

"Breeze, where are you? I need you to show me the way. I'm lost, please come back to me."

"This way, Jesse, follow my voice, come to me. Let me love you."

"What!" Jesse shouted, opening his eyes to see blurry shapes around his bed.

"Jesse, can you see me?" David asked, concerned.

"Yeah, Dad," Jesse said, rubbing his eyes as his vision returned. He looked at the group gathered around his bed and was surprised to see Zeela, Gran, Cami, Mr. Chambers, and Jim Slater.

"What happened to me? How long was I out?"

Zeela stepped to the foot of his bed so he could see her better.

"Jesse, you mind-talked to blood fairies?"

"I didn't mean to. I was just bored and curious, so I decided to try something I had wondered about. I call it mind travelling. As soon as I saw the evil little bastards, I tried to pull out. I guess it was too late."

"All you have to do is touch someone of magic with your 'mind travels', as you call it, for them to lock on to you. It is like the emotions that Tazeron uses to track and trap mortals playing the games. There are many ways to use your mind to explore, but none that I know of are undetectable.

The blood nymphs could send a dart of searching after you, dipped in a potion of forced magic. Basically, they turned your own magic against you. If Breeze hadn't pulled you away, you would've wasted and died, with no hope of returning to your mortal body. There was nothing we could do for you. If you had not eaten the Naqisha fruit before entering the game world, you would not have survived. It gave you time and made it possible for us to do what we could. Breeze saved your life, Jesse."

Shocked, Jesse whispered, "How long was I unconscious?"

"Three days," Zeela said, looking at him with a sad expression.

"Zeela, am I ever going to get it? Am I ever going to become the person you all think I can be?"

"Yes!" said a determined voice.

They parted, and Rambo entered the room. To Jesse's surprise, Zeela and the others backed away and bowed, allowing Rambo to take their place at the foot of Jesse's bed.

"Minor setbacks will not stop us, Jesse. We will succeed, by the gods, we will succeed."

"Rambo," Jesse sputtered, then broke down into sobs.

All the frustrations, all the pain of the last three days, all the indecision and fear flooded him. His sobs consumed him, as Rambo moved to the side of the bed and Jesse melted into the winged embrace of his friend and defender.

"Rambo, my dear, Jesse needs to rest," Gran gently patted the dragon.

"Indeed, but first I must tell him," Rambo gently lifted Jesse's tear-stained face with his clawed wing. "I have much to tell, but I will not until you are well enough to hear along with the Council. Sleep now, my friend, get the rest you need to continue recovering."

"I will," Jesse peeped, wiping away tears. "And thank you all, especially you, Breeze, wherever you are."

To the surprise of the gathering, the ethereal being landed on Jesse's chest. She stayed there until he fell asleep. All he could do was smile at her, resting in her dreams of relief and comfort.

Jesse dreamed of a soft, gentle wind on his face. He saw a lovely girl, bright-eyed and laughing as she ran down a hill, trailing ribbons of light. The sun shone on her golden hair as it bounced softly against her pale green skin. His heart ached for her, but she was not to be found in his world.

"I will be in your world someday soon, Jesse, but the time is not yet. Sleep now, my love, soon we shall meet in the flesh, and we will blend our worlds to defeat the evil that threatens us all. Sleep..."

Jesse slept a long time. When he finally awoke in his apartment, he felt rested and eager to return to his studies. Jesse was sure that much had happened and was anxious to get caught up. But, as nervous as he was for all that, Jesse was especially keen to talk with Breeze and discover more about her. Jesse tried mind searching, but she wasn't to be found. Testing his strength by walking to the door and peeking out of the room, Jesse instantly felt more than a little weak. He returned to the bed and sat down, panting.

"Well, that sucked," he said, disappointed in his strength. *"Rambo, where are you?"*

Jesse mind-searched for his friend and discovered Rambo sleeping in a large round bed of pure gold, moulded to fit his massive body. Fairy guards were on duty at the door and patrolled the hall. Jesse pulled his mind back, giving Rambo privacy.

Jesse wondered what time it was. There were no clocks in this world that he knew of. With just a hint of reddish glow coming through the room's window, it was either becoming morning or evening. It was impossible to tell, since he had slept so much. He would wait until he heard movement before venturing out again. Perhaps someone would bring him some food. He was suddenly starving.

"I wonder if there are any flowers in this room," Jesse thought as he looked around briefly. Not seeing any, he lay back down on the comfortable bed and drifted back to sleep.

Jesse woke up to sounds in the hall outside his door. He had no idea how long he had slept, and he jumped up. There was a tray loaded with delicious-smelling food on a side table, and that distracted him. After he ate and dressed in new robes, Jesse peeked out of his door and was surprised to see people walking around, visiting with each other. He was relieved that there was no weakness this time.

"Hey," he called to a couple of girls chatting across the hall from his door. "What's going on?"

"Hello, are you new here too?" one of them asked.

"Yes and no. I've been here a few days, but I've only had one day of training. I've been… sick."

"Oh, you must be Jesse Finch. I'm pleased to meet you. We've heard of your adventure into the game world. Amazing—you must have been very brave to fight off the attack of the blood fairies like that."

"Yeah, I guess," Jesse stammered, confused.

"I'm Julia, and this is my new friend Ginger. We're training as bards. It's so exciting," she giggled. "Well, we must go now. Master Isomer is expecting us at the Place of Learning. I'm sure we'll see you again later."

Jesse stepped out into the hall, watching the two girls disappear.

"I wonder how I'm supposed to find my way around this place."

Without warning, a small silver ball appeared a couple of feet in front of his face and beeped twice. The appearance surprised Jesse, but he quickly recovered and examined the device. Curious, he asked it, "Can you show me to the Place of Learning?"

Again, the ball beeped twice.

"Excellent. Show me to the Magician's Place of Learning."

The small silver ball moved forward, matching Jesse's pace. If he sped up, it sped up; as he slowed, it slowed.

"Awesome. Can you show me anything I want to see?"

The little ball beeped once and changed from silver to red.

"I guess that means no," Jesse said. The ball beeped twice and turned back to silver.

"Cool. Are there others of your kind that will show me things you can't?"

The silver ball beeped twice as they rounded a corner and started down some stairs that Jesse recognised.

"Are you only allowed to show me things in this building?"

The silver guide beeped twice as they stopped in the arena, which was now full of people practising their skills.

"Man, this place is crowded," Jesse scowled.

The silver ball beeped twice, still hovering close by.

"Can you show me a quiet place in this building?"

Again, it beeped and took off. The silver orb led Jesse to a large room full of books and tables, and people everywhere reading.

"This isn't quite what I had in mind. Show me a quiet place, without all the people, please."

The director beeped and off they went, Jesse jogging this time. After a few minutes, they entered a grassy atrium, with trees and sunlight shining through the open ceiling. Birds sang in the trees and bees buzzed around large, colourful flowers. It appeared to be part of the same building. Jesse was amazed at the size of a building that could house something like this.

"Wow, this is outstanding. Thank you. If I need you again, can I call?"

The ball beeped twice, still hovering in front of him.

"Very well, you can go now—and thank you."

With two beeps and a small pop, the little silver globe disappeared.

The quiet was soothing to Jesse's mind. He sat there in a shaft of sunlight with his eyes closed, soaking up the peace that surrounded him, enjoying the birdsong and bee buzz.

"Jesse, my friend, I'm happy that you are feeling well. May I join you?"

"Rambo...! Of course, please join me. And Rambo—how did you know I was awake and where to find me?"

"I was alerted by the director ball. Breeze told the director ball to alert me when you were awake. She knew that you were stirring. I have been waiting for you."

Jesse felt embarrassed that he hadn't thought of contacting his companion when he woke up this last time, but they would visit now.

After a few minutes, the reduced version of Rambo landed in the grassy courtyard.

"It's time to address the Council, Jesse. Shall we go?"

Stunned, Jesse agreed, and Rambo once again became his greater version, placing Jesse on his back and launching into the sky. It was enjoyable to be with Rambo once more.

Flying over the city of Rodashu was unbelievable. Jesse was impressed with its size—it was much larger than he had imagined. Locating the Great Library of Learning, Rambo landed, becoming smaller as they walked up the steps. Walking through the front doors, Jesse and Rambo entered the courtyard with the beautiful white dragon. Rambo walked up to the statue and bowed deeply. Jesse was surprised to see a tear on Rambo's face as he turned to stride up the staircase.

"Rambo, I can't help but think there is more to your story of this White Druid."

Rambo was silent for several minutes as he kept walking.

"Jesse, it is a sad story and very hard to talk about. Someday soon, perhaps, I will tell you. For now, my friend, let us leave it at that."

"I'm sorry," Jesse said meekly. "Of course—tell me when you are ready."

"Thank you for understanding."

Jesse burned with curiosity, but he was smart enough to let it go. Realising that even his thinking about it might be painful to his friend, he wrapped up his curious thoughts and stuffed them deep into a side pocket of his brain. He tried to focus on the upcoming meeting with the Council instead.

As they approached the large, ornately carved doors of the Council chambers, all the fairies took flight, circling Rambo's head and landing on his shoulders.

"Ah, my lovely ladies, how are you today?" Rambo asked in a soft voice, full of affection.

"We are blessed by your presence, Milord," one of the fairies replied in a high-pitched voice, full of respect. "We were instructed to show you and Master Jesse in as soon as you arrived."

Jesse was impressed with the greeting Rambo had extracted from these fairies. Once again, his curiosity was inflamed, but like his other thoughts, he stuffed it into a back pocket of his mind as well.

As they entered, everyone in the room stood and then bowed. Jesse was sure it was for Rambo and shuffled back a few steps, but Rambo wrapped a wing around him and pulled him forward. Rambo returned the greeting bow, as did Jesse.

Jesse was escorted to a seat on Nexlucimus' right, at the head of the table, by one of the larger fairies, and a fluffy chair pulled itself out and beckoned him to sit. As he sat, everyone else in the room—except Rambo—sat.

That was weird, Jesse thought.

Rambo quickly added, *"Politeness and honour are never weird, my friend."*

Jesse fidgeted, trying not to think any further.

"Rambo, it is indeed an honour to be in your presence again, my dear friend," Master Nexlucimus said.

"The honour is mine, sir," Rambo gave a quick nod.

"We are anxious for your report. I hope you don't mind that we invited others to attend this meeting."

"Not at all. You are welcome," Rambo nodded in the direction of the guests.

Chapter 15

Council Meeting

Jesse was happy to see Gran, his dad, Mr Chambers, Jim, Sara, Cami, other members from his school, and a few he hadn't met yet. Looking at the councilmen, Jesse saw his friend Tommy, who was smiling at him. Jesse resisted a strong urge to wave. He was determined not to embarrass himself any more than usual.

"Now, Rambo, we are anxious for your report," Nexlucimus said.

Rambo bowed slightly. A few papers appeared on the table in front of each council member, and the flat-screen double-sided monitor lowered so that all could see.

"I have prepared a written report, in addition to the visual one I will now give. What you see on the screen is what I saw as I witnessed the events within Tazeron's camp. As the Council knows, I was sent on a reconnaissance mission, to infiltrate and spy on Tazeron and his minions."

"What I will show first is when I arrived at the camp. Then we will view what happened three days past. Nothing reportable occurred between the two meetings."

The big screen came alive, and everyone's attention was directed to it.

What the audience saw surprised Jesse very much. He had expected Tazeron's camp to be a wilderness setting, with barracks and maybe tents. Jesse was not prepared to see a walled city with buildings and vendors. It reminded him of one of the towns he had seen in a game—but it hadn't been evil at the time of his visit.

They travelled to a large building, and on the third floor, they arrived in a meeting room. Several men and a few women sat around a table; blood fairies patrolled the area. Jesse scooted deeper into the security of his chair, which wrapped its arms around him. Nexlucimus looked over and smiled, patting Jesse's arm.

They watched a small goblin approach the table and bow very nervously.

"What say you?" a rough, gravelly voice snarled at the goblin.

"We are still looking, Milord. Those sympathetic to our cause search the records of learning in the Great Library. We have narrowed the search to records of the Great Splittings. That is where the oldest histories are found. Our oracles are confident that we will find what we need in those accounts."

Rambo told them that the person the goblin had spoken to was one of Tazeron's generals.

The scene changed, and another messenger approached a medium-sized man, whom Rambo informed everyone was Tazeron. There was a collective gasp from the Council at his appearance. He was dressed in robes that must have been magnificent at one time. Now they were scorched and torn in places; his hair and beard were unkempt.

"Speak, fool," Tazeron spat.

"Yes, Milord," the messenger bowed, clearly excited. "We have discovered a riddle."

Tazeron sat straighter in his chair. "Tell me how it was discovered."

"One of our followers, still on Xanthara in the capital city, placed pages of giving in a book being copied for the coming Splitting. After they were removed, they were taken to those that can decipher. They work on them as we speak. This is the last piece—they are sure."

"At last," Tazeron smiled a wicked smile. "Leave me."

The goblin bowed his way out of the chamber.

Tazeron sat sulking. His thoughts burdened him.

"I need the answers I seek to enter the mortal world. Once I am there, I will involve their anti-gods and have complete power. They will be my slaves, along with the mortals," he laughed—a high-pitched, manic sound that made Jesse shiver.

"The people of Xanthara will pay for what has happened to me. They will see that I was right all along… fools. If they had listened to me, all the mortals and their world would be saved. Now, they will all be destroyed."

The room brightened as the screen receded back to where it was stored.

A long time of comprehensive silence passed. When Nexlucimus finally spoke, his voice was subdued and cracking.

"Do you have a copy of this riddle, Rambo?"

"Yes, it is among the papers I gave each of you."

"Very well." Looking to his left, the Elder addressed one of the other councilmen. "Heralon, my friend, you are well?"

Jesse noticed that the man, Heralon, was very pale despite his dark skin. He looked like he might pass out at any moment.

"It's just such a shock—to see him like that. It seems as if his goals have changed to be more destructive than we thought."

"Indeed, Father. I'm glad that Mother didn't see this presentation," Tommy added.

"Wolfa would've been very saddened indeed," Heralon said.

With a jolt, Jesse began putting all the pieces together. *Heralon is Tommy's and Tazeron's father, and Wolfa—my magic teacher—is their mother. She is Nexlucimus' sister, and Meriloc is their little brother. Wow, so complicated.*

Rambo's voice broke through Jesse's thoughts. "I will read the riddle out loud, and perhaps it will make more sense as I do." Jesse followed along with his own copy.

"Dewdrops of honey they travel from far but go nowhere. Time is of the essence.

Two worlds are joined and form one blood, take no mercy, deliver no threat.

Arches of pain are needed for gain; use this to see what only ears can hear.

Stir swiftly, lest it drowns in its own dreams of travel, on light faster than wings.

Two worlds, one blood, let the key that walks before you guide the way.

Travel far but go nowhere to the world of mortal man.

Open you must, to no one give trust, beware their heir may eat you."

"How very odd," said a thin woman.

"*Indeed,*" whispered several others.

One little man cleared his throat.

"We have known from records revealed to us by the gods that there was a way for Tazeron to create a portal to the mortal world. It appears that they will now have the answer, once this riddle is solved. We must solve it first, to stop them."

"Well spoken, Trusol," Nexlucimus agreed, and then added, "We must be the ones to solve it first. The goblin said they retrieved this riddle from the old records, with pages of giving. I have not heard of those for many millennia. It is most shocking that they still have sympathisers in this world, when everyone knows what happened to his other followers. I am amazed at Tazeron's influence.

"We must continuously be on watch, and more guarded in what we do and say outside these rooms. If this is indeed the key to opening a portal to the mortal world, we must increase our efforts. It also increases the Keepers' duties. I suggest that we keep Tazeron's minions stirred up. Perhaps they will have less time to solve riddles. What say you, David?"

"That might be what we need to do—to make time for our own riddle-solvers. I will consult with my captains and devise a stratagem," David said determinedly.

"We must be diligent, never resting until this is solved. We must not fail in this test of our devotion. We cannot fail the mortals and all the gods," Nexlucimus said, looking resolute.

Jesse had the feeling that someone was watching him. Looking up, he saw her. A pale mist clung to an upper corner. He smiled—and he felt her smile back, sadly.

Nexlucimus glanced at the corner, then at Jesse, his eyes questioning. He addressed his council.

"Now, I believe—unless we have other business—we will adjourn. Rambo, my friend, as always, you have exceeded my expectations. We are deeply in your debt. I would like to have a brief meeting with all the Keepers present in this room. Please remain, if you would."

After the council had been dismissed, Nexlucimus addressed the remaining Keepers.

"It is uplifting to see all of you together. You will be some of the captains in this battle. It is important that you are able to communicate with one another."

Nexlucimus moved away from the table. "Cami, please come forward. I require your talisman."

Cami came forward, seated in a gliding chair. After removing the talisman, she handed it to Nexlucimus. She turned to leave, but the Elder stopped her.

"Please stay here, Cami. I have a gift for you."

She watched him curiously. Nexlucimus placed the white dragon ring on her head. He began to hum the same tune that she had used in Gran's house, and that Rambo had used before giving Jesse the dragon's blessing. Shock registered on her face. The air became charged, like just before a storm—electricity snapping and crackling.

"Cami Chambers, stand and receive your gift."

She stood. Others in the room gasped.

"I bless your body to be whole, that you may perform your duties as will be required of you, as we face this most critical time in all our history. I bless your mind to be clear and sensitive to what will be vital, to accomplish your distinct role in these most terrible times. It is done."

Cami was so overwhelmed that she hugged Master Nexlucimus and cried into his robes. He hugged her back and then kissed the top of her head.

Everyone stood and clapped.

"Yes, yes," Nexlucimus waved them into silence. "We still have matters of urgency to finish here. I must say, however, that this is as good as it gets sometimes," he smiled at them all.

"I want all of you to please roll your left sleeves up past your shoulders… good. Now face your left arms toward me—you too, David."

They did as they were told.

The High Priest then bowed his head, holding out the talisman on his open palm.

"Mistress of the sky, transmitter of all things good and pure, consent your spirit to enter the hearts of these brave souls here this day. Fill them with the power to communicate, and the determination to defeat the evil that lurks at the door of both our worlds."

There was a flash of bright light, and the dragon ring took flight, touching each Keeper briefly on the upper left arm below the shoulder. Each of them now bore a small, exact copy of the white dragon taking off in flight, etched into their skin.

As a bonus—surprising everyone in the room—the talisman circled Jesse's head, and a thin silver chain appeared around his neck. It felt warm and seemed to pulsate with its own life force.

Jesse fingered the chain's smooth, delicate surface, feeling its natural, vivacious warmth. He then placed a hand over the small dragon drawn on his flesh by the talisman. It, too, felt warm to the touch.

Nexlucimus was stunned. "I am… astonished." He motioned Jesse to come to him.

Jesse stepped up to the Elder, and Nexlucimus examined the chain without touching it.

"Remarkable… Rambo, come look at this."

Everyone in the room was staring at the trio, but not a word was uttered.

Rambo gasped quietly. "How is that possible, Nexlucimus?"

"Ah, my friend, please stay and visit with me when we are done here," Nexlucimus whispered, so only Rambo and Jesse could hear.

Then louder, the Elder addressed the gathering, "I will tell all of you in this room that something extraordinary has happened here this day. Let me explain."

"Jesse, keep the silver chain covered. Do not let anyone touch it. It will be explained to you soon. Act like it never happened. This

is important. All but the three of us will forget," Rambo said directly to Jesse's mind.

"I will do this, my friend. I trust you."

"Now, I must tell you about the talisman that you wear," Nexlucimus continued. "This talisman is a gift from the gods—a guardian to guide you. She will protect you and assist you in your quest. It will alert you when anyone wearing her is in danger. She will give you transport anywhere you wish to go, whether in this world, the game world, or the mortal world. If you contact any part of another person not wearing her, you will be able to transport them as well."

"Awesome," Cami, Jesse, and a few others whispered.

"Indeed, it is a special gift. All you need to do is touch the talisman with your mind, and it will respond. But I must warn you—as this gift is a protector to you, you must be a protector to it. Do not show this talisman to anyone not here right now, in this room. There are those who would kill you if they knew you wore this. It identifies you as a champion of freedom. Do you all understand? Are there any questions regarding this?"

There were no questions.

"I wonder what my mum would think if she knew I had a tattoo," Jesse said.

"I think she would be pleased to know that her son was fighting for the freedom of the mortal world, and all of our immortal souls," Nexlucimus said solemnly.

"I never thought I'd see you wearing a tattoo, Gran."

"Me either, to be truthful," Pearl said, amazed, studying her upper left arm.

"I even have one—how is that possible, Master Nexlucimus?" David asked.

"It is printed on your soul, David, as it is with all of you. It will be a part of you through all eternity, so that others may know of your service. No one can erase it, not even you, even in death.

"Very well, my friends—unless there is anything else—I release you to your training."

"Excuse me, sir," Cami said. "What are the 'pages of giving' that were mentioned in the presentation?"

"They are a very ancient method of copying. They were used in eons past when the Elders were preparing the records for a splitting. They would place a 'page of giving' on top of something being copied and then rub it. The page would be copied and then transferred to a clean page. Once the copied text was removed, the 'page of giving' would vanish—thus 'giving' itself.

"We have other ways of copying now. We have learned from you mortals and have something like your copy machines—but of course, we have no such devices here."

"Thank you for your question, Cami. Are there any others?"

There were none.

"Good day to you then. Learn your lessons well. Rambo, please come with me."

Jesse watched curiously. Rambo gave him a meaningful look before he reduced in size and stepped into a side room with the Elder, closing the door.

Chapter 16

Shadow Dreams and Food for Thought

As Jesse exited the council chambers and walked past the fairies on the door, he noticed them waving goodbye. He smiled, returning their farewell with a quick bow. Waiting outside the door was Tommy, with a big smile on his face.

"Tommy! It's great to see you again, dude. What's up?" Jesse grinned, excited to see his friend.

"I'm going into training with you. Since my skills don't require magic, I'll be able to do anything in the game world that I can do anywhere else."

"Awesome, dude! That's totally wicked!" Jesse grinned.

"Indeed it is—I mean… ah, totally. Did I say that right?"

Jesse smiled at his friend. "Good enough. Nice to have you back, man. I've seriously missed you—and the laughs."

"Yeah, me too," Tommy said. "And Cami, it's amazing to see you standing there, knowing that it's not going away."

"Yeah… hey, I'm sorry, guys, but I'm kind of emotional right now. I might have to join you later."

"That's understandable, Cami. But before you go, there's something I'm sure you'll enjoy seeing." Tommy jogged over to a box he had up against the wall. When he opened it, Brutus jumped out and began yipping and turning tight little circles. Gran trotted right over and picked up the little mutt, who started licking her face as fast as his tail was wagging.

"Sorry, Pearl, but Brutus has been reassigned."

"I understand," she said, hugging the little dog. "Where's Brutus going—any ideas?"

"As a matter of fact, I do," Tommy said. "Cami, this is a day of surprises for you. This fuzzy little mutt is now your companion."

"Ooh, he's so cute. What am I supposed to do with a tiny dog?"

Tommy, Gran, and Jesse all shared a look and backed up.

"Cami, would you step over here with us for a moment, please?" Tommy said, winking at Brutus.

At the signal, Brutus morphed into a beautiful snow-white griffin the size of a Clydesdale horse. Cami shrieked in delight, hugging Tommy, and then hugging Gran and Jesse too.

"It was decided that you would be the perfect choice to receive Brutus' service," Tommy told her. "He has many abilities, gifted to him by the gods, like Rambo. He won't lose those skills in the game world."

"Oh, how can I thank you, Tommy?"

"It wasn't just me—it was the whole council. Maybe you and Pearl can bake us some of her famous cookies."

"Well now… I don't think cookie baking is on our schedule anymore, kiddo," Gran added.

"True, true," Tommy laughed. "I vote we all go get some lunch and have a long chat."

They all agreed that they were starving and left to find a vendor—except for Jesse.

"I have something I need to do. I'll join you in a while," Jesse told the gathering.

He was not going to miss another opportunity to chat with Breeze, not even if it meant skipping lunch with his friends. He found a secluded bench and sat down, closing his mind to everything but the silver mist that warmed his dreams. Calling to her mentally, he felt her soft caress on his cheek and smiled at the sound of her sweet voice in his thoughts.

"Jesse, my love, how I have dreamed of this day when we could talk. It is my fondest fantasy."

"It is a pleasure to talk to you, Breeze. Please, tell me again about yourself and how we are connected."

"Jesse, because Tazeron has entered the game world, the gods are monitoring that world and the gamers who play there. I was part of the monitoring, assigned by the gods. Once I documented you as a Finding, the gods commissioned me with the great honour of preparing you for this quest. I did this with dreams. As I spent time giving you these thoughts, I realised that never has another being sent ripples across my essence as you did."

"I don't understand how that works, but I must confess, I have felt something too," Jesse said, blushing slightly and looking down at his hands.

Never in his life had he ever said anything like that to a girl—and Breeze wasn't even a girl. There was just something wrong with this picture, but it felt so right.

"How can this work, Breeze? You don't even have a body. All you are is thought—and yet it feels so normal."

"Jesse, you have seen my mother. Soon I will leave you to be born. It is not yet… but soon. I will not always be a Shadow Dream. I will have a body, and then we will be together in that way."

She sent him the image of a pale green girl with golden hair, laughing in the sunshine. She smiled shyly as she waved to him from a shadow in the marketplace, before flying off on gossamer wings.

"This is who I will be; this is what my mother looks like."

With surprise, Jesse recognised the beautiful girl he'd seen on his first day, right before he and his father met Master Nexlucimus.

"That was your mother? How can this be? I'll be an old man by the time you're grown."

"I am fairy-kind, Jesse; it will be possible. Trust me. Do not think about it now—only believe. All things are in the hands of the

gods. So it is with this quest; so it is with our lives. If we do all we can, as required, we will be blessed."

"Do you know how this quest will end, Breeze? Have the gods said anything to you in all your contact with them?"

"I know things I am forbidden to talk about—but not the outcome of this quest. Some of what I know will be given to you at a time when needed. The gods are aware of you and what you are capable of. Know this: nothing in this life is by chance. I must go now while you join your friends. Great things are near, Jesse, and I will be with you as I can. Farewell for now."

Jesse was left feeling lonely and cold. A hollowness settled over him that he had never felt before—an emptiness only his Shadow Dream could fill.

He stood and walked to the food vendor before rejoining his friends. He arrived at the lunch spot carrying two giant sandwiches, two fruit sticks, and a sixty-four-ounce pineapple slushy.

"Wow, man, you hungry? Is there anything left at the vendor?" Tommy snickered.

"This is just a snack to tide me over until the real food shows up. Dang! I should've grabbed one of those apple pies. Oh well, maybe next trip. Man, I love buffets."

"You're gonna get fat if you stay here too long," Cami giggled, tossing Brutus a piece of her sandwich.

"No, I won't…" Jesse said, tapping his leg. "Got a hollow leg—good storage spot. Hey Gran, how's it been since I've been gone? Pretty dull, I bet."

"Yep, very quiet. Nice for a change. Oh, by the way, your mother says 'hi', and don't give your father a hard time," she chuckled at Jesse's gaping mouth.

"Close your mouth, dear. I've told you before—it's rude."

"Are you serious about Mum, Gran?"

"I certainly am. I wouldn't tease about something like that."

"How… how…" He just couldn't get anything else to come out.

His dad moved over to join them.

"I can talk to her through dreams, Jesse. She's a worrier, as you know, but she's a believer in dreams. That's why she never questioned yours through the years. That's how I can help her. That's how I introduced her to Bill. That's how I explained why you and Gran needed to live together. It's very convenient, really. She's very easy to talk to in her dreams," David shrugged, then addressed the group.

"OK people, as soon as you're done eating, I need to have a meeting with everyone. Just tell your director balls that you want to go to Conference Hall Number Eight, and it'll get you there. I need to run ahead and make some preparations. See you all soon."

Jesse watched his dad jog off. As he sat there, listening to the idle chatter of his friends and companions, he noticed Jim and Sara standing off to the side, talking to Zeela. Sara appeared to be crying, and Zeela was trying to comfort her while Jim kept an arm around her waist.

Jesse watched his grandmother move into a sunny spot by herself and decided to join her.

"Mind if I talk to you for a minute, Gran?"

"As long as I don't have to move… What's up?"

"Several things. First, do you know what's going on with Sara? Is she OK?"

"She's having a hard time. I think I told you that she and Jim lost a baby a couple of years ago. They can't seem to have another. She's talking to Zeela about the problem. With all the many kids here, it's difficult for her. What else is on your mind?"

"Do you remember Breeze, and that she's my Shadow Dream?" Jesse didn't really know why he asked—he just wanted to know. Then Gran surprised him, which was nothing new.

"She came to talk to me a couple of nights ago. OK, we're going to have to do something about that mouth of yours, dear. It keeps dropping down to your chest. One of these days, it's going to fall right off."

"Why would she come to you? And how can you talk to her?"

"She had a question, and Nexlucimus told her to talk to me. Her way of talking is quite pleasant. She has a very soft, musical voice—rather soothing, hypnotic. It's nice to listen to, especially right before you fall asleep. Splendid for dreaming."

"Did she say anything… about me?"

"No. Is there something wrong, dear?"

"No, I was just curious. Wow, everyone else has gone to the training—we'd better get going."

"My lands, get me talking and the world could end… Just kidding," Gran added, seeing Jesse's face.

Jesse smiled and shook his head at his wonderfully strange little grandmother.

They found the meeting place without trouble. Jesse was surprised to see about fifty people there. David was just explaining what they were doing.

"I wanted to introduce you to just a few of the Xantharaians. These people are helping us get established in the game world. There are other Xantharaians performing tasks in the game world and unable to meet with us now. They have put in a lot of effort and will be helping with your training. There are also local soldiers guarding the Shield already, all eager to assist you as you move into your assignments. If everyone involved in this campaign were assembled, there wouldn't be a building large enough to hold us all—except for the capital buildings and the Great Library, of course."

"Wow," a girl to Jesse's left whispered, along with several others.

"I will now introduce the Xantharaians who will be joining us in this quest. There are many others already in the game, as I mentioned, but these magnificent warriors are highly skilled through their experience and training. You will notice that some of them have magical abilities which they won't be able to use in the game; however, each of them brings other special talents to the arena."

He approached a blue wood nymph. "This is Shaza; she's an enchanter—very skilled in potion-making and disguises."

Moving on to a dwarf with a long braided auburn beard, he said, "This is Zealoc. He is a warrior extraordinaire." The little man huffed, but his ruddy skin deepened in colour.

"Oh my," Gran whispered.

Jesse glanced at her and noticed her grinning behind her hand.

"What's wrong, Gran?"

"Not a thing, dear… not a thing."

Jesse shrugged, his attention returning to his dad. David was standing next to a tall man dressed in shiny chainmail.

"This is Paylag—also a very skilled warrior and a Xantharaian war hero from ages past."

Moving to the next person in line, David introduced another blue fairy-kind. "This is Malleesa. She is a rogue, most skilled in laying and detecting traps."

"*Sweet,*" one of the people Jesse didn't know mumbled from behind him.

David continued, "This is Toolle, also a rogue and Malleesa's brother. Next, we have Faber, a priest of the shadows. Faber is also Malleesa and Toolle's brother. As you will see, we have several different groups of family members. They know each other's style, skills, and weaknesses—excellent things to be acquainted with in a battle."

David moved down the line. "Ginnea is a very skilled hunter. She could track a mist beetle in a haystack. She is also a potion master—and Tomitobas's sister."

Jesse glanced over at his friend and saw him smiling proudly at his sister.

David stepped next to another dwarf named Beloe—a warrior, and Zealoc's cousin. Next to Beloe were Zeela and Tommy. Past them stood five other Xantharaians: Mesola, a shaman; Geezale, a warlock; Pluergo, a holy priest; Isomer, a bard; and Tanzi, a paladin.

"These respectable people are some of the guides and comrades from Xanthara. Get to know them. As each assembling group grows, we will be assigning Xantharaians to assist. There are many from this world willing to support the Keepers in their quest, and as more Keepers assemble, more Xantharaians will join us.

"We will soon divide you into parties—just like raid groups in the game. Balancing out skills as much as possible is our goal, but in real-life play, that isn't as important as it was in the computer game world. Likewise, your party won't be held to a strict number. If there are people that you are more comfortable with, please let us know. Everyone will have the training they need. Are there any questions?"

"Yes, sir," said an Asian girl as she raised her hand.

"Please tell us your name, and then your question."

"I'm Flowergirl—an enchanter in the game—but Mi Kang in real life. I was wondering if we will be advancing in level, like on the game?"

Jesse found his attention wandering back to Breeze and their strange encounter.

I wonder where she had to go. Ugh! I have so many questions to ask her.

"We'll start assigning you into groups now," his dad's voice cut into Jesse's thoughts. "I want you to stand with the people you would like to group with. It doesn't matter if you don't know anyone—we'll take care of that."

Jesse was pleased with his group. It consisted of all the people he was most familiar with: Tommy, Gran, Cami, Sean, Jim, Sara, and himself. That gave them two hunters, a rogue, a cleric, a warrior, a druid, and a mage.

What they needed was another melee fighter, and for some reason, Gran wanted the dwarf, Zealoc. She trotted over to him and, to Jesse's surprise, Zealoc came back with her—along with Tommy's sister Ginnea (another hunter) and Zeela (another druid).

They had their group—soon to include Rambo and Brutus.

Chapter 17

Into the Game

After many gruelling days of duelling each other, beating up and frying practice dummies, David graduated Jesse's group. They were ready to start the quest—into the game world—towards the southwest corridor. Their first assignment was to remove anything unfriendly and seal the area, from the Shield to Tazeron's camp. They would be under the direction of Zealoc who, because of his experience in the live game world, would be their party leader.

Pearl, for one, seemed delighted with this decision. Jesse overheard a conversation between her and Zeela, right before their departure.

"Zeela, dear, what can you tell me about Zealoc? He seems to be a very humble, charming and capable leader. So strong and steady, plus… he is one of the most handsome and fascinating men I have ever met," she enthused.

"He is a great man and brilliant warrior, Pearl. He has defended our fair city from the primitive tribes that live in the surrounding areas many times," Zeela explained.

"What people are you talking about, Zeela? I was under the impression that everyone in your world was peaceful."

"They are the people who, over the generations, have provided the wood and stone needed for construction in our buildings. They have recently rebelled against their station, because of Tazeron's influence. Thank the gods, they have no magic. Zealoc has tried to re-establish relations. Unfortunately, they refuse friendship to any but their own kind—and the elves, who also share the forest with them. It has not always been this way," Zeela added sadly.

Jesse was shocked at this revelation, and he stepped away from his eavesdropping, making a mental note to talk to Zealoc about it later.

As they prepared to leave the city, other groups were almost ready to travel to the game as well. They met several of these advanced teams. Zealoc's cousin, Beloe, was heading the group that included Savana and Peter from their school and home guild. Jesse met with them briefly. It was an exciting time, as the different groups gathered their needed supplies and packed up.

Each member was given a flying animal to ride. Jesse and Cami, of course, had Rambo and Brutus. Tommy and his sister Ginnea had matching Firelings that they had raised from chicks. Jesse thought they looked cool, with their flaming wings. He was disappointed to learn that it was an illusion and not actual flames.

Zeela could fly herself, of course, and Gran rode behind Zealoc on his war eagle (because she didn't feel comfortable alone). Zealoc didn't seem to mind. The rest of the party had flying steeds like Pegasi and flying lizards. They were set.

After loading their gear and passing through a game portal, they mounted up and launched into the beautiful game-world morning. It was fun for Jesse to see his mortal friends morph into their game toons. Mr Chambers became his cleric—a barbarian lady—which Jesse found very bizarre. For a female, she was big and burly, which was going to take some getting used to. Even though Jesse knew her from their game time together, it still felt weird. Gran was a dwarf hunter, which made her a bit shorter than Zealoc. Cami's rogue (which Jesse had never seen in the game) was human.

All of them enjoyed flying over the countryside. While it was familiar, there were subtle differences. For one thing, you couldn't fly through birds and trees. If they got too close and hit one, it hurt. While Rambo and Brutus were experts at flying around things, not all the mounts were. There would be many bruises and minor scrapes for the healers to tend to later.

The first day of their flight was uneventful. They decided to spend the night in a real inn, with real beds, before pressing on. After checking into the *Snuggle Bug's Inn and Tavern*, they went to get something to eat. Gran wouldn't let Jesse order any alcohol because she said it would stunt his growth. He didn't see a problem with that, since he was already taller than everyone else (except for Mr Chambers' lady barbarian character). Gran explained that it was final, and she ordered him milk.

Later he learned that it wasn't cow's milk. Zealoc refused to tell him what kind it was—even amid his snickers. Jesse wasn't sure he appreciated Zealoc's sense of humour. Gran thought he was hilarious.

The food was bland, even by game-food standards, according to Tommy—but the drop-dead gorgeous waitresses more than made up for it. Gran had to remind Jesse to close his mouth more than once. She finally threatened to use the talisman, warp back home, and grab a roll of duct tape—if he couldn't keep it shut on his own without being reminded.

As they finished eating, Zealoc filled them in on their assignment.

"I wish to convey my honour in leading this company. It is a very humble responsibility for me. Now to explain our mission. It will be our duty to patrol the Shield in the southwest corridor. After destroying the mobs by the Shield and magically sealing it against them respawning, we will advance to Tazeron's last known camp, clearing and sealing as we go."

"I'm sorry, Master Zealoc," said Cami. "But I'm having a hard time picturing this in my head."

"Perhaps I can help, Miss Cami." Zealoc took a piece of charcoal from the cold fireplace and drew a map on the tablecloth. He ignored the waitress glaring at him.

"OK… to picture this, imagine the surface of the world of stories and games as flat as this table—when in truth, it is a globe. Since I am no artist, this is the easiest way for me to explain."

He drew a map of two circles that overlapped in the middle. He then divided this chart into three equal sections using horizontal lines, creating a north pole, south pole, and a centre.

"Imagine the two circles folding together, creating the game-world globe. As the orb is formed and inflated, the areas of the games would expand. The Shield was designed to contain Tazeron. The centre area that you see here is the total area of the online games."

"Holy cow! That's huge, Zealoc—do we have to patrol that entire sector?" Mr Chambers and the others wanted to know.

"No, sir. Let me continue." Everyone relaxed somewhat as Zealoc went on.

"The upper and lower two areas are what we refer to as hardcopy fantasy. They are the written form of books and stories. We will not be going into those two-thirds—there is no need. They are sealed against crossover by the Shield. The part that we are concerned with is this smaller area."

He drew a circle within the middle section.

"This part of the central area is an approximation, but it is the area that contains Tazeron within the Shield. The online games in this field are MMORPGs—mass media online role playing games, as they are called. Suitable for teenagers to adults. Simple children's games are not included, even though we know that mature people play them, just as younger children play the ones designed for teens and adults.

"When the gods sealed Tazeron and his followers into the game world, they enclosed them in the mature games, to protect younger mortal children. Unfortunately, we can't control who plays these games," Zealoc sighed sadly.

"We are to remove unfriendly creatures and seal against respawning in this circle that contains Tazeron—wherever he happens to be now. To make it simpler, the circle has been divided into quadrants, marked northwest, southwest, northeast, and southeast. We are assigned to the southwest area, as I mentioned," he added, shaking his head contemplatively.

"We do have spies who send us updates, but the game masters are always changing things. Those playing the games in the mortal world have no idea what they are dealing with. We must find and destroy Tazeron before he enters the human world.

"Did that help, Miss Cami? It will make more sense as we begin the quest."

"Yes, thank you. I'm afraid you've made a big mess on this tablecloth now," Cami said, eyeing the charcoal dust smudged across the white linen.

Zealoc simply shrugged and continued. "In case you imagine this might be a simple task, let me assure you—it is not. There are hazards only a distorted or demented mind could create. Pure evil, and challenging almost beyond our skills. But we have one great advantage over Tazeron: we have each other, and the blessing of the gods."

Zealoc paused to take a drink from a huge mug and, wiping his hand across his bearded face, continued.

"The Shimmering Mountains are close to Tazeron—or so we were told in our last missive. They are surrounded by the Swamplands of Maritone. These will be our greatest challenge. We think we know where the mountains are, but they move. Don't ask me how that happens—you'd have to question one of the creators."

"I remember those names from the game. Are they the same ones?" Jesse asked.

"Aye, young Jesse. The Shimmering Mountains are the home of dust whelps and many other fearsome beasts—such as purple dragons and glass spiders."

Rambo hissed at this news, sending up smoke rings. Brutus growled. Jesse turned to ask him about it, but Rambo shook his head and simply said, *"Later,"* to Jesse's mind.

"Why are they called the Shimmering Mountains?" Cami wondered.

"They take their name from their appearance, Miss Cami. As the sun's rays reflect off the green and black glass that make up the mountains, the rising mist of the swamp makes them appear to shimmer," Zealoc explained.

"In those mountains, there is a network of caverns and many trails, made by ancient orcs and pygmy trolls. So there are paths to travel if we need them. The orcs and pygmy trolls have moved into the forests, allowing the dust whelps, purple dragons, and other creatures to take up residence.

"The swamplands, as you probably know, are home to mist lizards, worm witches, and log dogs."

"Joys," Jesse mumbled, to everyone's agreement.

"In addition to these two places of interest," Zealoc continued, "there are grasslands, deserts, and forested areas, all teeming with blood fairies, ogres, pygmy trolls, giants, and assorted other nasties."

"Exactly what will we be doing during our guarding patrols, Zealoc?" Mr Chambers asked.

"Now that the Keepers are here with all their magic, our duties will be to clean out our assigned segments—like a raid you would organise in the game on your world. As we clear an area and the Keepers seal it with magic, it is supposed to stay that way. Previously, the nasties would only respawn.

"We are also looking for mortals who have been pulled into the game. These may have escaped from Tazeron or were ignored by him because they were too low in level or skill. We will escort any mortals we find back through the Shield. We'll advise them to play in moderation until the 'bug' that pulled them into the game can be fixed.

"You'll know them by their fuzzy auras," he said, taking another drink.

"Excuse me, Zealoc," Jesse raised his hand. "What do you mean by fuzzy aura?"

"They will appear to shimmer, as if they're just barely out of focus."

"Ah... okay, thanks."

He continued, "As each group of Keepers clears out their region, they will move into other areas, assisting other parties. Once all the zones are secured, we will mount an assault on Tazeron—at least, that's the current plan. Plans are always subject to change in this world. Are there any other questions?"

There were no further questions, and Zealoc dismissed the meeting for the night. Everyone either retired to their rooms or returned to the lounge to sit by the fire and discuss their thoughts and feelings.

Forgiving Zealoc for his earlier teasing, Jesse asked if they might have a private conversation before turning in.

"Certainly, young Jesse. What's on your mind?"

"I overheard a conversation earlier about some primitive people who live near the capital city of Rodashu. Could you tell me more about them?"

"Aye, I can indeed. These primitives inhabit the surrounding mountains and forests. In the creation of Xanthara, the gods placed these people in our world to help us in our quest to assist mortals in their development.

"They provided us with raw materials, and we provided them with education, medicine, and other things they could not produce themselves. They were not blessed with magic and could not understand it.

"In the beginning, they were gentle people, happy with their station, and we were at peace. Unfortunately, they have been corrupted by Tazeron's influence. Greed and bitterness have changed them. They are not held to the same level of accountability as the highly developed immortals. We must care for them and help where we can.

"It is sad that we have failed them. Because of Tazeron, they have become a wild and ferocious people," Zealoc sighed, looking down at his hands.

Pearl, who had apparently been watching from a distance, joined them, sitting next to Zealoc.

"Zealoc, dear, I know that this troubles you greatly and that you have tried to befriend these people. Zeela told me about your efforts. Don't let this concern you. As soon as the trouble with Tazeron is under control, I would consider it an honour if you would allow me to assist you in working with these people," Pearl said earnestly.

"You would do this, Pearl?" Zealoc asked, surprised.

"Indeed... I would love to help you, in any way that I can," she said, placing her hand over his and staring into his eyes.

That was enough for Jesse. He had learned what he wanted to know, and for some reason, the way Gran and Zealoc were staring at each other made him uncomfortable.

"...I'm going to bed now, Zealoc. Thanks for answering my question. Night, Gran."

"Good night, dear," Gran said, smiling at Zealoc.

Chuckling softly as he climbed the stairs to his room, Jesse looked down at Zealoc and Gran, still holding hands, whispering with their eyes locked on each other.

"It's so strange to see Gran with a boyfriend!" Jesse smiled at the oddity of it.

Once in his room, Jesse dressed for bed and, slipping between the crisp sheets, was instantly asleep. As before, Breeze visited him in his sleep.

"Jesse, my love... my time is coming soon, and I will not be able to travel with you into the game world as we planned."

"When will you contact me again, Breeze? Will you even remember me after you are born?"

"I will remember you, but I do not know when we will once again talk. Farewell, my love, until we meet again. Remember me."

"I will remember." Jesse rolled over in his sleep and dreamed no more.

Chapter 18

The White Druid

In the morning, Jesse searched for his grandmother with a troubling question.

"Gran, how long does it take for fairy-kind, like Breeze, to grow up after they are born?"

"Approximately two mortal years, dear. Why do you ask?"

He decided to tell Gran everything, and she suggested he talk to Zeela, since she was fairy-kind herself.

"It's very unusual for a wood nymph like Breeze to pledge devotion while they are still in Shadow Dream form. You must have greatly impressed her, Jesse," Zeela stated, smiling.

"I didn't do anything and never encouraged her in any way, and yet..." Jesse sighed deeply. "I admit that I felt something for her also," he confessed, embarrassed.

Zeela watched him intently, as he seemed to struggle with himself.

"She will be mature in two mortal years, Jesse, and be able to enter a full commitment shortly after that. Just know that fairy-kind are very devoted, and if you have promised her your love, that is as binding to her as a marriage agreement. Have you done this?"

"No… but I wish I had, and I don't know why. It just doesn't make any sense to me, and yet it feels like the right thing."

"I suggest that you don't think about it right now. Concentrate on our quest line. We all have a crucial mission, and we need to be on top of our game."

He decided to talk to Rambo about it later as they flew.

Their morning meal proved to be a revealing experience. Jim and Sara made a compelling disclosure.

"Last night, Sara and I both had the same dream—at least we think it was a dream."

Jesse noticed Zeela's shocked expression, like she knew what was coming next.

"We had two children come to us in a dream, telling us that they were our kids-to-be-born—a boy and a girl. They were obviously azure elves, like Sara's game character… Anyone have any ideas about what this could mean?"

"Have you both been eating the Dumplumba, like I told you?" Zeela asked.

"Yes, we have been faithfully eating it," Sara said, smiling hopefully.

"In the fantasy world, children declare their conception to their parents. While in your game forms, you are a part of that world. You two are expecting twins. Congratulations! This would not have been possible if not for the Dumplumba fruit. Children are never conceived in the game world."

Sara let out an excited squeal, hugging Jim, who looked stunned.

"Oh my…," Gran smiled. "Well, I guess it took a change of scenery to have success, although I question the timing. Thank goodness they didn't take after their father. Ogre twins would have been nasty."

"Oh, I don't know. Ogre babies in that one movie back home were cute. Congrats, you two," Cami smiled.

"Congratulations," Jesse said. "Drinks all around—my treat."

They all laughed, catching the excitement. When the drinks arrived, Jesse was served milk along with Sara and Cami. He shot Pearl a dirty look, but she only raised her tiny glass of peach blossom tea in salute. Zealoc was chuckling.

He decided to order a large plate of cookies, and while he knew it wasn't cow's milk, at least the cookies made it taste better. He made a point of not sharing, except with Sara and Cami.

"Your children will be born of our two worlds, Jim and Sara, which has never happened before." Zeela's voice trailed off, a thoughtful look crossing her face. "This does complicate things, however. Sara, I think we should send you back to Xanthara, considering your history. Do you agree?"

"Perhaps that would be wise, but where would she stay?" Jim asked.

"I will settle her into Wolfa and Heralon's home in the central city. Wolfa is an expert midwife and, having had many children of her own, is an excellent choice. I advise you to keep eating the Dumplumba and add Naqisha fruit as well. I'm sure Wolfa would agree—she can get them for you."

"You will retain your game form while you carry the children, since they are to be born azure elves. Your pregnancy will be shorter as an elf. Hopefully, we won't be gone that long. But if we are, Jim, you may return to an extended family. The twins may even be crawling, since elves also develop much faster," Zeela smiled at their astonished faces.

"I wish I could go with you, babe, but it sounds like you will be in good hands," Jim said, giving Sara a hug.

Jim and Sara excused themselves and walked away from the breakfast, all thought of food gone from their heads. They seemed to be in elated shock as they took seats nearby and conversed softly.

"Zealoc, should I get a replacement for Sara while I'm in the capital?"

"That would indeed be an excellent idea, milady."

After a few moments of allowing Jim and Sara some privacy, Zeela walked over to them.

"Come, Sara; let's get you back to the city."

Turning to the rest of the group, Zeela waved goodbye. "I shall return shortly."

After watching Zeela and Sara depart, Zealoc directed the party to mount up, even though they were down two players. Rambo and Brutus more than made up for the short numbers.

Later, while flying toward their destination, Jesse and Rambo discussed the last day.

"Rambo, what should I do about Breeze, and what do you think about Jim and Sara's elf babies?" Jesse asked his friend.

"Breeze was a very devoted essence, a good friend, and companion. She will make a loving, faithful spouse."

"What! What do you mean?" Jesse gulped.

"I'm sure that's where Breeze hopes this is headed. What do you think is happening?" Rambo asked.

"Rambo, I've never even had a girlfriend. I wasn't allowed to date until I was sixteen. If I went home with a wife, my mum would kill me."

"You're sixteen now, correct?"

"Yes—have been for six months."

"Well, there you go. Problem solved. Stay on Xanthara for a couple of years, and Mum should be okay... right?" Rambo chuckled.

"Problem is not solved... this is so bizarre."

"Well, on the bright side—a couple on Xanthara can't have children until they've been married for one hundred years, unless they're elves or fairies, even if they eat the Dumplumba fruit. Oh, wait, you're an elf and she's a fairy." Rambo laughed so hard, Jesse nearly fell off his back.

"OK, amusing... Ha ha. We'll just drop this for now. You are absolutely no help at all. I don't want to talk about it anymore. What about Jim and Sara's babies?"

"I think it's wonderful about the Slaters," Rambo responded. *"I heard Pearl say that they've been trying for two years to have a baby—now they're having two. My concern is the riddle... this seems to fit in there somehow. Zeela said she was going to talk to Nexlucimus. I'm sure she's having the same warning bells as I am."*

"Wow, do you think Sara is in danger?"

"No, there is much security there. I'm sure that's why Zeela wanted to get her back to the central city."

"It would be sad if something happened to those babies," Jesse said, his mind on the riddle.

A few moments passed, and Jesse had another concern come to mind.

"Rambo..."

"Yes?"

"What about this silver chain I'm wearing? Why did I get it? What will happen if someone else touches it? It seems to have its own warmth and pulse."

Rambo emitted a deep, almost sad sigh. *"I think it's time I told you that story."*

Rambo slowed his flight, moving to the rear of the group, and Jesse sensed that his friend was struggling with something.

"Rambo, are you OK?"

"Yes, my friend. I am well," Rambo sighed. *"Jesse, there are many mysteries concerning this quest, and a considerable part of them seem to be focused on you. Master Nexlucimus has a theory, and while the gods neither confirm nor deny his opinion, he feels comfortable with it. To begin with, I will tell you a story, and perhaps it will help."*

"Over two and a half millennia ago, there was a young man, a prince, and he fell deeply in love with a beautiful maiden. She was also a member of royalty—a different family, from a neighbouring village. She showed great promise as a holy woman and warrior. They became best friends."

"She had powerful magic, profound spiritual insight, plus strength and stamina in battle. Her people wanted her blessings for everything—children, crops, sickness, animals, and direction. They also desired her leadership. Because of their dependence on her, the people started drifting away from their spiritual roots. Unlike

the gods, she was tangible. They could talk to her, use her abilities and see her, all in the present."

"Her fame caused her to be sought after, pursued, even hunted. They wore her down. Even though she couldn't die, she couldn't live either. She cared deeply for her people, but she didn't want the position that was being forced upon her. She feared that they were offending the gods. She tried to run away and escape from it. The young prince helped her. She fell in love with him, and they were secretly married in a distant city."

"After a time, a child was born to them—a daughter. They were happy in their hiding until they were discovered by a traveller. The people again demanded her service. They took the child and banished her husband. She was a prisoner of her talents, and she was heartbroken."

"Her husband petitioned the gods to intervene. He pleaded with them continually, day and night. He missed his daughter, he worried for his wife, and he was willing to do anything to change the situation."

Rambo became silent, apparently troubled by his emotions.

"Rambo... my friend, is she the White Druid of legend?"

"Yes... you have guessed correctly."

"And... you... are her husband?"

"Yes," he said, his voice thick with emotion.

"What happened?"

"The gods did just as I asked—only not the way I thought. I was willing to do whatever it took to restore some peace to Chaelea, my wife, and to have our daughter Trelesa return. What the gods did was take Chaelea and Trelesa to themselves. They changed Chaelea into the white dragon that you see in the Great Library. It was both a blessing to her and a protection."

"The people were shocked at the disappearances, especially since they were never told where they were taken. They had their suspicions, but since I was also changed, and remained, they were confused. To live with the gods, you must be altered to abide by them. Trelesa was an innocent, pure baby—she needed no change."

"Dragons are considered servants of the gods on Xanthara. I know that this is not always true in your world. It seems that dragons are either feared or revered by mortals. By changing Chaelea into one, she could live with the gods and escape the powers that imprisoned her."

"The gods blessed me with this form, as a reminder of Chaelea's love, and for my reverence and willingness to serve them. It also gave me specific abilities, such as shapeshifting—which happened once I entered your world to help prepare for this quest."

"While the gods solved the problem, it left a hole in my heart. One good thing, however—when Chaelea disappeared, the people saw it as a sign. They humbly returned to the gods. There have

been many splittings since then, and the pattern has been completely disrupted."

"Lately, Jesse, we have seen signs of Chaelea's work in you. Nexlucimus believes the gods are getting close to returning her to us. I pray this is true."

Jesse was speechless, and they flew in silence for several moments.

"The abilities that I have, and the silver chain—those are all from her, and the gods?" Jesse asked weakly.

"We believe so, yes. If a person tried to touch the chain, their hand would merely pass through it. This means that no one can take it from you. It would also signal to the dissenters that you could be a problem for them. We aren't sure how it will be used, but it has been confirmed to Master Nexlucimus that you are the only one with power over it."

Jesse forgot all his grandmother's efforts and allowed his jaw to drop temporarily.

"This story—this history of your life, Rambo... I am stunned and so incredibly honoured to be in your confidence. How many people know of this?"

"At one time, many knew, but over the eons, very few remember the real story. Master Nexlucimus, Zeela, and a few others. Our parents, of course, know. Some of the older members of our two villages, and the fairies."

"Trelesa had none of her mother's talents and was returned to her maternal grandparents when she was two years old. They raised her. She doesn't really remember that time, or her mother, but she knows who her mother is. She is now married with many children. I am a grandfather, with many greats and great-greats and great-great-greats," Rambo chuckled.

"Holy cow!"

"Jesse, I would ask you not to say anything about this to anyone, not even in jest."

"Of course, I will honour that request, my friend. And Rambo, thank you for telling me this story. I am humbled by your sufferings. It makes my problems seem trivial."

"I have grown used to the separation, Jesse. While it is hard, and I miss my family, I know that someday we will be united again, and our lives will be different."

"Have you seen your daughter and her family?"

"I have visited with her many times. She knows the whole story and has told her family. Someday we will all be together again."

"Amazing story..."

"We are almost to our destination, Jesse. Again, do not mention any of this, and keep the chain like the talisman, hidden."

"I will... on my honour."

After flying for the better part of several hours, the party finally arrived at their destination and was pleased to see a small camp of rough cabins next to a small waterfall. They decided to put up privacy screens around the waterfall and use it as a shower, since Skeedlers didn't seem to be in the game world.

Rambo morphed into a rooster, took a dirt bath, and headed into the woods to scratch up some bugs.

Jesse thought the cold water was very refreshing and wished he had some shampoo; he settled for foaming roots that Zealoc handed him. He didn't care much for the super sweet, flowery, girly smell. The flies loved it. He wasn't alone—everyone was swatting flies. At least they didn't bite.

"Man, Zealoc, what did you give us?" Tommy complained, swatting flies madly.

"Could be worse," Jesse said, grinning at Gran. "They could be a foot long and bite."

"Nope, those come tomorrow," Zealoc said, winking at Pearl.

She giggled at him like a schoolgirl.

Jesse wasn't sure if he was going to be able to stomach much more of the lovebirds. When Ginnea announced that she was going hunting for food, Jesse asked if he could go with her.

"Sure, if I miss the prey, you can fry it. It would save us firewood."

Ginnea headed out into the woods, sniffing the air as she went.

"Do you smell that, Jesse?" she whispered, after tracking for a while.

Jesse sniffed and detected a faint smell—like an overflowing public toilet. He gagged.

"Yep, that's the smell," she chuckled. "It's over this way. Try not to step on anything noisy."

After a short distance, the smell intensified, and Jesse pulled his robe over his nose, trying to filter it.

"Where is that smell coming from?"

"Dinner, I'm hoping," Ginnea said, smiling.

"You've got to be kidding," Jesse gagged.

"Nope. Hog rats smell terrible, but they are supposed to taste fantastic."

Jesse was doubtful—especially when they crept over a small hill and saw a gnarly-looking rat the size of a large Labrador. Ginnea had the rat down before Jesse even saw her equip an arrow to her bow.

"Now, we just need to find something to carry it back to camp. Any ideas?" Ginnea asked.

"Sure, watch this."

Jesse closed his eyes and imagined the beast floating behind Ginnea as she walked.

"Impressive... looks like dinner is on its way," Ginnea said, smiling at Jesse.

"All I can say is, I hope it tastes better than it smells, or we're all going to be very sick," Jesse said, trying hard not to puke.

When they returned to camp with the rat, they learned that Zealoc and Jim had left to scout the area.

"Man... this thing is disgusting, Ginnea. Are you sure it's safe to eat?" Cami gagged.

"Yep, they're called hog rats, and they're supposed to be a delicacy—if you cook them long enough to kill the parasites. Oh... by the way, be sure to wash your hands thoroughly after handling it."

"Lovely," Gran retched. "Can't wait to see how this turns out. If the mobs don't kill us, maybe the food will. I'm going to go find some herbs for the parasites and improve the flavour. Come with me, Sean. If I get sick thinking about the rat stew, I might need a good doctor along."

"Oh come on, Pearl, it couldn't possibly be any worse than that 'fish head stew' you cook up," Sean laughed, following her to hunt herbs.

"That's a good idea," Gram said. "Maybe we could find some golden bass tomorrow."

Chapter 19

Now you see them, now you don't.

After a short while, Gran and Mr Chambers returned with roots and herbs, which they added to the pot. Surprisingly, the cooking rat started to smell wonderful. Jesse hoped it would taste as good as it smelt, because he was starving.

"Man, that smells delicious. Every mob for miles is going to know we're here," Zealoc commented when they returned. He looked worried, but then added, "All we need is a loaf of bread and a jug of mead to round out the meal."

"Good, tomorrow you can make the meal, Zealoc," Pearl teased.

"Anything for you, fair lady."

Jesse turned his back on the happy couple. *"If I weren't so hungry, I'd lose my appetite right about now."*

While they ate the surprisingly delicious rat stew, Zealoc and Jim told them about their scouting trip.

"There's a small party of pygmy trolls not too far from here, about three miles to the north. They're being guarded by a group of blood fairies, which are no big deal," Zealoc said.

NO BIG DEAL? Jesse's mind yelled.

"Down the road from them were dust whelps," Jim added. "I'm confused as to why they're so far away from the Shimmering Mountains—unless the mountains are on the move."

"The dust whelps will be more of a problem," Zealoc said. "They can disappear and attack from behind. Ginnea, we'll need you to lay some traps for them when we get closer."

Ginnea nodded in agreement, while Jesse worried about the blood fairies.

"How can blood fairies be 'no big deal', Zealoc? They almost killed me," Jesse asked.

"Jesse, you were new to this game world, and you didn't have enough people to handle the situation—even with a warrior tank and two healers. It's different now. Either Jim or I will go in and grab the blood fairies' attention while the rest of you wipe them out. The pygmy trolls are easy to distract until they can be killed. Since those are the only mobs close to us here, I suggest we take care of them tonight, before we camp."

"Remember that Brutus and I are here also, my friends," Rambo added.

"Indeed, so—a piece of cake," Jim said.

It was agreed they would advance to the troll camp, but before they could set off, there was a loud crack, like lightning snapping. Seeing nothing nearby, they mounted and surveyed the Shield

Wall. They decided to split up—half heading south, the other half going north.

After a few short moments, Jesse's group found a single female player with a fuzzy aura to her appearance, indicating she was a real person from the mortal world. Jesse and Rambo landed near her, and she reacted by pulling out a bow and equipping a large arrow with alarming speed.

"Whoa… take it easy, I'm a friend," Jesse said, raising his hands to the lovely purple satyr.

Gran, Zealoc and Ginnea landed right behind him.

"Peace, fair maiden," Zealoc said, raising a hand as he approached her.

"Who are you, and what has happened to me?" the satyr asked, clearly confused.

"We are Game Masters," Ginnea said.

"And you, dear," Gran added sympathetically, "are in the game you were playing just a moment ago. Tazeron the Terrible captured you and pulled you into this world."

The girl looked as though she was going into shock. She blanched to such a pale purple that she was almost light lavender, except for the darker worry lines. She started to tremble.

They had her sit down. She did so weakly, and with help.

"But… h-how is that possible?" she stammered.

"May I ask you a question before we answer that? How long were you in the game before this happened?" Sean asked, curious. He handed her a cookie of peace and wisdom to steady her. Recognising the wafer, she accepted it and started nibbling.

"My… my guild was pulling an all-nighter. I've been on for about… twenty-two hours," she said, nervously looking around."

"We will show you how to get back home, but you must promise to play the game in moderation until the bug is fixed. This episode will appear to your guild as an internet disconnect. We suggest you rest for perhaps a day or two before getting back online. This could happen again," Gran told the frightened girl.

"How is that possible?" she asked again, though she seemed a little more at ease. The cookie was working.

They explained that it was a far-reaching bug in the game, and unless she followed their instructions, it could possibly kill her next time.

"Have you heard of the 'Lost'?" Jesse asked.

"Yes, I have," she replied.

"Well, right now you are one of them—or you could have been if we hadn't found you. The Tazeron bug has a way of pulling people into the games," Gran told the shocked girl. "Now that you've had this experience, go home and tell everyone about it. They might not believe you, but you can try. Perhaps you can save someone else from becoming Lost."

"I don't know what to say… I'm stunned," she said. Sean gave her another cookie.

They suggested that she tell everyone she knew about the bug. They recommended she post it on her guild's web page or any other internet forum frequented by gamers.

After the girl said she would do those things, they showed her to the portal she had created during her entry. They had her step back through, and she and the portal disappeared. By this time, everyone had gathered at the spot.

"That was so cool," Jesse sighed. "It gave me warm fuzzies all over."

Rambo snickered.

"What… can't a guy have warm fuzzies without ridicule?"

Tommy punched him in the shoulder.

"Ouch… Gran, Tommy and Rambo are picking on me!"

"Brilliant… I always knew I liked those two," Gran said, as she climbed onto the war eagle behind Zealoc, who was chuckling.

They all remounted and headed back to camp.

The group decided to wait until morning before approaching the mobs Zealoc and Jim had scouted.

Ginnea would take the first watch, and Tommy would take the second.

During the night, Brutus sounded a small whine, waking the camp, and cast a spell of calmness over everyone at the same time.

"Keep them covered with the calming, Brutus, while I pull Tommy away and try to revive him."

Jesse woke up unable to move. He heard the exchange between Brutus and Rambo, but it didn't make sense. At first, he wondered if the rat stew had poisoned him, but then he realised that everyone he could see by the light of their campfire—including himself—was tied up in ropes.

"Everyone be still," Rambo growled softly.

"What's going on?" Jesse whispered, struggling against the ropes.

"Quiet, Jesse. Don't move unless you want to die," Zealoc shushed him urgently.

"What are these things?" Cami whimpered, her voice shaking.

"Glass spiders. Don't move, and they will leave. If you move around, they'll poison you and take you home for supper," Ginnea murmured quietly.

"Where did they come from, and why did they rope us up if they weren't going to eat us?" Sean breathed.

"They are from the Shimmering Mountain, and we'll explain after they go," Rambo told them.

"Hush, everyone... be quiet and hold still. Try to act dead," Zealoc hissed.

"What would happen if I roasted a few of them? I only see five," Jesse asked.

"Jesse... shut your trap," Zealoc snarled at him.

Jesse snapped his mouth shut, thinking about the situation. There was something familiar... what was it?

They lay there for another thirty minutes (give or take a century), as massive, translucent, pure white, very creepy, big-butt glass spiders crawled over them, tightening their ropes. Jesse had to pee badly. He wondered if the spiders would know he was alive when he wet his robes. He was just about to ask when the spiders suddenly vanished, and Zealoc gave the okay to get out of the ropes.

That was another problem. The lines seemed to be made of durable fibreglass. Brutus again came to their rescue. The snow-white griffin morphed into his little dog form and started chewing through the ropes with diamond-sharp teeth, like they were soft butter.

After everyone was free, Jesse asked Rambo and Brutus where they had been, and why they hadn't intervened. Rambo answered his question.

"It was better for us to stay out of the way, except for removing Tommy. Our interference could have caused your accidental poisoning, as the spiders would've tried to kill us—which, of course, they couldn't have done. We could've taken them out one at a time, but many were invisible. Sometimes it's best to wait and let the situation rectify itself. You were in no danger if you followed your team leader. Always remember that."

"I believe that was one of your first lessons, Jesse dear. It's more important now than it was then," Gran added.

Zealoc explained the spiders: "They only eat live food, which is why they wait to see if you struggle. Their ropes have a mild stimulant in them which causes a weak or damaged victim to squirm. They only eat wriggling prey. Only the spiders that are working are visible—all the rest are invisible."

"Nice," said Gran, picking leaves and bits of spider web out of her long red braid. "I wonder if there has ever been a female dwarf with short spiky hair," she grumbled.

"Never! Such an atrocity has never been seen. Why would a beautiful woman deface herself in such a way?" Zealoc said, incensed by the thought.

"I was only kidding, Zealoc, my dear," Gran said, cuddling up to him.

"Oh, brother!" Jesse thought to himself, rolling his eyes.

Ginnea noticed Jesse's reaction and chuckled softly.

"Ah... love. Enjoyable at any age," she whispered to Jesse.

"Whatever..."

Standing, Jesse noticed Tommy—unconscious and lying on a bed of glowing white flowers. Mr Chambers dribbled purple liquid into his mouth. His darkly tanned skin was pale, and he was shivering.

"What happened to Tommy?" Jesse asked quietly, kneeling next to his friend, concerned.

"He tried to warn the camp, since it was his watch, but one of the spiders poisoned him. He's lucky that Rambo could pull him away from the spiders before they finished him off with another dose of their toxin."

"I'm giving him some Dumplumba mixed with Naqisha," Mr Chambers told them. "It's supposed to cause the poison to leave the body and be collected in the bright sponge flowers. I can then process the flowers and make another concoction that we can use against the spiders if they return."

"Tommy was very brave to try and warn us," Cami said, helping her father.

"We were very fortunate to have Rambo and Brutus with us," Ginnea choked, watching her brother. "I'm wondering why there are so many mobs from the Shimmering Mountains. The mountains must be very close."

Jesse remembered something familiar—something from the game, something that frightened him, but it might help.

"Rambo, could your bubble shield protect me from the darts of searching?" Jesse asked.

"Interesting idea, Jesse... I don't know."

"Could you burn the darts out of the air if I told you where they were?"

"Jesse, what's this about?" Zealoc asked, curious.

"Indeed, my friend," Rambo said, seeing Jesse's thoughts and what he had in mind. "In fact, all you would have to do is picture them."

"Zealoc, I have an idea, and with the help of Rambo, I think I can find the Shimmering Mountains. Rambo, can you talk to Brutus' mind like you can to me?"

"Indeed, I can, Jesse."

"Perfect. Zealoc, once we find the mountains, we could mount an offensive and clear that dungeon—freeing a wider path to Tazeron."

"No one can see the Shimmering Mountains when they aren't moving, Jesse. It's the swamp that makes them visible."

"Zealoc, my dear, I think Jesse might have something here. This whole situation does remind me of the Frozen Citadel found in one of the games. We must trust Jesse on this one," Pearl said imploringly. "All his life he has been sensitive to impressions, and since before we started this quest, he was deemed a Finding. He can find those mountains. I know he can."

Zealoc studied Pearl and Jesse for a moment, then nodded his consent—not looking very happy about it.

"This will allow more time for Tommy to heal, and for us to rethink our plans of advance toward Tazeron," Jesse said. "I'm impressed with the thought that they are throwing a different kind of magic at us—one that will take more thinking and fewer melees."

"I'm sure that we are dealing with not only a very skilled magician, but a brilliant, very evil mastermind. It reminds me of the last boss in the Screaming Caverns within the Frozen Citadel—like Gran pointed out," Jesse stressed to all of them.

"Oh, glory... I pray not," Mr Chambers stammered.

"Zealoc, you said when we first started this assignment that we would meet things that would test our skills—almost beyond our abilities. If what I'm thinking is true, that might just be a prophecy," Jesse said gravely. "I seriously doubt that we're going to have very many 'no big deal' encounters, my friend."

Jesse saw the truth of his words register in the face of the brave little man as he took Pearl's hand, and they both sat down hard on a log.

"Jesse speaks the truth. He does indeed possess a rare talent for seeing beyond the blocks in a puzzle," Zeela said, as she approached the camp.

"Zeela...!" Gran and Cami both squealed at the same time.

Jim jumped up excitedly, asking about his wife and how things were going with her, anxious to know. The others expressed their joy at Zeela's safe return and asked about Sara.

Zeela smiled at their greeting, but then became sombre.

"Sara and the babies are doing remarkably, but we must discuss what this development means to the success of our mission."

"What are you talking about?" Jim asked, now concerned.

David landed his steed near the camp.

"Dad...! I wasn't expecting you to return. What about all the new Keepers you needed to prepare?"

"We need to call an emergency meeting right now. The new Keepers who haven't been assigned a section in the game are helping back in the capital city," David said, dismally.

"What are you talking about, David? What has happened?" Zealoc and Ginnea both asked at the same time.

"We will explain. Please be seated, everyone," Zeela pleaded, urgency in her voice.

Everyone that could gathered around David and Zeela, finding places to sit in a tight circle. Rambo and Brutus reverted to their smaller forms—a small dog and a rooster—so they could get in closer. Rambo stood proudly by Jesse, and Brutus curled up in Cami's lap while she stroked his silky fur.

David and Zeela stood before them, looking tired and worried.

Chapter 20

Could it be that easy?

"The city was under attack when we left," David announced to his audience.

There was a collective gasp, and everyone shifted nervously, shocked.

"What about my wife?" Jim asked imploringly.

"Wolfa has taken her into the forest to be with the elves. She is as safe there as possible. The elves will also have a better understanding of her condition as the babies develop, since she is in elf form now. Please be at peace—she is well. Now, we have other urgent concerns."

Jim sat down behind the group, and Jesse noticed that he seemed to be having a hard time focusing on the meeting. Jesse didn't blame him one bit.

"What is happening in the city?" Zealoc asked.

"The primitive mountain tribes have started attacking the outer perimeters, taking prisoners. Two of the portals have been breached in the Outlands by Tazeron's followers—those who were trapped in the mortal game world when all this started. They escaped back into Xanthara, bringing with them mortals who are in sympathy with their cause. We also fear that Tazeron's mystics may have solved the riddle. Nexlucimus told us that our scholars believe they know the answer."

"Wow, so much news... unbelievable," Jesse murmured. "What is being done about all of this, Dad?"

"For now, our intercity militia and the Keepers have secured all of the portals," David told them. "There is an intense search for those that have escaped from the game, but we fear that they have united with the primitive tribes."

Then Zeela added, "Because of their past crimes, we feel confident that they will soon be dealt with by the gods. They were, after all, promised a banishment into outer darkness before they entered the game world. Why they would want to come back is a mystery to us.

The mortal sympathisers, when located and captured, will be sent back to the mortal world and blocked by the shield. It will be tuned to their essences, making it impossible for them to play the games as well. If, by chance, they aren't captured and join with the primitive tribes, they will be treated as enemies of our world," Zeela told the group.

"The solving of the riddle is another matter—and perhaps a greater concern," David added. "If what the scholars have told the High Priest is true, we have grave concern for the possibility that Tazeron could pass into the mortal world. Nexlucimus didn't tell us what was translated, but he said to increase our efforts to capture—or even better, kill—Tazeron and his minions."

"This makes it even more vital that we get to Tazeron," Jesse said, his voice a mere whisper.

"Indeed it does, Jesse. I was most interested in your plan when we approached. Could you tell us what you had in mind?" David asked.

"We were attacked by glass spiders last night, Dad, and Tommy is gravely ill with their poison."

David whistled. *"Oh man."*

"While thinking about Zealoc's confusion—because we keep seeing so many beasts from the mountains," Jesse continued, "I remembered the Screaming Cavern in the Frozen Citadel.

The last boss there was Grieval the Harsh. She was a human that would morph into this colossal spider when she got to half health. Every time she was hit with magic or melee after she morphed, an egg pustule growing on her side would rupture and spawn more spiders. The only way to kill her was to alternate freezing and nuking her while managing the little spider add-ons.

She wasn't the nastiest part of the problem, however. Her mate, Nakmaul, could mind control. He could also fear everyone in the room. There was no avoiding him. What you had to do was mind control him first, as soon as you saw him.

It wasn't easy, because it required one of your raid members to sacrifice themselves to the destruction of Nakmaul to save the group. That meant you were fighting one person short as you took out Grieval.

Another thing—even though Nakmaul was controlled, he could still pulsate waves of freeze that affected your intelligence and stamina. The more waves you collected, the less efficient your spells and damage became. There was also the possibility of being randomly silenced so none of your spells would work, or he could send you into an alternate plane, ultimately taking you away from the battle."

"How did you ever get past those two?" Zeela, David, and the other Xantharaians wanted to know.

"Our guild never did," Sean said sadly. "I was aware of only one group that downed the evil pair, and I never heard any reports of their strategy. I'm sure that the finest and highest-tiered armour was an important part of their success, along with the best enchantments and strongest magical gems of imbuement."

Jesse added other thoughts to the equation. "I was impressed that we are chasing a boss that is like those two. I'm not saying that it is those two, only that whoever it might be is a thinker—not just another 'you'd better stay out of stuff on the floor' melee boss.

They are moving Shimmering Mountain just out of sight, but close enough to be a staging point. I believe that their sole purpose is to keep us distracted as we try to get to Tazeron.

If what you say is true, and Tazeron has the riddle solved, they will be turning up the heat so we won't get close enough to interrupt them. We must keep after Tazeron—just like the flies after Zealoc's foaming soap," Jesse said, with seriousness.

There were a few nervous snickers.

"I think I can get close enough—especially with Rambo and Brutus, which means Cami too. Ginnea, as a hunter, I would like you to come. Your traps and potions of invisibility will be most helpful.

Zeela and Dad—now that you are here—your skills are needed.

Jim, my friend, I think you are too distracted worrying about Sara."

Gran and Zealoc, you should stay with Mr Chambers to protect him while he works on Tommy. Zealoc, we will need a plan for when we get to the mountains.

David studied his son for a moment. "You know, Jesse, I believe you've grown since I saw you last. This sounds like a good idea, son. I'm assuming you planned this to be a short reconnaissance adventure?"

"Yes, sir. I'm hoping it doesn't take too long, but that will depend on what we find there. We should be able to keep in communication with our talismans, but we've never used them before, so this will be a test. Rambo and I will be mind-talking, and if I forget to keep you posted, I apologise now before we start."

"Jesse, we must go, my friend," Rambo said.

"OK, if there are no questions, we need to get going," Jesse said to the group.

Rambo and Brutus changed back into their superior battle-active forms, and Jesse and Cami scrambled aboard for take-off.

As they took to the air, Jesse tried the talisman to explain in greater detail what he had in mind. He found that if he first thought of the talisman, then the intended person, he could communicate with just that person. If he thought of the group, he could link to all of them at once.

"I'm going to have Rambo encase me in a bubble and make me invisible. I will be mind-searching the area, looking for anything unusual. Dad and Zeela, I'd like you to hang back while Ginnea stays close to Cami. Rambo will tell Brutus to cast the protection bubble and invisibility on Cami too, which will help."

Shortly after take-off, Jesse encountered an anomaly—an enormous black spot, like a black hole in the atmosphere. It wasn't there, and yet it was. He probed it, trying to break through the magic that surrounded it.

"Could it be that easy?" Jesse reached into his medicine pouch and pulled out a handful of Greater Sight Dust, sending it into the air with his mind. It coated the area and revealed an astonishing view.

He had expected a floating mountain, but what they found was a floating castle. Complete with ramparts and turrets, it appeared to be covered with a blanket spell of invisibility.

"What the heck..." David said.

"What do you think, Rambo? Should we head in and explore?"

"That sounds like a good idea, Jesse," Rambo concurred.

"Zeela and Dad, keep watch here and let us know if anything alarming happens. Ginnea, invisible yourself and accompany Cami to the west of the compound while Rambo and I search the east side."

"Will do..." Ginnea replied.

Zeela and David were already getting into position.

"OK, let's see what secrets this place holds," Jesse said to the group.

Flying over the wall towards the central courtyard, they saw only a few soldiers and armaments. Jesse asked Rambo to shrink in size so they could go inside and have a look around. Jesse noticed that not only did Rambo shrink, but he, Jesse, did too. That was an exciting discovery.

They flew down corridors and into rooms, seeing quarters for troops, a galley, a sizeable healing facility, a prison compound, and an armoury. They were shocked at the lack of individuals. It was a skeleton crew—preparing for something.

"Cami, where are you?" Jesse asked using the talisman.

"We're flying over a training area, but there isn't much going on here."

"Head back to where Dad and Zeela are—we'll be right behind you."

"OK, we're on our way."

Once they were all together, they had a brief conference.

"I'm not sure what they're preparing for," Jesse said. "I think we should continue looking for the mountains and maybe check back here before we head to camp."

Zeela and David thought that was a good plan.

"Oh, one more thing. Rambo and I discovered that when I'm riding him and he shrinks, I shrink also. Can Brutus do that too?" Jesse asked Cami.

"Brutus and I don't communicate the same way that you two do—I don't know," Cami said.

"His mind works differently. They won't be talking, but he can shrink if I tell him to. Let's try it," Rambo said.

They watched as Brutus morphed to a smaller size, but Cami didn't shrink—so that idea wasn't going to work. Brutus was either a cute fluffy little dog, one in-between size, or an impressive griffin. Cami was OK with that.

Jesse thought about the harness and leash he had put on Brutus back at Gran's and wondered if that might come in handy. He felt Rambo chuckling softly. He would talk to Rambo about that later.

They all agreed to head farther out and see if the Shimmering Mountains were in the area.

As they were leaving the castle, Jesse saw a chilling sight. Purple dragons were approaching them from inside the blanket that shrouded the area. The others didn't seem to notice them. He sent a picture to Rambo. Jesse let the others know they were being pursued and to take evasive action.

As the dragons passed through the veil of invisibility, they came into view for all to see.

"Hang on, Jesse—we're in for a rough ride. They will attack us, even though it will do no good. It'll be bumpy," Rambo cautioned.

"I trust you, my friend," Jesse thought back.

Rambo banked hard to the right and then went into a steep dive. Just as suddenly, he shot back up, directly in line with the other dragons. Rambo was on a collision course with the leader and gaining speed.

Jesse closed his eyes. He trusted Rambo, but it was still scary. Through his eyelids, Jesse saw the glow of a ball of flame. Opening his eyes, he watched Rambo's fire engulf the two lead dragons, sending them spiralling towards the ground. The other dragons turned around, leaving the area.

Jesse hooted with laughter.

"That was spectacular, Rambo—you totally rocked."

Rambo laughed. *"I was just showing off, but thanks. It was fun."*

"We're going to keep flying deeper into the area while I search with my mind travel. Stay alert, everyone, in case I scare up some nasties," Jesse told the group.

Flying around for what seemed like hours, Jesse didn't find anything that could be mountains. They decided to head back towards the camp. They were all becoming anxious because of the time away.

About halfway back, Jesse felt something trailing them. He had Rambo stop mid-flight. Searching the area with his mind, Jesse was surprised to find a small invisible ball, similar to the director balls back in the city. Tossing a pinch of greater sight dust in the direction of the ball, Jesse heard Zeela gasp. Puzzled, he looked over at her and was startled to see her panicked expression.

"What is this thing, Zeela? What does it mean?"

"It's a telewave ball, Jesse. A message from the Council—but I've never seen one so small or concealed under cover of invisibility."

Zeela approached the ball and tapped it like Gran had done back at the house. There was no video, only an audio message with this small device.

"Zeela, my dear, I'm sorry to alarm you in this fashion. The situation is even graver than we thought. The Council has been dissolved; it is all we can do. Most of the members are either missing or in hiding. I have moved our household into the safety of the forest with the elves, along with Heralon and a few others.

Our militia is holding out as well, with the brave Keepers' assistance, but they are ill-prepared to fight a battle in Xanthara since their skill and training lie within the Game.

We have little hope if Tazeron is still influencing the primitive tribes. I will launch an embassy to those misguided people soon. You and the remaining Keepers must be successful. You are our only hope.

We will continue to do all that we can from here. The elves are unyielding, and their magic is of the highest quality. Tazeron has little hope of success in this forest, but we must not become too confident.

Tell Jim that Sara has been delivered of the babies. They are all doing fine.

Please be safe, my love. All of Xanthara depends on you—and the Keepers—to discover and stop Tazeron. I'm sorry that this is a one-way message. I have a great need to see your face and hear your voice. I look forward to our reunion."

The message ended, and Zeela landed on Rambo's back with Jesse, her strength gone.

"Zeela, do you need to go back to camp, or can we continue? It is even more urgent that the mountain is cleared, and then we proceed to Tazeron."

"We proceed, Jesse. Xanthara is in danger—as well as the mortal world—unless we destroy Tazeron and his plans. He has become even stronger than we thought. He must not succeed... he cannot succeed."

As the day began to wane, Jesse continued to search. He was heartsick, and his head was aching. He was finding it difficult to concentrate, and yet he knew it all depended on him and his talents.

"Rambo, I'm having a difficult time concentrating. Is there anything you can do to help me?"

"I can remind you that you are a unique blend of this world and the world we are trying to preserve. Reach deeper inside, Jesse. Perhaps there is something that has been overlooked. I will search as best I can, but the soul that you possess is stable and capable of more than you ever thought possible."

Jesse took Rambo's words to heart and stretched farther into their surroundings. Deeper and deeper he delved, focusing more clearly, tuning the lenses of his mind to a sharper aim.

He found it.

Hiding in plain sight, under cover of the castle, Jesse could just make out the outlines of the mountains. An image hiding within an image. A puzzle within a puzzle. A face made of faces. The peaks were finally visible to him. It was indeed a mind game.

The others couldn't see what he was seeing, and he had a hard time convincing them that it was there, layered underneath the façade of the castle—even with sight dust in the air.

Then Zeela began to see, along with Rambo and Cami. Once they started seeing through the smokescreen—which was magically in place—David and Ginnea saw it too, although not as clearly.

"How ingenious," David said, awed. "A picture hiding within a picture. We had it right in our hands from the start. No wonder mobs were so close, and the purple dragons chased after us. Now we need to separate the two, so we can make a path to Tazeron."

"We need to get back to camp," Jesse said, feeling anxious. "We need to tell the others about Nexlucimus' message, and prepare a plan for separating the mountain from the castle—and destroying them both. I feel like this mountain will be here for a while."

Chapter 21

Oh My Gosh

It didn't take them long to get back to camp; the castle was closer than they thought. Everyone was glad for their return and eager to hear of their discovery. A meeting was called to discuss the message from Nexlucimus and what it meant to the quest.

They were saddened to hear of the Council being dissolved and the dire situation in the city. There was concern for the Keepers left helping the militia, but Cami reminded them that, while most of their training was for magical skills, many of the Keepers were non-magical classes such as warriors, death knights, rogues, hunters and other melee types. They played more first-person shooter games, and because of their non-magical orientation, their training had concentrated on those skills under David's direction.

"They will be better prepared than the primitive people or the recruited mortal supporters of Tazeron, who have not had the training we have had on Xanthara," she said, bringing a positive feeling to an otherwise dismal report.

There was also concern about the way the mountain was concealed and what that could mean in finding Tazeron's camp and destroying it.

"I have never heard of such a thing—hiding something in plain sight. Blasted wizards!" Zealoc snarled into his beard. "You were indeed correct, young Jesse. This is a brilliant tactical thinker that

we are facing. The strange thing is, I'm sure it isn't Tazeron. Perhaps it's one of his captains. This is someone familiar with the mechanics of the Game. Tazeron is a stranger here; this is a foreign world to him. He is far more comfortable in Xanthara or the mortal world. He is only in this place because he is trapped, not because he knows it or wants to be."

Zealoc's words brought a sombre mood to the group, and they sat in silence. Then Zeela remembered the babies.

"Jim, we have fantastic news. Your children have been born, and they and Sara are doing remarkably well."

"How is that possible?" Jim asked, stunned. "How could they be developed enough to be born? I know that pregnancies progress faster in elves and fairies, but Sara was barely into her pregnancy. That couldn't possibly be long enough for two babies to develop," he whispered in astonishment.

"Jim, she was in Game form, and she was eating Dumplumba and Naqisha fruits. Pregnancies progress faster in fantasy than in mortal worlds, even under normal conditions. War and stress speed up those pregnancies in elves and fairies. She was also very healthy."

Jesse paled at this disclosure. It just hit him what this could mean for him. "Fairies develop faster too. Oh... my... gosh!" He felt light-headed.

"All of that contributes to a faster delivery time and growth rate once they are born. Now, Jim, as much as we all know that you want to be here with us during this time, I feel that you should travel to the forest and spend time with Sara and the babies," Zeela said.

"Are you serious?" Jim could hardly believe what she had just said.

"Yes, my friend. Your level of concentration right now could possibly be a safety concern for all of us. So, with that being said," Zeela added, smiling, "we all wish you well. Spend time with your wife and children, and please tell my husband..." She choked on her emotions.

"Please tell my husband that I will return as soon as I can."

"I will do that, Zeela. Thank you all."

Everyone gave Jim their best wishes to send to Sara, then watched as he warped to the forest with his talisman. Shortly after Jim left, the meeting was adjourned while the evening meal was prepared.

Jesse was glad to be back at camp and to see Jim so happy with the news of his wife and children. It made him, Jesse, nervous to think that they were down one more person, but they did have Rambo and Brutus. He was also concerned about Tommy; the poison wasn't leaving as soon as Mr Chambers and Zeela hoped, and that worried them all.

"Is there anything else that can be done to help Tommy?" Jesse asked.

"Not here, no," Mr Chambers and Zeela both agreed.

"We need to send him to the elves," Zealoc interjected. "I feel that it is necessary. That way, we can concentrate on what's happening here, and Tommy can get the in-depth help he needs. Zeela, I think it would be good for you to accompany Tommy to the forest. That way, you can tell the healers what happened, what's been done to help him, and then give a report to Nexlucimus. Sean, since you were also involved with his care and can warp Zeela, I want you to go also, but come back as soon as Tommy is settled," Zealoc said.

"Yes sir," Sean said. "Zeela and I will prepare Tommy for transport and leave immediately."

During the evening meal, Zealoc let the remaining Keepers know of the decision.

"It has been decided that for the sake of the quest and Tommy's recovery, he needs to be sent to the forest of elves. Zeela and Sean will accompany him to the healing facility." There was a collective sigh of relief—Tommy's condition had been a concern for all, especially his sister Ginnea.

Zealoc continued, "Zeela and Sean can explain Tommy's situation to the healers. Sean will stay just long enough for Tommy to be settled with the elves and then he will return. Zeela, on the other hand, will stay and explain our predicament to Nexlucimus and gather any new information that might help us in our quest."

It was the right decision, Jesse thought. Ginnea was glad that her brother would be on his way to better help. They were down three people now, but Jesse felt they should still head to the mountain.

David and Ginnea had the first watch. Rambo and Brutus would circle the area from the air. Just knowing that the mountains were so close, and the high chance that they would be attacked again, had everyone on edge—like waiting for the other shoe to drop.

"What plan do you have for tomorrow, Jesse?" Zealoc asked as they relaxed around the fire. Gran sat close to Zealoc and listened.

"I want to explore the mountain on Rambo in the morning. Alone."

"Are you sure that's a good idea?" Zealoc said, looking pensive.

"We can shrink down to a tiny size, Zealoc, and become invisible. It worked before, and I'm thinking it would be a good way to get the facts we need without endangering the whole party."

"That might be true, Jesse, but remember, improved sight works both ways. They might have guards posted who can see through invisibility. I think this person we're up against is very aware of us. They might even have guessed what we are planning."

"I realise that, Zealoc, but I've got to try, and if it gets too intense, I can warp us out with the talisman."

"I don't like the plan, but I'm willing to let you try."

"Thank you, Zealoc," Jesse said as he stood up. "I think I'm going to try and get some sleep. Good night, Gran, Zealoc."

"Night, Jesse, sleep well," they both said, watching him walk to the edge of the firelight.

Crawling into his bedroll, Jesse tried to sleep, but it was almost impossible. Too many thoughts were chasing each other through his head. Too many nightmares were demanding his attention. He decided to try some mind travel. As he let his mind wander into the night, he became aware of how beautiful the sky was in the game world. It was so different from the mortal night sky, with its two softly glowing moons. He was just starting to relax when he felt his mind being touched in return—it felt familiar.

"Jesse, my love, I am here."

Shocked, Jesse sat up, surprising Pearl and Zealoc, who were still facing him as they snuggled by the fire, whispering and waiting for their turn at the watch.

"What is it, Jesse? What did you see?" Pearl asked, standing—always sensitive to his moods.

"Breeze just talked to me. How is that possible? She must still be a toddler."

"Um... I don't know how it all works, but the Slaters are having a similar situation. Why don't you ask Breeze?" Pearl suggested, sitting back down.

Jesse lay back down and focused on talking to Breeze.

"Breeze...? Is that you? How can that be? You aren't very old, are you?"

"War affects us differently, Jesse. Fairy-kind and elves mature faster during times of stress such as war. I am young by mortal terms, but I can reach out to you and touch your mind. I can no longer give you dreams, but I can still be close."

"This is so bizarre... how old are you, Breeze?"

"That has no meaning to me, Jesse. We of Xanthara do not count age the same way mortals do. We look at the soul of a person. Do not think of me as you would a human, Jesse. I could never be a suitable partner if you did."

"What do you mean?"

"Jesse, it will be best to talk about this at another time when we can meet in person. I will come in a few days, and we will talk then. In the meantime, be safe."

Breeze ended the conversation and once again disappeared into his thoughts. He was shaken by their interchange, but now he felt lonely for her. She was real—more than a dream—and yet she was not with him. This was an extraordinary world.

Climbing out of his bedroll, he went to sit by the fire with Gran and Zealoc again.

"Gran, why do fairy and elf babies develop and grow up so fast during times of war? I know what was said earlier, but it doesn't make sense."

"I don't really know, Jesse. Can you tell us more about this, Zealoc?"

"Dwarf babies do not respond to these times the same as fairies and elves. I have heard that many millennia ago, when the world was a wilder place, those races developed faster, and more boys were conceived than girls. That it is happening again is not a good sign."

"Did she say anything else?" Gran asked.

"Only that she would be here in a few days, and that I wasn't to think of her the way I would a mortal, because she would never be suitable for me if I did. I'm not afraid to admit that she scares me more than going to the castle-mountain tomorrow. What am I going to do?"

"Well, I guess you better decide what that means to you. It sounds like you're going to have an exciting time in a few days," Gran chuckled.

"Gee, thanks. I guess I'll go back to bed."

"That's a good idea. Night night, dear," Gran said as she snuggled back into Zealoc's arms.

Nestling down into his bedroll, Jesse wrestled with his thoughts for a long time, finally drifting off into a restless sleep.

Rambo woke Jesse as dawn broke the morning sky. Urgency pushed them as they gathered a few supplies and launched into the refreshing air. Soaring towards the mountain, soft red clouds clustered on the horizon, signalling an impending storm. Jesse hoped the weather would hold.

Birds flew in and out of the clouds in patterns that reminded him of geese heading south for the winter. Watching the birds for a moment, Jesse was struck with an unusual thought.

"Since when did in-game birds follow a migration pattern?"

Jesse searched the sight with his mind and was startled to see riders on the birds. He sent the picture to Rambo.

"Eagle Riders, unusual indeed," Rambo confirmed. *"I wonder why we didn't see them yesterday. We must shrink and go invisible. They may have seen us already."*

As they got closer to the castle, Jesse sent out a wave of sight to dislodge the mountain from its hiding place within the castle's cover. As hoped, the mountain began to shimmer and then focus before their eyes. The impressive size and structure of the mountain amazed them. The gleaming black and green glass caught the beams of sunlight streaking through the red-tinged clouds, creating a fiery glow.

"Beautiful," Jesse breathed. *"Never have I seen such evil shine so astonishingly."*

"It is magnificent, my friend, but we must remember our quest and stay focused."

"True, Rambo. Let's go in for a better view of the mountain and explore our options."

While Jesse and Rambo were exploring, they saw many beasts and creatures that were initially on the mountain in the game. In addition to the usual animals, there were many other races such as pygmy trolls, orcs, blood fairies, dark elves, and oracles. This indeed was a place of gathering. The mountain seemed to be on a slightly different plane than the castle. Jesse noticed the mobs accessing both levels, using what appeared to be escalators. The moving stairs ferried the different races, like people at a shopping mall, travelling between levels. The riders even carried packages like weekend shoppers.

Jesse and Rambo didn't try to penetrate the cavernous areas. They didn't want to meet a guard or something that could see them with their own form of improved sight. There were many possibilities, and they didn't want to engage any nasties by themselves. More and more, Jesse was impressed that their diminished group was ill-prepared to handle this situation on their own. They needed to enlist the help of others and combine their skills to raid this fortress. Back home in the game, they would gather larger groups to attack bigger dungeons like this, and that's what they needed to do this time as well. At least here, they wouldn't have issues with computer lag because of the graphics.

"Rambo, I think we've seen enough. Let's head back to the camp and tell everyone what we discovered. We need more people for this situation."

"Indeed, Jesse, I agree."

Arriving back at the camp, Jesse and Rambo talked to Zealoc, who called a meeting with the others to discuss what they had found.

"We were able to access the castle-mountain and explore some. We didn't want to engage the enemy, so we didn't penetrate the compound too deeply. We saw enough to tell us that our group here will be unable to take it down on our own."

"Dad, you said that the new Keepers were aiding the militia on Xanthara, but I was wondering if we could pull some of them in to help us with this."

"I'm worried that if we pull those Keepers away, we will weaken the army. I think it would be better to gather people with us who are already in the game. There are also guards patrolling the outer regions that we could use if needed," David said.

"Another thing you need to remember, Jesse," Mr Chambers added, "once a mob is killed here, they won't respawn or return. Even though Tazeron is gathering troops to the castle-mountain, he only has so many that he can draw on. The game does have limitations."

"That is true, but I worry about any mortals that he might have captured for his cause," Jesse added.

"Ah... good point, I had forgotten about that," Mr Chambers said.

"Zealoc, is contacting your cousin Beloe possible?" Jesse asked.

"Aye, they are in the Northwest section. He and his party would be honoured to assist. I am sure of it. Pearl and I will leave immediately."

"Thank you, my friend. Gran, you be careful out there. With all the preparation that Rambo and I saw, I believe that the enemy is focused on the activities at hand. We are safe enough for a while, but hurry back."

"We will, dear, and you take care as well." She gave him a hug before she mounted the war eagle behind Zealoc, and they took to the air.

"Ginnea, I think it would be a good idea to bring in Malleesa and her family, what do you say? We need to remove that mountain, and the more people we can get to help, the better."

"I agree, Jesse. I'm sure that Tommy would agree with that plan as well, if he were able." She paused to control her emotions.

"David, do you know what section Malleesa and her family were assigned?" Ginnea asked.

"I believe that they were assigned to the Northeast section. If you head that way, be sure to fly wide-ranging, keeping to the south as you go east, Ginnea, so you don't alert Tazeron's compound or any of the other mobs that might be watching the sky."

"That's good advice," she smiled at him, "and even though we will fly under the mantle of invisibility, I will do as you say."

Ginnea mounted her Fireling, and as the remaining members of the party watched, they shimmered invisible and began their mission. Jesse looked at the camp, and even though he wasn't alone, he felt exposed and vulnerable. It wasn't a feeling that he enjoyed.

"I suggest that we become as small as possible," David said. "No fires, and Sean, please give everyone some potions of invisibility. Jesse, even though you felt like the forces on the mountain were too busy to bother us, I still think that someone out there is watching us. I'm sure they would consider our reduced numbers the perfect chance to cut us further."

As Mr Chambers passed out the potions, there was an odd sound in the surrounding area. Rambo decided to investigate on his own since he didn't need a tonic to become invisible. He was gone only a short time before returning with news of a small group of humans, probably from the mortal world, except they didn't have the fuzzy aura around them.

"That's strange," Cami said, concerned. "Let me go look since I have stealth."

"Rambo and I'll go with you, Cami, just in case you need some crowd control," Jesse volunteered.

Being careful not to step on anything crunchy, they picked their way through the underbrush and found the camp of strangers that Rambo had seen. They silently watched the small group.

"What do you think we should do now, Nebo?" A tall, skinny kid with red hair and tattered clothing said to another skinny kid who was a little shorter than himself.

"I have no idea, Slicer. We probably need to keep moving, or else we'll be discovered. Since we don't have creators anymore, I don't think we would be able to manage. What do you say, 'Booter'?"

Jesse jumped at the name and was startled to see another character, an erudite, sitting off in the shadows. He recognised this person.

"No way, I can't believe this, it's too weird. Stay here, Cami," Jesse said.

"Absolutely not. I'm going wherever you go."

"Suit yourself... I really don't think these guys are a problem. I just need to settle something, even if it's only my own curiosity.

Rambo, it might be a good idea if you stay behind and watch from the trees, just in case something is hiding we can't see. I don't think there will be, but you never know."

Rambo nodded in agreement. Jesse stood up and he and Cami walked into the clearing where the three characters were sitting.

"Hey, guys... what's up?" Jesse said, approaching them.

Jesse had to chuckle as the three jumped and then tripped over their own feet trying to get away.

"Whoa... wait a minute, we're friends. Hey, Booter, it's me, Nophule, what's up dude?"

"Wow... is that really you, Nophule?" The erudite asked Jesse, in a shocked voice.

"Yep, it sure is. What's up, man? I thought you got deleted because your creator wanted to move into a different game or something. At least I never saw you again."

"Yeah, I got dumped because he was bored. A stupid reason really, but what could I do? There used to be lots of us running around, but then this Tazeron boss started taking over and making all the abandoned and deleted toons join his forces. We didn't want to join that loser. Because we were high enough level to start thinking for ourselves, we went into hiding."

"This is so weird," Cami whispered.

"Tell me about it... totally weird," Jesse whispered back.

"Would you guys be interested in joining our party? We're planning a massive raid on the Shimmering Mountain. Our guild is launching the attack."

"No way, dude. That mountain is evil. It's been taken up and overrun by Tazeron's general, Geezlouise — she's pure insanity. How come there are so many of you guys? I don't understand," Nebo said.

"It's okay if you don't want to join us. At least come back to our camp where there is safety in numbers, and we'll explain everything. Sound good to you?"

"Yeah, that sounds cool. We can hang with you guys for a while. I would love to have a good meal. We haven't been able to stop long enough to eat anything except bugs and berries," Booter said.

"Eww... gross," Cami shuddered.

"Hey, you do what you can," Slicer said, giving Cami a big smile.

"We'll see what we can find. How many other deleted or abandoned characters are there in this area?" Jesse asked.

"There used to be lots of us, but most of the others have disappeared. Tazeron has this way of pulling toons to him with the people still attached... it's creepy," Nebo said.

"Hey, that isn't what happened to you guys, is it? Because if it is, I think we'll pass on coming with you," Booter said nervously.

"No, that isn't what happened to us. We'll explain it to you when we get back to our camp," Jesse said.

"Okay, dude, I'll trust you, because you were always a good guy."

Jesse and Cami led the three deleted players back to their camp, picking up Rambo in rooster form on the way.

"Hey, look at this," Slicer said. "Dinner decided to join us."

Rambo hiccupped, and a flicker of flame sparked in their direction."

"Whoa... that chicken just tried to fry me," Slicer said, jumping back.

"No, if he'd wanted to cook you, you wouldn't be standing there talking about it. I suggest you don't mess with the rooster."

Slicer nodded and stepped behind Cami.

Arriving at their camp, Jesse introduced the deleted characters to David and Mr Chambers, who were very interested in their story and how they happened to be wandering around the area. A different view of the situation could be helpful. David tried to explain what was going on in the game, but the players had a difficult time following what was said. Mr Chambers figured it was because they didn't have a healthy brain in their heads. They possibly were running on stored power that was running low.

"So, Nebo, how long did your creator play the game before you were deleted?" Mr Chambers asked.

"I was a level sixty-five shaman when he deleted me, Slicer was an eighty-two magician, and Booter was a seventy-one warlock. All of us were pretty high up, which makes no sense, but what do we know?" He laughed without humour and then looked sad.

"I wonder if characters would be abandoned or deleted if creators knew that as they gave them personalities and intelligence, they would continue on," Jesse asked so only Mr Chambers and Cami could hear.

"They wouldn't think about it, Jesse, because to them they aren't real, they're only part of a game," Mr Chambers answered.

"Maybe after this is settled and we win the war, and this story is out to the mortal world—assuming we do and it is—things will change for them," Cami mused.

"Maybe, but I'm not going to hold my breath," Jesse said.

"Interesting idea, Cami. I, for one, hope to never venture into another game. Nope... give me the quiet, boring life, please," Mr Chambers sighed.

"Bah! Two weeks after we get done with all of this, you'll be going stir-crazy and begging for something to do with your time. Just wait and see. Besides, I think you like being a buff girl," Cami teased.

"Some of that could be true," laughed Mr Chambers as he flexed his female toon's muscles.

Nebo, Slicer, and Booter watched the exchange, trying to follow the flow of the conversation but, after a while, finally gave up and fell asleep.

"What are we going to do with these guys?" Jesse asked. "I feel responsible for them now that we have them here. Especially Booter — he was such a smart kid, just young, only twelve or thirteen, I think. I'm hoping that once we get involved with battle mechanics, they will understand what's going on and can help. Except... none of them is high enough level, nor did they want to go to the mountain. I guess we'll just have to see what happens."

"I think that's the best plan, son," David said. "They have helped us to understand a little better what's going on out there and that Tazeron has a General in control of the mountain. With the name Geezlouise, it must be a mortal sympathiser. That's a good piece of information because now we know that he is still in the centre of the zone. I think our plan needs to be: defeat the mountain and crush Tazeron as soon as possible. Then we can get back to Xanthara and chase the primitive tribes back to their areas and reestablish peace in the world."

"Dad, you and Zeela said that there had been prisoners taken. Nexlucimus mentioned that many of the Council were missing or hiding. What's going on there?"

"Some of the Council just disappeared. We don't know what happened to them, except for a few notes left behind. One or two were for ransom, asking for medical supplies or odd things, like art materials. All the letters were written as if a grade school student had composed them, making us think that the primitive tribes were responsible. Other than those few messages, we didn't see any reasons or demands for their release. It was confusing on many levels."

"So, you don't really know why the city was attacked other than to confuse and distract the leadership?" Jesse asked.

"That's the only reason we can think of," David said. "The scholars did believe that they had the riddle solved, but I never saw what they thought it meant. Maybe Zeela will have more information when she gets back. While we are talking, Jesse, I just wanted you to know how proud I am of you and the way you have stepped up to the plate. This is precisely what you were chosen for. I am sure."

"Thanks, Dad. It helps to be surrounded by trustworthy people, and it means a lot to hear you say that." After a few moments of silence, Jesse curled up next to Rambo, enjoying the warmth radiating from him. It wasn't long before they were both asleep.

Chapter 22

Kidnapped

In the morning, Jesse was surprised to see Slicer, Nebo, and Booter preparing a large rabbit-type animal for breakfast. It smelled delicious, and everyone's stomachs growled in response.

"Where did you get that?" Jesse asked, remembering the hog rat Ginnea caught when they first started. It felt like forever since they had eaten that huge rat. Jesse chuckled, thinking about how awful it had smelled and yet how delicious it was once cooked. That made him think of Gran and their time before the game. Jesse had no idea how long it had been.

"Slicer is an excellent hunter for a mage when there's game about. He just nukes their feet out from under them, and there you go," Nebo laughed.

"Wow, outstanding," Cami praised.

"Thank you, Milady," Slicer blushed.

"Careful, Cami," Jesse whispered in her ear.

"Nonsense, there's nothing wrong with a compliment, especially to a toon."

"Whatever..." Jesse said, watching Slicer, who was looking at Cami.

"That smells delicious, Slicer," Cami complimented again.

Jesse had little warning bells going off in his head, but he decided to keep them to himself since Cami didn't think there was a problem.

"Let's eat," said David. "These rarebits are delicious, and I'm starving."

"Hey, Dad, I just realised that you can eat now. How is that, after so long without being able to?" Jesse asked.

"Excellent, only I do miss pizza."

"What's pizza?" Slicer asked.

The rest of the meal was spent in small talk, wondering when the other troops would be arriving so they could begin their siege of Castle Mountain.

Jesse watched as Slicer offered to show Cami where he caught the rarebit and what herbs he used in cooking. They walked out into the forest. Jesse felt immediately nervous. It helped him to know that Brutus was with her. Nebo and Booter were happily talking with Mr Chambers about spell rotations, and David was sharpening his axe.

After about an hour, Jesse decided that they should have returned by now and started searching for Cami with his mind. After an exhaustive search of the area, he determined that she and Slicer were both gone. He couldn't detect where she was.

"Mr Chambers, Dad, did Cami tell you where she was going with Slicer?"

They both looked up from what they were doing and asked him what he meant.

"Slicer was going to show Cami where he caught the rarebit and the herbs he cooked with. They haven't returned. Do you know where they might be? It's been over an hour."

Everyone was on their feet now, including Nebo and Booter.

"The talisman would warn us if she was in danger," David stated.

"I don't know, Dad. I have searched the area and can find no sign of her or Slicer. Rambo, where is Brutus?"

"I will call him Jesse. I'm not sure where he is."

Rambo searched the area for Brutus and then announced that he had found him about a quarter sector away, tied up and unable to move in his little dog form. Everyone was instantly alarmed. Jesse was feeling intense guilt because he had sensed something wrong but had not acted for fear of upsetting Cami.

"Stupid, stupid, stupid..." Jesse badgered himself.

"Jesse, don't blame yourself," David tried to comfort him. "Cami is a big girl. She can take care of herself. Her judgement was weak this time, but we can hope for the best."

Mr Chambers was worried beyond reason. They decided to take off and search the area where Brutus was tied.

"Nebo and Booter, what do you know about Slicer? Has anything like this happened before that you know of?" David asked.

"We don't really know him that well; he only joined us a few days ago," Booter said. "He did say that his creator really liked the cute girls. He hoped that he could meet one."

Again, warning bells in Jesse's head. He hoped that Slicer's creator was a decent person, but they had no way of knowing. They had to find Cami fast.

After reaching Brutus, Jesse untied him, and Rambo asked what happened. Brutus told Rambo that he had no memory of what happened or where Cami and Slicer had gone. Brutus had been in his small dog form following Cami and Slicer as they tracked another rarebit. He had sensed no danger until he was tangled. He had no memory after that.

Jesse tried searching the area for clues but came up blank. Rambo had the same results, but trying to find someone other than Jesse was tough.

Jesse decided that he and Rambo would take flight and search the area near the mountain alone. The others weren't sure it was a good idea, but he argued them down. Mr Chambers was desperate enough to agree with Jesse's plan. It made sense that they should go alone. Everyone else headed back to camp to wait.

They searched for a long time without success and were about to call it off when Jesse felt something. Deep inside his mind, there was contact with someone. He wasn't sure who; it didn't feel like Cami. He decided to follow the trail this person was putting down, unsure if that was the right course.

"Rambo, what do you suggest we do?"

"I don't really feel the same thing that you are feeling, Jesse. However, when you search this path with your mind, and I tap into your thoughts, I don't feel danger. I suggest we follow it."

The path led them closer to the mountain. In fact, it prompted Jesse and Rambo into the mountain. They both began to feel very uncomfortable about the situation.

Rambo morphed down to his smallest size before the rooster, keeping Jesse's bubble and invisibility spell up. With their smaller size and invisibility, they were able to travel deeper into the zone.

Once they were deep inside the mountain, Jesse was finally able to make solid contact with the voice trying to reach him.

"Who are you?" Jesse asked. *"Do you know my friend Cami? Is she here, and can you help?"*

"My name is Clarisa. I am a friend. I know of Cami; she is safe. She asked me to contact you if you looked for her. You must leave here; you are in danger. She is safe. Do not try to find her now. Go quickly. Go now while you can; she is safe."

"Rambo..." Jesse started to say.

"I know. We are leaving. Hang on, my friend, and trust me."

Rambo morphed into his full battle form, scattering mobs everywhere and reapplying the bubble as Jesse watched for darts of searching. There were blood fairies everywhere, as well as dark elves and pygmy trolls, all of which had ways of attacking a retreating dragon and his high elf passenger.

Jesse, using his mind-searching ability, watched for darts and saw many coming. He transferred what he saw to Rambo, who turned to face them, sending a massive fireball in their direction. Many of the blood fairies and several of the dark elves fell victim to Rambo's fury, along with their weapons of war.

As they broke away from the mountain, Rambo told Jesse to warp them out. Jesse touched the talisman with his mind and sent them to the first place that came to him. Warping was strange; it was like seeing your life flash before you, only backward. Instead of watching yourself grow older from a baby, you saw yourself getting younger. Since Jesse was only sixteen, there wasn't much to relive, but it was still fun. He especially enjoyed the scenes that included Breeze and wondered why he hadn't thought to go where she was.

Why had he thought of Gram's house in the mortal world? There wasn't even any food here, except maybe a can of beans or some tuna—and he wasn't a fan of either. Even though he knew this place, it didn't feel like home anymore. As he walked around the house, it felt foreign, almost uncomfortable. He couldn't imagine living here any longer. His mind drifted to his mum and Bill, reminding him how much he missed them. He imagined warping to them. How bizarre that would be—showing up on their doorstep with a full-sized dragon or even a small one. Heck, a rooster that blew smoke rings would be fun too. He fought the urge to laugh.

"Let's head back, Rambo. Should we get that harness and chain leash that Gram had me use on Brutus? Would it be good to have on hand?"

"I don't think so, Jesse. Brutus can change without the harness. That was just for effect," Rambo chuckled. "It was just to get you in the mood."

"What...! Why, that sneaky old lady. What a fraud. I've got to get her back," Jesse fumed.

Rambo roared with laughter. "Be careful, my friend. I'm sure she has more tricks up her sleeve than you could ever imagine."

"Oh, I'm sure. I never could sneak up on Gram. Let's get going. We need to let Mr Chambers know about Cami. I'm sure he's worried sick."

"Indeed… all aboard."

Jesse settled into place on Rambo's back and touched the talisman with his mind, sending them back to their camp in the game.

Everyone had arrived while Jesse and Rambo were gone. The camp was busy, with all the added recruits making meal preparations and getting bedding laid out and ready for the night. They were all anxious for his report, especially Mr Chambers.

"Welcome back, Jesse and Rambo. Were you able to find any signs of Cami?" Zealoc asked, concerned.

"Yes, we discovered where Cami is, and if our contact is correct, she is safe."

Mr Chambers breathed an enormous sigh of relief. "What contact?" he asked, confused.

Jesse explained, "After flying around, getting closer to the mountain and not finding any signs, we thought about giving up. Then I felt someone trying to reach me. I knew it wasn't Cami. We decided to follow the path and find out who it was. As we went deeper into the mountain, I continued to search for the other mind.

I discovered that it was someone named Clarisa. She said she was a friend, and that Cami was safe. She warned us not to look for her right then. We were to get out while we could." Jesse noticed Mr Chambers' grim expression.

"Mr Chambers, both of us felt that Clarisa was to be trusted and that, for the time being, Cami was safe. We decided to evacuate until we could make positive contact with her."

"What has happened to her?" Mr Chambers asked.

"I don't know, that's all I can tell you. Cami is inside the mountain, but Clarisa repeated three times that she was safe. We had to take Clarisa's advice and get out of there while we could. It was much easier getting into the mountain than out. By then, every mob in the place was aware of us and coming after us.

I'm sorry. I wish there was more I could tell you. All we can do now is trust that Cami will be okay until we can rescue her."

Mr Chambers collapsed to the ground. David and Toolle helped him to his bed.

While this was happening, Zeela arrived back from her trip to the forest just in time to hear Jesse's report. She, like everyone else, was concerned for Cami but felt no need to panic. She gave Sean a potion that would send him into a dreamless sleep.

With Mr Chambers settled, Jesse wanted to hear her news.

Zeela told them all about Jim and Sara's babies.

"They are adorable, little blue bundles of energy," Zeela chuckled. "They made me think of blueberries, crawling all over the place, trying to climb trees already. They are so small. It's amazing to see what they can do. Jim and Sara can hardly believe that they have been so blessed. Nexlucimus is fearful for them, however, and that is why we left Jim there with Sara."

"What's wrong, Zeela? Why would Master Nexlucimus have concerns about the babies?" Pearl asked. They all wanted to know.

"Because of this," Zeela said, pulling a piece of parchment out of her medicine bag.

"This is a more exact translation of the riddle, and it is indeed a worry. As I read this to you, you will notice that it is slightly different from the one Rambo read at the council meeting. Our record keepers located the riddle in an ancient book, and it appears more accurate. Since all of you are aware of this riddle and what solving it means, I will read it to you now and give what we believe is the translation."

Zeela took a seat on a log and read from the parchment as the others gathered around her.

"Dewdrops of the morning; they travel from far but go nowhere.

Like morning dew, the mortals appear but aren't meant to stay. They come from far but go nowhere because it's all virtual—over the internet. Just recently, mortals are in the game world either as captives of Tazeron or as Keepers.

Time is of the essence.

Time will be sped up... look how fast these babies developed and were born, and how quickly they continue to grow even now.

Two worlds are joined to form one blood, take no mercy, and deliver no threat.

Because Jim and Sara were in their game shapes and yet still mortal when the babies were conceived, two worlds were joined to form one blood—the infants. The one blood will be taken without mercy or threat. We don't know yet what this means or how it will happen; we hope to prevent it.

Arches mark the way; blood opens the door.

The Arches in the puzzle are the portals between the worlds. Again, we don't know what this refers to, but we think it refers to the babies' blood. We aren't sure how their blood is needed to open the portals. I know this sounds horrible, but we still aren't sure how this will happen, and of course, we hope it never does.

Use this to see what only ears can hear.

This riddle is solved by reading with eyes, but listening to it will help discover its deeper meaning, as we pay attention to the facts and understand.

Take care to stir swiftly; lest they drown in their own dreams of light faster than sound.

We think this refers to a potion of some kind. There are still many unanswered questions. From the beginning, Tazeron's goal has been to return to the mortal world, to gain control. The fastest way for him to do that is through the Shield. It's instant—more rapid than sound or light—and on the other side of the portal are the dreams he has been drowning in or obsessing over.

Two worlds, one blood, let the key go before you, to guide the way. You will travel far to the world of mortal man in a blink.

Two worlds are the game world and the human world; the one blood is the babies, but we aren't sure how they can be a key or a guide. In a blink, Tazeron and his minions will enter the human world, travelling far.

But beware; the holders of the heir can eat you.

Tazeron is being warned that someone can destroy him.

Open you must to no one give trust, beware their heir will eat you.

Again, Tazeron is warned that someone will destroy him.

To unlock the portal of mortal pain, a riddle must be gained.

This is telling Tazeron that the portal may bring pain by opening the mystery. It's unclear whose pain this is referring to."

After Zeela had presented the interpretation of the riddle, there was silence as each member of the group processed what had been said and what it meant.

"Are the scholars entirely sure of this interpretation, Zeela?" Pearl asked solemnly.

"Indeed, Pearl. Nexi has taken it to the gods and asked for confirmation. Sadly, it was confirmed, although many parts are still a mystery. What we are sure of is that the one blood is the twins, and, in some way, they are needed for Tazeron to pass through the portal."

"I want to know where this riddle came from. Who wrote it, and why does it have to be true?" Jesse asked.

"We aren't sure, Jesse, and it doesn't have to be true. We can still stop Tazeron. We must do our best to keep the babies safe. But he also has this translation, or one similar. He will constantly be looking for a way to get them. He will hunt them their whole life; he is that obsessed. We must guard them while we find a secure way to contain Tazeron. We have no choice."

Chapter 23

Riddles and Recruitments

"We have so many things going on right now; how will we ever be able to solve everything?" David wanted to know, sounding discouraged.

"We will do our best, David," Zeela said. "Helping trapped mortals and finding Cami and the missing Council is important, but protecting the babies is imperative. Stopping Tazeron must be our focus. If we think about it too much, we can quickly feel overwhelmed, and that is a tool in the hands of discouragement."

"We will not fail. We will capture the flag. We are the only ones who can do this," Jesse said with conviction. "We were never told it was going to be easy; in fact, I think we were told how hard it would be. What we must do is have faith in each other and master our ever-expanding quest line."

"Amen, Jesse," Zealoc stated, standing up and helping Pearl to her feet to stretch out their stiffness. They moved to the back of the group.

"Jesse, now that we are all here, why don't you tell us what we are up against? Since you and Rambo explored the area today," Pearl added.

"Before we do that," Jesse said, "I haven't heard anything about Tommy. How is he doing with the elves?"

"It's a very insidious poison, Jesse," Zeela told them. "His vitals and colour are getting better, but he still isn't as responsive as the healers would like. The toxin coats the nerves, so they respond slowly to incoming stimulus. Nexi promised to keep me informed."

"Thanks, Zeela," Jesse said sadly, thinking of his friend desperately ill in a healing facility. Then, shaking his head to clear his thoughts, he continued.

"It's my feeling that our main push should be the castle-mountain, to weed out Tazeron's general. That compound stands in our way. Because the two have been joined, it now covers a large part of the west and southwest segments of the game, within the Shield."

There was a shock of surprise at that revelation.

"I thought of pulling in Keepers who were still in the capital city, but David suggested that because of the militia's need there, that was not possible. This has grown beyond the ability of one group in this area; we need to create a raid. We have gathered information that explains the changing mechanics of the game. Tazeron has a general who is one of the creators. Once we get rid of this general and the other minions, we will be light years closer to getting Tazeron, and that, as Zeela said, must be our focus. What I would like to do now is have each team leader introduce their people, and then we can decide how to organise this raid."

Jesse noticed Zealoc, Gran, his dad and Zeela sitting together in the back; they seemed to be having a separate conversation, looking in his direction and smiling. It made him very nervous.

"Beloe, would you please introduce your people, their classes, and the skills they bring to the table?"

"It will be my pleasure, young sir," said the little man, who looked very much like his cousin Zealoc, with his long-plaited beard and hair.

"Peter, you know from your mortal world, is a skilled magician and a master of potions and herbs. Savana, also from your school group, I understand, is a skilled shaman, experienced in healing, slowing the movement of mobs, and with the help of her pet wolves, she can deal ranged magic of destruction. Jeremy is a mighty warrior and master of distraction; he can redirect anything to anywhere. Shosho, as a fairy and a hunter, is a significant asset to any arsenal with her darts of searching. Leapin, another hunter, has tidy skills in misdirecting and stealth. Sheela is a talented warlock, and together with her conjured friends, she can help with whatever we need."

"Toos is an enchanter. She isn't a magic imbuer as you would think. Her form is very uncommon; not many like her exist in the games, only a handful, which is a real shame. Toos is a shapeshifter, but she can shapeshift others in her party, so we can all look like furniture or bugs. It's a very useful skill, primarily since shapeshifted characters generate no threat, but of course, they can't cause any damage either. Our next addition to the party is Tonic, a bard; he is our crowd control professional. And finally, Wisdom, a wizard of unmatched range and power. That, my young sir, is the proud team that we present to you at this gathering of Keepers."

"Beloe, we are honoured to receive you into our company. We express our gratitude that you accepted our invitation."

"Our pleasure, good sir," the little man bowed and sat down.

"Now, Malleesa, would you be so kind as to introduce your excellent team to us?"

"I am honoured to present our family. While we are not all related, we are still all family, and as we get to know the rest of you, our family will grow," she gave a small bow to the gathering.

"First, my brother Toolle and I are at your service as Rogues. Our other brother, Faber, is a skilled shadow priest, and while he practises some of the healing arts, he is more comfortable walking with stealth and cunning, as are Toolle and I. We are all skilled in traps and poisons and in appearing where the enemy would prefer we stay out. As our race would tell you, we can use the darts of searching," she smiled towards her brothers.

"Excellent," several of the Keepers, including Jesse, whispered.

"Now, I will introduce the rest of our party. Rose is a bard of skill and cunning; she spins songs around foes so tightly, they sleep through any battle and die twice as fast. Pumpkin is a delight—small and agile. This gnome is a necromancer of unique skill in dealing death with death, as he challenges all mobs with his pet skeletons. His bone buddies make a mighty army of their own. Brainanator is also a wizard of incredible skill. As an erudite, his intelligence is the highest of any race. Even imbued items on another player would not raise stats to equal his. Because of this, his mana or magical energy never runs dry, and his spells are always at their peak."

"Clarice is a cleric capable of keeping any party healthy, skilled in herbs and potions. Healamonster is also an exceptional healer; he comes to you as another shadow priest, able to disappear into the folds of his robes and attack the enemy as he heals his party. Dropdead is a mighty warrior, capable of taunting and then hiding to confuse the mobs; he can be either the primary tank or sub-tank. Either way, the crowds won't know what hit them. Rykan is a Paladin, and as you know, a good Paladin can tank and heal, and Rykan is an excellent Paladin. He is also skilled in mining minerals, which is useful for making and repairing weapons. That, my friends, is the outstanding group we offer to your service."

Malleesa bowed and then sat next to her brothers at the end of her presentation.

"Thank you so much for coming. Beloe and Malleesa, we are deeply indebted to the two of you and the amazing people you bring with you to this quest line. I will take just a moment to introduce the members of our group and explain what is going on with us, and why we reached out to you for your help."

Jesse introduced the members of their group, including Rambo and Brutus, and described what they had experienced since entering their assignment. The different groups discovered that their experiences had been similar, which would make it easier to blend them into the raid. Jesse would be the raid leader with several captains.

It was decided that, just like in the game, attacks didn't happen immediately; there was planning involved. And while time was sped up and it felt critical that they get at it, the groups needed to relax and rest. Nothing could be done until the morning anyway. The team leaders and Jesse would each consider their options and formulate a plan, and in the morning they would pull together the final strategy.

So much had happened to them, and yet it felt like yesterday that they launched into the game. Jesse tried to remember how long they had been in the game, but he couldn't. Time moves differently here. Others talked about how fast time seemed to be moving. They worried that they weren't accomplishing enough to stop Tazeron or protect the Shield.

David reminded them that since the arrival of the Keepers, all mobs that they killed stayed dead. They didn't respawn unless, of course, they were mortal sympathisers.

Thinking of that fact, Jesse wondered about Tazeron's general, who they were sure was a mortal. "How was that going to affect the battle?" It was something they would deal with when they faced her.

After the group broke up, Jesse walked outside the camp and enjoyed sitting by himself as he ate dinner. It was a delicious stew of some kind. Someone had made bread, which was a pleasant treat. It was nice to be alone and allow his thoughts to trail over the events of the day. He watched Rambo wander off into the forest to forage for bugs.

"It must be nice to be a rooster; dinner is always close."

"Yep, but it's a good thing roosters don't have taste buds. Some of the bugs here are nasty-looking things that puke slime or other foul stuff as you try to eat them. I wouldn't want to taste that. They do fill the stomach, however." Rambo chuckled as Jesse gagged at the thought.

"Thanks for the visual, Rambo."

"No problem, bro. Hope you enjoy your stew," Rambo laughed as he walked into the forest.

Enjoying this quiet time, Jesse mused over the current events and once again puzzled over the way time seemed to be so different here. He marvelled at the fact that three babies had been conceived, developed, and born. Breeze was one of them, and the other two were in mortal danger. How sad that they would never live a normal childhood. Jim and Sara's babies would never know their parents' world.

Jesse felt different thinking about all of this. He felt older and confused about what was real and what was game. Mortal life seemed surreal and far away; even his and Rambo's brief trip back to Gran's house felt strange. Jesse wondered if he would recognise normal when he saw it again—if he did. Maybe this was normal. Perhaps his life before this was a dream, make-believe, fantasy.

His head and heart ached. He wondered what his mum and Bill were doing—probably touring Europe. What was wrong with him? With all these people here, he felt... lonely.

"Jesse, I am coming."

"Breeze...? Where are you? When will you be here?"

He felt instantly alert, happy, scared, nervous, confused, but primarily excited.

"I will be there within the next hour. We will talk then. I'm sure that I can help in this most important battle."

Jesse felt unsure about this meeting with Breeze. He decided to talk to Zeela, since he figured Gran was a bit twitterpated. Jesse wasn't sure what his dad would think. He stood and walked back through the camp. So many people here, and all because he called for them. It was fun to watch them interact as they renewed friendships and caught up on what had been happening in different areas. The reality of what was coming felt overwhelming, and he thought back to when just the idea of the game being 'real' made him nervous.

What would he have done back then if he'd known what he was about to oversee now? Maybe Germany wouldn't have seemed like such a bad idea. No, this is where he needed to be. This was what he wanted to do: to be of service to the world. Sure, the responsibility was daunting, and he would probably make mistakes, but he felt the burning desire to complete the quest. Thank the gods that he had such an amazing group of people to help him.

Thinking about all of this, Jesse saw Zeela sitting alone a little way from the camp. He stood and approached her.

"Zeela, I'm sorry to bother your solitude, but I was wondering if I could talk with you."

"Of course, Jesse, please sit down. Is everything okay? Is there a problem?"

Jesse wasn't sure how to answer those questions—that's why he needed to talk to her.

"Zeela, Breeze is coming. She seems to think that there is something between us. Sometimes I like the idea, but other times, it makes me nervous. I'm just not sure."

"Oh, I see." Zeela paused, looking down at her hands, thinking. "Jesse, people develop relationships at their own pace. Mortals tend to need more time, which seems odd to me because they have the least amount of time of all the beings. Breeze is different because she attached to you while still a Shadow Dream. I would suggest that you wait until you get to know each other. Have a friendship first. Breeze will be receptive to that idea. I'm sure. If she isn't, let me talk to her; I'm sure it will be okay. In the meantime, let's concentrate on our quest line. Don't worry about things of the heart right now."

After his talk with Zeela, Jesse felt slightly less nervous at the thought of meeting Breeze in person for the first time, but with all that was happening with the quest, he felt Zeela's advice was what he needed to hear right now. They would concentrate on what was important now and worry about a relationship when Tazeron and his minions were taken care of.

He excused himself from Zeela, thanking her, and walked out into the forest to find Rambo. He didn't get very far when Rambo approached him.

"Jesse, come with me."

Curious, Jesse followed Rambo, the rooster, deeper into the forest.

"Stop here and search the area with your mind. Tell me what you find."

"What's this all about, Rambo?"

"Just do as I ask—trust me."

Jesse sat down on the forest floor and sent his mind into the area, searching. He saw animals, small and large; he saw various plants, trees, flowers, bugs, spiders, snakes—and large holes in the ground, too big for anything but an enormous animal. Curious, Jesse explored closer. He was surprised to see some of the holes had doors, camouflaged to look like parts of trees or rocks.

"Holes in the ground with doors—is that what you're talking about?"

"Yes," Rambo said, sounding excited. "Go inside and see what made them."

"You are so weird," Jesse smiled at Rambo.

Jesse sent his mind into one of the tunnels and was shocked to find a large room with many mortals, complete with fuzzy auras.

"Wow, that's incredible. I wonder what the mortals are doing there."

"Go back and listen to them," Rambo said, sounding impatient.

Once again, Jesse travelled back to the holes. This time, he tucked himself into a corner and listened to their conversation.

What he and Rambo had discovered was a group of game players hiding from Tazeron. These players had decided to stay hidden and help anyone else captured by the game bug. Some of them had read about the virus and set out to activate it. Now they were searching for a way to get back to their world, along with the kids they had rescued.

"Wow, Rambo, let's go back to camp and tell the rest. I'm sure we could use the help of these gamers to continue searching for trapped mortals. That would really lighten our load."

"Indeed, those were my thoughts exactly."

Entering the camp, Jesse and Rambo made an announcement, telling everyone about the mortals they had found. David and Toolle decided to go back into the forest. They would contact the gamers and bring back the leaders to discuss a plan of action.

After a while, David and Toolle returned with about six others. A meeting was called. The leaders introduced themselves, amazed at the size of the gathering.

"How many of you are there, that you know of?" Toolle asked.

One of the leaders told them there were twenty-five in their group, but that there were twenty-six other teams they knew of—maybe more. Some of the circles had as few as three people, and others as many as seventeen. Their assembly was the largest. The bands were scattered throughout the game world, contained by the Shield.

The Keepers were surprised by the number of mortals captured by the game and sucked into this world. They were told there were hundreds more. That was a shock to them. The gamers were just as surprised to learn of Xanthara and the mission of the Keepers. They had heard rumours, but this was the first contact they knew of.

"If a player is drawn into the game, they can return through the same portal they created within a couple of Earth hours," the leader of the gamers said. "But if they don't, the portal disappears. If we can find them before then, we can help them. This is our only purpose. We were mainly interested in helping the younger kids."

"We commend your efforts. It's an honourable thing that you're doing," David said.

Except for the part about other gamers trying to help kids and the numbers involved, this was information the Keepers already knew. Because of everything else going on, the mortals hadn't been as much of a priority as they should've been. The guards still patrolled the Shield, but with the problems back on Xanthara and the increased need, more and more Shield guards were being called back to the city.

"Do you think we could get these return groups warp stones from Nexlucimus? Then they could transport snatched gamers back to their own world," Jesse asked.

"We might be able to arrange something like that," Zeela said, "but we'd need to be careful and make sure the stones weren't misused. We still need to guard against Tazeron and his followers gaining access."

After the meeting, the return group left the camp and headed back into the forest. At David's suggestion, they took the two deleted toons, Nebo and Booter. They promised to find a place where they and others like them could hide and wait out the war.

"That was a fantastic find, Rambo—and Jesse," Zealoc said.

"That will lighten our load," Beloe noted.

With so many people around them, there was a smaller chance of being attacked at night. The atmosphere was more relaxed; there were games and music and laughter. That was good to hear. There was even dancing, as the different people got to know each other. It was a fun time, but Jesse craved solitude, and Rambo came with him to the edge of camp to enjoy the night sky. It was beautiful.

As they sat there, listening to the sounds of music and laughter, a soft voice came to Jesse's mind.

"Jesse, I am almost to the camp. When I arrive, could we fly to a quiet place?"

Jesse was surprised at the request and asked Rambo what he thought.

"I see no problem with that, Jesse. We will let Zealoc know."

"I'm not afraid to admit that I'm very nervous about this meeting, Rambo."

Rambo smiled at his friend. *"No doubt, Jesse. No doubt."*

Chapter 24

Trip to Clay

Jesse let Zealoc, Gran, Zeela and his dad know that Breeze had contacted him and requested some alone time. They would be flying out on Rambo, and he had no idea how long they would be gone. Jesse hoped it wouldn't be too long. Zeela took him aside and asked if this was what he wanted to do, and—surprising even himself—he felt comfortable.

Rambo prepared to take off as soon as Breeze arrived. The two of them sat waiting for her at the edge of the forest, just out of sight of the camp. After a few moments, Jesse saw a soft glimmer in the distance. It slowly grew, filling the air around them with light. Gazing into the centre of the light as it landed near him, Jesse was amazed to see a beautiful girl, about the same size as Zeela. She stepped out of the glowing bubble of light and smiled widely at him and Rambo. He was stunned by how lovely she was—and how mature she appeared.

"Breeze...?" Jesse asked lamely. Who else could it be?

"Yes," she said, giggling softly as she stretched out her arms and beckoned him to come to her.

He had absolutely no problem stepping toward her and hugging this stranger—this fairy creature, this mystery of his dreams.

"Wow... I can't believe I'm finally meeting you. I feel like you've been a part of my life forever, and now you're really here."

"It has been forever, Jesse. I've been waiting for you... forever."

He studied her lovely pale green face with its softly pointed features, framed by golden hair that flowed down her back to her waist. How could someone—even of fairy kind—develop so quickly? There were many questions. He hoped she would be able to answer them.

"I know we have much to discuss, Jesse," she murmured, as her delicate hand came to his face and traced his cheek, creating so many feelings—so many uncertainties.

She continued talking, pulling him from the trance she had spun around him.

"There is much to learn about each other. But before we can do that properly, this war with Tazeron must end. The safety of the mortal world must come before our own lives."

This was true. There was much to building a friendship, but the quest line was a priority—even if he now wished they could fly off on Rambo and never return.

"Jesse, I know in my heart that I've always loved you, and that will never change. I also know that you're not so sure."

He was starting to wonder what he felt. *"Slow down... breathe,"* he told himself.

"We will have time, Jesse. But the quest line must be completed before any of us can continue with our personal lives."

How could she be this age... *his* age? He was having a hard time thinking of her as anyone different than what she appeared to be now. Perhaps that was all he needed to do.

"Breeze, I'm having a hard time understanding how one moment you're a Shadow Dream and then, the next, you're here—a mature girl, whom I just hugged. How is that possible?"

She smiled at him as though hiding some great secret. He hoped that she was—and that very soon, he would learn what it was. He wanted her to have the answers. He wanted her to solve the mystery—to make it real.

"Come, Jesse. Let's go for a ride on Rambo. I'll explain it all—in a place where it'll make more sense to you."

Rambo helped them get seated comfortably on his back. Breeze sat in front of Jesse, and leaning forward, she whispered a few words into Rambo's ear that Jesse couldn't understand. Rambo sucked in a surprised gasp of air at her words, but he nodded in acknowledgement before launching into the night sky.

Rambo placed a bubble around them as they flew deep into the outer atmosphere. It was as beautiful to Jesse as it had been that first time, flying to Xanthara, so long ago. He had experienced so many memories and adventures since coming to the worlds of Xanthara and the games.

Spending time with Breeze as they travelled didn't feel awkward like Jesse had thought it might. Breeze turned to face him, her legs crossed in front of her. Jesse created a tiny globe of light that hung in the space beside them. They couldn't see the stars anymore, but at least they could see each other.

They chatted like old friends—comfortable with one another. Perhaps it was because they had been linked through thought while she had been his Shadow Dream. Whatever the reason, Jesse was happy there were no walls of apprehension between them. Breeze didn't want to talk about where they were going—or why—but she seemed happy to answer all his other questions.

She appeared to know all about Jesse, but he felt like he didn't know her at all. He asked her about her family and how she had become a Shadow Dream. He learned that she had been chosen by the gods for that assignment, based on her abilities as an essence to absorb and retain information.

During their visit, he discovered she had many siblings. In fact, she had a younger brother now. That was just crazy—impossible by any other known standard. She told him that the capital was under siege; many people had fled to the Forest of the Elves. That was why so many children had grown to maturity at an alarming rate—mostly boys.

Histories had contained stories of these times, but this was the first advent in several millennia that anyone could remember. Many of the citizens wondered what it meant for the safety of their people. As they talked, he learned that her family had remained in the city—and that worried her.

The thought of the central city being brought to this point of conflict left Jesse torn between wanting to go there and help, or completing their quest line. He knew, of course, that they would finish their first assignment—the quest. Nothing was more important. Everything would return to normal after they destroyed Tazeron. Jesse just hoped it wouldn't take much longer. Wars typically didn't go away fast—but he could hope.

After talking for an extended period, they lapsed into silence, drifting into their own thoughts. Breeze turned to face forward, and Jesse extinguished the tiny globe of light. He was puzzled over his feelings for this beautiful creature who sat so close, leaning back against his chest. She stirred emotions Jesse had never felt before. There were so many questions. He hoped this strange trip would answer all his troublings. He wondered why she didn't want to talk about where they were going—or why.

"How are you doing out there Rambo?"

"I'm just enjoying the scenery. Everything okay in there?"

"Oh yeah, it's just great! She doesn't want to tell me where we're going. Can you?"

"Nope, I've got my orders."

"Great, I've been kidnapped, and my best friend is the taxi."

"Sorry."

"Yeah, yeah, I see how you are."

They flew for a long time, and Jesse resisted asking if they were almost there. Where were they going? It was all so peculiar. As he stared out into the vast expanse, Jesse noticed a dark spot, void of any stars—and it seemed to be growing.

"We are almost there, Jesse," Breeze said, startling him from his thoughts.

Rambo banked to the right, and as he did, they seemed to be circling a giant sphere, like Earth—only different. It had appeared as a dark spot at first because they were in its shadow, like an eclipse. Now that they were skirting its outer edge, the light from its sun made vision possible. The sphere did appear to be a new world.

"Why would we come here, Breeze?"

"Wait. You'll understand."

As Rambo entered the atmosphere of the world, it grew bigger and bigger, now filling his entire vision.

"What is this place?" Jesse asked.

"This is a new mortal world that was created, Jesse. It is just now ready for human habitation. The mortal gods haven't placed their young ones on it yet, but I was given permission to show you this—and something else."

"Something else?"

"Yes."

"Rambo, take us to Clay," Breeze said.

"Clay...?" Jesse questioned.

"Clay is a new world of fantasy, Jesse, created for the people chosen for the splitting from Xanthara and one other world, Moerlen. They will now help the mortals that will inhabit this new world the mortal gods have created."

"Wow, I remember hearing about how this happened from Nexlucimus," Jesse whispered softly. "But seeing it is amazing."

Rambo climbed higher and higher, breaking through the atmosphere and heading directly into the sun of this new world. Jesse watched in amazement as another world suddenly appeared—out of nowhere. It looked familiar to him.

As they approached the planet, Rambo slowed and then dove toward the surface. The bubble kept Breeze and Jesse from feeling any wind as it rushed past them. Jesse could tell that they were moving at high speed. Rambo's scales began to glow. Jesse wondered if they looked like a comet to the people of this new world of fantasy.

Once they glided close enough to see the surface, Jesse noticed that it was without buildings, and yet many people moved around. Rambo flew closer until they could land and then removed the bubble that had encased them, helping them off his back. Jesse heard the familiar rumble in the distance. He turned quickly to look at Breeze. He was surprised to see her with her arms outstretched, eyes closed, and a smile on her face.

"Welcome to Clay, Jesse," she giggled.

He barely had time to wonder about this when they were all over him. Skeedlers—everywhere! Breeze had disappeared beneath her own covering, and he could hear her intermittently laughing and gagging.

"Strange girl," Jesse said to himself, smiling, as he too was covered with the fuzzy critters.

For the first time, Jesse noticed that Rambo was also receiving a thorough cleaning from the little scouring professionals. Rambo's scales, darkened by their entry, were starting to shine brightly in the crystal-clear air; his crown of spikes glistened like diamonds.

After a few minutes, the Skeedlers were done and had disappeared into the distance. People started gathering around the travellers, welcoming them to their city. Jesse wondered what they meant when they said 'city', because there wasn't any city that he could see—not so much as a teepee.

Breeze thanked them and asked where the council room was. A tiny lavender lady, even smaller than Breeze, volunteered to show them. She seemed familiar to Jesse—mainly as he watched her and Breeze flutter side by side ahead of him with their dragonfly wings. Jesse rode a reduced Rambo.

After a period, they arrived at the council room, which was nothing more than a clearing in a field. The little woman excused herself and left them. Several men and women were sorting out what looked like building supplies.

As Jesse and Breeze moved toward them, a jolly, plump little man with a long blond beard and hair broke away from the group and approached them.

"Ah, Breeze, welcome to our city."

Jesse was surprised as the round little man gathered her into a big bear hug. He didn't know why, but having that man hug Breeze bothered him.

"Who is this handsome sir, and this magnificent dragon that accompanies you?" He gave a small bow to them, making him look like an inflated ball with legs.

"Good day, Master Osuweep. This is my friend Jesse, and this is Rambo."

"Indeed, amazing! I am honoured to make your acquaintance, Sir Rambo. I have heard many truly remarkable accountings of you."

Rambo nodded to the little man.

"And young Jesse, it is a pleasure." The friendly little man shook Jesse's hand.

"Pleased to meet you, Master Osuweep," Jesse said, weakly.

"Breeze, it is delightful to finally meet you in person, dear."

"The pleasure is mine, Osuweep. Jesse, this man is the Nexlucimus of this world. He will manage the organisation and building of this city."

"We have known each other for a very long time—although this is the first time we have met in person. I was his Shadow Dream, two millennia ago, and he was my Finding."

Jesse just stared at her, and then at the man.

"Her Finding... two millennia ago?"

"He and two thousand others have been my charges. Most were mortals—some, like Master Osuweep, have been immortals. All of them have been from different worlds."

"What!"

Jesse was stunned, and he was glad that Gran had taught him how to keep his mouth closed.

"Breeze, my dear. It has indeed been a delight to see you and your friends. I was so excited when you sent me the message. I wish I had more time to visit and get to know you all better."

"I must, however, leave you now and tend to my duties. We have much to build and prepare before the young ones come to the mortal world below us."

"Master Jesse and Sir Rambo, it has been my pleasure to meet you. Please excuse me now."

"Of course, Osuweep. Thank you for meeting with us. We can see that you're busy. It was wonderful to see you in person, and to learn that you have turned out so well," Breeze giggled.

Chuckling, Osuweep returned to the field, waving farewell to them as he walked away.

As Jesse watched Breeze say goodbye to the man, the shock of what she had just revealed to him began to settle and slowly wear off. Irritation started to fill him.

"Breeze, did you bring me here so that I could be impressed with how old you really are? Or did you bring me here so that I could feel small and insignificant in your presence?"

"Careful, Jesse..." Rambo whispered into his thoughts.

"Butt out, Rambo."

"As you wish, my friend... but don't say I didn't warn you."

Rambo wandered off and morphed into a rooster, pecking around for bugs.

Breeze studied Jesse, who was glaring at her, for a long moment before answering. He began fidgeting under her scrutiny.

"Jesse, you asked me how old I was. How would you answer that question now that you better understand who I am—and what I was?"

She let him think about that for a moment. He had no answer.

"I brought you here so that you could understand how important I felt you were. In the eternal view of things, I have always been. Age and time have no meaning to me. When your mortal body dies, and you are reborn again into your immortal shape, age and time will have no association with you either."

"I love you, Jesse. After all my travels, through all my experiences, you are the one that I have grown to care for in this way. You are that important to me. You are the reason I petitioned the gods for a body at this time. Never has there been someone I would like to share my life with.'

"If you decide you don't want me," she choked, "if you decide you don't want me, then I will serve the gods forever, alone."

"I thought that if I brought you here, to where a new world was getting started, perhaps you would understand that time, and age, and existence are all wrapped up into one eternal round—with no beginning and no end."

"It doesn't matter how long it took me to be conceived into this body and then be born, because I have always existed in one form or another. And so have you. You just can't remember."

"It's essential for you to lose your tunnel vision, Jesse, for you to see the future. It's all about who we are, and how we live. We must remember that. We can't concentrate on time and age, or who has had what experience. We must focus on the abilities we have been given by the gods, and how important those talents are for us in the whole scheme of life, until it is completed."

"There is much distraction around us, which can interfere with staying on course. Defeating Tazeron is our challenge now—but if we didn't have that problem, life would throw other things at us. It's all part of the experience, the growth, and the development of who we are, as we strive to reach our goal of accomplishing our life with integrity."

"We must return to our gods with honour. It should be our highest quest, no matter the challenges we meet. We are all here to help each other. We can do this, Jesse. You must believe that—no matter what our perceived ages are."

"I know you don't want my interference, but listen to her, Jesse. She speaks wisdom," Rambo's soft voice echoed in Jesse's mind.

Jesse stood silent, amazed and humbled, as Breeze finished talking.

She watched him, a tear leaking down her perfect face. Perhaps she was afraid she had said too much.

"Breeze..." Jesse wasn't sure what he wanted to say.

She took his hands. "Jesse, I didn't have much time with my mother, and she would probably be horrified with me right now. Even as a Shadow Dream, I was headstrong and audacious. I do not mean to offend. I only wanted to help you see how important all of this is.

"I have never been good at hiding my feelings, and I don't want to lose you on details. I was only trying to open your mind. Forgive me if I have upset you."

Jesse was amazed that, of all the people she had influenced down through time, he was the one she chose to be with. Him—Jesse Finch, small-town boy, hard-headed and slow to learn. How many lessons did it take for him to capture the whole vision?

He hoped this was the last one. The final exam.

Once again, he was being shown his path—blessed by a dragon, challenged by a demon, gifted by the White Dragon, and now loved by a fairy.

There was no reason why they wouldn't succeed.

Surprising even himself, he reached for Breeze and embraced her. Then, meeting her eyes as she looked up at him, he kissed her. It just seemed like the right thing to do.

It sure felt good.

"I'm not offended, Breeze. I'm just slow to recognise a good thing when it crosses my path. Thank you for not giving up on me. I think I understand now why you brought me here. And honestly, I don't think any amount of talking would've opened my eyes like coming here has. We will succeed—and when we do, we'll continue this, perhaps right here."

"Indeed we will, Jesse. Indeed we will..." she whispered, and then she kissed him again.

Chapter 25

Storming the Castle

"Ahem..." Rambo cleared his throat. "Now that that's all settled, I want to introduce you to a few people before we head back."

Rambo led them through the city that was being built. Holding hands, Jesse and Breeze followed him, wondering where he was headed. Arriving at a small gathering of vendors, Jesse and Breeze acquired some food before continuing after Rambo a little farther.

Jesse noticed Rambo stopping by the little woman who had led them to the council room earlier. She looked familiar, and Jesse wondered why. Now, perhaps, he would find out.

"Jesse, Breeze," Rambo said, morphing back into his smaller dragon form, "allow me to introduce you to Amber. She is Zeela's mother."

"I am honoured, Milady," Jesse said with a smile and a bow. He understood now why she looked familiar. Breeze also smiled as she curtsied.

"I am indebted to your daughter," Jesse continued. "Zeela is a real friend, and teacher, to me."

"The pleasure is mine. It is an honour to meet you two. I know that there are many challenges left on Xanthara. My daughter and her husband are capable people. It would have been a treasure to have them here at this splitting, but their course is different. What they, and the Keepers, do will affect us all. We pray for you."

Jesse was once again struck by the importance of the quest.

Rambo then introduced them to Zeela's father, Patonious—a friendly little man with bright blue hair and freckles on his light tan skin and wings. A few others, friends of Rambo, were eager to make their acquaintance and show them the work being done. It was fun to meet so many and to see the beginning of this new world as they laid it out and started construction.

Rambo explained that no magic would be used in the creation of the city. The buildings needed to be constructed slowly and precisely. Building it by hand gave it more importance. It allowed the people to feel ownership—more than magic ever could. He explained that more than just buildings were being constructed here.

While they were there, a refreshing began, and bubble shelters appeared to keep them dry. The storm was impressive, and having an unobstructed view was breathtaking. Rambo took a nap in his own little rooster-sized shelter. It even had a straw floor and a perch. Jesse and Breeze sat on a conjured, overstuffed couch in theirs.

"This is unbelievable, Breeze. Thank you for bringing me here—not just to open my eyes, but to be a part of this with you."

"Perhaps someday, we could be a part of our own splitting, Jesse."

"Is that possible?" Jesse said, astounded at the thought.

"If the gods wish it, anything is possible."

"I suppose I'm still trying to wrap my head around the fact that all things are possible—if the gods wish it. I don't understand how they could allow Tazeron and his followers to do what they are doing. I know it's a test. I understand that. I guess I just prefer it when things are easy."

"We really wouldn't prove anything if it were easy, Jesse," Breeze said with a yawn. "I think I'm going to take a little nap before we head back."

She kissed him on the cheek, then curled up on the couch with her head on his leg and fell asleep.

Jesse absently stroked Breeze's hair as he sat there watching the refreshing create small rivulets around them. He could barely see the other bubbles as he stared out into the surroundings. It would be fun to come back here in a year or two and see what the city looked like as it developed.

To think that right below them, another mortal world was just getting started—it was incredible and exciting to consider. If there were more time, Jesse would ask Breeze and Rambo to give him a tour, but they needed to get back to camp. They needed to rest before the assault on the castle-mountain. Perhaps he should take a nap too.

After the rain stopped and Breeze stretched awake, Jesse spoke to Rambo's mind.

"Rambo, we need to get back to camp. As soon as we're seated, I'll warp us back."

"Whenever you're ready, Jesse. It'll be faster that way, and now that you've been here and have the flight path, you'll be able to come back anytime, using the talisman."

"Awesome. I'd like to come back sometime. I was just thinking about that."

"I know."

"I keep forgetting that our minds are connected. I sincerely hope I don't think about anything too embarrassing."

"I'll just slap you if that happens."

"I hope so, my friend. And Rambo... thanks for slapping me earlier. I'm thick-headed, I guess."

"Happy to be of service... again," Rambo chuckled.

Jesse smiled as he and Breeze settled onto Rambo's back, and they warped to camp.

Once they arrived back, Jesse helped Breeze get settled after introducing her to everyone. The teams were just starting to settle down for the night, so their arrival was perfectly timed. Jesse excused himself from Breeze as she went to bed in the shelter shared with Ginnea. He headed over to the group that included Gran, Zealoc, his dad, and Zeela. He had much to tell them.

"I wanted you to know that Breeze had Rambo take us to the new world of Clay," Jesse explained to them.

Zeela was surprised, and as Jesse explained what had happened, she was excited to hear they had met her parents.

"It's very unusual for people to be allowed to travel between worlds, Jesse, but I understand why Breeze wanted to do it."

"It was a very effective way to open my eyes to the entire situation. I don't think any amount of talking would've gotten through this thick head of mine. Zeela, I am fortunate to have her. I know that more surely than I've ever felt anything in my whole life."

David, Pearl, and Zealoc sat listening quietly.

"You know, war does strange things to people, Jesse," his father said. "It grows them up faster, fleshing them out in ways never thought of. You and Breeze are starting a relationship under adverse conditions. Get to know her before you make any promises—that's my advice."

"I would agree with your father on this one, dear," Gran added, concern in her voice.

"I haven't made any promises, but I did kiss her. I know that emotions during war can be challenging, but I just wanted you to know that my feelings are strong. And unless something highly unusual happens, they will not change. Even though I've been unsettled and scattered in my thoughts in the past, I feel like I've changed a lot in the last little while. I understand the whole scope of life better."

"We hope so, Jesse, because there are many hard times yet to come. We have watched you mature, and we have faith in you," Zealoc said.

"We are all impressed with how you've stepped up to the battle plate, son. Go get some sleep—you'll need to be fresh in the morning," David added.

Jesse felt them watching as he walked over to where Rambo was waiting. As he and Rambo settled in for the night, Jesse had a couple of pressing questions for his friend.

"What do you think about all this, Rambo? Do you think I'm being impulsive with Breeze? She is beautiful."

"I don't know about impulsive, but I would agree with your family—give it some time before committing. Breeze is a brilliant person, and as a fairy-kind, she isn't impetuous. When she commits, it will be forever. I see great things ahead for you both—after Tazeron, of course."

"Now sleep, my friend. Tomorrow will come fast."

***

Rambo was right—morning came quickly. People were stirring in the camp, cooking meals, packing gear, and visiting with each other as Jesse climbed out of his bedroll.

"Welcome to the waking world, sleepyhead," Breeze smiled at him as he straightened his robes.

"Good morning to you too," he said, kissing her. "You're looking all cheery this morning."

"Jesse, get over here. We need your input," Zealoc called to him, causing Breeze to jump.

"He can be a bit pushy sometimes—come with me," Jesse smiled at her.

"Pushy, am I...?" Zealoc laughed.

"Just kidding, oh noble one..." Jesse bowed.

"Humph..." Zealoc snorted. "Whippersnappers."

"Geezers," Jesse retorted, smiling as he and Breeze sat down where the team leaders were gathered around David and Zealoc. Rambo and Brutus were also there.

"Jesse, I was wondering about something. What if we cleared out the castle before the mountain? Could we keep the two of them separated? Didn't you say that while it looked like they were preparing for something big in the castle, there really weren't that many people there?" Zealoc asked.

"That's true. I don't know, Zealoc—it might work. We could also try coming in from three different directions. It might stir up a hornet's nest, though, with the mountain people joining forces, but that's kind of what we wanted with this raid anyway. How's Mr Chambers doing today, by the way?"

"He's much better. In fact, he's eager to get started," Zeela told Jesse.

"Excellent, I'm glad to hear that. Whatever we decide to do, Zealoc, I vote we get started. It isn't going to get any easier. With so many things going on, we need to get to Tazeron before he moves out of our reach. And taking out his general will deal him a serious setback," Jesse said.

They all agreed and quickly worked out the battle plan details, with the three groups coming in from different directions. Zeela would ride Brutus into battle—even though she could fly herself—because they wanted Brutus accessible in case they found Cami and she needed to fly out.

Zeela handed out invisibility potions to the mages and other magic casters. The warriors, hunters, and rogues all had stealth and didn't need them.

The bards would float songs that would calm and confuse the mobs and give spell haste and stamina to the team members. Poisons and traps were loaded by the rogues and hunters. Ranged weapons and spells were prepared. Healers packed their fish-head and sushi roll snacks for increased mana. The wizards had their escape spells poised, and the enchanter was ready to turn everyone into poufs and end tables—complete with flower arrangements and doilies—as needed... or into bugs. They were prepared.

Zealoc gave his battle shout, and they all lifted into the air. Jesse wouldn't be using his spell this time, so only the castle would be visible to them. Jesse noticed the determined look on Mr Chambers' face and hoped he would be able to focus on the battle.

As they approached the castle, they came under enemy fire—darts and arrows leading the way. Rambo handled them quickly, sending them back as fiery missiles. The hunters targeted the blood fairies with their traps and snares, as the rogues and warriors began taking the offensive on the ground. Ranged spells were sent to disrupt any healers and mob casters, while misdirect and disruption were aimed at pets and companions. Healers had no trouble keeping everyone healthy.

Jesse was impressed at how well the teams worked together as they sliced through the castle's defences. It was almost too easy.

Zeela approached him and asked if he would join her on a trip into the castle to search for Cami. He was fine with that but suggested perhaps he should search for Clarisa first. She agreed. He backed away from the battle with Rambo so he could concentrate better.

Jesse found it easy to drift down corridors and into rooms—there weren't that many people. The deeper he went, the surer he became that Cami and Clarisa weren't in the castle. There was a healing facility and a jail, but both were empty. He reported his findings to Zeela.

"I wonder if we should go into the mountain," she asked.

"Let me talk to the team leaders. If I send out a true sight spell, the mountain will become visible to everyone."

Jesse sent a message to Breeze, asking her to have all the team leaders meet him just outside the castle. The battle was almost over anyway, and the remaining mobs could be taken down quickly without much effort.

"Strange," Jesse said to Rambo. *"That was too easy."*

"Indeed."

After a few moments, not only the team leaders but the entire assault team met him outside the castle.

"That was way easier than I thought it would be," Jesse told the assembly. "I'm pleased, but also kind of disappointed. Any thoughts on why we cleared the place so fast? I really thought there would be more resistance."

"Nah... we're just uber," one of the wizards said. Jesse remembered his name—Brainanator.

Jesse presented his and Zeela's thoughts about sending out the improved sight spell and bringing the mountain into view. The assembly agreed that, since the castle had gone down so quickly, they might as well give it a try.

Rambo and Jesse flew closer to the castle and launched the spell. To their surprise, the mountain wasn't there. It was gone.

"That would explain why the castle went down so fast. There was only a skeleton crew to confuse us. Now we've wasted valuable time," David complained, slamming his hand down on the horn of his saddle.

Jesse told them he would comb the area with his mind. Breeze said she could also search the area, cutting down the time considerably. During the break, some of the younger members held a duelling contest; others hunted for herbs and meat.

Jesse and Breeze explored for a while without success. The group decided to move forward, hoping the mountain would resurface.

Mr Chambers was distracted, worrying about Cami. Jesse was very concerned and decided to try Clarisa. Reaching out to her as they flew towards Tazeron's last known location proved to be a good idea. About halfway between the two places, Jesse contacted her.

"Jesse, Cami is still well and comfortable. Do not try to find her now. This is important, Jesse—listen to me. Trust me on this."

Shocked, Jesse asked, *"Why... Why should I trust you on this? Why are you telling us not to come for Cami? What's going on in there? What's happened to her?"*

There was a moment of silence, frustrating Jesse even more. What was going on?

"Jesse, Cami was damaged during her capture. Her body is safe now, but her mind is... missing."

Jesse was so shocked at this news that he yelled at Rambo to stop flying, while he gathered his thoughts.

"What do you mean... her mind is missing?"

"Shortly after we got her, and she asked me to find you, she became... unresponsive. Nothing we do brings her awake. She is missing."

It sounded so odd—like she was in a coma or something. Jesse had to talk to Zeela and the rest. Clarisa now seemed almost childlike to him. The more he spoke to her and thought about it, the more convinced he became... but he couldn't be sure.

Because he and Rambo had stopped in their flight, the others gathered around him.

"What's going on, Jesse?" David asked, concerned.

He told them what Clarisa had said, and as he feared, Mr Chambers became highly agitated by the news.

"We must find her and get her out of there. We can't just sit by while some child takes care of her. I can't lose her. She's all that I have."

Mr Chambers acted as if he were going to charge the mountain by himself, but Zealoc and Beloe stopped him. Brutus cast a calming spell over him.

"Listen to me, Sean. We must plan better—we can't just go charging in there. What would Cami do if she woke up and discovered that you had died trying to save her? We will find an answer to all of this. Please, have patience, " Pearl said, seeking to reason with him.

"I think there's something that all of you are forgetting here," David added. "It might not be what you want to hear, but it is an answer to this problem, like Pearl said. What if we helped Cami die?"

They all looked at David as if he were mad. Then Zeela's face brightened, and she grinned widely. The others were now certain Zeela had joined David on the loopy farm.

"Rambo, could you and Jesse shrink and become invisible to find Cami?" Zeela asked.

"Indeed we could, Zeela. What do you have in mind?"

Zeela pulled a small vial out of her medicine bag and explained to the group that it was a tonic of renewal. One of the other healers, Healamonster, gasped in understanding.

"In other words, it's a potion of death," Heala told the group.

"Whoa! What are you talking about?" Jesse asked, confused.

"No, Jesse—this could be just what we need," Mr Chambers said.

Jesse was stupefied. "I must be missing something here if Mr Chambers is okay with this."

Chapter 26

Sariah

Smiling, Zeela said, "What David and Sean are trying to say is... well, maybe I'll just let them explain."

"How many times did all of you die in the game?" David asked the group.

Everyone agreed that, in some cases, dying had been a way of life for them. Then, some of them began to understand better.

"Cami has to die so she can become whole and live?" Jesse asked.

"Yes," David said. "Jesse, take the renewal tonic of death to where Cami is. Tell Clarisa that it will make her better, and she needs to give it to Cami immediately. After Cami dies, use the talisman to pull her body to you—you should be able to do that, since she won't have physical form. Then resurrect her, and the three of you warp out."

Jesse took the small vial and studied it for a moment, unsure how he felt about doing what they were asking. Then he reached out to Clarisa's mind again.

"Clarisa, I have a potion that will help return Cami, but I need you to tell me where she is so I can give it to her."

"Jesse, she is in the Queen's chambers. She is under constant watch. They wanted her there because of the dragon's mark on her arm. What is that mark, Jesse... no one will tell me."

"Whoa... that changes things," Jesse said to the group.

"What does?" Zealoc wanted to know.

Jesse explained what Clarisa had said to him. They were stunned.

"So Clarisa saw the talisman. I wonder if they know what it is. Are they waiting for us to rescue Cami, hoping to wipe us out? I wonder if they know that we can die and resurrect," Pearl asked.

"I bet this Queen is the general 'Geezlouise', and if she is, then yes—she knows about death and resurrection. She is a mortal player. Nexlucimus told us when we were given the talisman that there were people who would kill us because of it. Perhaps she knows—or maybe she doesn't. Possibly, she's just curious," Jesse said.

"I doubt that, son," David replied. "I'm sure Tazeron knows, and if she is indeed his general, I'm sure he's told her."

"What do we do now?" Mr Chambers asked, troubled.

"I vote we storm the mountain," Jesse said, "just as soon as I find it, that is."

The majority cheered at that suggestion, and it was agreed they would follow Jesse. There was a scramble for mounts and a flurry of excitement. Jesse sensed the mountain not too far beyond where they were, and he sent a spell of improved sight towards it with his mind. They all watched as the mountain shimmered into view.

"*Unbelievable,*" several of the members breathed.

"Beautiful," others said in awe.

"Too bad that a thing of such beauty carries so much evil inside," Pearl added to their comments, bringing many nods of agreement.

"I suggest we proceed as we did with the castle—except for Rambo and me going to find Cami. Is everyone ready?" Jesse asked.

Zealoc and Beloe bellowed their battle cry. Pearl even tried her hand at it, which brought a smile to Zealoc's face. The party advanced on the mountain to the reception of darts and arrows, which Rambo once again returned as fiery missiles. Warriors landed in the courtyard and taunted from different directions, causing the mobs to have confused focus.

"I love playing Ping-Pong," Rykan said with a chuckle.

Melee settled in close by, with ranged attackers firing spells and weapons from above. It was nice that each of the different games the Keepers had played in the mortal world had brought talents and abilities to the one game court.

When it looked like the battle was under control, Rambo and Jesse signalled Zealoc that they were going in. Under the cover of invisibility, they shrank as small as they could and headed into the mountain.

"Clarisa, where are the Queen's chambers? We are coming in."

There was no answer, and that concerned Jesse and Rambo. The chambers could be anywhere. Jesse sent his mind into the mountain, searching for Cami. He found her deep inside, on an upper level—but what he saw surprised him. She was all there—mind and all. She was simply under the guise of feigning death, only modified to feign sleep.

"Odd... when did she learn that ability?" Jesse wondered.

Jesse tried to reach her mind, but couldn't—probably because of the spell she had placed on herself. He decided to pull back, but stay close enough to watch her and observe what she was doing. He and Rambo found a secluded and empty hallway in the fortress. They settled in. Jesse sent a talisman message to his dad, explaining what they had seen and what they were doing. David acknowledged his communication and said that they would pull back until notified again. Now it was a waiting game.

Jesse watched the shadows flatten out and then grow longer—several hours had passed. Then he saw a small person move out of the shadows towards Cami. It was a female Azure elf. He watched as she placed her hand on Cami's arm and shook her slightly. She then acted like she was talking to someone and stepped out of the room.

"That was unusual."

"Clarisa, are you with Cami at this moment?" he asked.

"Yes," she said sadly. *"She is still unresponsive. I am sorry."*

"Is she in any danger? Are there others nearby?"

"I am the only one here now, but the Queen is due back soon. Since the attack on the mountain, she and her guards are returning from Tazeron's hiding place."

Jesse sent this updated news to David. He and Rambo would continue their watch.

"Sorry, Rambo. This is a pretty dull assignment. Can you see what is happening in Cami's room too?"

"I can, Jesse. Most interesting. I do not find it tedious. It will be fascinating to see this Queen when she arrives."

As they watched, there was increased bustle in the corridor, not too far from where they were hiding. Jesse shifted his mind over to the activity. He was surprised to see an enormous, hideous, male troll with an equally massive dog. The dog seemed very interested in the hall where Jesse and Rambo were hiding.

"What do you sense, my pet? Outsiders, perhaps? Would you like to explore?" the troll asked his canine companion.

The dog became very excited and started coming towards Jesse and Rambo at the signal from the large green man. Just as they were in danger of being discovered, a panel opened in the wall behind Jesse, and a little Azure elf waved them in.

Jesse was relieved to see her. Rambo morphed into a rooster so he could fit.

"Are you Clarisa?" Jesse asked, very grateful to whoever this was.

"No, I am Sariah, Clarisa's friend. We are healers in this facility. While we do serve here, we are not loyal to these evil people."

Jesse was pleased at this disclosure and extremely intrigued by the possibilities it presented. Sariah led him through a tight little tunnel, using a torch as light. He was delighted that Rambo could become so small and that he, Jesse, wasn't much bigger. As he followed, he asked Sariah where Cami was and how they could get to her.

"She is not far from here, but it would be dangerous for you to get to her. If you are patient, we promise that you can rescue her. Cami has asked us to tell you that she is safe; she is in no danger. We had to say to you that her mind was missing because that's what our main healer believes, and she is loyal to the Queen. Cami wanted you to know that when her mind was blessed by the head Elder, she gained this ability that she is using. We have assisted her with our knowledge.

We are more skilled with herbs than our chief because of our origin. We know of shadow sleep. Cami appears to be sleeping, but she can leave her body and explore. She thinks it might be an excellent way to get information. We are sorry that we couldn't tell you more, but we are not trusted," she giggled nervously.

"Sariah, is it possible for me to warp out and then back into this place? Is it safe for me to do that?"

"It is as safe as anywhere on the mountain. These tunnels were created as escape routes for the pygmy trolls that built this city. The larger races can't fit in here, and there aren't many smaller races that know about them."

"Tell me about the Queen. What is she like? Where did she come from?"

"She comes from your world. She is a giant troll and very skilled in the games. Some call her a game master, a creator."

"Uh, oh... that's not good," Jesse said to Rambo.

"Indeed..."

"She has been controlling the mountain for Tazeron, to occupy the Keepers, keeping them away from his fortress. I will tell you this: he has plans to leave the fortress soon. It has almost fulfilled its purpose. Tazeron has promised the Queen great wealth and power in your world for her loyalty. Many mortals follow him for promises of riches and control. Fools... evil cannot reward with anything but evil," she spat.

"When you say Tazeron is going to leave the fortress, where does he plan on going?"

"We do not know that yet, only that it will happen soon."

"Sariah, where did you and Clarisa come from? Are you abandoned or deleted game characters?"

"I am abandoned, but Clarisa is deleted, which is pretty close to the same. Abandoned characters don't lose all their stats. Unlike most deleted characters that have been stripped of their equipment, abandoned characters have the possibility that their creators will return. I don't hold much hope of that happening; it has been a very long time, but I guess it is possible. Clarisa and I were both high level, which makes it possible for us to do what we do here. I have given her equipment to help maintain her stats."

"What do you do here?"

"We tend to the injuries that are brought to us. When we can, we help mortals that are brought here against their wills, like your Cami."

"Sariah, what would you suggest we do at this point?"

"As hard as it would be, we would propose that you pull back. Act like you gave up. Do not try to rescue Cami. Let her gather intelligence for the Keepers. It will be of greater value to your cause if you allow this. Both Clarisa and I can talk to you or others of your party. We can communicate the information that Cami acquires since we cannot spy ourselves."

"How many other mortals do you have here?"

"There are many mortals. Some are in Tazeron's service. Others are in prison because they refuse to serve. The Queen does not want them freed because of what they know."

"Wow... this is crazy. What should we do, Rambo?"

"I suggest that we follow Sariah and Clarisa's advice. Perhaps pull back for now. Let's return to the front and consult with the team leaders."

"Thank you for your help, Sariah. We are indebted to you and Clarisa. Thank you for caring for Cami; her father will be happy to hear of her good condition. Thank you also for the valuable information. I will be in contact. Tell Cami we wish her well in her efforts."

"You are very welcome. We delight in helping the Keepers whenever we can."

"I guess we should warp back to the front and then disappear off Tazeron's radar, Rambo. What a change of plans! I think the party is going to be surprised and perhaps disappointed with this information."

"Indeed, they are, my friend."

Jesse held the talisman with his mind as he touched Rambo, and they were once again at the front. As expected, Mr Chambers didn't take the news well.

"I can't believe that you want us to turn tail and leave. That's malarkey, Jesse."

"Jesse, do you and Rambo feel like they were telling you the truth?" Pearl asked.

"Yes... we watched, listened, and talked to these two toons for a long time. Nothing that they did or said gave us an impression that they were anything less than honourable."

Unknown to anyone except Jesse and Rambo, Breeze returned to the place where Sariah and Clarisa were.

"Jesse, I will be there soon. I have more information," Breeze told him.

"While we have been talking," Jesse said to the group, "Breeze went back to the mountain to contact Sariah and Clarisa. She just contacted me saying she had more information. She will be here soon."

"Well, I guess we wait then," Zealoc said to them.

Jesse noticed that Mr Chambers was still distraught. Zeela tried to talk to him.

"I know that all of this is completely against what we have been told. We were, above all, to guard the Shield, but it isn't in as much danger. Our focus now, considering the riddle, needs to be protecting Jim and Sara's children," Zeela told him.

"What about my child? What are we doing to protect her? She's all that I have," Sean said, his emotions close to the surface and pain etched on his face.

"If we redirect our focus and prepare for Tazeron's attempt on the twins, then we can basically head him off at the pass. Mr Chambers, I feel your pain, even if you don't believe me," Jesse said. "I think we all do. Cami and I have been friends for many years, and I would never do anything to hurt her or put her in danger. It only makes sense for Cami to stay where she is, with Sariah and Clarisa, gathering information to help the cause," Jesse said.

"You must believe them, Sean," Pearl said, joining the group. "We wouldn't leave Cami there if we thought she couldn't handle this. She's a smart girl, and she has many gifts working for her right now. Remember, we are here for you too; you aren't alone."

Mr Chambers was looking at the ground as they talked to him. He took a deep breath and let it out slowly. Looking up, he appeared more resolute.

"Ok... for Cami... I will move forward. But if any of those bastards hurt my little girl, I'm going to personally rip out their black hearts."

"Awesome! I'll be right there with you," Jesse added.

"We all will be, Sean," Pearl and Zeela said.

When Breeze arrived, Jesse turned the meeting over to her.

"I know that I am a relative newcomer, but I have known several members of this party for thousands of mortal years. I am trustworthy."

Rambo, Zeela, Ginnea, and Zealoc all concurred, as did several others.

"Tell us what you found out, Breeze," David said.

"I returned to Cami's bedside and talked to her while she was in her shadow sleep. She is indeed well and confirms what Sariah told Jesse. Tazeron is abandoning his fortress shortly. He might be making plans to invade the forest of the elves with his supporters in the world of Xanthara. As soon as she is sure of this, she plans to warp out and help us."

"Sariah and Clarisa are what they said they are. They are concerned for the welfare of all people trapped in the game. One more thing—the character that was with Cami when she was abducted was also seized. He is in prison. He was innocent; I checked on him as well. He shares proximity to someone else that you know, Jesse. I believe you knew a boy by the name of Mckay Palmer? I remember an incident involving some graffiti at Pearl's place. Mckay is a very lonely and scared boy; he regrets his past and desires to change."

"Oh brother," Jesse said. "He was always flirting with jail time. I hope this will have a positive impact on him."

"I believe it will," Breeze smiled.

After Breeze's report and some discussion, the camp decided that they would leave for the forest of elves in the morning and prepare for Tazeron's attempt on the twins. After the evening meal, everyone retired to their beds in preparation for an early departure.

Later that night, as he slept, Jesse had a dream in which he saw a mist-shrouded deserted island, covered with cages. On closer examination, he discovered that the pens were full of men. They had bloodied, mangled bodies covered with festering battle sores. They were emaciated and crying for help, begging for food and water, growling and grovelling like animals, pleading for relief.

As he watched, a man walked among the cages, promising release and help if the captives would only serve him. They had to do what he wanted—anything he wanted. Some agreed; their suffering was so great. Others refused, opting to die or continue suffering. The man laughed at them, taunting them, cruelly sneering at their misery.

As Jesse watched the horrible scene, another man arose out of the miserable masses—one-armed and pathetic. This stranger challenged the arrogant man.

The sneering man laughed wickedly but then seemed to recognise the man challenging him and appeared fearful. When the evil one discovered he could do no harm to the one-armed man, he ran, taking his slaves with him. They ran through a blue-splattered wall.

Jesse trembled awake. He was surprised when the chain at his neck warmed, and a peaceful feeling blanketed him. He fingered the thin metal, thinking about the White Druid and the meaning of the dream. For the first time since receiving these thoughts, he was impressed that this vision was not to be shared. Puzzled, he lay there in the dark listening to the night noises and thinking, *"What does this mean?"* Gradually, Jesse drifted off to sleep again as the chain he wore continued to pulsate warmth and peace to him.

Chapter 27

Forest of Elves

The trip to the forest was uneventful, considering that everyone either had a talisman or was standing next to someone who did. It was a solemn reunion with Nexlucimus and others who had survived the attack on the capital city. Zealoc filled them in on their mission and all that had happened. Jesse and Zeela added details as needed.

"It's apparent that solving the riddle has shifted Tazeron's focus," Nexlucimus observed.

"We must redouble our efforts to capture or destroy Tazeron," Heralon, Tazeron and Tommy's father, said with a pained expression on his face.

"While that is true, my friend," Nexlucimus said sadly, "I believe our focus must be protecting those children. Perhaps we can discover a way to accomplish both goals."

"What of the capital city?" Zealoc wanted to know.

"Ah, there too is a problem," Nexlucimus sighed. "The main population of the city is managing as best they can, with no on-site leadership. What's left of the Council has been relocated to this forest. Of the fifteen members of the Council, only seven of us remain. Tommy, as you know, is recovering, and that leaves seven others unaccounted for."

"Where do you think they are?" Beloe asked.

"According to the ransom notes we discovered," Trusol, a Council member, stated, "it is believed that five are being held captive by the primitive tribes. They are hoping to negotiate for products and services. We have no idea where they are being held. The other two have just vanished — it's very peculiar. Another thing: the refreshing cycle has been disturbed."

There were exclamations of shock and disbelief.

"How is that possible, Nexlucimus?" Breeze whispered, clearly shaken. "Never, since the beginning of our records, has that ever happened. Have you any ideas?"

"The only thing we can discern is that the magic which protects this world and directs its functioning has been disrupted by this war. It's the same reason so many children are being born and developing so quickly. We consider it another sign of the sickness that Tazeron has infected us with," Nexlucimus said, sighing heavily.

An intense feeling of gloom was settling thickly upon everyone.

"I suggest for now," Zeela spoke up, "we all get something to eat and rest. Perhaps later, we can further discuss what is to be done."

"I agree," Zealoc said. "I believe some food and rest sounds like a great idea."

He took Pearl's hand, and they headed towards the vendors.

Jesse watched them go. "I'm glad Gran has Zealoc Rambo, she seems happy."

"Indeed, Jesse, she does seem content."

"Come, Nexi, we have much to discuss, and I need to visit the Slaters," Zeela said, pulling gently on her husband's arm.

"Indeed," the Elder sighed again, tiredly, as they walked off together.

After their meeting with the Elder, Jesse and Breeze went to the healing facility with Ginnea and Rambo to visit Tommy. They found him in a herb-induced coma.

"We must keep him quiet so that his brain can heal from the poison at its own pace. If we don't sedate him, he thrashes around, and we fear he will injure himself," the healer told them.

It made Jesse feel depressed, seeing his friend so sick. Ginnea started crying so hard that one of the healers took her away. Tommy's recovery was taking impossibly long. The whole situation made Jesse fume. It was incredibly unfair. He stormed out of the facility. Breeze and Rambo ran after him.

"Jesse, slow down, let's talk," Breeze pleaded with him, as she flew to catch up, Rambo right beside her.

"People have had babies, and those babies have grown, and still Tommy is lying in a bed unconscious. I'm seriously going back and killing every freaking spider ever created!" Jesse growled.

"Think about what you are considering, Jesse. Be reasonable," Rambo told him. That only made Jesse madder.

"Don't tell me to be reasonable. Dang it, Rambo, we are making no progress. We have accomplished nothing, except for following smoke trails. Tommy is poisoned, Cami is captured, and half of the Council is missing. Tell me how we are doing any good. Tell me."

"Wars aren't won in a few days, Jesse. Casualties are to be expected..."

"Oh, don't give me that, Rambo. All we've done since starting this is lose people and fall into traps. It's like we're a bunch of stinking noobs."

"Jesse, my love, you are upset about your friend, but remember your dreams. Do you not remember the one I gave you from the gods? You saw Tommy waving to you. Is that not a testimony to his recovery? We must be brave and patient. We will triumph."

"Jesse," Pearl said, as she and Zealoc approached from behind. They all jumped, not having seen them before this.

"Gran... I'm sorry, but this was a private conversation."

"Well, for a private conversation, you were being very public. I just wanted to remind you of one thing, and then I will butt out of this 'private' conversation."

"What is it?" he sighed, loudly.

"How many times did we have to go into an endgame dungeon before we killed the boss? Think about it, that's all I'm going to say."

With that, she took Zealoc's hand, and they walked off.

Jesse stood there, speechless.

"She's right. I'm such an idiot."

"No, you are not..." Rambo said, to Jesse's mind.

"Breeze, you were right. I'm sorry." He kissed the top of her head as she hugged him.

"Rambo, I know you were trying to help too. I am sorry that I got mad at you. Even though it's so real, and so much depends on our succeeding, I keep forgetting that game rules apply — except for when Tazeron's minions interfere, that is," Jesse groaned and kicked at a clump of grass. "It's just so frustrating. Forgive me, again." Jesse sighed and then knuckled Rambo's head.

"Hey! Don't mess with the hairdo!" Rambo said, flipping his head.

Jesse laughed and shoulder-punched him. The action only bruised Jesse's hand.

"Ouch, you freakin' bucket of bolts, that hurt my hand."

Rambo shrugged.

"It sure takes some people a long time to get the obvious."

"Isn't that the sad, hard truth," Jesse said, smiling at Breeze.

"Soft skin, hard head — there has to be a connection in there somewhere," Rambo laughed.

Breeze giggled at the two as they ambled down the path, their banter continuing.

After a short distance, Brutus stepped out of the trees and approached Rambo. Apparently, they were having a silent conversation. Jesse and Breeze watched, curious. After a few moments, Rambo nodded, and Brutus continued back towards the healing facility. Jesse asked what was going on. Rambo explained that Brutus wanted to see Tommy. He had an idea that might help. Rambo couldn't tell them any more than that, but it was exciting news to hear.

When they reached the central area of the village, Breeze expressed a desire to visit Jim and Sara. Pearl and Zealoc voiced the same wish; they all decided to walk together.

"Gran, I'm really sorry I got so mad at you. You were right."

"I understand, dear. We're all under a lot of pressure."

As they travelled together, Jesse filled Gran and Zealoc in on Tommy's condition, creating a sombre mood.

"He will recover," Breeze told them. "Of that, I am sure."

"I believe you, Breeze. We must have faith and trust in the gods," Pearl concurred.

When they arrived at Jim and Sara's place, they were astonished to see Sara still in game form. She explained that it was just more comfortable for the twins and more acceptable to the forest community. She told them that it was possible to stay that way forever — or so the elves had said. Because of the circumstances of her pregnancy and how she had changed with that experience, she seemed very well fitted to the race.

That surprised the group. Another surprise came when Jim told them that Sara was expecting again — a boy this time.

"He could arrive at any time," Jim said.

"I guess this world suits you two," Gran said, smiling at them.

"It certainly does — embarrassingly so," Jim added, giving his wife a tight smile.

"Well, before this new child is born, may we meet the other two?" Gran laughed.

"Of course, we would be delighted," Sara said.

Jim called the children to the main room, and the two teens shyly entered the room full of strangers. They were small and slim, with softly pointed features. With their azure blue skin, they looked just like Sara — perhaps a little lighter in hue. They were quiet and very polite, and after a brief visit, they asked to be excused. They went back to their friends, who were playing a game with them in a back room.

"All their short life," Sara explained quietly, "they have heard of the many brave people trying to rid the world of the evil Tazeron. Only recently has their part been revealed to us, and now them. It terrifies us and worries them, but they see it more as an inconvenience because now we have more restrictions on them. I don't really think they understand the danger they are in. And from what we know, this new baby will be subject to the riddle as well. Zeela told us that this afternoon," Sara looked concerned.

"It's so hard to believe that they are teenagers in their development. They crave their independence. We are struggling with how fast they are developing. At least they aren't alone. There are many children here the same age and growing at the same rate. We are friends with many parents, also wrestling with the same situation. And now we have this new one coming," Jim said. "We are feeling overwhelmed. They grow so fast—if it weren't for magic keeping them in clothes, I don't know what we'd do. And, thank goodness for vendors."

Jesse stepped toward them. "Jim and Sara, this is my friend Breeze. She, like your twins, was born only a few months ago."

"How nice to meet you, Breeze. And you are one of the Keepers now?" Jim asked.

"Yes, I am."

"Breeze," Sara began, sounding hesitant, "would you be willing to talk to the twins? With your unique connection and situation, perhaps you could help them better understand their feelings and the danger they face."

"I would be happy to. Would now be OK?"

"Oh yes, and thank you, Breeze. Come, we will take you to them."

The children were just finishing their game, and their friends were leaving as the adults entered the back room. It was a pleasant room with a table and chairs in the middle. The walls were lined with bookshelves. Jesse noticed several pictures hanging on the walls that showed Sara and Jim in their mortal forms, and scenes from the mortal world, including one showing Jim standing next to his patrol car. There were also pictures of Gran, and Jim and Sara's parents. Breeze and Jesse were drawn to the pictures. The twins watched them, curious.

"When did you get these taken, Jim?" Jesse asked.

"I warped back to our house and collected some things that would be helpful when telling the children about our world. It helps them understand where we came from, and a little about their ancestry," Jim explained.

"Jason and Mary," Sara addressed them, "we have asked Breeze to talk to you both. She, like you, was born just a short time ago and understands, perhaps better than we do, what it's like for you. Would you be OK talking to her?"

The twins, Jason and Mary, seemed eager to visit with Breeze.

"Yes, Mother, we would like that. It would be fun to talk with Breeze, since she is close to our age," Mary said, and Jason, shaking his head in agreement, seemed eager too.

Jim and Sara left the room, thinking the twins would feel more like talking if their parents weren't watching.

As Breeze talked with the twins, it was clear that they had many things in common.

"We understand our parents' concerns, but we really hate being restricted and always watched—it's so embarrassing," Mary said, with a sad little pout.

"I can't even go fishing with the other boys my age. No one follows them, and they don't understand why we are being followed. It's tough to explain, because we can't tell anyone what the real reason is," Jason expressed.

"I can appreciate how you feel, but I will inform you that in just a few days, you'll understand better, and you won't need to be looked after as much. I remember all I wanted was my independence. I was always struggling with my parents' rules, but within just a few days, I felt different. I still wanted to be independent, but the rules didn't bother me as much—they made sense. Then my little brother was born, and I felt so old, even though by the seasons I was still very young. I understand the challenge you face," Breeze told them. "Especially now that you have another brother coming any day."

It helped Jesse to listen to her tell the twins these things. He felt like he had a better appreciation of what it must have been like for her.

Later that night, the group sat around a campfire discussing what they should do next. It was decided that for the next few days, until the whole team could be reassembled, they would hang out in the forest helping as needed. As soon as everyone was gathered, they would work up a plan.

Nexlucimus was still trying to put together a delegation to go to the primitive tribes and arrange peace. Zealoc wanted to go, and so did Pearl, but it was decided that they were more valuable in their present assignment.

"Perhaps later, Zealoc. After this horrible travesty with Tazeron is over, you and Pearl can help in rebuilding those relationships," Nexlucimus said.

"Zealoc, my dear, I would love to help you rebuild relations with those people," Pearl said, snuggling up to him.

Zealoc wrapped an arm around her. "And I, fair lady, would be honoured to have you at my side."

Zealoc kissed Gran right there, in front of everyone. It made Jesse smile. Apparently, size didn't matter in their case, since Gran in her non-game form was much taller than Zealoc.

"This war has certainly changed all of our lives."

He looked down at the beautiful fairy sitting by his side, her head leaning on him. He tightened his arm around her waist, and she looked up, a radiant smile on her face.

"Rambo, are you happy? I mean... do you miss your wife so much that you can't be happy?"

"You do ask difficult questions sometimes, Jesse. Yes, I miss my wife, but we have been apart for so long, I have adjusted. It does make me sad that I can't hold her and talk to her, especially when I see that kind of happiness around me. I do have peace of mind, knowing I will see her again."

"You are the bravest person I know, Rambo. Now that I have Breeze, and I realise that I do love her, I can't imagine how hard your life must be."

"Do not think of me, Jesse, enjoy what you have—you don't know what the future holds. After we are done with this war, I will petition the gods for our reunion. I believe it is time."

"I will add my voice to yours, my friend," Jesse said sincerely.

"Thank you. Now, enjoy the moment."

"You were having a conversation with Rambo, weren't you?" Breeze asked, looking up at him.

"I was. I was telling Rambo how much I love you, and how I couldn't imagine life without you."

"So soon you have decided this?" she asked, amazed.

"Indeed, I have. When this is over, I will ask your father for your hand. If that is agreeable to you, and if that's how it's done in your world."

"Your world now, my love, and yes, it is very agreeable to me." She had tears in her eyes as she kissed him. Jesse noticed Gran watching them with a big smile on her face.

Jesse had never felt happier.

In the morning, after a restful night's sleep, Jesse walked out of his tent and joined the gathering party members. Some were still absent, including Gran and Zealoc. Jesse chuckled at the idea of Gran having a late date night. Breeze came over and kissed him good morning, handing him a plate of fruit and fresh bread.

"Wow… bread, what a treat! Thank you, Breeze."

"You are welcome, my love. I must keep you healthy."

They walked over to a table and started eating their meal.

"I was wondering if you would like to take a little trip with Rambo and me, if he is willing. I want to go to the capital city and see for myself what's going on there," Jesse said to her.

Just then, Rambo walked over to them. He was in rooster form, carrying something big, green, and fuzzy, wiggling in his beak.

"Rambo, after breakfast," Jesse eyed the bug Rambo was trying to eat.

"How would you like to take a trip to the capital city with Breeze and me?"

Rambo finished the bug, which he had to beat into smaller pieces to swallow, before answering.

"It would be my pleasure. I have been thinking of that myself."

"Jesse, would you mind if we went past my parents' home, so you could meet my family?"

"Sure, Breeze, I would love to meet your family."

"Holy crap! It's Meet the Parents Day—yikes! I should've known this would happen someday soon."

Rambo chuckled. Jesse glared at him.

"Sometimes having you eavesdrop on my thoughts is annoying."

"I try to avoid them unless you say my name first, but sometimes, they just jump right out there and grab me." Rambo chuckled again.

"Shall we go, Jesse, or did you have something else you needed to do? You have a pensive look on your face," Breeze said.

"No, it's fine," he gave her a smile. "I was just thinking of something—not important."

"Liar..." Rambo added, morphing into his battle-ready form.

"Shut up, you big lizard, mind your own thoughts." Jesse scowled at him, and Rambo laughed again.

"You two are having a conversation in your minds. This is something I'm going to have to get used to. What were you talking about?" Breeze wanted to know, a smile playing on her lips.

"It was nothing, Breeze. Rambo was being a dork."

Rambo chortled again.

"A dork...?"

"Yeah. Shall we go, Rambo? Quickly, before I'm in trouble."

Snickering, Rambo helped Jesse and Breeze onto his back, and they launched into the morning sky, flying toward the capital city.

"I was wondering about something, Breeze."

"What's that, my love?"

"Why can you listen to and talk to my thoughts sometimes and not others?"

"I can only listen to and talk to your thoughts when you allow it, or if it's crucial. If it's a private conversation, like with Rambo, I'm not allowed in. So, what's a dork, and why was Rambo one?"

"That's hard to explain. Maybe I'll figure out how to tell you later."

Breeze turned to look him in the eye and smiled broadly.

"You're embarrassed."

"Kind of. Can we drop it?"

"As you wish," she said, as she snuggled back into his arms.

"You're the best, Breeze," Jesse said, as he kissed the top of her head.

It didn't take long to fly to the capital, and what they saw was very disturbing. For the most part, the city looked the same—it was just silent. There were almost no people on the streets and very few vendors. Andy's gardens were dug up, and the prized Naqisha trees were gone, as were the Dumplumba trees. Grass and flowers were drying out, and the sparkling was absent. Everything was still spotless, but it looked abandoned and dying. The Great

Library of Learning seemed cold and empty; several windows were broken.

"I need to go in," Rambo informed them. "I must see Chaelea. You can stay out here if you choose."

"No, my friend, we will go with you."

Chapter 28

Love and War

As they walked up the stairs of the Great Library and approached the high doors, they didn't automatically open as before. Breeze unlocked them with her magic, and as the doors swung open, the friends walked in.

Rambo stopped and emitted a soft cry. The white dragon statue was gone—not merely damaged, but gone. There was no sign of vandalism, no broken stone or cracked fountain marble. She was simply not there, with no indication as to how or why.

"Why... why would anyone do this thing?" Breeze whispered, not expecting an answer.

As they stood there pondering the situation, an enormous troll came racing towards them with a wicked-looking spiked mallet held high above his head. The whole room seemed to shake as he charged. Jesse and Breeze scrambled onto Rambo, and they took to the air as flaming arrows flew at them from other locations. Rambo formed a bubble around Jesse and Breeze and dived deeper into the building. The bubble deflected the barrage of ancient weapons. Jesse tried to speak to the trolls with his thoughts, but either their language was too primitive, or their heads too thick—he had no success.

"Let me try, Jesse. Sometimes these ancient tribes will talk to fairies."

"OK, have a try."

"Rambo, let me out of this bubble."

"What! No, Breeze, wait, they'll kill you."

"Trust me, Jesse. Rambo, please."

Rambo dropped the bubble, and Breeze fluttered to the most massive, meanest-looking troll in the room. To Jesse's surprise, she landed on his huge nose and talked to him, eyeball to eyeball. The troll raised his big ugly club and acted as though he wanted to hit the tiny fairy, but wasn't sure how to do it without killing himself. He was puzzled for a moment, then lowered his club. His shoulders slumped in submission. Breeze continued speaking to him for a few more moments before he puckered up his giant lips and blew an ear-splitting trill. All the other trolls began moving towards the big one, their weapons at their sides. Then, like a group of schoolchildren, they lined up and marched out of the building.

"I think I've seen everything now," Rambo said, amazed.

"I'm just glad we didn't nuke any of them," Jesse said, stunned.

"Truly spoken, my friend," Rambo replied. "She is a very talented lady. No wonder she was a Shadow Dream for so long."

"Amen..." Jesse said, still amazed by what Breeze had done. "Maybe she can find out where the missing Council was taken, or what happened to the White Druid's statue."

"Possibly. Shall we go see where they went?"

"Definitely. I want her back with me."

"You and she are progressing then?" Rambo asked as they flew through the building in the direction Breeze and the trolls had gone.

"Yes. When this is over, I want to marry her, Rambo."

"My, my. What happened to the frightened Jesse I used to know? Who couldn't date until he was sixteen? Whose mother would kill him if he came home with a bride?"

"OK, I get it. I'm jumping into it, but Rambo, it feels so right. And when I'm with her, I know it's right."

"You must go with your heart, Jesse. Now, shall we find your heart?" Rambo said as they exited the big building.

"Yes, indeed. Ah... Rambo, I don't see them. Where could something as big as a troll go?"

They were amazed to find no sign of Breeze or the trolls when they reached the outer steps of the Great Library.

"No idea, Jesse. Strange."

They flew around for a long time, but still there was no sign of Breeze or the trolls. Jesse decided to search for them with his mind. To his surprise, they weren't in the city. Instead, they were in the forest with the troll tribe.

"Rambo, they must have warped back to their village. I didn't know trolls could do that," Jesse said, bewildered.

"They can't," Rambo replied, stunned.

"I've got to get closer to talk to her. I'm not sure how I can feel her even now. We're warping back."

Jesse touched the talisman, and they returned to the elven village.

"Breeze, where did you go?"

"Jesse, the most amazing thing has happened. I will be coming back shortly—trust me, my love."

Jesse and Rambo decided to get some food while they waited for Breeze to return. Rambo morphed into his rooster form and scratched his way into the forest, while Jesse enjoyed a huge sandwich and a steamy bowl of soup. Just as he was finishing, Breeze appeared beside him at the table, making him jump.

"Welcome back, Breeze. How did your trolling go?" Jesse snickered, and she looked puzzled.

"I found out some fantastic news, and I need to talk to Nexlucimus right away. Come with me?"

"To the ends of the world," Jesse said, grinning. *"That was cheesy—but she liked it."*

Rambo snickered in Jesse's mind.

Breeze was in such a hurry that she popped out her wings and took off, leaving Jesse jogging behind.

"Whoa, slow down, little lady—you're leaving me in your dust."

"Oh, sorry Jesse, I'm just so excited."

"What has you so excited?"

"Oh, there's Nexlucimus and Zeela—what luck! Hurry, Jesse, and I'll tell you at the same time."

They stopped in front of the Elder and Zeela, surprising them with their swift arrival.

"Master Nexlucimus, and Zeela—I have made a surprising discovery in the troll village, not fifty leagues from here."

"Good heavens, Breeze, what were you doing there?" Nexlucimus asked.

"Jesse, Rambo and I went to the capital to see for ourselves what was going on. We went to the Great Library and were shocked to see that the White Druid statue had been removed."

"What! Could you tell what happened to her?" Zeela asked.

"Not at the time, because our visit was interrupted by an attack of trolls. Jesse tried to mind-talk to them and couldn't. I tried—and I was able to."

"She was amazing—she had those trolls marching in a line like schoolchildren," Jesse said proudly.

"You did?" Nexlucimus asked, impressed.

"I learned a trick or two as a Shadow Dream. The truly amazing part was when they walked outside—they warped back to their village."

"They did what?" Zeela said, shocked.

"They warped. I'll explain in a moment. I had moved to the back of the troll's head and was hiding in his thick hair. He forgot I was there. Nexlucimus, I found the missing Council. All of them."

"What? They are all in the troll village?"

"Yes, and some of them—two, it looked like—were walking around and talking to the trolls. The councilmen seemed to be giving orders, and the trolls were following them. It was the two defectors who transported the trolls into and out of the city. The rest of the Council are in huts, chained up. Since I could only see what the troll I was riding on did, I became invisible and flew around. The chained ones seemed to all be in good health and, except for the confinement, they were comfortable. There appeared to be an aura around each of them—probably some kind of containment spell to silence their magic.

"I talked to one of the missing Council, and she said they heard a rumour that Tazeron was coming. The camp was preparing a place for him. But that can't be true, because the gods would take him if he did. Wouldn't they? My guess is it's some of his mortal leaders—maybe that Queen. I told the Council lady that we would free them as soon as we could. I hope that was okay to say."

"Yes, my dear, and thank you for this information. You've been a great help to us, thank you."

"My pleasure, sir. Please excuse me now—Jesse and I have some unfinished business to tend to."

"Indeed. We will talk to the team leaders about this information," Nexlucimus said.

Jesse looked at Breeze, curious, but followed her into the forest.

"Breeze, what's going on? Where are you headed now?"

"I need to find Rambo."

"I can do that for you—wait a minute."

"Rambo, can you come to where Breeze and I are right now?"

"Certainly, I'll be right there."

"Okay, he's coming. What's this all about?" Jesse asked.

"Patience, my love," Breeze responded.

"Okay, I'm here... what's going on?" Rambo questioned.

"Rambo, I found the White Druid! Well, I found where her statue is."

"What? Where is she?" Rambo asked, shocked.

"The trolls took her into the game for Tazeron. He's afraid of her. He wanted her guarded where he could keep an eye on her."

"Why would he go to all that trouble to defend a statue?" Jesse asked, curious.

"Because," Rambo said, "it's a favourite story among some people that if the capital city is ever attacked, the White Druid would come to her statue. In years past, people attacked the city trying to bring her back. This is the first time her statue has been stolen, however."

"Is that real, Rambo?" Breeze asked.

"It's a story. No one knows for sure if, or when, she will return." Rambo gave Jesse a meaningful glance. Jesse looked away, trying not to think of the story Rambo had told him.

"Another puzzle piece?" Jesse asked Rambo.

"Indeed."

"Jesse, I would still like you to meet my family. Could we do that now, Rambo, or should I have Jesse warp us there with the talisman?"

"I believe I will let you two go on your own, if you don't mind. I need to talk to Nexlucimus."

"No worries, my friend. We'll see you later then," Jesse said as he held Breeze's hand. Touching the talisman with his mind, Jesse warped them to Rodashu.

When they arrived at Breeze's family home, children were playing in the front yard. A couple of Skeedlers scurried around with them in a game of hide and seek. Jesse couldn't see how that would work, but the children seemed to be having fun with it.

"Breeze!" a small teal boy fluttered up to her, with his tiny pale green wings. "Mother... Breeze is home, and she has a Keeper with her!" the boy shouted at the top of his voice.

"So much for a surprise," Breeze said to Jesse, as she embraced the boy who had made the announcement.

"Jesse, this is my youngest brother, Ammon. Ammon, this is my friend Jesse. You be nice to him."

"I will, Breeze. I'm nice to everyone, just ask my Skeedler. Jokel, I'm nice to everyone, am I not?"

To Jesse's amazement, a bright orange Skeedler jumped on Ammon's head and appeared to be tickling him. Ammon collapsed into laughter as he fought off the Skeedler.

"See, that means yes—I told you," Ammon said through his giggles as he stood up. "I'll go get Mother; she was baking."

"That's okay, Ammon. We'll just go in. You and Jokel go play with your friends."

"Okay, it was fun to meet you, Jesse." The little boy bowed before running off, the Skeedler following close behind.

"Nice to meet you too, Ammon."

"So... he has a pet Skeedler?"

"All the children on Xanthara get a Skeedler when they are born. The Skeedlers keep the children clean and entertain them—like a mortal nanny. When the little ones can entertain themselves and take care of their own needs, their Skeedler shifts its attention to the general population. They will still visit sometimes. Ammon will outgrow his Skeedler shortly, the way he's developing. He was just starting to crawl when I left."

She had a sad little smile on her face, and Jesse couldn't help himself—he gave her a kiss.

At that moment, Breeze's mother came to the door.

"I saw that, young man. I hope you have a good explanation."

Both Breeze and Jesse jumped, their cheeks flaming.

"Mother, I've missed you!"

"Somehow, I doubt that, daughter." She glanced sideways at Jesse.

"Mother, this is my good friend Jesse. He's a Keeper."

"Ma'am," Jesse gave a bow, "it is my pleasure to meet you."

"Welcome, Jesse-who-is-a-Keeper." She was smiling now, and Jesse had the impression she had been teasing them.

"I believe I've seen you before, Jesse—in the marketplace, a little over a year ago."

"Indeed, ma'am. I remember seeing you in the market, and Breeze has shown you to me in a dream."

This information surprised Breeze's mother very much.

"I knew that my daughter was a Shadow Dream, but I've never heard any of her stories. Please come in—we can visit until your father comes home, Breeze. I'm sure he'll be delighted to meet your friend Jesse, the Keeper."

Jesse, smiling, took Breeze's hand as they followed her mother inside.

After what seemed like a short time of visiting, Breeze's mother, Miranda, jumped up. She announced that it had been a couple of hours, which surprised them all, and said she needed to start dinner. Breeze offered to help her, and Jesse wandered into the forward room.

While he was sitting there, looking through a book, a tall, impressive man walked into the home.

"My, my, a stranger is in my home—and who might you be, young sir?"

Jesse stood and bowed.

"I am Jesse Finch, sir. I'm a friend of Breeze's."

"You are a mortal as well, so that must mean that you are a Keeper. Am I correct in that assumption?"

"Indeed, sir. And are you Breeze's father?"

"I am. I am called Dalaron." He offered Jesse his hand, and they shook. "What brings you to my home?"

"Father!" Breeze ran to her father and hugged him tightly.

"My Breeze, you are such a delight and always my favourite."

Breeze giggled. "You say that to all of your daughters."

"And why should I not? For it is the truth."

"Now, my favourite child, tell me why there is a mortal called Jesse in my forward room. He tells me that he is a friend of yours?"

"Ah, my husband, it goes farther than that. I caught them kissing," Breeze's mother added.

Breeze was horrified and stood silently, watching her father's reaction.

"Sir, may I explain..." Jesse tried to say but was stopped by Dalaron's raised hand.

"Sit, children. We will discuss this."

Breeze and Jesse sat on separate chairs, waiting for her father to say something; instead, he left the room with Breeze's mother.

"Breeze, what's going on? Are we in trouble?"

"I have no idea, Jesse. I'm sorry if I've caused problems."

"I'm the one that kissed you. I should've been more careful. I'm so sorry."

Breeze's father returned to the room with his wife. They sat across from Breeze and Jesse, each holding a small white box.

Dalaron spoke. "Breeze, we didn't have you in our home very long before you left to make your way. This world is in trouble, and because of that, you never had a proper childhood. Many of the traditions of our people were lost to you. We are sorry beyond grief for this fact."

"Father, I..."

"Do not interrupt me, child."

"Yes, Father... sorry," Breeze murmured, staring at her hands in her lap.

"One of our traditions is a ceremony of commitment. It is usually done between families as their children choose mates and seek permission to marry. So many things have changed in our world. The old ways are being forgotten. Breeze, your mother and

I would like to give you and Jesse the commitment rings, if you wish. In days past, such public displays of affection, such as a kiss, would have been a sign of engagement. I don't know what it means anymore. Jesse, if you love our daughter and wish to marry her, I must know it now. If you are only playing with her feelings, I should be aware of that too. What do you say? Before you answer, I will have you take this ring and hold it."

He gave Jesse a small silver ring.

"Sir, I have only known your daughter a short time as she is now, but I have known her as my Shadow Dream for longer than that. I love her, sir. I hoped to ask for her hand in marriage. I don't know your customs, but Breeze and I are fighting in a war, and we cannot marry until that battle has been won. Would you grant me your permission to marry your daughter when this war is over?"

Jesse looked down at the ring, and to his surprise, it had changed from a plain silver band into a white dragon, like Cami's talisman ring.

"What the..."

Jesse looked over to Breeze; she had tears in her eyes. He then looked at Breeze's parents and noticed their shocked faces—her mother also had tears.

"*Jesse, my son, we dare not refuse you,*" Dalaron whispered. "Your marriage to our daughter has been given the blessing of the White Druid. How this can be, we do not know, but it is so. We will plan a wedding for after the war. May the gods of both worlds bless you, our children."

Jesse was told to wear the ring until it could be exchanged for the wedding ring at their marriage ceremony. Breeze was given one too. When they opened the second box, it was discovered that her ring had also changed into a white dragon. It appeared they were meant to be a couple.

They all stood and embraced. Miranda invited them to the kitchen for a light meal to celebrate. They had visited for a long time before anyone noticed that it was dark, and they had missed a refreshing for that day. The world was changing.

"Jesse, come back to the forest immediately. There has been an attack on the Slater children. Jason has been taken, and Pearl is gravely wounded."

Rambo's message came so suddenly and unexpectedly that Jesse jumped, surprising everyone. When he explained, they were all anxious for him and Breeze to return to the forest. After hugs and farewells, Jesse and Breeze warped back to the village, unsure of what they would find.

***

"As the story of life unfolds, there will always be challenges, and sometimes, tragedies. But with these—providing balance—arise happiness and joy. At times, they come together; more often, we must wait to discover the answers and the reasons.

May the gods bless each of us in our journey, and in our understanding."

—Quoted from a sermon given by Mistress Qiana, as recorded in the Archives of Learning and Faith. She was the first counsellor to Master Jaysar, High Priest of the world of Clement, and her words were recited during a time of great sorrow by Nexlucimus, High Priest of the world of Xanthara.

Chapter 29

Give Them Hell

Jesse and Breeze were stunned by the message from Rambo telling them about the attack on the Slater twins. The news that Gran had been severely injured was alarming, and after a hasty farewell to Breeze's parents, they warped to the Slater home in the Elven village.

They were shocked at the sight that greeted them. Bodies of the dead and wounded were scattered around the yard of the house. A quick glance told them that none of the fatalities they could see were from the village or Keepers, but a few of those who had been guarding the Slater home were wounded. Elven healers were tending to the injured, and others were gathering the dead for burial preparations. The horrible sight temporarily stunned both Jesse and Breeze into silence, until Ginnea approached them.

"What happened, Ginnea?" Jesse asked solemnly, eyeing the casualties.

"The assault was well-planned and quick. The invaders cut a hole in the back wall. It came at a time when Sara was napping, and Jim had gone to the vendors for food. They surprised the Keepers who were guarding. Rambo and Zealoc were in the main part of the village talking with Nexlucimus. Sara woke up and tried to intervene, but her condition prevented her. The stress and shock were too much—she collapsed, which probably saved her life and the life of her unborn child.

The hole weakened the back wall of the house, and it fell in, covering Pearl and Mary with the wreckage. Jim heard the noise and ran there to help, but it was too late by then. The minions who weren't killed or grievously wounded had already captured Jason. They must have warped to their camp because there were no other signs or tracks outside. Pearl was found covering Mary with her own body—that's probably what kept the attackers from seeing Mary and taking her too."

Ginnea's voice cracked.

"Pearl was so brave, Jesse. She and Mary were both buried under debris when the roof partially collapsed and the bookshelves fell. Neither of them were conscious when we found them. They have been taken to the healing facility. Jesse, you must hurry, please go. The elves don't hold much hope for Pearl. Because she wasn't in the game world when this happened, she didn't have the advantage of her character form. She has extensive internal and head injuries. The elves also worry about Sara and the baby. The stress caused Sara to go into premature labour. They are trying to delay the delivery, but aren't sure if their efforts will work."

"Why didn't my talisman tell me something was wrong?" Jesse asked.

"That will be explained when you get to the healing facility. Nexlucimus is expecting you. Hurry, Jesse, Pearl needs you. I bid you farewell. I must join the others in pursuit and hope to see you soon."

Ginnea ran to her Fireling and launched into the sky.

Jesse took Breeze's hand and warped them to the healing facility, where they were met by Zeela.

"Come, Jesse, hasten," Zeela said, flying ahead of them down a hallway.

Travelling down the long corridor, they came to a room busy with people. Pearl was resting on a wooden plank bed, covered with a mattress made of woven grass, padded with soft feathers. The healers had blanketed her with a blue quilt, embroidered with silver dragons. Her face was badly bruised, and there were many bandages. Zealoc was standing at her side, lovingly holding her hand, his face tear-stained, his jaw quivering with the effort of holding back sobs. Rambo, in rooster form, was lying on her other side, his head resting on her chest as he made that soft clucking sound. Pearl's arm draped over him like she was cuddling a teddy bear. Her eyes were closed, and her breath came in short, shallow gasps. She was deathly pale.

"Gran... what happened to you?" Jesse asked weakly, his voice breaking as he approached her bedside.

Pearl's eyes fluttered open; her ashen face lifted into a shaky smile.

"Ah Jesse, my dear, come give me a kiss goodbye. I'm afraid I won't be finishing this quest with you."

Jesse and Breeze walked to her side, by Rambo. Jesse kissed the top of her head, stroking her red hair as tears ran down his face.

"Give them hell for me, Jesse..." she whispered.

"That's a given, Gran," Jesse said, as he wiped his tears and chuckled softly.

"I love you, Jesse, I always will, and if the gods let me, I'll be watching this to the end."

"Gran, what am I going to do without you? I need you to kick my butt and tell me to shut my mouth."

Pearl snickered at this, and weakly responded, "I solemnly surrender my butt-kicking and mouth-closing duties to Rambo and Breeze. I noticed the commitment rings—I approve."

Several people turned to look at him and Breeze with this disclosure.

Pearl looked up at Zealoc, who was watching the floor, his eyes blurry with tears. She seemed to gather strength for a moment.

"Dearest Zealoc, look up, not down, and remember the wonderful times we have had. No matter my past, you are where my heart is, because of your love... and this world."

Through his tears, Zealoc kissed Pearl's hand, then bent forward and kissed her forehead, and her mouth.

"Two millennia I have walked alone because I could find no woman that understood me. Now I have found you, a mortal, and you must leave," he could talk no more.

"Zealoc," Pearl said feebly, "like the two sides of a coin, our love will never be separated."

She smiled at him weakly and feebly squeezed his hand.

"I promise you, that when this is over, we will be together. Never again will we be apart. I feel this strongly."

Zealoc kissed her one last time before giving in to his sobs.

Gran peacefully passed away a short while later. The elves took care of preparing her body in the custom of ancient mortals, who, they said, treated the dead with reverence and honour. Because she was so well thought of, she was given the highest regard. Her memorial was planned for the following morning at sunrise.

At dawn, Gran was gently lying on a platform that had been prepared for her funeral pyre in the centre of the village. She was dressed with great respect, in a traditional elven costume—pure white leather, decorated with many designs of the native wildflowers. Her hair had been brushed and adorned with downy feathers of different hues. In her hands, she held a bouquet of red and white forever roses.

The service was a beautiful, spiritual experience, with many tearful eulogies given, including one from Nexlucimus, who praised Pearl for her years of loving dedication to the Keepers' cause and the Xantharaian people. Jim Slater tried and failed to express his gratitude and indebtedness to Pearl for her sacrifice, but tears and the inability to get his voice to work prevented him from communicating his feelings. Mary stepped forward with the help of others and tearfully told how Pearl had defended her with her own body and tried to assist Jason.

"She was so brave, taking no thought for her own safety."

After the others who wished to express their feelings and appreciation to Pearl had had their turn, Jesse was given the honour of sending her remains home to the gods. Rambo, in full battle form, assisted him. With the help of their magic, the blaze took only seconds to release Pearl's essence. Zealoc and Breeze stood with them, along with David, who had arrived in time to say goodbye to his mother-in-law.

After the memorial, it was another elven tradition to hold a great feast, during which the loved ones' favourite dishes were prepared. Following the feast, there was energetic music, and the elves performed many of their traditional dances. Jesse wasn't in the mood for all the gaiety, but Breeze wanted to take part. After a few dances, he had to admit that he felt better.

Zealoc had a harder time releasing his grief until a young elven girl asked him to dance with her. He refused at first, but she was persistent. He finally agreed, and like Jesse, Zealoc began to feel lighter with the participation. After a while, Zealoc felt well enough that he and his cousin Beloe, who had come to support him, did a dwarfish jig. Jesse could almost see Gran there clapping her hands. It made him smile.

"This is the way she would've wanted to be remembered — full of life and love," Jesse said to Rambo.

"Indeed," Rambo sighed sadly.

The memorial party lasted all day and well into the early evening, but Jesse only lasted a few hours before he needed to get away. He asked Breeze and Rambo to join him, and the three of them walked to the shore of Lake O's.

Breeze and Jesse sat just inside the forest on a downed log, while Rambo, in rooster form, continued down to the lake. When he reached the water, Rambo crowded loud and long before morphing into his small dragon form and going silent. Surprised by this action, Jesse and Breeze said nothing. After a few moments, Jesse stood, watching Rambo sitting silently on the beach by the water.

"Breeze, I think I need to be with him for a while. Will you wait for me here?"

"Yes, I will wait for you here."

He kissed her and then walked towards the grieving dragon.

"Rambo, my friend, do you mind if I sit with you?"

As Jesse sat next to his friend, Rambo remained silent for a long while before acknowledging him. When he finally spoke, it was with difficulty.

"I am immortal, Jesse. It's not supposed to be like this. I am so tired of losing people that I love. I can't cope with it anymore." Rambo's voice broke with these last words.

Sitting at the edge of the forest where Jesse had left her, Breeze watched the two friends sitting close to each other on the beach. Rambo and Jesse talked and cried for a long time, thoroughly venting their grief. They even sat through a much lighter-than-usual refreshing rain that had returned that day. It wasn't enough to soak them, and it wasn't at the correct timing, but it did help to wash away some of their pain. When they finally got to where they could just talk and even laugh some, they decided it was time to go back.

Jesse stood nose to nose with Rambo's reduced dragon form and hugged him. Rambo embraced him in return, with his wings.

"Someday, my friend, I hope to give you a proper hug, with arms instead of wings."

"Oh, I don't know, Rambo, I kind of like the claws. Besides, your elf form is probably so short you still won't give a proper hug," Jesse snorted.

"You think so, do you?" Rambo morphed a little bigger and whacked Jesse so hard he did a complete flip and landed face down in the sand.

"I'd punch you back, you big bucket of bolts, but I'd only bruise my hand again," Jesse said, spitting sand out of his mouth.

They laughed all the way back to where Breeze had fallen asleep on the forest floor.

"Let me see that commitment ring, Jesse."

Jesse showed it to Rambo, and the dragon emitted a deep sigh at the sight of the White Dragon.

"It's like the talisman ring that Cami wore — another sign that Chaelea's hand is in all of this."

"Hey, Rambo, what's that out in the water?"

"What? I don't know. It does look out of place. Let's go check it out."

Flying over the water, they were surprised to see a black panther swimming rather weakly.

"Poor thing, I wonder where it came from?" Jesse questioned.

"We have to do something, or it'll drown," Rambo said.

Jesse reached out to the cat with his mind and was surprised at the answer he got.

"Rambo, throw a bubble around him... hurry."

Rambo did, and Jesse magically towed the bubble to the beach.

"Rambo, it's Jason — he got away!"

"Jason? How is that possible?"

"I have no idea, but this is a blessing for sure!"

Jesse dismounted and ran to the weak panther.

"Jason, how did you get away? And how is it possible that you can shapeshift?" Rambo asked.

The exhausted twin collapsed on the sand without answering. Rambo removed the bubble. Immediately there were Skeedlers everywhere, but Rambo yelled at them in his loudest voice.

"LATER!"

The Skeedlers scurried out of sight, but not far away. The yell had awakened Breeze, and she ran down to the beach to see what was going on. They explained to her who the panther was.

"Jason? How is this possible?" Breeze questioned.

"We aren't sure, but we need to get him back to the village healers. Breeze, would you fly ahead and alert Nexlucimus about this? We will take him to the healing facility."

"I will indeed," Breeze responded as she flew to alert Nexlucimus and the healers.

Jesse helped Rambo get the exhausted young cat onto Rambo's back, then climbed on behind to help keep him secure. Arriving at the healing facility, there was a small gathering of concerned and curious people. Nexlucimus greeted them along with the healers who were waiting.

Jesse and Rambo watched as the healers removed Jason to an examination room. Jim, having been alerted to his son's arrival, came running down the corridor, joining Jesse and the others who had gathered.

"How did he get away? Is he okay? It's another miracle, Jesse, because of Pearl and now you and Rambo, our children are once again safe," Jim said gratefully, his voice breaking.

"We think he is fine, Jim, just exhausted from his ordeal," Rambo said.

"The healers are checking him over now," Jesse added. "After he rests, I'm confident he will give us the details. Go see him, I'm sure it is okay."

Jim thanked Jesse and Rambo again and then stepped into Jason's room as Jesse turned his attention to the Head Elder.

"Master Nexlucimus, I have some questions for you, sir," Jesse said, taking Breeze's hand and facing the Elder.

"We can go into this empty room here, Jesse. I have some questions for you as well. Would you permit my wife to join us? And I believe that your wife should be included," Nexlucimus smiled, observing Jesse and Breeze.

"I would like that, and you too, Rambo," Jesse said.

Zeela joined them in the small room, and Nexlucimus closed the door for privacy.

"You first, Jesse," Nexlucimus said as they all took seats around the carved wooden table.

"Why didn't our talisman tell us that Gran was in trouble? It also didn't warn us when Cami was abducted," Jesse questioned.

"The talisman can be turned off by the person in distress. We didn't understand that at first," Nexlucimus sighed sadly. "Cami, who is back, was rendered unconscious at first. When she became aware of where she was, and the great advantage it gave the Keepers, she didn't want to be rescued."

"She's back! When did that happen?" Jesse asked, surprised.

"Cami returned not too long ago. She said she had information to relate to us, but was tired and saddened about Pearl, and wanted to rest first. I believe that you three had been gone for several hours by that time. Now, let me tell you why I think Pearl's talisman didn't warn you. I believe that Pearl was so involved with protecting Mary that she felt nothing of herself. I'm sure that when she was mortally wounded, her thoughts were still not of herself, but of protecting Mary and, in her own way, you. She blocked the talisman from alerting you, not through any conscious effort, but through her love for you, Jesse."

Jesse felt the sting of tears filling his eyes again, and as they fell, they hit the commitment ring on his left hand. Breeze took his hand as she leaned her head against his arm. He kissed the top of her head.

"Is there anything else that I can help you with, Jesse?"

"No, sir."

"Then, I would like to ask you and Breeze about your commitment rings. May I see them?"

"They are from Chaelea, Nexlucimus," Rambo said.

Zeela gave a soft gasp as she and Nexlucimus were shown the rings.

"We can see that. Tell me, were the rings in this form when you first received them?" Nexlucimus asked, curiously.

"No, sir, they changed as I talked to Breeze's parents. They were very shocked. Her father said that our marriage agreement was blessed by the White Druid. We told them this conflict with Tazeron needs to be won before the wedding. They will be planning it for after the war."

"Breeze, do you know the history of the White Druid?" Nexlucimus asked.

"Yes, sir, I do. I know that she was taken to the gods to protect her and that she lives with them now. She can act as one of their messengers and she has great influence and power because of these blessings in addition to her own natural talents and skills. I know that she is the wife of Rambo and that they were both given the shapeshifter ability. Chaelea was given the ability so she could live with the gods and serve them. Rambo was given the ability as a sign of her love for him and his devotion to the gods and their service. I know that while he has the shapeshifter ability, he is denied his true form. Even though many things were lost to me because of my rapid development, I do have additional knowledge because I was a Shadow Dream. Rambo and I have become good friends through the ages, and I know much about his past. As a

Shadow Dream, I also had close contact with Chaelea." She smiled sadly at Rambo.

"My friends, I must admit, I don't fully understand how, or why, Chaelea is so involved with Jesse's life. I do know that it can only mean good things. You are a very blessed young man."

"I know it, sir," Jesse said, as he squeezed Breeze's hand and patted Rambo's shoulder. "I know."

Nexlucimus smiled at them as he started to stand.

"Sir, there is one more thing. I feel like we, the Keepers, must launch a more aggressive march toward Tazeron. I would like to call a meeting of the Keepers. We all need to learn what Cami and Jason have to say if they are able. I also want Breeze to tell them about what she discovered in the troll village. Your attendance would be appreciated as well."

"That can be arranged, Jesse. Would tomorrow morning be okay with you? That will give young Jason more time to regain his strength."

"Yes, sir."

"Very well, it will be arranged. Until then, good night to you."

"Good night, sir, and thank you."

Chapter 30

The Rescue

Leaving the healing facility, the three friends walked towards the village centre and the vendors for a late snack. Rambo, the rooster, wandered off into the woods. While Jesse and Breeze were eating their food at one of the outside tables, Zealoc approached and spoke to them.

"Jesse, I must apologise for abandoning you in the leadership of our group. You are an accomplished natural leader, but that is no excuse. The only reason I can give was my finding Pearl. Now, I have lost her to this war," Zealoc grew silent as he struggled with his emotions.

"Zealoc, my friend," Jesse said, "you gave Gran love and happiness, and I can't fault you for that. She was a very lonely person before you. You gave her purpose and companionship. We have all suffered a great loss, and now it is time to remember her words and 'give them hell.' All of us grow tired of this war. It is easy to feel like we are making no progress; however, like an end-game dungeon, when it feels like we have been beating our heads against a wall, we have been learning from the experience. Tomorrow we will gather all our people to discuss our next move. I want everyone, including the twins, at that meeting if they are able."

"Thank you for your words, Jesse," Zealoc said humbly. "I agree that a meeting to plan is needed. Until tomorrow, good night, Jesse, Miss Breeze." Zealoc bowed.

"Good night, Zealoc," both Jesse and Breeze said as they watched the grieving little man walk away.

While Jesse and Breeze visited at the table, Sean and Cami arrived. They conveyed the good news that they had been to the healing facility and that Sara had delivered the baby. The baby was healthy and vigorous. There was much relief felt by all at this happy news. Cami expressed her shock and grief at Pearl's passing and the way it had happened. They sat for a while reminiscing before Cami said that, despite her nap, she was tired and left for her room.

"Jesse, come with me," Breeze said urgently, tugging at his arm, smiling. "I wish to visit Sara and the baby. I think we need to do something enjoyable."

"It's late, Breeze, are you sure?"

"Yes, come," she said, tugging harder on his arm.

"Ok… Ok, I'm coming," he laughed.

They warped to the healing facility and walked to the busy nursery, which was experiencing a population explosion. Unable to distinguish one tiny bundle from another, they went to Sara's room and found her there with Jim and Mary, who was sitting on a side chair. Sara cradled the baby in her arms.

"Jesse, we are so sorry about your grandmother," Sara said, her voice thick with emotion. "She was a wonderful person and a thoughtful neighbour. We will forever be grateful for her bravery in saving our Mary."

"I'm very grateful to her also, Master Jesse," Mary said, a tear running down her cheek. "I wish there was some way to repay her sacrifice," Mary added. Jim nodded his agreement.

"Mary, there might be a way for you to help us. I'm calling a meeting tomorrow morning with the Keepers. I would like you and Jason to meet with us, if Jason is well enough, that is. Your father will be there, but your mother is excused for obvious reasons." Jesse smiled at Sara, who didn't smile back.

"I will be there," Jason said, as he walked into the room and was happily greeted by his parents and sister. "I was just exhausted, but I am feeling much better now. The elves gave me a potion of renewed strength and stamina. That, and a good power nap, was all I needed to feel refreshed and eager to help with this quest."

"What is this all about, Jesse?" Jim wanted to know.

"Jim, this chasing Tazeron around and getting nowhere has got to end. We are wasting too much time and accomplishing nothing. Gran's last words to me were 'give them hell,' and it's time to do that. We will discuss all this tomorrow, but I will tell you this: your twins are grown now, and the best way to protect them is to let them be a part of this war that centres on them."

"Yes, Father, listen to Master Jesse. I feel he speaks the truth. Mary and I have had training in the way of the elves; let us help. We need to help." Mary stood and stepped beside her twin. "Indeed, Father, we must be allowed to help, as Master Jesse has said."

"I feel so old when they call me Master. I know it's for respect, but it still feels weird," Jesse mind-talked to Breeze.

"You'll get used to it, love." Breeze smiled at him.

Jesse could tell that Jim was struggling with the discussion—seeing the truth and yet wanting to protect his children.

"We will be at the meeting, Jesse, but I make no promises."

"Agreed. Now, Breeze and I would like to see this new little one, is that okay?"

"As long as you don't want to take him off to war. I believe it will be okay," Sara said, with a worried smile, as if she expected Jesse to whisk the child off and fit him with armour.

"Not to war, Sara," Jesse chuckled, "but it might be wise if we transport you and this child to Clay for greater protection."

"Clay?" Sara looked confused. "What is that?" she asked.

"Clay is the new world of fantasy that was created for the splitting. It would be a safe place for you and this new child," Jesse explained.

"I'm not sure that is necessary, Jesse. I feel that, for now at least, we are safe. The elves, while very busy with new babies and wounded, are enough deterrent for any more attacks. Surely, Tazeron's minions wouldn't try anything again so soon while everyone is on high alert, would they?" Sara asked, looking hopeful.

Jesse, feeling uneasy, simply said, "We can discuss it tomorrow after everyone has had time to rest. I urge you to think about it."

Sara, satisfied with Jesse's response, handed the baby to Breeze, who smiled and cooed at the little one, which made Jesse nervous. Then Breeze, smiling big, passed the baby to Jesse. The tiny blue bundle was light as a feather, but he had lungs like a gale wind when he cried, demonstrating his displeasure at being passed around. Jesse was unnerved and quickly gave him back to Breeze.

"Get used to babies, my love, because I want to have many of them," Breeze grinned mischievously at him. Jesse groaned softly at her but smiled despite himself.

The next day, in the morning, as planned, the Keepers gathered in an outside amphitheatre. Jesse explained that the purpose of the meeting was to hear the experiences of different members who had recently returned and then make plans. They listened as Jason, Breeze, and Cami gave their accounts. Jason was the first to brief them.

"I was taken to the troll village which now houses ogres and other supporters of Tazeron, not fifty leagues from here." There were expressions of surprise at that disclosure.

"Mary and I have known for some time that we had our mother's talent as druids, and that is where our training has been. My captors obviously didn't know this, because they chained my hands and feet to a wall and left me, alone." Jason snickered at this.

"All I did was morph into my cat form, slip out of the chains, then cast stealth on myself and sneak out of their camp. I'm sure some heads rolled. It was almost too easy. I just wish that I had a flight stone, to change into a raven or a hawk. Maybe Master Lamb will think I'm ready now. I sure got tired swimming Lake O's. It's huge! I owe my life to Master Rambo and Master Jesse." He gave a bow in their direction before sitting down.

Breeze gave her report next.

"Rambo, Jesse and I went to the capital city and were attacked by trolls in the Great Library, the same village that captured you, Jason. I managed to talk to one of them, and after that, I hid in his thick hair. He forgot I was there. All of the trolls were warped back to their village by the two missing Council members, who, it seems, are sympathisers to Tazeron." There were voices of outrage at this disclosure.

"I also discovered the other council members who were chained to walls like Jason. There appeared to be an aura around them as well, probably blocking any magic. I don't understand why they didn't do that to Jason, but we're glad they didn't. The council members seemed well taken care of and, except for the chains, they were comfortable.

One more thing that not everyone appears to know: the statue of the White Druid has been taken from the Great Library." There were more stunned expressions among the gathering.

"We discovered that fact when the three of us went to the Great Library and were attacked. While I was in their camp, I learned that the trolls had carried the statue and placed it in the game for Tazeron. He wants it guarded in case the White Druid returns, as the tradition says she might."

Rambo explained the old tale that the White Druid could possibly return to her statue in a time of conflict. There were a few who hadn't heard of the tradition.

After that, Cami stepped forward with her report.

"Most of what I was able to learn, you already know. There was some uncertainty as to when Tazeron would make his move on the children, but as we have seen, that has happened. I'm sure with Jason's escape there will be other attempts, and they won't be so careless next time. I am wondering if Jason's easy escape was because many of Tazeron's supporters had warped to this village to help with the abduction of the twins. The supporters that captured Jason and chained him to the wall apparently forgot to cast silence on him, or maybe they couldn't, so he was able to use his magic to escape. We are all very happy for that, Jason." She smiled at the young man.

"My most significant information is the fact that the Queen seems to be the one making most of the decisions. She, as most of you know, was a game master-creator. This makes her very dangerous to our cause. She not only knows how to change the game landscape, as we saw with the mountains, but she has the power to control all aspects of the mechanics. We need to get rid of her, permanently. We cannot merely move her to another location or even kill her — she would only resurrect. She stays in her chambers most of the time, surrounded by protectors. She relies on messengers to relay information."

"Another thing," Cami said. "Tazeron has absolutely no magic, neither do many of his followers except for those who were the former council members that joined him. Tazeron depends on these two sympathisers who still possess their magical abilities. I will say this: we also have sympathisers for our side within their ranks, but I can give no details at this time, for security reasons."

After Cami finished her report, Jesse stood before them.

"Since we started with this quest line, we have seen many changes. Our focus has shifted all over the place. Now, as we have learned, our priority besides the Slater children must be this Queen. She needs to be silenced, entirely and permanently, as Cami has said. We must be prepared for anything. I'm sure with her knowledge and command of the game we will meet some extremely nasty aspects in the game.

We are running out of time, people. With the information that Cami gave us, and help from the inside, we will head back into the game and attack the Queen's chambers. Some of us will lead directly in, destroying everything in our path, while others will travel through the secret passages that the pygmy trolls carved centuries ago. Either way, our goal is the same. I will be talking to the team leaders, deciding who will do what, then we will chase this black-hearted bitch into another existence.

Except for the team leaders, you are all excused to pack for our offensive. We will leave in one hour."

Just as they were regathering and Zealoc was getting ready to give his battle shout, everyone at the meeting with a talisman experienced burning in their left arm. A message was sent directly to their minds: Sara was in danger; she and the baby had been kidnapped. Zealoc could sense something was wrong when most of those in attendance cringed and jumped to their feet.

"Our plans have just been changed, people," Jesse announced to the group, explaining what was going on so that those without a talisman would know the situation. "This child has just become more critical than getting rid of the Queen. He must be rescued first, then we will destroy this evil woman."

Jesse noticed Jim and the twins having an animated discussion off to the side and plans formulated quickly in his mind.

"Jim, I want you to come with me to rescue your son along with Rambo, Breeze, Cami, Sean, and Ginnea. We will go to the place where Sara is. Since we have no idea where that might be, I think it's best if only a small group warp there."

"Zealoc, I want you to take the twins with you to the mountain where the Queen is. The rest of you," Jesse spoke to the gathering, "will go with Zealoc. All of you that have a talisman, link with those that don't. Make sure everyone has a link; we don't want to leave people behind. When you get to the Queen's Mountain, wait for us there—do not engage her. Ok, everyone, gather your supplies and good luck."

Jim warped ahead of the team rescuing his wife and son and was waiting there for them, visibly shaken. He sat on a nearby stump as the team quickly formulated a plan.

"Jim, you are so big," Jesse said, eyeing Jim's Ogre game form.

"Jesse, I have shrink and invisible potions, so Jim's size is no problem," Sean told them.

"Ok Sean, thank you." Jesse mind searched for the fortress and found Sara in one of the upper towers. He talked to her through the talisman. The baby was not with her. She was relieved to hear from them, and that Jim had come. She wanted all their effort directed to her son's recovery, but she didn't know where the baby was.

Not knowing where the child was made it difficult. Jesse decided that a better plan would be for Sean, Ginnea, and Cami to recover Sara. He, Jesse, would go with Jim and Rambo to look for the infant. Sean made sure that they had plenty of the concoctions needed. When Sean's group found Sara, they were to warp her to Clay and wait for the rest there. Since Jesse and his talisman had been to Clay once, and they were all linked through the party, travelling there would be no problem. Jesse's group would go to Clay once they had the child.

They were ready.

Rambo morphed to his smallest dragon size and cast the bubble and invisible spells for extra measure. They started searching the stronghold, beginning with the lower levels. They found those areas pretty much vacant.

As they moved higher into the fortress, they started seeing more people, including blood fairies. Rambo's invisibility spell seemed to be holding, and so far, they hadn't excited any nasties. Breeze flew off on her own, searching rooms. She planned to contact the tiny child, knowing that it would be hard to do.

Jesse and Jim flew around hoping to hear the baby crying, fearing that they might have drugged him to keep him quiet. Jesse tried again to mind search. By pure luck, with his mind search, he saw a suspicious-looking goblin as it came out of a room carrying blankets. Jesse's mind jetted into the room before the door could close, and a terrifying sight greeted his senses.

Stretched out on a marble bench was a tiny naked azure elf baby, tied down like a frog on a dissecting slab. His mouth was stuffed with what looked like cotton. The monster at the head of the table had a knife, ready to use. Tazeron was there, and they seemed to be performing a ritual on the blade.

Jesse pulled his mind back, badly shaken by what he saw. He made a note of where he had been, directing Rambo and Breeze where to go. They raced there, knowing that the child's life was in peril.

When they arrived at the location, Rambo blasted the door with his fire, blowing it off its hinges. The villains scattered everywhere. Breeze sent darts of confusion to those in the room and then freed the infant as Tazeron and his followers tried and failed to get to her. With the baby in her arms, Breeze landed on Rambo's back and handed the baby to his father. Jesse and Rambo incinerated the chamber. As they did so, Tazeron briefly made eye contact with Jesse. The madman screamed in a fury before he seemed to drop through the floor. Jesse sent a message to Sean and Cami as his group left for Clay.

It took Ginnea, Cami, and Sean only moments after receiving Jesse's message to get to Sara. They needed to be in contact with her to get her to Clay where the rest of the group had warped. She broke down in tears as they too travelled to the new world.

Getting Sara and the baby safely settled at the healing facility on Clay relieved everyone's mind. Jesse and Breeze contacted

Master Osuweep; they explained what was happening and made sure that bringing the Slaters there was alright.

"It is our pleasure to assist the Keepers in any way we can, Master Jesse. Breeze, my dear, it's always a delight to see you. If I may be so personal, I notice that you two are wearing commitment rings. May I see them?"

Without any hesitation, Jesse and Breeze showed this kind man their rings. As expected, he was stunned by them.

"The White Druid... how very curious. When do you plan to marry?"

"As soon as this war is won, Master Osuweep," Breeze told him. "We would be honoured to have you attend, along with your household."

The Elder was pleased with the invitation. He assured Jesse and Breeze that he and his family would be there.

Jesse decided to leave Jim on Clay with Sara for now. Jim promised to join the battle with the Queen as soon as Sara and the baby were settled in their new surroundings. The other citizens seemed delighted to welcome Sara and the baby. Jesse had one more request to ask of the Elder before they left, then they warped back to the Queen's chambers.

Jesse, Rambo, and Breeze arrived at the mountain right behind Sean, Cami, and Ginnea. Sean ported to the forest to retrieve his mount, which he and Cami would be sharing since Brutus was with

Tommy. Zealoc let them know that the lower two levels of the compound, including the central courtyard, had been cleared without much effort. It seemed like the fortress wasn't expecting any trouble and had sent their troops elsewhere.

The advance team of Keepers didn't try to clear the prison or the other work areas, such as the galley or the healing facility. Those areas were lightly populated and of no consequence right then.

Rambo, Jesse, and Breeze travelled into one of the small connecting tunnels as Jesse searched for Sariah and Clarisa through mind talk.

When contacted, Sariah had a warning for Jesse.

"Beware, Jesse, the Queen has changed her protectors. They will now morph to match your strength and abilities. They will be like mirrors, reflecting to you what you do to them. They will respawn at a faster rate because they will no longer be sealed by your magic. There is nothing we can do to assist you, other than communicating this way only."

"How many protectors does she have?" Jesse mind talked.

"That will change. The Queen will start at seven, and each time one dies, two will spawn in its place. The best strategy will be to control them, holding them to one area."

"Is there anything else that you can tell us at this point?"

"Only that Tazeron is recruiting others to take the place of the Queen, if you should destroy her. He may have others of her skill or greater on their way here now."

"Are these others also mortal?"

"I think so, I'm not sure."

"Can you find out, please? It's crucial."

"I can't promise, but I will try."

"Thank you, Sariah."

Jesse relayed the correspondence he had with Sariah to the other Keepers and asked if anyone had any ideas.

Malleesa spoke up, "My brothers and I can use stealth and invisibility as we work our way into the chambers, Jesse. Druids can also do this. Even without magic, we have concoctions to help us. We have several druids, including the twins that joined us today, and their magic seems to be working perfectly, even with their lack of experience. The songsters — or bards, as you call them — can charm the mobs to follow them out of the chambers, and then perhaps they could warp them to a secure location."

"Those are all excellent ideas, Malleesa. What we don't want is to use magic that will bounce back at us, as it's being reflected. Toos, can you change us into anything besides furniture and bugs?" Jesse asked.

"Only furniture and bugs, Jesse. Sorry."

"That's okay, it was just a thought. We need to get rid of those protectors without killing them. What do you think of this idea, Malleesa?"

"Please, Jesse, call me Mally."

"As you wish, Mally. It is easier to say," Jesse smiled at her. "I would like you and your brothers, and Jason and Mary, to stealth in, just to the outer chamber room doors. Toos, you go with them. As they advance into the inner chamber, change them all into bugs. Breeze, Zeela, and Shosho — since you are fairies — I want you to go right behind Toos with the Bards. Breeze, I want you to target the Queen with a dart of sleep. Shosho and Zeela, I want you two to muddle the protectors with darts of confusion, as the Bards sing spells of calm and charm, then pull them out to the tanks with their tractor spells."

Jim Slater quietly joined the group to many thumbs up, nods, and smiles.

"I've heard most of the plan, Jesse. What would you like me to do?"

"Welcome back, Jim. It's always nice to have a warrior drop in." He smiled at the big man. "As the singers pull the protectors out to you, I want you and Zealoc, Beloe, Rykan, and Dropdead to buddy up and each grab one or two, then warp them to a moon, or the bottom of an ocean, or something, and leave them there. Remember to hold your breath." Jesse chuckled.

"In the meantime, the rogues and druids will snare and trap the sleeping Queen until we can warp her to Clay, where Osuweep is waiting with a security crew."

It was such an unusual plan that they thought it might work. It was nice to have the abilities of many of the different games at their command. The team voted to give it a try. Each of the tanks decided where they would travel to and who was going to grab one or two. Then they launched their attack.

Jesse told Sariah what they were doing, and she was impressed, thinking it was an excellent plan. She would watch from a closet and let Jesse know what was going on.

If that plan didn't work, the backup was for all the magic casters to storm the room and incinerate the place until there wasn't a crumb left. They might still do that. Jesse was starting to think maybe they should burn the place down no matter what happened.

Most of the mountain had already been cleared out, so getting to the Queen's chambers was relatively easy for the advancing parties. With the talisman ability, Jesse, as the team leader, was kept informed in the tunnel where he and Rambo waited for reports on how the battle was progressing. Breeze left them to join the other fairies.

The rogues and druids used their stealth to reach the outer doors of the Queen's chambers with the enchanters close behind. The fairies and bards lined up right behind them. As soon as Mally, her brothers, and the twins entered the chambers, Toos changed them into giant beetles. The protectors ignored the bugs.

Zeela, Breeze, and Shosho entered after the bugs and sent their darts of searching to the Queen and her guardians. While the Queen slept, the bards sang calm and charm spells to the protectors. Those songs allowed the singers to pull the big, ugly thugs with their songs of snare into the waiting arms of the tanks. Each tank then grabbed their quota and warped them to destruction in another dimension.

The rogues and druids did an excellent job of trapping the very sleepy Queen. Other Keepers, with talismans, waited outside the chambers to warp her to Clay. When they arrived, Osuweep was waiting with several burly guards.

Once the Queen was out of the game world, she reverted to her small mortal self. She would have no contact with anyone, nor have magic at her disposal while on Clay. She would remain there until the war was over, and her fate could be decided.

Jesse had Sariah and Clarisa guide the Keepers to the working areas of the mountain. There they decided what to do with the prisoners, cooks, healing facility staff, and anyone else they found who wasn't a real part of Tazeron's minions. These people, including Jesse's ex-nemesis Mckay, were all transferred to places where they wouldn't have contact with computers or Tazeron.

Mckay appeared very humbled by his experience, and when he saw Jesse, he was shocked and repeated many times how sorry he was for his past. He was still sent to a detention facility on Clay to remain until proven trustworthy to return home. Mckay understood the conditions and promised to comply with the guards. He seemed honestly repentant. Jesse hoped so.

If the people they found were merely game characters who were trapped, or children who had been sucked into Tazeron's world, they were released to the rescue groups. The children were then returned to their parents, with instructions that they were grounded from the games because if it happened again, they could die.

Sariah and Clarisa went with the rescue groups where they offered their services. Slicer attached himself to Clarisa, and the two of them seemed very content.

When the mountains were cleared, Jesse gave the order, and everyone who had functioning magic threw all they had at it. It took several hours to destroy the fortress, but they had a whole lot of fun doing it.

"Hey, Rykan... I have a new title for you," Jesse shouted at the paladin who loved to collect trophies and armour in the game.

"Oh yeah, what's that?"

"Mountain killer..."

"Naw... that's okay, I'd rather have a new dress to add to my collection."

Jesse laughed until his sides hurt, and it sure felt good. After everyone had finished congratulating each other and the mountain fire died down, they started talking about what to do next.

"Hopefully, we got rid of most of Tazeron's spies by destroying the mountain," Rykan said as he munched on a piece of Breeze's conjured pepperoni pizza.

"I wonder why we never thought about conjuring pizza before," David asked.

"Probably because we didn't have Breeze with us before, and no one thought about conjuring it from the Xanthara side and bringing it in," Sean said, with his mouth full.

"Maybe I should travel to a tavern and get some beer," Healamonster chuckled.

"Now that we have a better understanding of the possibilities, there are all kinds of things we can do. I don't think beer is going to be one of those options though, Heala. Sorry man... you need ALL your intelligence," Jesse laughed, thinking of Gran and her stories.

"Aw, man... that sucks," the healer said, taking a big swig of cold milk. "What kind of milk did you say this was?"

Jesse shared a smile with Zealoc as they continued to eat, not answering.

Just as they were finishing their meal, there was a tremor in the ground.

"That was weird," Dropdead said. "Makes me think of the earthquakes we used to have..."

Before he could finish his sentence, a huge worm came flying out of the ground and ate him.

Chapter 31

Captured

"Whoa... that's new!" Heala choked, jumping on his steed.

Just then, another quake happened, and another worm shot out of the ground. Jesse fried it, and several smaller larvae spawned from the big one.

"Everyone up in the air... NOW!" Zealoc yelled at them.

"It looks like the Queen's replacement has arrived," Savana shouted over the roar of the worms that were everywhere now.

"What game did these slimy demons come from? Anyone know?" Jesse yelled at the group.

"There were some in my game, and they were a nightmare," Pumpkin called back. "Everyone hated that dungeon."

"My game had some too... I can't remember what we did to get rid of them, though," Clarisa responded.

"Watch the sky, people!" Rambo shouted, as a multitude of bats started swarming them.

"Everyone get behind Rambo!" Jesse yelled. "Have your mounts back in so that all heads are out. Then blast them with everything you have."

As the Keepers killed bats, the downed bats were eaten by worms. It was an eerie sight.

Right in the middle of the battle with the bats, Dropdead reappeared and announced to the Keepers that when he was eaten, he was ported to Tazeron's Fortress.

"Wait, stop fighting. You ended up in the Fortress?"

"Yeah, weird huh?"

"Maybe..." Jesse said.

"What are you thinking, son?" David asked.

"I think that might be a fast trip to our target."

"Everyone back on the ground, and when you get eaten, stay at Tazeron's Fortress."

"Eww..." Cami wasn't impressed with the plan.

"Jesse, why don't we just warp there?" Zeela asked.

"Okay, if you want to warp, go ahead. I'm taking a worm. I want to see exactly where I end up. Rambo, meet me there. Breeze, are you coming, or are you going to warp with Cami?"

"I love you, Jesse, but I'm going with Cami. See you there."

Most of the Keepers warped; only a few brave souls opted to take a worm. Jesse stood there watching the travellers and the ones being eaten. Nothing happened to him. Worms came and went, and still, he was standing there. He was all alone.

"Amazing how quiet the forest gets when you realise you are all alone. Rambo, can you hear me?" There was no answer. He tried to warp, but he didn't go anywhere.

"Okay, now my creep alert is starting to freak me out. What the heck is going on?"

Darkness engulfed him, and there was an extreme pain in Jesse's left shoulder. He crumpled to the ground, gasping. Jesse passed out, and when he woke up, he had no idea how long he had been unconscious. His left shoulder throbbed, and he couldn't move his arm; it was as if his arm was stuck to his side.

Jesse was still trying to figure out what was going on when a disembodied voice answered his question.

"I'll tell you what's going on, my young fool. You are in my territory now, and you have no power here."

"Who are you?" Jesse asked. Trying to sit up, he felt unbalanced and nauseous. He vomited.

"Your worst nightmare..."

Somehow, Jesse got to his feet, and staggering, he started to walk as the voice in his head laughed at him. He was so hot. It was like being in a scorching desert with no shade. Why was it so hot here? The scenery didn't seem any different, but it was so hot.

He needed to get out of here, only he wasn't exactly sure which way to go.

"Maybe travelling south would take me to the Shield and our first camp. But which way is south?"

If physically getting to the first camp were possible, then just perhaps the warp stones would be there. It was a long shot, but something had to work.

As Jesse continued to walk, the heat made him sweat like he'd been tossed into a fire. He felt so weak and unstable but determined. He noticed that he wasn't hearing the voice.

"Can you still hear me, weirdo? Voice in my head, nightmare guy?"

There was no answer. *"I must be outside the voice reception range. I wonder where the zone line is?"*

He started slowly walking in a circle pattern, he guessed. As he walked, he tested the voice. He still couldn't travel with his talisman. He started feeling like he was staked to a tether and walking at the end of his rope, marking out a circle. Two inches in and he could hear the voice, two inches out and he couldn't. Five inches out and he could hear it again. This could be a zone path. If he stayed on the track, he didn't hear the voice, but if he got off the trail, it laughed at him.

"It reminds me of a rat in a maze. If I keep figuring out the path, I wonder what weird reward will await me at the end."

Curious, Jesse sent his fire into the area, then had to duck as it rebounded and bounced all around him. He sat on the ground and shot it up; it kept going. He shot it forward, and it jumped back at him. Jesse experimented by walking into the laugh zone and shooting it; no magic would work in there. If he stepped onto the path, it worked again but bounced back.

Jesse had an idea. He conjured a ball of light like he did when Breeze and he were riding on Rambo. He tossed the ball of light into the air and whacked it with his right hand since his left wasn't working. He watched it bounce off the walls of his path. He followed it until it vanished, and he couldn't reconjure it. The pain in his left shoulder was draining his energy.

"I wonder what I did to my arm. Could it be nerve damage? I'll figure it out later, once I get to the zone. I wonder if I can mind search." His head was beginning to pound. *"Oh, if I had just packed some pain pills."*

Jesse tried to search the area with his mind. He was surprised to find that he could, even with his pounding head.

"Finally, something that works."

He used his mind to go straight up. Looking down, he saw himself. He looked around from his higher viewpoint at the landscape, like a map. Right in front of him on the ground, he saw the light ball. When he was inside himself, and not mind searching, he couldn't see it.

"That is so bizarre. Okay... I'm beginning to wonder if I got sent to the two-thirds of the game world that are a hard copy because this doesn't make any sense. The game doesn't act like this. Of course, I haven't played all the games, so I guess one of

them could be this weird. If this were my game back home, I would cancel my subscription."

Jesse started feeling desperate and more than a little frightened.

"Gran, when I was a small boy staying overnight at your place, and I got scared, you often said all I needed to do was pray to feel safe. All the bad feelings would go away. It always worked when I was with you. Gran, I'm feeling frightened right now, and I need to know what's going on. This just isn't right; something is terribly wrong. Please, someone, help me. Breeze, talk to me, guide me out of this."

Jesse felt compelled to sit in the meditation pose and think about Rambo coming to rescue him. He sat there for a long time. He didn't know what else to do.

He must have fallen asleep because he saw himself floating in a pool of gelatin, trying not to go under yet sinking. There was a rope over his head, and he knew that grabbing the rope and pulling himself out of the gelatin could be possible, but if he sat up to reach the line, he would sink faster.

"Trust me, Jesse, reach out and grab the rope."

"Rambo? I need you, bud, where are you?"

"Trust me, trust yourself, look within and search for who you are."

Jesse looked up; there was a rope hanging over his head. He reached for it.

As he grabbed the rope, it snaked around his arm, pulling him up out of the maze. It drew him higher and higher until he could see the whole game world—the forest, the burnt mountain spot, and Tazeron's Fortress. Then the rope released him, and he fell. He flailed and shouted, but no one heard him.

"It's okay, sir, please be still. George trying to help you. The more you move, the more you hurt."

Jesse's eyes popped open, and for a moment he wasn't sure what he was seeing. He thought he was staring into the face of a purple, one-eared goblin. *But that couldn't be. Could it?*

"What the heck! Where am I? Who are you?"

"You talk to George, sir. George help you mend."

"Help me… what? What are you talking about?"

Jesse tried to sit up; a wave of nausea hit him, and he had to puke. George was right there, with a bucket and a cold cloth to wipe his mouth and head. Jesse realised that his left arm was bound tightly to his chest, so tightly that it almost seemed like it wasn't there. With a shock, Jesse remembered the dream of the one-armed man.

"No… please, no…"

He reached around with his right hand and felt his left shoulder. His arm was gone. He fainted.

When Jesse woke up, there weren't as many bandages on his shoulder, and his head didn't swim as much when he tried to move.

George wasn't in the room, so Jesse decided to see if he could stand. It didn't work out very well. He slipped to the floor with a loud thud. George opened the door and quickly came to his aid.

"Oh sir, you must not do that. You will damage your other side. If you want to get out of bed, you must call George. Please call George. You are all George has..." He actually started to cry.

"Um... George, don't cry. I'll call you next time. Ok?"

"Oh, thank you sir, that makes George happy. Does sir want any food today? George has been giving you soup with herbs for pain and sleep while you mending. Would you like real food, sir? You have been so sick, sir. You talk in your sleep when fever blazing. You cry for Breeze and Gran and Rambo to help. You no need those names, sir, George here to help. George feared for your life, and for George's. If you die, George loses head. George likes head, sir."

Jesse watched as the little goblin talked animatedly and realised that while George was still purple, he had two ears.

"I must have been hallucinating. Maybe I still am," he laughed, and that surprised George.

"Is sir ok? Did George say something wrong?"

"No George, I'm all right, and you didn't say anything wrong. I would love some food, but only if you agree to eat with me. Is that allowed?"

"Um... George not sure, George asks, will bring back food. Please stay in bed, sir. George does not want to find you on ground, with a booboo on head."

Jesse chuckled, "Ok George, I will stay right here in bed, and thank you."

"George's pleasure, sir, George be right back."

As Jesse sat on his bed waiting for the little goblin to come back, there was a small knock on the door.

"Come in. I think the door is open."

Surprising Jesse, a small lady mist lizard flew in. She was flying like she was drunk.

"Sorry to bother you, sir, I has fresh linens for George. I will put in closet."

Her arms were full of towels and sheets, but that didn't stop her from speeding across the room and slamming into the wall. Jesse would've helped her, but George came running in, probably thinking it was Jesse.

"Oh, it's you Cazi, George tells you and tells you, go slow."

The lizard lady looked sheepish.

"I know George, but I forgets."

"That's ok, George remind again."

"George, are you and Cazi deleted game characters?" Jesse asked, curious.

"Yes... George fifteen levels, Cazi twelve. Creators left, and we are alone, we only have each other," he started to cry again, and Cazi joined him.

"George, where are we? What is this place, how did I lose my arm?"

"This place..." George looked around anxiously; Cazi brought her hands to her mouth.

"This place belongs to King."

"Oh George... you bad boy," she whispered. "Master don't want the guest to know these things."

"There are more people here?"

"Yes..." she giggled nervously.

"How many and where are they?"

"We must not talk about these things. George be in big trouble. George does not want big trouble."

The door pushed open, and Jesse was startled to see Tazeron walk in. Both George and Cazi fell to the floor, grovelling. Seeing that made Jesse feel sick again. Tazeron kicked both little toons aside as he walked closer to Jesse. Jesse noticed that Tazeron was wearing different robes than Rambo's memory had shown—he was cleaner and less rumpled.

"It's so hard to find good help anymore, why do you think that is, Jesse?"

Jesse didn't answer.

"It's a shame about your arm; it couldn't be helped. I needed the dragon for my collection, and I discovered a fascinating thing. Your blood works for my purposes too.*"*

Jesse felt the colour drain from his face.

"Yes, Jesse, I want to thank you for giving me what I wanted. I still need other ingredients, but your little fairy lady will give me what I want, soon enough."

"What do you mean, Tazeron?" Jesse spat out.

"Breeze... you see... she was my Shadow Dream once upon a time, and I know her very well. What! She never told you about me? My, my... keeping secrets already. Oh, well, she's not my concern anymore. I saw that you were wearing commitment rings. You brought me two dragons for my collection. That was very kind of you, Jesse. So, how are dear old Dalaron and Miranda, anyway?"

Jesse was stunned; he couldn't even come up with a reply. He had forgotten that the commitment ring was on his left hand.

"By the way, Jesse, don't get too comfortable in this room. After you recover from your... accident, you will be moved to other, more suitable... accommodations." Tazeron laughed, gave a little nod, and exited the room.

Jesse had never felt such raw evil in his entire life. The man reeked of it; his foul essence stunk up the whole room, polluting the air. Jesse found it hard to breathe, and his strength was drained—just being around Tazeron sapped his energy.

"Wait a moment; I just realised that I'm not wearing my robes and other things. What am I wearing? A hospital gown?"

"George, where are my clothes?"

"They much damaged, sir. George tries to fix them, but... too much blood. George tries to wash it out; there were many holes. I found you this lovely dress, sir. George thought you'd like a new dress since yours is ruined."

Jesse groaned; it wasn't even worth trying to explain why his robes were different from a dress.

"George, when will I be moved to another room?"

"Not room, sir... cage."

"The dream..."

Jesse's worst nightmare was coming true; his next room would be a cage. When that happened depended on how fast he healed.

Might as well enjoy this luxury hotel while I can. I wonder if George can get me out for a while.

"George, my friend..."

"George is sir's friend?"

"Of course you are. You have fed me and clothed me and kept me company. You are my friend."

"You make George happy, sir. George never has a friend before... never," George started to tear up again.

"He's going to make me cry in a minute."

"George, can you take me for a walk? I need some sunshine."

"Oh, George can't do that, sir. George loses head."

"Well, I don't want you to lose your head. What else could we do that would be fun?"

"Catch bugs and stuff them into the wall cracks. George likes that—big fat cockroaches or the orange spiders that spin webs on George's nose at night."

Jesse just stared at George, then shuddered. *"You have got to be kidding me."*

"George, could you get me something to eat, maybe some fruit?"

"Oh, George do that; George be right back. George checks bandages while Sir eats."

"Lovely..."

While George was gone, Jesse tried to touch the talisman on his amputated arm, but it was no good.

"Probably all dissected and shrivelled up somewhere. Maybe it's floating in a jar. That's just disgusting." He shuddered at the thought.

Jesse tried to search the fortress with his mind, but that didn't happen. He didn't have any luck trying to reach Rambo or Breeze either. Then he felt a warm pulsation on his neck.

"The chain! I forgot about the chain, and it's still there. What does it do? I guess it just keeps me warm. Is it my imagination, or did the chain just get warmer? It did. I wonder what that means?"

George came in with a bowl of hot soup, a plate of fresh fruit, and some bread.

"Oh George, you're a lifesaver, thank you, my friend."

"George likes it when you call George friend. George checks bandages now."

It didn't hurt as much when George changed the dressing this time, though Jesse still couldn't look at the wound.

"It's healing good, sir. George knows... George sees lots of injuries. You be moving to nice cage soon, sir. Are you excited?"

"Sure, George, really excited," Jesse said dryly. The goblin didn't notice.

"Oh, George likes when people happy. People live longer when happy."

"Somehow I don't see how 'nice' and 'cage' can go in the same sentence. I must remember that this is a person who likes to stuff cockroaches and spiders into wall cracks... gross."

"George, why did Tazeron go to all the trouble of healing me? Why is he putting me in a cage?"

"Master likes to show kindness to guests, so they remember what they have if they serve him."

"Oh... I get it."

Jesse spent another ten days in the room with George. He was becoming attached to the little guy. He never saw Cazi again; linens just showed up.

"George, will I see you again once I go to my cage?"

"Oh yes, sir. George brings you food once a week, like other guests, sir."

"Once a week?"

"Yes, the master doesn't want you to starve to death. Master is very kind."

"Yeah... I see that."

"Well, George, I just want you to know, it's been a real pleasure getting to know you. I will look forward to seeing you... once a week."

"Oh, thank you, sir, you make George happy. Maybe," his voice lowered, "maybe George can sneak you some extra food." He gave a conspiratorial giggle.

"Good George, don't do anything that would cause you to lose your head."

"Oh no, sir, George likes head."

Two more days passed without any change, but then on the third day, Tazeron waltzed into Jesse's room.

"George tells me that you are healed. I was happy to hear that... it's time to move you to your new room. George will prepare you.

Oh, by the way... Breeze sends her love." Tazeron laughed a loud evil laugh as he left the room. It sent chills up Jesse's spine.

"I wonder why a 'king' would deliver his own messages. And why does he keep bringing up Breeze? I certainly hope she isn't in this place. I don't feel like she is... I wonder why the chain just warmed up when I thought that. Interesting."

Soon after Tazeron left Jesse's room, George showed up with a platter of roasted meats, fruits, and vegetables. There was also fresh bread and a large pitcher of something that smelt like alcohol.

"George, what is the liquid in this pitcher?"

"Oh sir, the master sends the finest wine." The little purple goblin smiled and added quietly from behind his hand, "It has herbs to help you. That is George's gift."

"Thanks, George. Could I have a jug of pure water to drink?"

"Of course, sir, George makes last day comfortable."

After Jesse had eaten, George brought in a large tub with warm water and several different soaps. He seemed to have limited magic at his command.

"Sir's bath, George will help."

"Is getting my wound wet okay, George?"

"Oh yes sir, you all healed."

George helped Jesse get out of his gown and into the large tub. It felt terrific.

"You want George to wash back and hair, sir?"

"That would be wonderful, George, thank you."

"George likes to help friend, sir."

"George, are there any women prisoners here?"

"Oh, yes sir, but they are separate from men. Master doesn't want any... funny business," he giggled.

"Is there one named Breeze here, George?"

"George is not telling names sir, but George not remembers Breeze."

Jesse felt relief at the answer. He sensed the little goblin was telling him the truth, as the goblin knew it. Somehow, Jesse wasn't sure yet, but the chain was confirming the fact.

Almost embarrassed, George had a question for Jesse.

"Sir... what is chain you wear?"

"It is a gift from a special friend; it brings me comfort, George. Why do you ask?"

"Master is afraid of it sir, and he isn't afraid of anything. Master tried to take, but no one can touch. Like air to everyone, even George."

Jesse wasn't surprised by George's answer; it was precisely as Rambo had told him.

"George, does Tazeron have a giant statue of a white dragon in this fortress?"

"How you know sir? Is secret."

"A friend of mine talked to some trolls; they told her."

"You friend of trolls?"

"Not friends, we are... neighbours."

"George understand, you over with bath, sir?"

"Can you heat the water, George? I'd like to soak a little."

"Yes, must go soon, before dark. There are dangers, cages will protect. It is master's kindness to guests on island."

Chapter 32

An Island of Friends

"Where I am going is an island?" Jesse asked George.

"Beautiful island, you like. Trees and animals and birds are beautiful. Island flood every day. It is a blessing. You bathe in water, drink water, water washes away bad smells."

"Will I still be in my... room when it floods?"

"Oh yes, sir. You be glad, will keep bad things away." George gave a little shudder.

"What bad things, George?"

"George is not allowed telling sir, is a surprise."

"Wonderful."

"I think I'm done soaking now, George."

George helped Jesse out of the tub, dried him off, and then dressed him in a pair of linen pants.

"Man, I miss my boxers."

George then helped him get into a rather lengthy tunic and handed him a thin blanket.

"This, is it? No boots, or a hat?"

"No sir, water rots boots."

"Great," Jesse groaned.

"One more thing, George, could you do something with my hair, please?"

"You want George cut?"

"No, just braid it, for now, thanks."

George braided Jesse's long hair. As an elf, he didn't grow a beard.

"George pleasure to serve a friend. George goes now. George sees one-week sir... I bring surprise," he whispered.

Jesse was left to himself after George went, with nothing to do but think about the dream and wonder about its outcome. He was beginning to think that everything that had happened to him was because of the new game master. They could do just about anything within the game, and the worms and everything else could have been under the direction of the game master. Even Jesse losing his arm — but that was probably under the direction of Tazeron.

"Breeze, you certainly were right when you said life throws experiences at us to help us grow. I wonder what this gift of experience will bring my way. I can't wait to find out... just kidding. Breeze, I hope that you're okay, hun. I miss having you around. Hey, the chain warmed up. I think it likes it when I think about you. Yep, it just warmed up some more. I love you, Breeze. We'll figure out this mess. I promise you that."

Jesse drifted off to sleep, and a short time later, he was shaken awake by a rough hand.

"Let's go, scum, no more lollygagging," the huge man laughed like he was listening to a comedy act.

"As you wish, sir," Jesse said as he got up. He was rewarded for his kind words with a punch to the back of his head that nearly toppled him over.

"No talking."

"As you wish, you freak show maggot."

To pass the time, since talking wasn't an option, Jesse studied their surroundings as the guards marched him out of the compound towards a small dock. The complex reminded him of one of the towns he had seen in the game, only that city was filled with friendlies. It reminded him of the one Rambo showed the Council. If that was true, then Jesse was sure he could find his way around — unless this fortress was in a different game than his. He didn't think it was. His game was a big one and very popular around the world. He tried mind searching without any success.

"I wonder what has changed that I can't mind search."

As they approached the docks, Jesse saw a small boat — dinghy came to mind.

"I wonder how the three of us are going to fit into that thing."

When they arrived at the dock with the dinghy, Jesse noticed a rope tied to either end.

"A ferry?"

"Get in, scum. Chops will meet you at the other end." The rough hand pushed him, and Jesse nearly fell face-first into the boat. The guard thought it was hilarious.

Once Jesse was in the boat, it started moving forward towards a small dot on the horizon. He decided to try and nap on the boat bottom as he travelled. Jesse clumped his thin blanket and used it as a pillow. With the soft rocking of the small vessel, he had no trouble drifting off to sleep. After what felt like a short time, a gruff voice spoke sharply to him, waking him up.

"Wake up, worm, move your miserable hide, before I dump you in the lake."

"Wow, a whole sentence, this one must have gone to Loser College. If this is the island George was talking about, they must have used the trees for firewood," Jesse thought, looking around at the stark scenery.

With the guard prodding him, Jesse marched down a path that led around a small knoll. On the other side of the hill, there was a thick forest, edged with about fifteen cages. He couldn't see them all to get a good count; there seemed to be another row on the other side of the first. Then the stench reached him, almost as soon as the sight did.

"This can't be healthy. Oh, please give me strength; I'm not going to make it through this without help."

To Jesse's surprise, the chain warmed up and started pulsating soothingly. He hugged his thin blanket to himself, trying to block out some of the smell, and doggedly plodded forward.

It was about half a mile, as near as Jesse could figure, from the dock to the trees. The closer they got, the worse the smell became. It was a combination of an open sewer, sweat, and rotting flesh. Jesse puked twice during his walk to the cages. The guard kept punching him if he slowed down.

"How can the gods allow this? Why don't they do something?"

As Jesse and the guard walked closer to the cages, Jesse could better see the men that occupied them. The dream was staring him in the face. The men in the cages gave the appearance of something from a horror film... pale, starved, swollen with disease and festering battle injuries. Only a couple watched him with interest; the rest lay on the floor of their confinement, unmoving and uncaring — and that was just the ones he could see. The whole place smelled of death and decay.

Jesse's 'new room' was a 4 x 4 x 4 foot cube of heavy-gauge wire mesh. He couldn't thoroughly stretch out, and he couldn't stand up. It was about twelve inches off the ground and not entirely under the trees. He considered himself lucky because his cage was on the outer perimeter of the camp. He at least had an unobstructed view of the water.

Jesse's nearest neighbours were either comatose or dead. They didn't move, and he couldn't tell if they were breathing. There wasn't a whole lot of talking going on—mostly mumbling and crying. Jesse counted the cages: they were in three rows of fifteen, just far enough apart that the men couldn't reach out to each other.

After the guard had left, Jesse called out to the camp.

"Hey, I'm Jesse Finch. Do I know any of you?"

There was a groan in the distance, but no answer.

"Oh well, it was worth a try."

As Jesse stared out over the water, he noticed that the waterline was getting closer. He knelt up to get a better view of what was happening. His cage was going to be one of the first the water reached. He figured that was an advantage, since all the filth on the ground would be washed away from him. As he watched the water rise, he thought about poking his blanket up through the top of the cage so it would stay dry. He noticed several of the prisoners doing the same thing. Others either didn't care or couldn't move to do it.

"There must be something I can do to help these guys. What would I want if I had been here a long time?"

"Hey guys... I'm Jesse Finch, and my raid group just took out Tazeron's Queen, 'Geezlouise.' She went down like a paper aeroplane in a windstorm, and then we torched the mountain."

"SHUT UP, Jesse Finch. No one cares!"

"I care!" one man, several cages over, answered.

"So do I. What else is going on out there?" another shouted.

"First, tell me about this water. How high does it get?"

"About two feet. Try to keep your blanket dry—you'll be glad later when the bugs come out and start to bite."

"And the snakes," there was a short burst of laughter.

"Don't forget about the hog rats. They actually make the place smell nice." There was another burst of laughter, this time from more than one person.

"I've actually eaten a hog rat. It was delicious," Jesse said. He wasn't sure if this was good information or not, since most of these guys were probably starving.

"I said, SHUT UP, Jesse Finch."

"Who is telling me to shut up? What's your name, friend?"

"I've never been your friend, never wanted to be your friend, and I could care less about becoming your friend. Now SHUT UP!"

"Your voice sounds familiar. What's your name?"

"Rusty Daniels... happy, little bird?"

"Holy cow! Rusty Daniels ... now I understand why I didn't see him with the other jerks the night they graffitied Gran's shed."

"You're right about never being a friend, Rusty. What's it like being one of the 'lost ones'? What I don't understand is why you're here, and not out there with the bad guys."

There were a few snickers at that. Rusty didn't answer.

After a while, the water was lapping at the bottom of Jesse's cage. He realised that, even though it was hitting his cage first, it was like filling a swimming pool—there was still stuff floating. Jesse wondered how he could hang from the roof of his cage with just one arm. The idea that he could drink this water or bathe in it made him want to puke again, but there was nothing left in his stomach.

Watching the other prisoners, he noticed a guy a couple of cages over had made a sling out of his blanket and was climbing into it. Another man was tying strips of material from his tunic onto the cage wires. Most of the prisoners were resigned to sitting in their cages and letting the filthy water cover them. Others stayed lying on the floor and didn't move.

"I wonder if those guys are still alive."

"Hey, what are the strips of tunic for?"

"The fabric filters out the chunks," the guy laughed.

"Oh..."

"That's really disgusting... but it might be an idea to keep in mind."

"Was it hard to tie the blanket to the wire for your hammock?"

"It took me a few tries to get it right. It was hard with one arm."

"How'd you lose your arm?"

"I had a tattoo the boss wanted."

There were a few snickers at that.

"Actually, the pub owner told him if he didn't leave his wife alone, he'd cut it off."

There were more chuckles.

"Where are you guys from? Are you in here because of the games or because you're Keepers, or some other reason?"

There was silence again.

"What is it with these guys?"

Then finally, from across the compound, a weak little voice:

"I'm from Ohio. I was sucked into the game by a bug."

"What's your name, Ohio?"

"Frank... I've been in here about two months, as far as I can figure."

"My name is Chaise," another voice called out. "I'm from Michigan, and I've been here for two weeks. I got sucked into the game like Frank. When I refused to join the evil dude in charge, he had me tossed in here."

"My name is Sam. I'm from Australia, and I was a Keeper. Did you really get Tazeron's Queen down?"

"Yeah, it was so cool. I can't wait until we take down Tazeron."

"Ha! Good luck with that one," another Keeper named Travis from Utah yelled. "That guy has more ways around destruction than any of the boss mobs we faced in the game. And we were a top-tier raiding guild."

After that, the guys started opening up, and conversation was no longer a problem. Jesse learned that there were ten other Keepers, but only six others—besides him—had lost an arm. It seemed not all the Keepers had tattoos.

The hammock guy's name was Garrett, and he was from England. Garrett had lost his arm like Jesse—it was just gone after a weird dream, or hallucination, or whatever it was. Jesse wished he was closer to him so they could talk without yelling.

Jesse tried to tie his blanket the way Garrett had told him, but it wouldn't hold him. He'd have to work on it.

As the water rose higher, bugs and snakes began to appear in their cages. Jesse tried catching a snake but missed. Several of the guys were successful, and their shouts of accomplishment echoed through the camp. Bugs were easy to grab, but Jesse couldn't bring himself to eat one.

"Maybe when I'm a little more starving, I'll be able to do it."

Four more days passed, and Jesse figured out how to tie his blanket to the roof wires. He found it was comfortable to just sleep there—fewer crawly things in his bed that way. Still, he couldn't bring himself to eat one of the giant beetles that came in with the water.

"Be sure to take the blanket down when Tazeron comes to visit, or he'll take it away from you. He doesn't want you to be too comfortable," Antonio from Canada said. "That's what happened to Brian over there."

Tonio, as he preferred to be called, was seventeen and a Keeper, but he still had his arm.

Jesse looked over at the guy who never moved.

"Is he OK? Hey Brian, you OK?"

There was no answer and no movement.

"The only time he moves anymore is when the water gets so high he can't breathe, and when his mender brings him his weekly meal," James, a Keeper from Ireland, said. James had also lost his arm.

"Hey guys, I was wondering, do any of you know why my magic doesn't work here?"

"What class are you?" Brandon from Georgia asked from a few cages over. He was also a Keeper but still had his arm.

"Red Mage. Does that make a difference?"

"I don't know. I was just curious, and I haven't been curious about anything in a long time."

"Look up, jerk," Rusty ended his long silence. "What do you see?"

"Hey Rusty, long time no hear. How's it going over there?"

"You always did talk too much, Jesse Finch. Always tweeting like a little bird."

"Is that why your guys tried to graffiti my grandmother's shed, Rusty? Because I talk too much?"

"He's right, Jesse, look up, man," one of the other Keepers named Jose said. He was from New Mexico and had been in his cage for about six weeks. He still had his arm.

Jesse looked up and was shocked to see a massive bubble, like the one that Rambo would cast on them.

"Wow, what kind of magic is this? That thing must be several miles wide and high."

"Hey Rusty, I'm sorry, man. Thanks for the help in solving the puzzle. Now we just need to figure out how to break that thing."

"I always knew you were an idiot, little bird," Rusty snorted.

"Nothing is impossible; it just might take a while," Jesse said, reminding himself of Tommy, and he wondered about his friend.

"Yeah, yeah... always talking, never saying anything. Some things never change."

"Rusty, you can badmouth me all you want, but you can't stop me from caring or hoping."

Silence.

As Jesse relaxed in his hammock, he noticed a flock of crows or ravens in the tree above his cage. One of the big black birds seemed to be watching him. They were eating some pods that grew on the trees every day right after the flooding. After a few moments, the big bird flew down to the roof of Jesse's cage and poked one of the pods through the wire. It landed in the hammock.

"Hey, thanks, buddy."

Jesse bit into the soft pod and was surprised to find it had a raspberry flavour—kind of sour, but very delicious.

"Wow, this is delicious. Can you pick me more of these?"

The raven bobbed its head twice and flew to the top of the tree. The big bird picked a few more bunches and laid them on the roof so the fruit dangled through the wire. Jesse gobbled the delicious fruit. They filled him for the first time in many days.

"This is wonderful. Could you pick some for my friends in the other cages?"

The raven looked around at the other cages. Bobbing its head two more times, it cawed and flew off into the trees.

"Hey guys, some friends of mine are going to be bringing you some fruit. Don't scare them away, or you'll miss out. The pods are delicious and filling, and you can eat the whole thing."

The prisoners sat up and looked around.

"What are you talking about, Jesse?" John, a Keeper from South Africa who had also lost an arm, wanted to know.

"Trust me, don't frighten them away. They might be able to help us."

"He's hallucinating. Ignore him," Rusty shouted.

Many minutes passed, and still no birds. Jesse began to wonder if he had hallucinated—but his stomach felt full, and he didn't feel sick. In fact, he felt great. Some of the guys started giving Jesse a hard time about teasing them with food.

"Bad joke, dude," Michael said. He was a Keeper from California who had also lost his arm.

"Cruel..." said Philip from Germany, who had been sucked into the game while off duty at his army base. He was worried about how he'd explain what happened to the officers if he ever got back. Jesse wished they could talk—he wondered which base Philip was from.

Then, off in the distance past the trees next to their cages, Jesse saw an unusual sight. A whole flock of ravens, flying silently. Jesse hoped their beaks were full of pods. Soon, hundreds of birds were landing on the cages, poking fruit down to the starving men. They began laughing and crying and stuffing their mouths with raspberry-flavoured pods.

When the fruit was consumed and everyone was full, the birds flew away, and the men were silent.

"Jesse..." the familiar voice of Rusty said. "I have never in my whole life said this, but... thank you. I'm sorry."

Jesse was stunned, and apparently, so was the whole camp.

"I knew it was in you somewhere, Rusty. We need to help each other to survive this, and we will survive this."

Softly at first, then gaining strength, the whole camp broke into applause.

Then the big black bird returned. Everyone stopped to watch as, once again, the bird landed on the top of Jesse's cage. In his beak, he carried a larger pod. He rubbed it on the cage before poking it through the wire.

This pod was harder; Jesse couldn't bite into it. The raven squawked and shook his head, wiping his beak several times on the cage top.

"Oh... I get it. I need to rub it on the wire to open it."

The raven bobbed his head twice.

Jesse rubbed the hard husk along the top of his cage, scraping it like you would grate a carrot. After a few moments, a green liquid shot out of the top, as if under pressure. Jesse quickly put it to his mouth and drank in the most amazing juice he had ever tasted. Everyone was watching for his reaction.

"Oh yes! We need this too! Please, my new friend, bring all of us more of this liquid!"

The raven, having waited for Jesse's reaction, cawed once and flew off.

"The pod has liquid, guys—the purest you have ever tasted. The raven has gone to get us all some."

Jesse expected to hear cheers at this, but what he heard instead was silence—and then sobs. In some cases, he thought he heard prayers.

After several minutes—perhaps almost an hour—the flock returned, poking the pods into the hands of the thankful men. Many whispered thanks to the big birds as they demonstrated how to scrape the seeds open. Their thirsts were all satisfied.

"Thank you, my friend—to you and your family, who have saved many lives this day. I would hope that you and they will return once again to nourish those of us who can't do it for ourselves," Jesse said to the big black bird as it sat on his cage, watching.

On impulse, Jesse stuck his finger out to the big bird as a gesture of trust and friendship. To his surprise, the bird bowed his head so Jesse could scratch his neck, then cooed softly and bobbed his head twice.

"My name is Jesse Finch. Would it be OK if I called you Bob?"

The bird bobbed twice, repeating, "Jesse Finch," as he flew off.

Later, as the camp quietened down, Jesse offered his own prayer to the gods—who certainly had been watching this day.

Chapter 33

Unexpected help

The morning brought new hope to the men, after a good night's sleep. Jesse noticed that the cage with the man named Brian still had fruit and water pods untouched. He wondered once again if the man was alive.

A little before noon, judging by the sun's shadow, there was some clatter coming from around the knoll. All heads turned in that direction, as several small figures walked towards them.

"It's the menders—everyone act hungry."

There were snickers. As they got closer, Jesse recognised George and he waved to the little purple goblin.

"Hello, sir. George so happy to see you, you look well. Master is pleased when he comes tomorrow."

Several of the other menders looked horrified at the disclosure. Jesse guessed that George wasn't supposed to tell them that Tazeron was coming.

"Hey George, that guy—Brian," Jesse pointed at Brian's cage, "is he OK? He hasn't moved since I got here, except to barely keep from drowning."

"George check."

Jesse watched as George unlocked a small door and crawled into the cage with Brian. When George saw the pods, he quickly gathered them up and put them in a pocket.

"Brian breathing, sir. George don't think for long."

George stepped up to Jesse's cage and, checking to make sure none of the other menders were watching, quickly handed Jesse the pods he had collected from Brian's cage.

"These fell from tree... hide them," George whispered.

"What are they?" Jesse whispered back innocently.

"Food, sir," George grinned.

"Food? Wow! Thanks, George," Jesse said, as he wrapped the pods in his thin blanket. Then, curious, he asked, "Are you taking care of anyone else since you healed me, George?"

To Jesse's surprise, George acted nervous and, checking again to make sure they weren't being watched, leaned in.

"Master tell George... he tell George... um, he say that soon there be many more to care for, because—"

"George, we leave, hurry," another little goblin said from behind Jesse's cage, making both Jesse and George jump.

Then in a loud voice, George said, "George likes to see sir. Here is food."

George handed Jesse two hard rolls and two strips of jerky. No water or anything else.

"George goes now. Boat leaves fast. Oh, George almost forgets surprise," he giggled. He handed Jesse two dried cockroaches.

"Excellent for sir to eat," he smiled like it was a fantastic gift.

"Thank you, George. You are very... thoughtful."

The little goblin waved heartily as he and the other menders left. Jesse noticed that no mender visited Brian. He was left wondering what George had been about to say before they were interrupted.

Shortly after the healers left, and before the flooding started, Jesse could smell something different in the air. Looking around, he was surprised to see probably twenty hog rats coming out of the trees.

"Great... more stench to add to the outhouse bouquet."

Jesse watched along with the other men and was horrified to see the hog rats pawing around and under the cages, rocking them. Jesse stood so the hog's bristly hair wouldn't touch him or his clothes.

"What are they doing?" Jesse asked.

"Sanitation duty," Tonio laughed.

"That's disgusting."

"That's hog rats—and you say you ate one?" Brandon said. There were guffaws all over camp.

Jesse felt sick all over again, and then he had a thought.

"If I can talk to the ravens, I wonder if I can talk to the hog rats too." He decided to give it a try.

"Hey, hog rats... stop trying to turn over our houses. Don't dig in the sewage—you're better than that. All of you go to the lake and take a bath."

Curious, Jesse looked around to see if his instructions were going to be followed. After a few minutes, all the hog rats stopped digging and walked over to the lake, swimming out into the water.

"That's a first. Are you talking to those things, Jesse?" Raku, a trapped player from Taiwan, wanted to know. Raku was only fourteen and had been in his cage two days longer than Jesse.

"Yes, I am. I told the hog rats to go take a bath because they were better than digging around in sewage. I wasn't sure if they understood me."

"This gift that you have—talking to animals—have you always been able to do that?" Chaise asked.

"It's a long story... but not always."

"We have time—we aren't going anywhere," Michael joked.

There were laughs all around.

"To be honest, guys, I can't talk about it. Maybe after we get out of here."

The silver chain became warm and started a soothing pulsation.

"I'll keep your secrets, little one." Jesse could almost hear the dragon's hum.

After a short time, the hog rats returned to Jesse's cage, clean from their swim. They looked at him expectantly.

"You will still do your sanitation duties, but instead of wallowing in it and eating it," he gagged, *"you will be digging holes and burying it. You will come back before the flood. You will dig holes, bury the waste, and then swim out to the lake and take a bath. Do you understand?"*

There was a mixture of grunts, squeals, and snorts. They started digging around the cages and moving the waste into the holes. They completely buried all the waste before the flooding began.

This time, as the water filled the cages, it was clean, and Jesse and the other men washed off. They still didn't drink it. Jesse stripped naked and rinsed out his clothes and then his blanket. It was a hard task with one arm.

Jesse decided not to dress right away and let his clothes dry entirely. He hoped the sun would warm his skin.

After the ravens' meal had been delivered and consumed, Bob visited for a while.

By trial and error, Jesse learned—through head bows and shakes—that Bob had a large family. Many of his children had fed them. His wife had died a couple of years earlier, but he was thinking of courting again. Ravens, Jesse learned, were long-lived birds—and brilliant.

Jesse told Bob all about Breeze and Rambo, and all the other friends he had. He told Bob about Gran, and his dad, and how much he missed them. He talked about his mum and stepdad in the mortal world. It was nice to have a conversation that wasn't shouted.

After Bob and his children had left, Jesse stretched out as best he could and took a nap.

Jesse woke to a sniff near his ear. As he rolled over, the breathing turned into a growl. Fully awake now, Jesse sat up straight in his cage and found himself staring into the eyes of the most beautiful cat he had ever seen in his life. It was the size of a super-sized tiger and was light blue with golden stripes. Another white tiger with green stripes stood by Brian's cage, licking a hand dangling through one of the wider wire squares on the floor. Jesse had the feeling that it was receiving a bath before being chomped off.

"Leave the man alone, he is not food for you. There are plenty of fish in the lake, and there are hog rats and other things for you to eat in the woods."

"But if we eat the man, he won't suffer anymore, and it is hard work to catch fish and rats."

"You can talk to me?" Jesse was so surprised he nearly forgot how small the cage was and tried to jump up, banging his head and scraping a knee. He also realised that he had spoken out loud and not to the cat's mind.

"We have been listening to you talk to all the beasts. We were curious. I am Oongo, and this is my wife, Purja. We will not hurt the man; she was cleaning his skin. We feel the White Druid in you, young Jesse. Tell us why."

Jesse was wholly astounded by these cats, their knowledge of him, and the White Druid. He showed them the silver chain as it warmed and pulsed in greeting to them. They bowed to the chain when Jesse showed it, and they offered Jesse their services as they were able.

"The evil man is ruining this beautiful world, and we are delighted to hear that Chaelea is involved," Oongo stated.

"She is a wonder to behold, and we have had the blessing of talking to her many times. We were originally from Xanthara. We came here to see what service we could offer to rid the world of this evil," Purja added.

"If you know the White Druid, do you know Rambo?" Jesse asked.

"Indeed, we do. You surprise us, Jesse Finch. Are you by chance a Finding? That would explain many things about you."

"Rambo and I are brothers; I have received his blessing. I wear a commitment ring—or I did—to a wood nymph named Breeze. She was my Shadow Dream, and I was her Finding. Tazeron took my arm that had the ring."

Jesse noticed several of the men listening to the conversation.

"We are shocked at the closeness of our world, Jesse, brother of Rambo. We know of Breeze and are glad to hear of her. Why does this evil man, Tazeron, keep your arm, and why are all of you in these cages? We have wondered this."

"Tazeron took my arm and the arms of others in this group because we are Keepers of the Shield. The others are here because they refused to join in Tazeron's evil plans."

The two cats growled softly and bobbed their heads in acknowledgment.

"Our arms bore the talisman of Chaelea; it was a threat to Tazeron. This chain also frightens him, and he would've taken it too, but no one can touch it. Tomorrow, Tazeron comes to this camp. Would you protect us if we need help?" Jesse guarded the chain by talking to the cats in his mind.

"We can do this. Watch."

Oongo morphed into a white spotted frog and then went invisible.

"How... how can you do that? I thought all immortals from Xanthara were forbidden their magic. I have been blocked from using mine because of the bubble of silence above us."

The cats looked up at the sky and then laughed—or Jesse thought it was laughing. It sounded like a snort, a cough, or a hiccup.

"We can use our magic because we chose it. We were dragon-blessed by Chaelea before she left. With that gift, we can use our magic no matter the world we are in. She also blessed us with the shapeshifter ability. Young Jesse, there is no bubble of silence above you. You believe the evil lies given you. You must reach inside and see that your magic is still whole. We can see it. You must believe. The dragon's blessing protects the magic, no matter what world you are in. It cannot be taken without your permission. Evil only succeeds when goodness and courage give way and step aside. Be strong. You are a chosen Prince for these times of darkness. Believe in yourself—others do."

The big cat's words caught Jesse by surprise. How could he keep forgetting all the blessings that he had received? How could he be so naïve and gullible? Why was he in need of constant reminding of who he was and the importance of his role?

"Grr, I am so thick," Jesse chided himself.

"I have been foolish, Oongo and Purja, you are correct. I am dragon-blessed, and this chain I wear is a reminder. I can't thank you enough for reminding me. I must once again find myself and believe. I need time to think on this."

"One more thing—there are others in these woods that would like to meet you. Would you grant them an audience?" Oongo asked.

"Of course, it would be my pleasure."

"We will return tomorrow, Jesse, brother of Rambo." They turned and were gone.

"Jesse, you talk to birds and they feed us. Rats clean our area so that we can clean ourselves. Now you talk to great cats. Who are you?" Garrett asked, across the cages.

"I told you, I'm Jesse Finch, a Keeper, taken by Tazeron, and I lost my arm because of a tattoo. There is nothing more."

"You aren't telling the whole truth, Jesse Finch," Rusty said. "We aren't stupid; we know something else is going on."

"Of course, you aren't stupid. I know you can see what's happening. You think I'm not telling the whole truth, and you are right. But I am under oath to not tell any more than I have. Until I am released from that oath, I will keep it."

"And we will all respect that," Rusty shouted to all the men, surprising Jesse exceedingly.

"You are an honourable man, Rusty Daniels. I'm glad I got to know this side of you."

"I'm not yet, Jesse Finch, but I promise everyone here that I will try."

Jesse struggled over the next hour to get his clothes back on. One arm missing, and not being able to stretch out properly, was a considerable handicap. Garrett gave him some pointers. With that advice, and after many attempts, he was finally successful.

Just as the sun was setting, a terrifying sight greeted all the caged men. Approximately forty large apes walked out of the forest, all of them heading towards Jesse's cage.

"Uh oh..."

"Fear not, young mortal, we only wish to meet the child of Chaelea."

"What? I am mortal, as you said. I'm not her child." Again, Jesse could speak out loud, and they understood.

"Mortal you may be, but her child you are."

"What do you mean... for real her child, or figuratively speaking her child?"

"You have been adopted, as you mortals would say. Has no one told you that you wear Chaelea's kiss on your forehead? Do you not wear her mark on your neck?"

Jesse fingered the chain and felt its warmth and the vibration of its pulse.

"What can I do for you, since I am in this cage?"

"We wish only to meet you, young sir, and wish you well in this battle of all battles. We, like Oongo and Purja, are not of this world; we came here to assist as we could. We have heard of you, and we are at your service."

Jesse was flabbergasted at this announcement.

"I am honoured by so many hands to help in this quest. There are many Keepers besides me. We all appreciate your gift of

service. What are you called, that we may summon you in a time of need?"

"I am Molo. I am chief of this clan. We will hear when a Keeper calls, Jesse Finch, son of Chaelea."

The giant apes filed past Jesse's cage, bowing in turn as they headed back into the forest.

Jesse looked over at the men in his company; they all, to a man, gaped at him with their mouths open.

"Oh, come on, guys, didn't your mums tell you it was rude to stare with your mouths open? Now get some sleep, we have a busy day tomorrow."

One lone inmate started to laugh, and soon most of them were. Some still looked like they were in the company of a rock star, and that made Jesse very uncomfortable. He tried to ignore them. As he wrapped himself in his thin blanket, he found the pods that George had given him and wondered what would happen to the little toon.

Jesse lay there a long time, thinking over the day and its revelations. Straining to sleep with the buzzing mosquitoes flying around him, Jesse finally drifted off.

Early in the morning, the hog rats were at the camp, tending to their sanitation duties. After they were done, they headed out to the lake and went for a swim before returning to the forest. That afternoon's flooding happened as usual, with perhaps fewer snakes and bugs. The consensus was that because the place was cleaner, there were fewer bugs, and since there were fewer bugs to eat, there were fewer snakes.

Everyone was in a pretty good mood when someone reminded them that Tazeron was making an appearance today. That soured the camp real fast. Then someone suggested to Jesse that he have one of his animal friends eat the old bastard. The mood improved considerably, even when Jesse explained that wasn't an option.

While the men bantered back and forth, Jesse sat brooding over what the big cats, Oongo and Purja, had told him about there being no silence bubble.

"Believe in yourself, others do." Jesse played the cat's words over and over in his head. As he thought of their words, he decided to look inside himself, and to his surprise, he did see the familiar red bands of light still flowing through him. Jesse pictured them growing stronger and more intense and felt the familiar warmth spreading down his arm to his hand. Jesse focused on a lone tree some thirty yards away and released his fire on it.

The tree exploded, and his fingers were smoking.

He hooted and hollered, surprising everyone in the camp.

"Hey Rusty, buddy, guess what?"

"I just saw, dude! How'd you do it?"

"Who here is a magic caster?" Jesse asked, and thirty-one were. Fourteen were not. Brian had jumped but didn't answer. However, someone knew that he was a warlock.

"How many of you were trained at the place of learning in Rodashu?"

All the Keepers, and none of the others, answered affirmatively. A few wanted to know what Rodashu was.

"Tell me your classes," Jesse requested.

Of the forty-five prisoners, six were healers, fourteen were warrior/tanks, three were bards, two were necromancers, one was an enchanter—"excellent"—three were warlocks, seven were mages, two were rogues, three were druids, two were shamans, and two were hunters.

All the inmates were experienced players, and after seeing Jesse's display with the tree, they were excited.

"How did you get past the silence bubble?" one of them asked.

"There never was one. Tazeron and his followers are such accomplished liars. All they did was tell us, in our weakened condition, that it was there—and we believed. What you believe or don't believe significantly affects what you can or can't do."

"How did you think to test it?" someone asked.

"Remember the big cat? He told me that there wasn't a bubble, and I decided to check it... short story."

"Look inside yourself, and do your best to focus, then release the magic away from the group."

"What do you mean, look inside? I usually just think of the spell I need, and where I need it to go. That works for me."

"If that works for you, then... go for it."

"I want everyone to work their magic. We can't be sloppy in this war. We've been sitting around on our lazy butts for too long. All of you healers, I want you to concentrate on Brian here. I want to see him dancing in a few days."

"I'm going to concentrate on getting out of these cages," Jesse thought.

Jesse still couldn't mind-search, and he wasn't sure why that was, but right now it was a minor problem. A more significant concern was what they were going to do once they got out. They could probably storm the compound, but he hoped that other groups of Keepers were already doing that. Besides, none of them had the proper equipment, and that was going to affect how they fought. It would also be tough to battle against Tazeron and his minions without flying mounts to help them get there.

Jesse missed being able to mind-talk with Rambo and Breeze. Being able to speak to people through the talisman was a bonus too.

Suddenly, there was a significant explosion and a loud yell of excitement. Someone had succeeded with a spell, and a limb fell from an overhead tree. It crashed onto a couple of cages, startling the inhabitants.

"Hey, watch it, dude... that just increased my laundry for tomorrow!"

Laughter and excitement filled the camp.

"Sorry, man, but that felt totally awesome. I just need to aim better; I'm kind of out of practice."

"No duh... we all are."

Jesse didn't listen to the banter around the camp, as spell after spell went off. There were even some conjured pets running around. Jesse just sat in the corner of his cage and focused all his magic on his index finger, until he had a beam of fire the size of a small laser penlight.

He remembered Mistress Wolfa's lesson on focus and detail, and how she had wanted him to draw pictures on the wall with his fire.

"I think she would be proud," Jesse thought, as he drew red lines through the wires of his cage.

Chapter 34

Jesse's Promise

As Jesse focused on his magic, and everyone else practised, someone called out that there was a party coming around the knoll and they had better clean up. They could see about ten people approaching, and there was speculation as to why there were so many.

Jesse noticed two white-speckled frogs hopping toward his cage. There were ravens in the trees, as well as great apes in the shadows.

"This is going to be interesting," Jesse thought.

As the party got closer, Jesse recognised Tazeron and the two guards who had taken him to the dock the day he came to the island. There were two men dressed in chainmail and two others in cloth robes. The other three people—two women and a man—didn't wear magical clothes or battle gear, and that confused Jesse. They looked like average citizens on a mortal street.

"Greetings, my friends," Tazeron's rough voice rang out. "Such a pleasure to see you all this beautiful day. Let me introduce you to my associates."

Tazeron didn't introduce the two guards flanking his every step, but he did introduce the two wearing chainmail and the two in cloth. They were all friends of his from Xanthara. Jesse thought he recognised the two cloth-wearers as members of the Xanthara Council.

The three street-clothed people turned out to be from the mortal world—recruits of Tazeron's followers. Tazeron explained that they were there to show the prisoners what awaited them if they chose to serve him.

They represented wealth, power, and popularity. As Tazeron explained, they morphed into examples—a magical show and tell.

One of the women, probably in her mid-thirties, became well-dressed and evidently very wealthy. She wore gem-studded jewellery and gold chains. The other female seemed to be about eighteen or in her early twenties, Jesse guessed. She wore a skimpy, very tight, revealing outfit and high heels, which made absolutely no sense—even to her, it seemed—as she lifted each foot in confusion, then simply shrugged. Apparently, she was supposed to represent popularity. There were several wolf-whistles, and she flashed a radiant smile.

The man, probably in his forties, was dressed in a general's uniform with many medals pinned to his chest. He also wore a crown, seemingly representing power.

As a further demonstration of goodwill, Tazeron had one of the cloth-wearers walk over to Brian. He pried open his mouth and poured a purple liquid between his parched lips. He then cast several healing spells, to which Brian groaned.

"Leave me alone... I just want to die," Brian moaned.

The healer shrugged and walked back to Tazeron.

"We will not force anyone to follow us, but if you don't..." his eyes took on a demonic glint, "you will be forever sorry."

Jesse noticed two spiders—one light blue and one white—crawling up Tazeron's robes as he began talking. Fascinated, Jesse watched as they crept inside Tazeron's collar.

"There will be no more..." Tazeron started to say, but instead yelped, surprising his followers as they, too, turned to look. Tazeron danced around, swatting at his robes. His skin began breaking out in a bright red rash with welts.

Jesse watched as the two spiders dropped to the ground and crawled toward their next victims. Soon, several followers were swatting, jumping, squirming—breaking out in various coloured rashes. Tazeron tried to continue his speech while digging at the itching welts, which pulsed as if something crawled just under the skin. He began drawing blood.

"This will be your only offer."

"Ugh! Give me something, you healers!" The problem with that request was that the healers were having the same experience and didn't seem to have a remedy for themselves, let alone anyone else.

"In one week, I will return to collect the ones who wish to serve me."

Tazeron fell to the ground, grabbing handfuls of mud to rub on his face and arms. Others did the same.

"If you will not serve me…" Tazeron now looked so ridiculous that the whole camp erupted into laughter. His unaffected followers looked confused and began to back away.

"You will all rot!" Staggering to his feet, Tazeron tried to look regal, but only managed pathetic. He and his company turned to leave.

"I guess that means no more scrumptious meals, maid service or massages!" Jesse yelled to the retreating Tazeron and his followers. "Oh well," he snickered.

"Hey Bob, do you think you and your children could show that evil idiot and his pack of losers what we think of the offer?"

Jesse showed the big bird a picture of what he had in mind, and there was a roar of squawking approval. The flock took flight and proceeded to deposit lovely raven poo all over the retreating dignitaries. The VIPs tried to run but weren't fast enough to avoid the splatterings.

When the girl in high heels tripped and fell face-down in the mud, losing her shoes, no one stopped to help her.

"I always knew birds could do that when they wanted," Jesse laughed.

The prisoners guffawed and hooted even louder when the large cats—now in their true forms—and the apes joined the chase.

As a final kick at Tazeron, Jesse focused his laser fire on the evil monarch's backside, burning a butt-sized hole in his robes and scorching his rump.

It was a lovely ending to a perfect day—if you lived in a cage.

As Jesse lay in his hammock that night, thinking about Tazeron's offer, he remembered the dream of the one-armed man.

"This could very well be that dream, only the situation in the camp is very different. We aren't as wretched as that vision showed, because of the animals. I wonder what that healer did to Brian."

Listening to the soft chatter of the men and the buzz of mosquitoes, Jesse drifted off to sleep.

In the morning, as the sun cleared the mountains, Jesse noticed that the sky was bluer. He tried mind-searching again, and to his surprise, it worked. He quickly sat up and scanned the area—and to his further surprise, Tazeron's fortress was on fire.

"Guys! Guys! Tazeron's fortress is burning! Someone made it in!"

"What... what are you bellowing about, Finch?" Rusty called to him.

"The fortress—a raid made it in and torched it. Look at the sky, it's bluer. The magic has changed!"

"What are you yelling about, young man?"

Jesse couldn't believe it. Brian was moving in his cage, talking to him.

"Brian! You're better! How are you feeling?"

"Not bad for an old guy who's been stuck in a cage for months and starved to death's door. Who are you? How long have you been in hell's paradise?"

"I'm Jesse Finch, sir. I've been in 'hell's paradise' for a while now. I'm glad you're doing better."

"Hey Jesse, how do you know that Tazeron's fortress is burning, dude?"

"I saw it."

"What do you mean, you saw it? The knoll's in the way!"

"You're just going to have to trust me."

Jesse felt renewed energy flowing through his body as he focused his attention on his magic. With the excitement of the incineration and the blueness of the sky, focusing seemed easier, and his magic felt stronger. Within a short amount of time, Jesse had one edge of his cage wall melted free. His fire beam acted as a welding torch. He worked on the bottom as hog rats reported for sanitation duty. He hadn't realised it was that time already.

"Bob, Oongo and Molo, can you hear me?"

"We can hear you, brother of Rambo," Oongo said.

"As can I, child of Chaelea," said Molo.

"My magic is working much better, thank you, Oongo. I mind-searched the area, and I saw Tazeron's Fortress on fire. Would you please check out the situation for me?"

"It would be our pleasure; we will let you know what we find."

Jesse could hear cawing in the distance and knew that Bob and his family were on their way too.

"Jesse, are you talking to the animals? I hear the ravens, and it isn't time for them yet."

"Yes, I've asked all the animals to check out Tazeron's Fortress. They're going for information."

"So, it actually is burning?" Chaise asked.

"Yes, it is. And I just got my cage open!"

Jesse pushed on the cut wall of his cage with his feet. He widened the small opening. He could barely squeeze through, but he made it. He tried to stand, but he was so weak from limited food and no exercise that his legs didn't want to hold him.

"Man, I need physical therapy."

After whooping and hollering while on the ground, Jesse lay there looking up at the sky. Everyone, by this time, was cheering and yelling, wanting their chance at freedom.

Now that he was on the outside of the cage, he could examine the locks that were keeping their cages closed tight. They were in the middle of a large metal plate. The wire was thick, but the padlock would be possible for Jesse's fire to cut.

After a few attempts at standing and holding onto cages as he went, Jesse managed to make it to Rusty Daniels cage, where he looked Rusty in the eye and addressed him.

"Let me see... Rusty Daniels, three years of a living hell during the sixth, seventh and eighth grades. I think you've been paid back by being in here. No one should be forced to live like this Daniels. I forgive you for all your despicable ways and will free you first."

To Jesse's surprise, Rusty broke down and sobbed. No one near them spoke.

After freeing Rusty and receiving a profuse apology from him, the two ex-enemies worked through the flood and were able to free seven others. Three of them were magicians that Jesse showed how to focus their fire, and the cages opened even faster. Some of the men had been confined so long their legs were too weak to stand. Everyone was thin, even with the food the birds had provided.

By the time half of the inmates were freed, Oongo, Molo and Bob were back with a report.

"There are two groups of Keepers fighting the Fortress. One of them has a mind searcher like you—his name is Baker. You might be able to reach him. Tazeron and his sympathisers have fled."

While talking with Oongo and Molo, Jesse had an idea.

"I was wondering something, Oongo and Molo. Would you be offended if I asked you and your families to give my friends and me a ride back to civilisation?"

"What you ask would be an honour for us," Molo responded. The surrounding apes thumped their chests and howled in agreement.

"My wife and I would also be honoured, young sir," Oongo said.

"Excellent. Once again, we are deeply indebted to you and your service to us. Thank you is not nearly enough to express our gratitude."

Jesse bowed to the remarkable animal players in this war—the ravens, cats, and apes.

The problem of weak legs seemed solved for the trip home.

"One more favour, if you don't mind. I would like to go to the Fortress and see if we can possibly help."

Both Oongo and Molo were pleased with this idea, and as soon as the remaining prisoners were freed, they mounted up and began the trip. Oongo and Purja carried Jesse and Rusty, while Molo and his clan brought the rest. Bob and his family followed.

Getting across the water was an interesting venture, since the apes weren't strong swimmers, but they made it. They could see the Fortress; it appeared totally engulfed. Getting closer, they saw several small figures huddling near a wall away from the flames. Jesse recognised George and Cazi locked in an embrace of pure terror. There were other healers huddled around the compound.

Rusty and the other men, with the help of the apes, looked for their own healers. Jesse moved toward George and Cazi.

"George? Are you OK, my friend?"

"Oh sir, you came! George hoped you would come. Master gave me a present for you, but George was too scared. Master says George would die if you do not get."

George pulled a small box out of a pocket in his tunic and handed it to Jesse.

"Did Tazeron tell you anything about this box, George?"

"Don't open it, Finch, it might explode and spray acid or something," Rusty said, returning to Jesse's side.

"Master said, you would understand."

Jesse gingerly lifted the lid on the box. What he saw inside so shocked him that he collapsed to the ground.

"NO... by the gods, no!" Jesse sobbed.

"What is it, man? Can I help with something?" Rusty asked, worried.

The little box slipped out of Jesse's hand. Rusty knelt and picked it up. Looking inside, he saw two white dragon rings, both stained with blood—one with green blood, the other with red.

Jesse was so grief-struck that he didn't notice when a great red dragon landed by his side. The other prisoners bowed and backed away. Rusty stayed.

"Jesse, my friend, what has happened to you? We have searched and searched, and only now we find you thus."

"Rambo, is it really you? No. It's another hallucination."

"No, my friend, it is I, Rambo. Much has happened since we lost you. You have been mistreated. I see that your arm is missing, and now this great shock. I see what the box contains. Please, Jesse, look deep inside and find the strength. I fear that to become whole and live once more, you must die, to be healed. We have much to do to win this war, and you, my friend, must recover what you have lost. I will help you. Trust me."

"I trust you with what's left of my life, my brother. I will gladly give everything to the cause. I am nothing without Breeze, Rambo. Without her, I have no desire to live. Take what is left."

With great difficulty, Rambo, with Rusty's help, opened the small flask and poured the liquid into Jesse's mouth. Jesse swallowed almost reflexively; the liquid felt fresh and smooth going down his throat. Then, with no pain, he felt himself floating above them.

He hovered there for a while, looking at the scene below him. He saw the iridescent green and red dragon and the skinny young man. They were sad—how strange. He felt... nothing. Why were they unhappy? Then he saw the body that they wept over. It looked familiar. It *was* familiar... it was him.

With a jolt, he remembered. He had to go back—but he needed to remember how.

"Jesse, my dear, you must go back."

Jesse turned around. *"GRAN! Oh, Gran, I have missed you."* He moved towards her and, with joy, he found that he could hug her.

"How can I hug you, Gran? You're an essence."

"You're an essence too, Jesse. But you must go back. You can't stay. It's not your time, and Breeze needs you."

"I don't know where she is. How can I find her?"

"The talisman will guide you."

"Tazeron took my arm."

"Jesse, that's why you needed to die, dear. Look at your arm."

Jesse looked at his arm—it was there!

"How...?"

"Remember... Nexlucimus told us the talisman was imprinted on our essences? It can never be removed, even by us, even in death."

"Gran, Zealoc loves you. He's a good man."

"I know. I talk to him in dreams. We will be together again soon. Now hurry, Jesse. Breeze is in great danger. To return to your body, touch the talisman. I love you, Jesse. I'm watching, and the gods are watching. Goodbye, dear."

Jesse touched the talisman. In an instant, he was lying on the ground, looking up into the faces of his friends.

"Jesse!" Rusty yelled, and forgetting himself (Jesse figured), he hugged Jesse, sobbing.

"Hey man, good to see you too—and it sure is nice to have this arm back."

"Oh wow, I didn't even notice," Rusty laughed, wiping tears.

"Rambo, my friend, it is wonderful to see you again. Please morph down, so I'm not looking up your nose."

Rambo chuckled and morphed to a smaller size. Jesse stood and hugged him tight, his own tears falling. Then Jesse asked for the little box. Rusty handed it to him.

"Oh sir, you have arm back. George is happy."

"Thank you, George. And thank you for taking such good care of me while I was... sick."

"Sir is welcome. Cazi and George leave—we go to the city not far. Live with her people. We be in love," the little purple goblin blushed a darker shade.

Jesse chuckled. "Congratulations, George—and you too, Cazi."

"Thank you, sir. Cazi very lucky—find George. I loves him," she blushed too.

"I'm thrilled for you two. Take care of Cazi, George—she needs a lot of reminding," Jesse smiled at the shy little mist lizard.

"George knows. George takes good care of her."

"And Cazi—see that George has things to do, so he's not stuffing cockroaches and spiders into wall cracks."

"Oh, I keeps him busy. No more bug stuffing," she shivered.

The two little toons waved goodbye as they walked off, hand in hand.

Jesse turned his attention back to Rambo and Rusty. "Gran helped me return to my body. While I was with her, she told me that the talisman would guide me to Breeze. She is still alive."

Jesse took his commitment ring and placed it back on his left ring finger. He then put Breeze's on his little finger. When the two rings touched, they glowed and warmed his whole arm. One glowed green, the other red. That was new—but made sense to Jesse. It was the colour of his and Breeze's blood.

Turning to Bob, Oongo and Molo, Jesse addressed them.

"My friends—especially you, Bob—have saved many lives with your kindness. That debt can never be repaid. We will yet face many hardships. Breeze, my intended, is taken," his words stumbled over his emotions. "But by the gods, I will rescue her—and we will end this war with Tazeron. We would be honoured to have all of you and your families at our sides."

The large black bird nodded his consent, and a reverberation of cawing filled the air, joined by roars, growls, howls and chest-thumping.

"My wife and I would be honoured to fight alongside you and your brother, Rambo." Oongo bowed.

"Likewise, child of Chaelea, we will follow you." Molo's clan thumped their chests and hollered.

Facing the burnt-out fortress, Jesse lifted his left arm. The rings glowed brightly as he shouted a promise to the evil monarch, who was no longer there.

"I will find her, Tazeron. I will. I also promise you, that I will hunt you down, and send your immortal soul into the gaping mouth of the hell where you will join all the other evil tyrants that ever lived."

The silver chain, the dragon rings, and the talisman all sent warmth and vibrations to Jesse's very soul, confirming that they too would be there—to help.

"Come, Jesse, there is much to do, but first you must heal," Rambo said soothingly, as Rusty helped Jesse to mount, before climbing aboard himself.

It was time to mend body and soul and complete the quest. A new day was dawning—one that carried promise, hope, strength and peace. Time for truth, and fulfilment of covenants to and from the gods.